ALSO BY PAUL MONETTE

POEMS

The Carpenter at the Asylum
No Witnesses
Love Alone: 18 Elegies for Rog

NOVELS

Taking Care of Mrs. Carroll
The Gold Diggers
Lightfall
Afterlife
Halfway Home

NONFICTION

Borrowed Time: An AIDS Memoir
Becoming a Man: Half a Life Story
Last Watch of the Night: Essays Too Personal and Otherwise

The Long Shot

PAUL MONETTE

A Citadel Press Book
Published by Carol Publishing Group

Carol Publishing Group Edition, 1995

The Long Shot was originally published by Avon Books-March, 1981

By arrangement with the Estate of Paul Monette

A Citadel Press Book
Published by Carol Publishing Group
Citadel Press is a registered trademark of Carol Communications, Inc.

Editorial Offices: 600 Madison Avenue, New York, NY 10022
Sales & Distribution Offices: 120 Enterprise Avenue, Secaucus, NJ 07094
In Canada: Canadian Manda Group, One Atlantic Avenue, Suite 105
Toronto, Ontario, M6K 3E7

Queries regarding rights and permissions should be addressed to:
Carol Publishing Group, 600 Madison Avenue, New York, NY 10022

Manufactured in the United States of America
ISBN 0-8216-2004-5

10 9 8 7 6 5 4 3

Carol Publishing Group books are available at special discounts
for bulk purchases, sales promotions, fund raising, or
educational purposes. Special editions can also be created to
specifications. For details contact: Special Sales Department,
Carol Publishing Group, 120 Enterprise Ave., Secaucus, NJ 07094

Another to Roger—
my fellow traveler

Feb. 26, Friday

My prickles or smoothness are as much a quality of your hand as of myself. I cannot tell you what I am, more than a ray of the summer's sun. What I am I am, and say not. Being is the great explainer.

—Thoreau's *Journal*, 1841

chapter 1

JUST BEFORE DARK, Greg turned the television face to the wall.
Which admittedly was childish of him, but at least he wasn't
out to get anyone's attention. He was deliberately all alone on
this, the first Monday in April—for the third year running, in
fact. He sat at the dining room table and wrote out envelopes.
He hadn't gone out all day, so as not to have to negotiate with
a grown man's line of credit. He figured to avoid in the
process any chance collisions with the past.

And all outside his windows, the world didn't blame him.
The spring air was stopped cold in a white haze over Hollywood. He couldn't have seen a thing if he'd wanted. The sun
broke through at last, like an afterthought on the lip of sun-
down. All of a sudden, the sky pumped up into orange and
rose. Greg glanced at the big arched window, caught off guard
by the colored lights—on edge, somehow, as if a tornado had
started to blow out of Beverly Hills. He got up and went to
the terrace, to see what it all might mean, and happened on
the way to pass across the Sony's line of vision. It was then
that he paused to flip it around, as if it ought to be ashamed.

Out on the terrace, he glowed like a peach in the setting
sun. He ought to have known it would never rain on Oscar

night. It didn't dare. At this very moment, everyone in the industry was on his way to the Music Center, and they had to know whether or not to wear their lynx, or to put the top down on the Corniche. The westering sun, Greg thought as he leaned against the balustrade, was a sign of benediction. Later on, he would say the day was rotten with signs, had anyone cared to take a look. But who had time to? One day a year, Hollywood had to make a seven o'clock curtain, so the rest of the world could watch. The city shimmered now with the air of being source and center, like Christmas Eve in Bethlehem. If anything else was fated to happen in the next few hours, a minor war or a market crash, well, that was its own hard luck. The Oscars preempted life at large.

Frankly, my dear, Greg thought, *I don't give a damn.*

He put an arm around the neck of the plaster sphinx and, trying to look as placid as it did, faced west to the ocean. He could have recited the winners in certain categories all the way back to the late twenties. There was a time when he had it all prepared who to thank when they gave him one of his own. Deep in his closet, he had the tuxedo he'd worn to his high school prom, and it hung at attention even now, waiting out a nomination. All of this before he failed. When he failed— didn't make it, as they said out here—he turned his back on movies once and for all. Wouldn't go, no matter what was showing. The golden age was done. In the new Hollywood, the Academy Awards had all the magic of a stockholders' meeting at ITT. Greg knew he wouldn't make a ripple, withholding his support. Neilsen wasn't gauged to register the silence on his Sony. But he stood on principle. Shoulder to shoulder with the sphinx, he tried to keep his mind on higher things.

Still, the whole thing hurt. He'd gotten fairly good at tearing his eyes from the titles in lights on theater marquees. The longing and remorse had abated some. Lately, he'd come to think he was practically cured. After all, he was only thirty-two, and he looked as if he'd settled in to look the same for twenty years—his body hard from tennis, sandy hair, and dreamy gray-green eyes with a haunting frown between. As if he were about to see things clearly, all at once. He stood five eleven and a half—in boots, six one. Got laid a couple of times a week, though rarely twice in a row. He generally came home late from the beds of strangers, because he liked to sleep sprawled out and keep his mornings to himself.

In the next ten days, he would pay out taxes on his last year's gross of twenty-four five. He even lived in a penthouse, sort of. In a building, to be sure, that had gone downhill—its common space grim as the Y, its apartments let to transients—but Hollywood Egyptian, all the same. If you shut your eyes till you got there, the eleventh floor was *Grand Hotel*, and Greg had the southwest quarter. With balconies off every room, and windows cookie-cut in a dozen shapes and sizes. There was ironwork and plasterwork, and an acre of Roman tile laid down wherever it would stick. All in all, he'd ended up in a reasonable life. It amazed him, therefore, still to feel the sequined taunts of Hollywood. Yet they welled up about him on Oscar night like two-bit music, till they scalded away the thick of his skin.

The doorbell called him back. He patted the rough right flank of the sphinx and turned toward the terrace doors. Ordinarily, he scarcely would have heard the bell. If he wasn't expecting someone, he didn't want to get involved. It must be the kid in 2C, bringing him up the book. As he came through into the living room, he locked the doors behind and shut out the sunset show. He was full of a sorrow cheaper than tears, but knowing it didn't diminish it any. The kid downstairs was safe. At least he had no ticket to Greg's other lives. Gary, was it? Jerry? Something with a *y*.

Until late last night, they were just two neighbors who met now and then in the lobby and passed the time, while they waited out the arrival of the weary, moaning elevator. For the longest time, Greg never dreamed the kid was gay. Then, two or three days ago, he asked if Greg had ever read *Walden*. That right there was the clue. It sounded so fucking Platonic, somehow. And Greg, who was not the reading kind, demurred as best he could. How was the kid to know he took a certain pride in *not* being philosophical? He liked life on the surface, and didn't need books at all. But he couldn't turn down a present either, now they'd gone so far. As he reached for the door, the name leapt into his head: Harry.

"For Christ's sake," said Edna Temple, barreling by in a housecoat and slippers, "we thought you must have died."

She didn't wait for an explanation. She padded across the foyer and left the fine points, as she often did, to Sidney Sheehan. Greg knew not to close the door just yet. He peered around at Sid, who stood in the hall and waited on ceremony.

"We blew a tube," he said pleasantly, right into the teeth of Greg's slow burn. "In the middle of *Mildred Pierce*." As if that was enough, he shrugged and jaunted along in Edna's wake. A shrug was by way of Sid's signature.

"Sid! Sid!" she called, to hurry him. "Greg's had to punish his television. I wonder what it did. You think it did a weewee on the carpet?"

"I told you to leave me alone," Greg bellowed, prepared to rail till he was hoarse. He cornered them standing on either side of the set, too old to pick it up and face it front again. "Of course you think you're adorable, don't you? Have a few laughs with good ole Greg. Can't you see I don't *want* cheering up? I told you—tomorrow morning I'll be the same as ever. You can do without me for twenty-four hours."

"But Greg," she begged him, "this is an emergency. It's got nothing to do with you. They're running these terrific clips of all the old best actresses. Can't we argue later? We already missed the bit from *Kitty Foyle*."

"Really? Sid said *Mildred Pierce*."

"Did he? Well, whatever." She shrugged, as if to dismiss a technicality. But she squinted at Sid as well, to let him know she'd go a lot further on her own. Sid lifted his chin and swallowed. The knot on his skinny tie did a little shrug.

"You're lying, aren't you? Your set's not broken at all."

"No," said Edna simply, one hand plumping the hair at the back of her head. "Besides, we got two. In case we don't agree."

"But we want to watch it in color. We *have* to," Sid said feelingly. Like he'd never asked a favor in his life, till now. "We'll keep it so low you won't even hear it."

He wavered, of course. He owed these two more than he ever let on. The summer before, when they landed in his life, they shook the hermit off his back. He'd had his share of lovers and amateur therapists, naturally, but not what you might call proper friends. Friends were usually people who got so close they tried to change him. But here he spent twenty, thirty hours a week with Sid and Edna, thrashing about in the madness that lay in heaps in his dining room, and he never seemed to tire of them. The rest of his life, sooner or later, put him to sleep with his eyes wide open. After so many years spent mooning in theaters, Sid and Edna began to seem like an ace in the hole of the real world.

"While you're deciding," Edna said, and reached around behind the set and snapped it on. It played to the wall without taking a breath, manic and jangled and dumb. Edna nearly disappeared, trying to reach the channel knob. She turned it to NBC with a second sight, and now they all listened to the noise of the crowd as the stars pulled up at the Music Center. An aura of arc lights and red carpet crackled in the air of Greg's apartment. It seemed the temperature itself began to rise.

"All right," Greg said, relenting fast. He crouched to the box and swiveled it round on the table, then nearly jumped away, as if the light from the tube could burn him. "But promise me this—you'll leave me out of it." He started to back up, as if to make his way to the safety of the dining room. Terrified, really, but they didn't see. They were already pulling up chairs. "Not a word about who wins," he said, "okay?" But not as if he expected much compliance. "I'm going to work on my taxes."

When he bumped up against the filigreed iron gate that divided the two rooms, he held onto the grille with both hands behind his back. The sting of failure tightened about his heart, as sharp as ever. All he had to do was flee the Oscars, and he'd be fine. And yet he was torn—caught in a fatal wish to be with the others. The part of him that still could breathe looked longingly at Sid and Edna, taking it easy a few feet off.

"Taxes," Edna sniffed ironically. "Isn't he fancy?"

"*I* never paid 'em," Sid said proudly.

"When I was waitressing," she said, "we never declared a tenth of what we made."

They weren't exactly talking to Greg, nor even to each other. They were more or less thinking aloud, airing their most firmly held opinion as to taxes, because taxes was what had come up. In fact, they had an opinion of everything, and kept at their fingertips every course of action ever taken, which they grabbed at the chance to tell in brief, whenever the context went their way. As if they needed to see how it sounded, now that the years had intervened. In any case, they'd taken him at his word. They sat intently, side by side, like space men bent at a radar screen. They let Greg be.

He fell back deadweight against the grille, and the gate swung in, to the high cool dark of the dining room. He did a sort of sleepwalk to the table and slumped in his chair, which tipped and rocketed on its springs. As he rode it out, the phobic state began to pass. From here on in, he thought, he'd better spend this half of April far away. He was asking for it, staying here. He could be flat on the sands of Maui even now, and still it would only be midmorning. He could hike to an inaccessible bay, where even a battery radio only picked up static. Surely a man could find the will to live without an Oscar.

Greg leaned forward across the cluttered table and drew the stack of envelopes toward him. Then he rummaged in the long drawer level with his abdomen, searching out a certain folder. He didn't hear a sound from the television, but couldn't entirely forget what was going on, since Sid and Edna were whispering madly. On the other hand, he'd done enough complaining. He took a dozen photographs out of the file, reached for his felt-tip, and began to sign. "Sincerely, Barbara Stanwyck," one after another. Then, by way of variation: "Greetings from Hollywood, Love, Barbara." The picture was a shot from *Stella Dallas*. Stanwyck wore a wide hat and a wide smile, one of which she was hiding behind.

It was really Edna's job that Greg was horning in on here. The division of labor was strict: She did all the ladies, Sid did all the men. Doubtless Edna would find Greg's signature work too cramped and cautious, incompatible with a name once written in lights. Greg was mostly left to the accounting work—publicity, banking, and postal rates. But not tonight. Taxes were a shade too gray and common, somehow. He needed to be in the thick of an outsize dream, whatever dream he wished. Stanwyck was just the ticket.

He'd fallen into mail order quite by chance. From the stroke of puberty on, to the day he went over the cliff at thirty, he was always shooting a movie in his head. He was his own most passionate apprentice, preparing the way for the grave and complicated artist he planned to be at twenty-five. At seventeen he took to sporting scarves indoors, with a clipboard under his arm, somewhat after the manner of a shot of Cukor on the cover of *Life*. In the suburbs north of Chicago, along the lake, it might have gone over as chic, but he lived too deep in the city. The wearing of berets could

7

only mean one thing: Greg Cannon was a fairy. Tight-assed and wholly alone, he got back at the bullies and toughs for the names they called him by standing apart entirely from the animal mess of sex. He shook the immediate wilderness —high school, no money, no car—by living his real life somewhere else, in the silvery dark of a movie house.

At seventeen, Greg would have been in a state of rapture to think he would one day autograph Stanwyck's picture. He wouldn't have given a second thought to the moral dimension at all—whether or not it was right to deal in phony artifacts, purveyed to innocent rubes at six-fifty a throw. On the contrary. Until he was twenty-five, he figured a film like *Stella Dallas* told a brand of naked truth you couldn't find in Illinois. In his formative years, he stuck with *The Late Show* all night long, while down the hall his workaday family dreamed in the properly Freudian way. The studio films of the thirties and forties served him much as a liberal education was supposed to, in the sense that it gave him something to say about anything at all. Of course, his College Boards were very low, since relative clauses and algebra had never made it big at MGM. Still, Greg at seventeen would have defended the morals of himself at thirty-two, most nobly. His was an essential service, after all. There were people lost in the middle of nowhere. They needed a dose of Hollywood something terribly. Besides, who was to say the autographs he sold weren't real, if the buyers out there thought they were? To Greg, an artifact was nothing more than how it made you feel.

By the time he finished the batch of Barbara Stanwyck orders, he realized he was signing a still from another picture. He couldn't place it right away. She looked a bit the way she did in *Sorry Wrong Number*, lonely and trapped, except here she wasn't in bed and didn't have both hands glued to the phone. Almost without thinking, Greg's hand shot out to the folder and patted it nervously, as if to measure its thickness. The moment gave him sudden pause—to think he'd used up all of what he had of *Stella Dallas*. Ever since the day he sank his savings in these stacks and stacks of photographs, buying out the back room of a camera store on Sunset, he'd never yet run out of any item. He'd vaguely assumed his stock was inexhaustible, but then, he hardly could have predicted how the whole thing would snowball. At the beginning, he could do the week's business Sunday morning, over a bloody mary. Now they were sending out a hundred and fifty packages every Friday. He'd even had to liberate a shopping cart at Safeway, just to truck his orders to the post office.

"Honey," Edna said, appearing at his elbow, "we're going to faint if we don't eat. We gotta stick to a schedule, see? Sid, he can't stand fluctuation."

She nodded over her shoulder, as if to say it was out of her hands. As to dinner, she didn't appear to be after anything fancy. Greg shouldn't lift a finger. She'd rather be left to herself in the zinc-lined kitchen, where she'd root around, carte blanche, among the tins and dry goods, throwing together enough for three.

"What's this from?" he asked her suddenly, holding up the shot of Stanwyck looking raw and anxious.

"Don't she look great?" said Edna, beaming. "Like she don't fool around with love at all." They seemed to be intimates, she and Stanwyck, in matters of the heart. "And while you're at it, please get a load of the shoes. Now *that's* what you call high heels."

Edna appraised the total look as if she'd had a hand in it. She was by her own admission the total fan, made special by indirection, like the moon. The candlepower of stars had been established by the loyalty of those who didn't miss the resonance of alligator shoes. From the beginning, Edna was hooked on the heavy stuff. Her first film was *Queen Cristina*. Though she was only fifteen—and overweight and pug-nosed

9

—she stared straight ahead for several days, totally expressionless, in homage to the final shot of Garbo. When she grew up to be temperamentally sassy, with a lilt about the eye and a cutting edge like Claudette Colbert, she went on loving every star, and not one kind or another. She didn't require them to be like her, for one thing.

"*Jeopardy*," she said, shaking her head with a little sigh. "But it wasn't really her." Though it pained her to have to give a bad notice, she seemed to feel there was something extra required of a star performance. She couldn't define it in so many words. She only knew when it wasn't there.

"Aren't you missing the best part?" he asked her, tossing aside the photograph. He meant the Oscars.

"They're having a slew of ads," she said, "and then they got the documentaries." She pinched her nose between two fingers. "The middle always stinks. Sid's gone down to get the bourbon."

"Why? Doesn't he know by now he can drink my liquor?"

"And bother *you?*" She was at the doorway into the butler's pantry. "Sid thinks you're very grand, you know, when you got a lousy mood on. He thinks you must be working on a script."

"Well, I'm not," Greg retorted with sudden annoyance. He snatched up the cap to the felt-tip pen, brought the two parts together, and scored a sea-blue line along his thumb. The second time he connected. "I bet I'm the only man in L.A. who's *not* knee-deep in a script. It shows a certain sort of valor, wouldn't you say?"

"You think so? It never seems to prevent you acting like you're *in* a movie, does it?"

She disappeared into the kitchen. He wiped at the mark on his thumb and determined not to care what Edna thought. The Moorish room he sat in was an octagon. It peaked above him in a beamed and vaulted ceiling pierced eight times by pointed amber windows. It was very difficult, frankly—what with the golden light forever flooding in and the field of vision ten miles wide off the balcony rail—not to feel tracked by a camera. All the scenes that had ever wised him up had been shot right here, in the same bright weather. The cast of thousands had all been drawn from the streets that gridded this neighborhood—recruited, Greg felt certain, right off the corner of Cherokee and Franklin, eleven floors below his terrace. Little wonder, then, he was all wound up like a film. Edna was right. Since the day he landed in Hollywood, he secretly thought he was in a story bigger than the sum of what he saw.

Edna called out from the kitchen, as if she'd followed his train of thought: "I'm not saying it's wrong, you understand. Maybe you *are* in a movie."

If this is a movie, he thought, it's a bomb. The next thing he knew, she was back. She gripped a can of tuna in the teeth of an opener, and winced as she cranked it round.

"If it's one thing I don't question," she said, "it's a person's right to get pissed. You don't see *me* before noon, do you? Sid's got his Jim Beam, don't he? You know what your problem is? You don't *enjoy* a crappy mood."

Abruptly, she fled away a second time, the oil spilling out of the sides of the tin. He raised one hand and made a vague gesture, as if to wave goodbye. Fuck that, he thought. Since when was *she* the authority on moods? Though he had to admit he always listened, he wondered why he bothered. It wasn't as if she altered his behavior. When he once got the word how he came across to someone, he usually dug in his heels and did it in spades. The clue to his darker hours was the art of acting opposite. Though he sometimes seemed on the edge of easing up, likely as not he was preparing for a further turn to the ornery.

He picked up the morning's second-class mail from a wicker basket at his feet. Then he settled back to get a bead on the competition. On top was a flyer from a dealer out in

Van Nuys who must have bought a lot of junk at auction. For three hundred bucks, a person could own the model boat they used for distance shots in *The African Queen*. There was a rusty gun from *High Noon*. Then a chaos of fans and batons and sparklers from various tin-ear musicals—including an actual Carmen Miranda headgear, all gourds and paper hibiscus. The whole package was terribly sleazy, but Greg put it all to one side, since dancing was Sid's department. Most of these offers he tore up in little pieces. The counterfeit autographs notwithstanding, Greg was a moral absolutist. He hated the gyps and fly-by-nights.

The Monday mail was always fat with movie mags. He riffled through them one by one and scanned the last few pages. There, among dog tags and rubber underwear, was where he took his ads. The market was hard, and the stuff back here was as actual as the real world, ever got. He spotted himself right off: *The United Fans of America*. "Who is the brightest star of all?" was written out in italic caps. Then there was a ballot attached, as if every vote were being gravely counted. Membership fee, six-fifty. And to the first five hundred lucky fans, a studio shot of the star of one's dreams would arrive in the mail posthaste. All of this spoken in breathless abbreviation, as space was at such a premium. Greg took a close look at his three-by-five bit of media, as if it were his own name seeing print at last. It was hardly *War and Peace*, of course, but the big thing here was going public. As things fell out, in two short years the UFA had grown to sixty-seven hundred strong, with no end in sight. There was a vast, undreamed-of market out there, burning for an autograph. The UFA was bidding fair to become the giant in the field.

Yet it didn't matter a whit to him as the night came down on April third. What mattered was this: The boy in 2C had broken his word, and it made him the same as anyone else.

When he left this morning, downing half a quart of milk while Greg put together a cup of coffee, he swore he'd be back before dark, to leave off the book. Nothing more. They weren't about to go another night together yet. They went out of their way, it almost seemed, to pretend the night before had hardly taken place. One or the other was still too shy. So they breakfasted on chitchat—no more intimate, all of a sudden, than if they'd met each other waiting for a bus.

So forget it, he thought. *Just let it go.*

He dropped the magazines back in the basket. He itched for something tough to do, so he wouldn't have to think. In the end he lit on Edna—i.e., what the fuck was she up to? It didn't take this long to doctor a can of tuna. He stood up and made for the butler's-pantry door, feeling all his juices rise to a wave of irritation. He only hoped she was doing something wrong, so he could go in hurling accusations. Halfway across the octagon, he suddenly saw an orange glow reflected in the mirrored wall. Of course: the TV out in the other room. He couldn't make the image out. It was all a blur. It had the effect of a manufactured sunset, packaged for use in the home. He came up close to the dusky mirror and peered in across the apartment, as if he didn't dare turn and face it straight on. As if it would turn him to stone. He could see two stars at the podium, having a bit of patter before they got to the list of nominees. They were too far off for him to see exactly who they were.

He was lost, and he knew it. His line of defense had vanished. Edna was all distracted now, layering a casserole half a foot thick. Sid was siphoning bourbon out of a litter of bottles on his bedside table. The whole day's drama of monk-ish unconcern, in which he had refused to be involved and changed the subject time and again, had fizzled now to a stop. The figures shining in the screen's raw light had struck him dumb with memories. He turned like somebody hypnotized. He walked across to the Sony, perfectly still inside, as rosy as a drowning man sent ranging through the flood of years.

What the hell, he thought, *why not?* The Oscar show was long ago his first real glimmer of life Out There. He'd never missed it once in over twenty years, no matter how broke and horny. He stood two feet from the screen and watched. *Oh kid*, he thought, *where are you?* Even now, if the doorbell rang, he could have torn himself away. As it was, he didn't stand a chance. The winner was named, the audience clapped, and a man ran up the aisle to get his prize. Greg didn't move a muscle.

The smell of lilies was so intense that after a while it began to seem not real—as cheap as the dollar toilet water they bottled to sell at the airport. Vivien's first few hours on the island were always more like a memory coming back than something happening here and now. The lilies were part of the given—a four-acre field on the side of the hill above the house. The view to Harrington Sound across the ranks of fat white blooms was literally out of this world, as her mother used to say, though nobody ever went up there anymore except for the farmer who leased the land. Every April, as soon as the plane touched down in Bermuda, Vivien swore she'd climb way up through the cedar grove, to stand again knee-deep in flowers. As things turned out, she never seemed to get around to it. Somehow, she had all the lilies she needed, just keeping the windows open.

She was all alone in her mother's house—a limestone cottage with a white slate roof, of an indeterminate age and breeding. The land it stood on, some four hundred acres along the neck between the sound and Castle Harbor, had been in the family since New Year's Day in 1615. Deeded by Governor Moore to the mate of the feisty ship that brought the Bermuda settlers here from the damps of England. Before he ran off to sea, this mate had done a season acting at the Globe. The letters he wrote to his cronies still on the boards in London, letters drunk on paradise, had made him the model for Prospero, or so the story went. Even as a schoolgirl, Vivien Willis understood that the island estate on her mother's side was classier in the way of pedigree than that which attached to her father's ancient lands—those flat square miles of desert scrub that grew to be Orange County, going up a hundredfold in value just in twenty years.

Vivien's mother had kept the Bermuda house as a refuge from her husband, Jacob Willis. There was no paved road or a telephone. The water was out of a pump. As she pointed out to Vivien every spring, the only guidebook a body needed to roam these woods and raw pink beaches was a copy of *The Tempest*. And though the warring parties of her parents' marriage were now long dead and done with, Vivien saw no reason to improve the old stone house. Not that she needed a place to hide from Jasper Cokes, the husband of her dreams. They were far too busy, she and Jasper, to bother each other with marital ties, skirmishes or otherwise. She came here once a year in April to flee the larger matter of herself.

But she couldn't always shake it. It was just after midnight on Monday the third when she gave up and got out of bed. She left the lights all off and took no robe. She made her way out of the house, down the overgrown path to the water. From the close and crooked bushes, she came to a ledge. The nearest lights were far away along the sound, the water as black as the moonless sky. She could have dived in without a light, since she knew the depth at every point for a quarter mile on either side. But she knew she'd never sleep at all if her hair got wet, and she didn't dare risk losing the thin gold chain at her neck, pendant from which was the Willis diamond.

A thing she only wore when she left L.A., in case she was caught in a world depression and needed cash in a hurry.

She knelt into a tangle of ice plant that cascaded along the ledge. She gripped a rusted iron ring that had been in the stone, for all she knew, these past three hundred years. Then she put a foot over the edge, felt for the first step carved in the face of the rock, and made her way down. She reached the water line between the sixth and seventh steps. The water lilted and lapped against her as she went in. Irresistible as ever, warm as the air and supple as silk. When she was in hip deep, she let go the ladder cut in the stone and lay back limply and floated out, like somebody sinking to sleep.

She started to drift, the diamond still as an anchor on her throat. Jasper wasn't the type, she thought, to swim on a sleepless night. If he had no boyfriend current, he still had Artie and Carl, his bodyguard and manager, right at the flick of an intercom. He buzzed them up on a moment's notice whenever he couldn't sleep, and they took up where they had left off in a running game of Chinese checkers. Jasper knew not to dial his wife's room after hours. It was one of the countless rules that allowed them to survive. What was strange just now was thinking about him at all, since she hadn't been home in over two months. Stranger still, she missed him.

They'd talked at ten o'clock, when she called him from a phone booth at the Mid-Ocean Club to let him know she'd detoured here. He'd finished shooting on the new film only a couple of hours before. Already he was beside himself with boredom. She told him to get coked up and go to the Oscars, but that was the one thing he wouldn't do without her. Besides, if you weren't awfully sure you were going to win, it was too much trouble just to get out of the parking garage at the end. Jasper was always the first to admit: He was a moneymaker, not a performer. He only got nominated now and again to put a pretty face in the lineup.

"So," he said, through the crackle of static, "you getting laid?"

"Not really. And you?"

"Me? I haven't got the strength."

"Not even to fuck?"

"It's not that," he said, and he seemed to grope for a reason that would travel all that way. For a moment she thought they'd lost the connection. Then: "It's the small talk, mostly."

Vivien fell into a lazy backstroke, covering thirty or forty yards from shore before she stopped to look around. In Harrington Sound, she was wholly without the fear of drowning. Not like the ocean she grew up on—the brute Pacific, chill as ice and churning riptide. In some unaccountable way, she felt safer here than anywhere, as if a place survived where she might recover the stillness she lived in as a child—where nothing seemed to happen unless she wanted, and never till she was ready. She paddled about in total darkness, under a sky that ached with stars, and puzzled out the paradox of being Jasper's wife. She didn't know she had it in her to think of the two of them' tenderly. Reading the gossip day after day, forever avoiding questions, she thought she'd surrendered *her* opinion long ago.

Jasper and I, she thought drowsily, turning wide and heading back to land. *Jasper and I are only—*

Only what? Friends? Perhaps it was best to call them partners. Colleagues in a single profession, successful all on their own, who decided to get together to make a deal. A deal too big for one to carry off. How else was one to explain the clash of cultures? That he, the highest-paid actor in Hollywood, should end up hitched to the zillionaire heiress whose every change of clothes was news. Between them, they had the cover of every magazine in the free world sewn up—and this before they even met. When they met, it was more of a merger than a meeting.

Now, for the first time in over two months, she missed him and wished she was back in L.A., so they could be at loose ends together. They had these occasional days when they stuck together like a comedy team. It was them against everyone else, and they loved it. And when it worked, they could always count on being good for about five days—generous, giddy, and tuned to somebody else besides the face in the mirror. It didn't matter what they did. They'd deck themselves in doubleknits and shades and order a platter of ribs at Bob's Big Boy. They'd browse around in dirty bookstores, or stand around on corners and watch the hookers traffic. Anything not to be stars.

The fucking was the least of it, right from the start.

She was just twenty-four when her father, Jacob Willis, missed the hairpin turn at a hundred and five on a road he'd graded himself, between his ranch house and his landing strip. Vivien, in fact, was the one who was landing that day—as it turned out, into the arms of weeping ranch hands. Always after that, she had a certain horror of getting off planes. It was cars she should have been wary of, since her mother got picked off too, just eight months farther down the road, by a taxi in the Place Vendôme. The last thing she ever said to her only child was, like the lady herself, entirely sugarless: "Whatever else is out to break you, baby, don't forget: You don't have to marry money."

Three weeks later, the orphan Vivien, last of the Willis line, fell heir to about a third of Newport Beach.

It was past time, meanwhile, for Jasper Cokes to take a wife. At twenty-eight, he ought to have had a first marriage over and done with. Not that the public suspected any irregularities. The public believed what it wanted to—that a man with everything ate up life like candy, girls included. Concern over Jasper's waking hours in bed came down direct from the executive suite, where the Gelusil accountants toted up the grosses. Given that Jasper Cokes was altogether too pretty for their taste anyway—the Apollo physique toughed up with a day-old beard, the jeans and moccasins tattered—

they wanted the satyr's lust he gave off channeled into a proper deathless passion for a lady. They had no evidence whatever of the men in his life. But they spied an edge of danger in his eyes and, for the sake of their investment, saw they had no choice but to fence it in.

When Jasper and Vivien caught up with each other, in the commissary at Universal, they both couldn't move a muscle if they tried. Each was stuck in the middle of a green banquette, pinned in by prattling fools on either side. Though she looked terrific in gray and dark green, the kinks of her chestnut hair stiff as a broad-brimmed hat, she was fading fast in the midst of preening moguls. She picked over a salad as dead as the days gone by. At the facing table, Jasper sat in a space suit minus the helmet, waiting out the shouting match between the publicist on his left and the producer on his right. He looked up at the selfsame moment Vivien did.

And there they were in person, the rich girl and the movie star. As they stared for a moment eye to eye, they passed the first level of liaison, moving all the way up to invasion of privacy. Seeming to understand on the instant that they, at least, didn't have to go to bed.

"I'll trade you," she said straight at him, "this whole shrimp salad for an onion ring."

Only Jasper heard her. It was the curve of the green banquettes, perhaps, that let their voices leap across the aisle—the way it is said to happen under a dome. They were suddenly all alone.

"It's a deal," he answered with a grin. "But you have to promise to come for a ride."

"Where to? Are you from Mars?"

"Not anymore," he said, wiping the sweat from his forehead with the Mylar sleeve of his space suit. "Now I live on the moon. It's less of a commute. You'll come?"

"Does it have enough closets? They say I have the most clothes of anyone on earth."

"You won't need them. On the moon, we go around naked."

"Well, then," she said, "I can't come with you, Captain. But let's have a drink when you're back in town. You can teach me to tell the stars apart."

She pulled the spotted carnation out of the bud vase next to the sugar bowl, snapped it off at the stem, and pitched it across. He dropped his fork with a clatter to catch it. The publicist and the producer, roused from their dogfight, looked at Jasper furiously, while Vivien's moguls gathered her up and bore her away to sign her proxies. As she passed in front of Jasper's table, he whispered: "Before I'm through, we'll find you a planet nobody's put a flag on yet. You can have it all to yourself."

"As long as it has a Bonwit's," Vivien said.

And that was that.

She sidestroked through the quiet cove to the ladder in the rock. She reached an arm up to pull herself out of the water, then climbed and swung from the second step, her legs still dangling in the sound below. She hung by her hands for a long moment—the breeze on her naked back, the coral rough of the rock against her palms—trying to think of something else but Jasper. She swayed like a pendulum, back and forth. At the end of the arc she bumped against something hollow, knocking it off the wall. It landed below her with a splash. An instant later, one hand let go of the ladder. She held on like somebody on a trapeze and reached around in the dark water. Whatever it was, it must have sunk.

Then her knuckles scraped against metal, and the sudden touch brought back a wave of memory. She dropped to the water and landed close. It was just a bucket—a brittle raw aluminum, with a rim of cork at the bottom to float it. It had hung on an iron hook in the rock for as long as she'd been coming here. She got her hands on it bobbing about and felt it all over. Her mother had used it to gather clams from the sandy floor under the cliff. Yet the overwhelming recollection here was not in the mother-and-daughter direction. The dead were as dead as ever. What seized her instead was a ravenous hunger for Harrington clams.

She put a hand to her throat and gripped the yellow diamond, then flipped and did a deep dive, forgetting her hair. It was only five feet of water, six at most, but she had to squish the sand between her fingers several times before she got one. Bolting up, she dropped the clam in the bucket as she gulped a draught of air. Then down again. In a while, she had half a dozen, enough for a midnight snack, when she stroked back over to the ladder to put the diamond out of danger. She had to shed it to free both hands. Treading water, she unclasped the chain from around her neck. Then climbed up level with the iron hook. As she hung it there, clicking the clasp together again, it seemed to wink dully in the darkness once, like a fallen star. For the moment she wasn't a Willis at all.

She made for the bottom again and again. She didn't really need a dozen, since they didn't taste half so good the next day, and besides, she wasn't hungry. But it wasn't logic that got her into all of this, and she paid no mind to reasons. By now, she was too out of breath to stay down more than a couple of seconds at a time. A band of white was pulsing in her head. She nearly tipped the bucket once—the next time cracked her head on it coming up. Half drowned, but she got all twelve. And twelve was what they always used to have when they sat at the cedar table having a feast of clams.

She gripped the rim of the bucket, her chin propped up on the cork. She wondered idly if the clam knives had survived. If they weren't in the white tin cabinet by the stove, she couldn't think how she'd eat her catch. The sea birds dropped their clams and smashed them on the rocks. She could always resort to a hammer, of course, but the thrill of it was eating them alive. Razored open with the proper tool, they split to reveal the muscle whole—peach-colored, quivering, scalloped—and they fought back when they were chewed, in a final undersea reflex all their own. She hadn't thought of the eating part in years. It was as if the memory only occurred in stages, step by step as she followed along. Just now, it seemed that nothing else she'd ever eaten since had tasted quite so new.

She drifted about for a moment more, to recover her strength before she moved to lift the bucket up the ladder. She wished the night would double, somehow, and lengthen out this still and private time in which she could simply draw a blank. When she was done with all of this, she could use eight hours of sleep before the sun came up again. Out in the water, the dark took away those minor things that got too close around her, even in Bermuda. Only an hour ago, she began to see she was moving into something new. She could feel it gather in the wide black air like a change of weather.

Something to do with Jasper.

When the lamp went on in the parlor up at the house, she didn't get scared at first. She was looking up the slope toward a windy grove of sea pines just in front of the cottage porch. She could see them roll their branches in the westerly breeze. The sudden glow of the lamp broke through the night like a burst of fire and put the house on the map again. More than anything else, she felt betrayed. If she wasn't safe here to be all alone, then there wasn't a place, not anywhere. Even the middle of the ocean wasn't as far as it used to be.

One by one, the rooms in her mother's house lit up. She supposed it had to be one of the servants, since who else knew she was even here? She clearly wasn't thinking straight. The house hadn't had any live-in help in the whole eight years that she'd been married. All but a week in April, the house was shuttered up. But wasn't there still a caretaker down the road, halfway to St. George's, who kept the keys of a couple of dozen millionaires? Or the outdoor man, perhaps, who did maintenance once a week? Well, no. They'd never drop by so late, or not without getting paid extra. Only last week, she had called from New York on two days' notice. The banker who handled her trust hustled up a maid and an underchef from the Princess. They'd been in and out all weekend, but today she let them go and fixed herself a salad, so it wasn't any of them.

She was scared, all right. She put an arm through the handle and made her way up the stone rungs slowly. At the top, she swung the bucket up and plopped it down in the ice plant. Then she scrambled up after. The blazing house awaited her, and she tried to believe it was nothing more than an island drunk, rifling her clothes for a little cash. Or a couple of teen-age lovers tired of going at it on the beach, who'd scouted out an empty house to break and enter. Somebody she could chase away. She steadied the bucket against her hip and headed into the trees. It was probably Willis business. She was always dogged with cables and mid-night messengers bearing sheaves of documents that had to be signed on the spot. Some lawyer who needed a proxy, or a money man's courier armed to the teeth. The branches whipped against her naked skin, the cones and needles fallen in the path jabbing her feet as she lurched along. The handle caught on a bush and yanked her off to the side. She ripped it loose and padded on faster.

She was wild with rage at the brokers and crooks who wouldn't leave her be, but here she was only whistling in the dark. She knew it could only be one thing: Someone had gotten to Jasper. The lilies high on the hill were rotten with scent. The sea at her back was thick with sharks. She bounded up the white stone steps and reached for the door of the lonely house. She knew it now as sure as she knew her face on the cover of *People*. Someone had stolen the only man who had as much as she did.

*   *   *

He stood behind Edna's vacant chair and rocked on the balls of his feet, ready to sprint at the first sign of either one returning. On the Sony, the special-effects award was being announced by a starlet of the new school—fresh from a million-dollar modeling deal with Clairol and looking like she'd slept her way to the bottom time and again. Her pitch about the wizard technicians who whisked an audience off to other worlds was full of a phony niceness—Disneyland by way of Vegas. The black-tie crowd was moved to minor applause, as a clip from the winning film came on. Greg could only guess, since he hadn't seen the picture, but it seemed to be the final minute of something like Pompeii. The burghers boiled and shrieked, the prisoners tugged at their chains, and a wave of red-hot tapioca swallowed up the villas in its path.

It had an instant tonic effect on Greg, who remembered all movie disasters fondly. His hands in his pockets, his shoulders shrugged, he bobbed up and down on his toes. He decided then and there to stay on through to the acting awards. The dread he'd felt an hour ago was gone like any other—vanished the moment he took a step forward. Hollywood didn't stick like a bitter pill at all, once the matter of self-esteem didn't hinge on it anymore. The Hollywood Greg had failed in—six years' peddling scripts, with the growing assurance that all they bought was dogshit—cured him of envying those inside. Watching now as a taciturn animator made his halting thank-yous, clutching the statuette, Greg found himself brimming over with forgive-and-forget. He was so perverse. He was bound to hate himself later—either at ten o'clock, when the Oscar show was over, or any minute now, when Sid and Edna reappeared.

As it happened, he had other things to do.

He really ought to have seen it coming, except he was such a dope when it came to sudden changes. Always the last to see a thing flash—a falling star, a red-bellied bird in a lemon tree, the plume of smoke when the hills caught fire. He had lousy reflexes. Somehow, he didn't seem to understand that he'd been in the eye of a storm all day, and the wind had built to a hurricane roar. He watched as an eight-year-old girl handed over an Oscar to a dead old man. A purely honorary matter, as far as Greg could tell, and meant to prove that Hollywood was nothing so much as a happy family. Standing there like a circus couple, the little-doll moppet and the stroke-slowed mogul fairly glowed with good intentions. Rated G. In a minute, no doubt, they'd sing and dance. Greg, who was all but lost by now in the Oscars of the past, gave off a dreamy smile. This bullshit didn't bother him a bit. He rather liked it.

I must be in love, he thought with a sudden queer and giddy twist. The word he never used was out before he had a chance to bite his tongue.

And at that, the screen in front of him went blank. For a moment he thought he'd shorted a circuit deep in his head. He glanced around the room to see if the lights had dimmed as well, and when he looked back a second later, the anchorman on Channel 4 was already going full throttle. At first he hardly took it in. It all blew up so fast.

"Steepside," intoned the anchorman, "the Stone Canyon mansion of Jasper Cokes, was the scene of a double suicide tonight." It was all the man could do to contain himself; this thing was better than a plane crash. "Cokes and a young male friend were discovered about an hour ago in the garden of the vast hilltop estate. They were floating naked in a redwood tub. Both had apparently slit their wrists and bled to death. Police on the scene have found a suicide note, said to be in Cokes's handwriting. Full text of that note has not been made available, but sources say that Cokes believed he had no other choice."

Greg knew right off who the young man was. It was Harry. He stood there face to face with the Sony, bathed in an awful certainty. Ordinarily, he didn't believe in anything out of this world, supernatural or otherwise. He wasn't much taken with the notion of fate. So how could he be so sure? They hadn't said Harry's name at all. There was some mistake, there had to be. It was just a trick of the airwaves.

"Cokes's friend," the announcer went on, "was an unemployed drifter, identified as Harry Dawes of Hollywood. No one seems to know how long the two men had been lovers. In the note, Cokes is quoted as saying they took this step 'to be left alone at last.' That's a quote."

Greg would have bashed in the screen with his bare hands, except he knew he couldn't stop it. It wasn't a nightmare a man could wake his way out of.

"The actor's widow, Vivien Cokes, sole heir to the Willis land empire, has been out of the country for several weeks. She is now en route to Los Angeles, but the Willis Company will not disclose the time of her arrival. There are no children." This last delivered like a punch line, as if they'd had the goods on Jasper all along. "NBC will present a special report at eleven-thirty on the life of this strange and tortured star. A man who earned two million dollars every time he went before a camera."

He clawed his way up for air and thought: *Somebody's got to be lying.*

As if anyone cared what *he* thought. The station flipped its inner beams and brought the Oscars on again. Greg swung around to leave. He couldn't bear the vast indifference of the normal course of things. He stumbled back to the dining room as if he could start all over—as if to see what he had left.

But just then, Edna came through the gated arch the other way. She was reeling under the weight of a tray piled high with the night's provisions. The two locked eyes for a long moment. She saw that he'd sneaked a look at the Sony. He waved one hand in the air like a white flag, a shot of panic quivering over his face, and backed away in terror. She might have gone forward to hold him if it hadn't been for the tray. But all she could do was make a joke.

"I should have suspected as much," she said. "You're mad for short subjects, aren't you? Just like my sister Ruth. She always said there's nothing like a nice little travelogue."

She advanced all the way to the television and slid the tray across the top. Greg knew he had to get out. This horror was all he had. If he stayed to tell it to Edna, it would end in grief and bitter rage, the same as every other failure he'd been through. He needed to cling to this hairline flaw that he alone detected. Something very specific that didn't make any sense. If he didn't go off and nurse it now, he'd lose it.

"I have to run," he said quietly, not looking her in the eye.

"Oh, good," a voice behind him said. "You decided to join us, did you?" Sid stood square at the front door, cradling a dollar quart of sour-mash. So Greg was caught between them. Even then he didn't clutch. The spring in his feet still held. He just had to wait for an opening. Meanwhile, Sid went on as always, a ready opinion for every occasion. "You might as well see for yourself," he said, "the crap they're giving prizes to. Believe me, you can write circles around them."

"Who asked you?" demanded Edna. "You never read a word Greg wrote. He'd write if he could, but he can't." She pointed a finger at the accused. "See how upset it's made him?"

In fact, he'd started to cry. Quite noiselessly, but the tears were there. And Sid and Edna thought he was having a bit of a crack-up, to do with his lost self-confidence. They were both convinced he could write his own ticket, if only he'd put his mind to it. He usually had to holler to make them stop. He didn't want to be believed in. The least encouragement set him to pout. And yet, as he stood between them choked with death, they seemed pretty harmless beside the violence sweeping down the canyons. He saw the sort of grief they'd pegged him with—the melancholy writer making scenes on Oscar night.

"Let's eat," said Sid, striding away from the doorway. He didn't need to be told things twice. What they needed to do was take the pressure off Greg. They all had days when they woke up watery. They just had to redistribute the weight.

Greg turned and went for the door, and they didn't protest or try to help. When he turned to close it behind him, he gave them one last look—opening both his hands like a man out of money, and shrugging his shoulders deep. His jaw dropped, his mouth made an *O*, but nothing at all came out. He couldn't put it in words. And Sid and Edna looked back at him without any expectations. They'd only stayed friends so long, these three, by taking nothing personal. He owed no logic and no explanations.

So he pulled the door shut and lurched across the hall to the waiting elevator. He thumbed the 2 button instead of the 1, though without any clear idea of where he was going. He thought he wanted to storm about in the empty streets of Hollywood. He pressed his forehead against the thick cool glass of the bottle-green door, and watched the seedy hallways come and go as he floated down. The wall reliefs of the pharaohs were pocked and crayoned, slapped at random with out-of-date notices. He heard no sign of life at all. This late at night, he usually caught the fragment of a drama, spilling out somebody's door.

It wasn't that he clung to the notion that Harry was some kind of virgin. Nobody went as far as that. But he hadn't been anyone's lover either. He was much too clumsy naked, much too shy. He'd probably had a little action here and there, but it must have made him sad. He seemed afraid that love did not come into it at all. Deathless love was Harry's game. Assuming Jasper Cokes was Harry's type, even assuming they'd had this wild affair, the kid would never have slit his wrists. With his gypsy eyes and his swimmer's build, he would have opted for running away if it got too hot. There wasn't a trace of Satanic abandon about him. He didn't act out these little plays.

The glass door released with a sound like a kiss and glided back. Greg stepped out onto 2, where he'd never set foot before. Directly across was apartment J, and he started counting down—moving from west to east, on around to the southeast corner. Behind each door was a television tuned to the Oscars. When he got to C, he didn't stop to rattle the knob, but hurled his shoulder against the door. Though the crash could have probably roused the cop at Hollywood and Whitley, the lock held firm. So he drew back without a pause, executed a kind of karate leap, and hit the door with the heel of one shoe, just inches above the knob. With a splintering sound, the door blew open and slammed against the wall.

He reached in and flipped on the light switch just inside, peering about to get his bearings before he stepped over the doorsill. He had no fear of ambush. The ruckus he'd made was his ace in the hole. Silence was a good deal more suspect here at the Cherokee Nile than noise. Banging along the halls, the tenants all went out of their way to announce themselves—on the theory that if they didn't, who the hell ever would? Besides, they were all as busy as Sid and Edna tonight. And as to fear, the business of getting from 11D down here to Harry's place had razor-sharped his anger and put aside his tears. If things were as fishy as he believed, he was up against very big money and had to work fast. He owed Harry better than a good cry.

All the same, the particular smell of a single man hit him hard as he came inside. It was ordinary stuff—gym gear and old books and lemon-lime cologne—that pinned down the kind of man Harry was. Like a hiker, even here in the desert city. A man not easily housed. He was taking a walk around the world, so everything he needed had to fit on his back. Greg swallowed a sob and wiped at both eyes. He padded across to the sink to get water, and let the cold run till it chilled. He bent and drank. The small view of life was right: No man could be free and safe at the same time. One's innocence played no part. Nor did being twenty-four. From where Greg stood in his furnished room, Harry Dawes had passed this way like a boy on a raft, so unencumbered was the place. And yet, for all of that, it turned out he was doomed.

Greg took it all in, but he already knew there was nothing here. The narrow bed unmade, a pair of disheveled wicker chairs, a bamboo table stacked with a week's dishes. What Greg was after was a well of details—things that, taken together, showed Harry Dawes completely whole, before the story of Jasper Cokes consumed him. Greg wanted clues. The signs of a struggle, or maybe a trail of popcorn starting here and ending up at Steepside. He picked up a pair of shorts from the floor, folded them once, and laid them on the bed. Then a T-shirt balled in a knot, still hot with sweat from an afternoon's run. He shook it out and draped it over the back of the chair. It seemed these bits of life could break his heart, but they couldn't prove a thing.

He sat on the edge of the other chair and tried to give it up. He was nobody, after all. So what if he turned up evidence that somebody'd kidnapped the modest man who lived in this bare room? Who would he ever take it to? The years of brush-offs had taught him one thing over and over: If you have no bureaucratic recourse—no producer's desk to put it on, no agent's name to drop—then whatever it is you've come up with doesn't really exist. And if Greg was a crummy detective, Harry Dawes was a crummy victim. Nobody really cared. It was Jasper Cokes who got top billing. Any one of a thousand unemployed actors would have done fine as the young male drifter. No one was going to bother much with why this Harry Dawes had ended it all in his twenty-fourth year.

He picked at the props for blowing dope that littered the wicker-table top. The eight-year gap between them figured forth wherever he turned. As a general rule, Greg wouldn't allow a man in his life unless he could prove he was thirty-two. More or less was a whole other generation. It was as if he had no patience with people who hadn't been through what he had. He ought to have known that a kid wouldn't leave any interesting secrets lying about. Twenty-four wasn't nearly eccentric enough. It took years. How could you track down the thread that led to their pimps and killers? A kid didn't leave any traces at all.

He and Harry had kept it clean from start to finish. Nobody lied to. Nobody scored on. The one night they spent in each other's arms had barely brought them out of hiding. If love was what you called it, Greg had only been in that far for a little under an hour. It seemed the moment he said the word, Harry Dawes was gone. No wonder he was pissed. Like anyone else, he'd lost a hundred men in his time, but he never lost one to death before. He'd always supposed that loving and dying went on in countries that didn't share borders.

Now the walls were closing in. There was nobody good to blame it on. He knew he had no other choice but to let it go.

The book was half under the telephone in the middle of the floor. He never would have noticed it if he hadn't wondered, as he walked away, what the hell the number was. He probably ought to have it, he thought, in case he found it written in somebody's book who swore he never heard of Harry Dawes. He knelt and peered at the dial, committing the seven digits to memory. He saw the phone was resting on a book, and he picked it up to read the title. No particular reason. When he saw it was *Walden*, he realized just how close he'd come. He probably would have been quite content to watch the rest on NBC, like everybody else.

Walden was money up front.

He crouched there testing the heft of it. Then peeled the back cover at the upper edge to check out the number of pages: 271. Print like a prayer book. Lucky for him, he didn't much need the inside part. He knew the gist of this old book from a C/C+ in American Lit: the shorefront cottage, the four pretty seasons out of Currier & Ives, and a man has to beat his own drum. When it came to reading, he preferred a thriller's pace and a Hollywood angle. Still, he liked the serious feel of it in his hand. He'd have to give it a shot some day, for Harry's sake. Then, suddenly, he saw his own name on the flyleaf. Dated today. And as he read the sentences meant for him, he felt himself grow oddly naked.

> *April 3rd. To my friend Greg. I can't find it right now, but he says somewhere how you can't pull up a single flower without the whole universe coming up with it. Maybe, after you read this, we ought to go pull one up together. You say when. Love, Harry.*

All day long, he'd been acting just like Edna said, as if he was in a movie. Then, tonight, he passed across some time zone, out of one story into another. April third was a double feature. From the moment Harry left this morning, to buy him this book and go running, Greg had played at the failed writer. All afternoon, if he thought of Harry at all, it was purely carnal stuff. Two men twined like creatures underwater, rolling through the chambers of a coral sea. But that was all in the background, waiting till after dark. Greg was much too busy feeling failed to get all wrapped up in the simples of love. He had no idea he would end the day as a friend of Harry Dawes. Now that it was so, he had to dog this story down. He had to find his way through all the contradictions, all for the sake of a small affair that had lasted twenty hours. Maybe it wasn't a movie at all. But if it were, there was one thing sure: A man didn't die without a reason.

He closed the cover on the final words and stowed the paperback *Walden* in his back pocket. Without another look, he left his friend's apartment forever, determined to find just one good reason why they had to kill two men to get rid of Jasper Cokes. He'd done this much for Harry Dawes already: The cops would stop and think twice when they found the door of 2C blown open. Meanwhile, Greg came down the hallway, looking kind of sleepy. No one could have guessed what speed he had stored for the days ahead. To anyone looking out, he was doubtless much the same as ever. Lost in a dream and vaguely alarmed. By the time he got into the elevator, the pain in his eyes was faded into the general air of wistfulness. By the time he got off at the eleventh floor, he looked like anyone else.

Vivien threw the door open and strode in ready to fight. The parlor was empty. She ventured in a couple of feet and drew a breath to shout. The bucket had cramped her arm, and the breeze that blew through the cottage shivered the skin on her naked back. She meant to bellow something like "Get out!" But even as the first sound broke, she froze. A burgundy leather briefcase stood by the Adam desk. A putty-colored trench coat lay on the chair. And a fear like a fit of madness knocked the anger out of her. "Jasper?" she whispered across the room, but not because they were Jasper's things. They were Carl's. What she wanted from Jasper was why.

Then Carl himself came out of her bedroom, his Brooks Brothers suit all out of place. He was zipping up a garment bag that he cradled in one arm. His steely eyes hid out behind his tinted glasses. He wore a bush mustache that wasn't there two months ago. Vivien had kept her distance from this man for the whole of her married life. The terror that had her by the throat, that kneed her in the belly till she thought she'd puke, came down to this: Carl Dana had finally cornered her.

"Oh, Viv," he said when he saw her—a trifle absent-mindedly, it seemed. As if *he* were surprised to see *her*. "I've started you packing. There isn't much time."

"Put that down," she ordered him tightly. Amazed at how little she cared for keeping up appearances. "In fact, why don't you fuck off? Your twenty percent doesn't cover me."

"Can we argue later? We got a plane waiting."

"I guess you better hurry, then. I'm not going anywhere."

She decided to act as if nothing had happened. She walked across the parlor toward the kitchen, seeming to forget she was numb with fear. It didn't appear to get in her way that she had nothing on. She'd got it into her head that Carl was here to bring her back for another round of publicity. A special appearance at the Oscar ball, with her and Jasper together again for the first time in over two months. If she'd stopped to think, she would have realized the show was over. At the earliest, they were seven hours' flying time from Hollywood, even if they started right away. But she was too scared to think. She only knew how sick she was of the stories Carl put out. She wouldn't play wife to Jasper Cokes. She wouldn't sit for pictures.

"Hey, Viv," he said as she passed abreast. The voice was so gentle she could have screamed. "Didn't Artie call you?"

"There's no phone."

"I'm sorry. I thought you knew. It's Jasper."

Of course she knew. But she kept on walking forward into the kitchen. She heaved her bucket and tipped it into the sink, till the clams all clattered out. Then she turned to the white tin cabinet. She jerked the warped door open, filling the room with a sound like cymbals. Years ago, these shelves were crammed with all the kitchen necessaries. She put out an automatic hand to the spot where the clam knives used to be. But no. She'd lost the thread of this whole idea. She stood there, rubbing the purpled crease in the crook of her arm, and started to cry at last, as if to palm the crying off on a patch of local pain. There wasn't any doubt she was naked now.

"How did you find me?" she asked him, still not turning around.

"He slit his wrists in the bathtub," Carl replied, as if trying to get what he could into just a few words. "Him and this other guy."

What other guy? The last she heard, he was unattached. They both were. Still, they'd only talked by telephone these last two months, and maybe Jasper never found the moment ripe for naming names. If he thought he had to keep her in the dark, it must have been awfully serious.

"Me, I've been in New York," Carl said. No time to wait till she asked him. "I figured, since I had the plane, I better pick you up. Otherwise you'd have to wait till morning. The press'd be all over you." When she didn't nod or say a word, he took another step and threw the blame on someone else. "It was Artie's idea," he said. "He promised to call and break it to you."

The name shot through her like a pang of relief. She realized all she had to do was hang on now till she got to Artie. *He'd* know. Whereas Carl, whose trade was hype, could only talk in lies. She turned around icy and dry-eyed, determined not to give him the satisfaction of watching her fall apart.

"There's no phone," she said as she crossed to the bedroom. "I'm all ready. The bank can send my things. What bathtub?"

"No, no," he corrected, two steps behind her. Leaning in at the bedroom door. "I meant the outside tub."

This wasn't at all what he said before. If he had, she would have asked him just how that could be. Carl knew as well as she did, surely. Jasper wouldn't go near it. He said it made him queasy to sit in hot water. It turned his muscles to rubber. So somebody must have got it wrong. Unless—did people bent on dying get so they didn't mind a bit of discomfort? Why was it she couldn't stop looking for holes? She felt like she wanted to answer back, to everything Carl was telling her: "You're *wrong*."

"What other guy?" she said out loud.

She slipped on a white silk dressing gown. Then packed a dark knit suit in a carry-on—shoes and makeup and all. She'd dress on the plane. She listened to what Carl said about Harry Dawes with only half an ear, assuming it was lies.

"You know the type," he said. "Kid drifts in from nowhere. Finds he can't make it. Gets attached." But all of this could wait. He had another case to plead. "Viv, I know what you're thinking. Me and Artie weren't careful enough. I don't say you're wrong. But you got to understand, this whole last picture was a real bitch."

"You'll have to tell me all about it," Vivien answered distantly.

She flipped off the light and walked towards him. He shrank back as she zigzagged through the living room, dousing every lamp. The darkness fell behind her as she left. Carl had to move double-time to keep up. He'd scarcely retrieved his attaché before she was out in the drive. But she didn't go forward toward the car—its headlights lost in the cedars, engine running high—until he joined her. She stood with her head turned up the hill. She looked to be checking the weather.

"Aren't you going to lock it?"

"What?" she asked. Pulling away from the scent of lilies reeling down off the upland field.

"The house. We have to close it up."

"Why?"

Why, indeed. She walked across the grassy court to the waiting BMW. The driver, whom she knew to be the pilot of the Willis jet, leapt out at his side and held the rear door open for her. As she scooped up the long white folds of the robe, she might have been setting out late for a party. And Carl, who'd lost the lead the moment she walked in, got in beside her now without a word. He'd had his fill of trying to second-guess her. Or perhaps they'd reached the point where they could keep a proper silence. The car pulled out, and he fiddled with the latches of his attaché, as if he had plans to bury himself in work.

"I never read the script," she said. "It's a western, right?"

"*The Broken Trail.*"

"And what's it about?"

She knew he wouldn't pass up the chance to talk a picture up. The word-of-mouth was everything. Besides, he was more than glad to take a break from the other matter. If he thought she was acting oddly unaffected by it all, he gave no disapproving sign. To him, she probably wasn't any odder than usual.

"It's about this loser," Carl began.

As to how she felt herself, she would have sworn she was going mad if she hadn't been gripped by such a sudden fury. The grief was nothing yet, but all her pent-up terror had loosed its hold when the rage came on. Her moods were usually rhythmed like the tides, by forces off the earth, so she wasn't much given to finding cause. But why this anger? What was wrong? Surely it was more than Jasper dying. She desperately wanted an enemy, and she wasn't sure Carl was good enough. She'd have liked to be all alone just now. But the fact that Carl was here as well insured one thing: He wasn't free to dispose of Jasper back at Steepside, changing around what didn't work like so many cuts in a script.

"So he follows this bandit's getaway route," said Carl,

"from San Francisco all the way to the Mexican border." Carl liked his stories two lines long, as tight as a joke. "He's trying to find the guy's last hideout. There's supposed to be a fortune buried there. The thing is, it's been lost a hundred years."

They reached the end of the cedar alley. The BMW turned off the dirt and tripled its speed on the main road. She thought how, in the days ahead, anyone peering in at her window would say she was only gone for a swim. She sat back now so the wind blew on her face. It suited her present air of disconnectedness that an aura of her lingered here. It meant she would return. When all the dying was over at home, she would bring the grief back here. For now, she let the whole thing go—the paradise bit and the island girl together.

Then, without any warning, the wind was full of nothing but the sea. She couldn't smell lilies, no matter how deep she breathed. It was as if they'd driven across a border where all one's finer sentiments withdrew. If she remembered right, the lilies had always grown more and more faint when she drove off long ago. They vanished by degrees. Tonight, the perfumed air stopped cold, and she caught the rougher scent of the world at large—blurred and nameless and raw.

"Well, does he find it?" she asked him finally.

"You mean the loot?" He sounded like he didn't know. "It's hard to say. The ending's kind of a trick." At that, he seemed to struggle. She wondered if he had his doubts as to whether he ought to tell the trick. He cleared his throat. "You know," he said, "we still have an awful lot to decide."

"Later," she retorted sharply.

It must have killed him to yield to her, but he had no say unless she asked, at least till Jasper was in the ground. By common consent, a widow still ran her own show, whether or not she had a publicist in residence. With Vivien, it was something even more. Her whole life long, she'd had this fear that came on her like a fever, such that she always failed in the maze of death at the first or second turning. Tonight there was none of that. The fury she rode would not be stopped. It made its own road over anything put in its way. Especially the likes of Carl.

"I'll tell you what," said Vivien brightly. "You just wait till we're over the Rockies. We'll still have a whole half hour to decide."

"Decide what?"

"Who to put the blame on, you or me."

"Vivien darling," Carl replied with a weary sigh, his temper razor thin, "don't you know a thing like this is never someone's fault?"

"Shove it, Carl," she snapped at him—meaning to tempt him further if she could. "You save that shit for the cover of *Time*."

They made the run to the airport. Far down the fields on either side, she saw the blue of landing lights. She could scarcely wait to be airborne—all locked up for seven hours, and nothing to do but fight. She looked across at his shallow profile in the dark. If she had it her way, they'd be rolling in the aisle—biting, pulling hair—before they reached the mainland. She burned to make him suffer it more than she. Burned to be, as between the two of them, the one who would survive it.

"You act like you're the only one got left behind," he said. "You think *I* don't hurt? I feel like I just lost a brother."

"What you just lost," she said, "is a job."

They came in under the wing of the Willis jet. A steward stood on the tarmac, a fat white towel over one arm—as if someone was just coming out of a bath.

"And I don't need you," said Carl, with a finger triggered as if between her eyes, "so lay it on someone else."

"What *you*'re going to need, Mr. Twenty Percent, is an alibi."

The pilot opened Vivien's door. The steward opened Carl's. For a moment, no one emerged from the back of the car.

"An alibi for what?"

"Whatever's been done," she said with a shrug, and gathered her things and left him there.

The night air all around was empty of every island flower. The breeze was soft. The sky full-domed. Vivien hurried across to the waiting jet as if she were in an awful rush.

She didn't know what she meant at all.

chapter 2

DESERT-GREEN, SNAKE-PROWLED, POWDER-DRY, they rise up here like the last of the West. In fact, as mountains go, the Santa Monicas play the wilderness part to the hilt. They front the coastal plain of the L.A. basin with something like the pride of ranges fully twice their size. And not because they can't be climbed, since that is all some people ever do. But they aren't pristine in the Tibetan way, removed forever from man's estate. One cannot get properly lost in them, or avalanched or height-sick. Still, there are stretches not yet built on that are empty as a dream. Money claims title and trees these slopes wherever it can, from Brentwood east to the steeps of Hollywood. Yet for miles at a stretch the stubborn ground persists, from crest to empty canyon. In a city where most of the people have scarcely a three-foot square to stand on, the scrub-covered ridge of the Santa Monicas is the closest L.A. ever gets to a thing like Central Park.

In the winter of 1919, Abner Willis was able to say that he bought Stone Canyon for a song. Nineteen hundred acres at eight cents a throw, to be precise. At the time it was so much dead-end dust, boxed in by mountains too steep to pitch a tent on, and not a cup of water as far as the eye could see.

Though it lay between Bel-Air and Beverly Hills, those heavily gardened districts turned their backs on nature in the raw, as if it were faintly embarrassing. But an old deed-trader like Abner knew a good deal more about land than how to turn it into the south of France. Long after everyone else had subdivided madly, he kept all his bottom land in orange trees and beehives, biding his time for twenty years, and never so much as breaking even on a crop. He put off deciding where to build his house, preferring to ride up all alone and living out of a sleeping sack.

In 1935, he convinced the county water district to use his canyon for the west-side dam and reservoir. He sold it back to the public at better than half a dollar's profit on the acre—a six-hundred-percent return over twenty years. Considering that he had a thousand back for every dollar he sank in Orange County, the canyon deal was next to philanthropic. Besides, if he'd charged the county any less, they would have been suspicious—maybe his canyon leaked, or it sat on a hairline fault. He couldn't have been more accommodating, frankly. All he was after was the view out over the water, with a bowl of hills around it. A wilderness all his own within the L.A. city limits.

He used to say he'd got a little corner of Wyoming. Doubtless no one from Wyoming would have seen it quite that way, but more and more, this was how Steepside came to see itself—wild as the last frontier. Abner Willis stood on his empty hilltop, pointing down the canyon toward the dam, and said to Mr. Wright, his architect: "Pretend this canyon's the middle of nowhere, and build me a house on top of it. Make sure it's open all over, so the Willises never forget it's the West down there."

Abner knew full well where the Mediterranean lower third of the state was headed. The people were pouring in so fast you couldn't count them. It wasn't going to end till every vacant lot was taken up. In twenty more years, Los Angeles wouldn't remember how far west it used to be. By then, as Abner saw it—turning to point the other way, east along the ridge of the Santa Monicas, high above the endless city—by then, the people here would all be living in the future. And barring some catastrophe—say an earthquake seven-five or better, which Abner knew was an old wives' tale—who was going to protest the future's being here? The rest of the world, as far as Abner Willis could ascertain, preferred to stick to the past.

On Tuesday the fourth, when Vivien Cokes, the last of the Willis line, came back to the hilltop she called home, she had to do the final leg in a company helicopter. She could have sworn the seats were upholstered to match the jet. But she had no choice. A crowd of upwards of a thousand was jammed so tight at the Steepside gate, it would have taken a car a good twenty minutes to inch its way through. If the widow herself had turned out to be in a given car, they probably would have flattened it. Just to get a close-up of her, red-eyed and bereft.

The helicopter whirled up over the dam and into the canyon, crossed close to the water, and then rose up the side of the hill, touching down on the west lawn. Vivien jumped out first. She ignored the half-circle of downcast types who waited to tell her how sorry they were. She threw her arms around Artie and tugged him away to the house. But he wasn't any help at all. He couldn't stop sobbing and asking her why—the very thing she'd counted on him knowing. As to where the blame should fall, he didn't leave an opening big enough for anyone but him. It was all his fault, he told her over and over. The mortal flesh of Jasper Cokes had been given into Artie's care. In the bodyguard line of work, a man made only one mistake.

Meanwhile, four sympathetic suicides—all of them thin young women—were laid to the Jasper Cokes affair in the course of the first day. It wasn't clear whether they died because they agreed the world was awful, or whether the knowledge that their particular star was gay had sent them over the edge. When at last the police came lumbering down the hall to Harry Dawes's apartment, they found it wall to wall with neighbors, all of whom swore the door was broken open when they got there. Nobody really cared. There was nothing to steal.

At Universal, a couple of jumpy executives scrambled around in the editing rooms and scooped up every scrap of *The Broken Trail*. This they locked in a vault, with an armed guard dressed like a chocolate soldier. The film's director, Maxim Brearley, announced to the press (before he went into seclusion) that all of Jasper's tortured final days were there to see in the picture.

Of course, you could hardly find an out-of-work actor who didn't have a story to peddle as to the kinks of Jasper Cokes. But most of the dirt was going to have to wait. In the follow-up work, they'd prove how his whole life reeked of death and the drift into moral corrosion. At present, the media had all it could do to bury him. Or, as it turned out, to burn him up.

It seemed he'd remarked to Vivien once that he wanted his ashes buried high in the hills at Steepside. Just like Abner Willis, who'd always had a horror of ending up another stone in a graveyard. At the time, Vivien simply laughed it off as one of Jasper's ironies. They were eating a mound of crab in the Cecil Beaton suite at the St. Regis, looking out of a big round window down the length of Fifth. Jasper had always been uncommitted, to place above all else. He didn't seem to require a permanent home. He preferred hotels. So when he spoke that night of a bare and windy grave site, she thought he was saying the opposite. Why would he care about afterwards? He'd had all his candy on this side.

But when they got together to iron out details, they found he'd made the same remark to Carl and Artie, too, years ago in a low-life bar miles from the nearest cemetery. They saw now that he must have meant exactly what he said. Ashes in the hills was the order of the day. It was only then, when Vivien gave the nod to release these plans to the press, that she first began to see herself as one of three around Jasper Cokes. She'd always thought of them before as three against Carl and his bloodless deals, though here it was she who usually stood and fought. Jasper and Artie tended to be amenable. Furthermore, she always supposed that if anyone split the group, it would be she. But now it appeared the mathematics were over her head.

They settled on a sunset service for Thursday the sixth, and decided to keep the mourners down to five, forestalling the overland invasion of the press by inviting the lady dean of the anchormen to film it from a hundred feet away. This was not enough for the swollen crowd at the bottom of the hill. By Wednesday noon, the police had pegged it at forty-five hundred. The boulevard up through Beverly Glen from Sunset to Mulholland Drive was all but impassable. Most had come expecting to file by an open coffin, thus to wail at the frailty of life. At the very least, they expected to watch a fleet of limos pass in and out. An urn let into the earth with only five in attendance seemed to them a lousy piece of theater. As the numbers grew on the boulevard, they put on a show of their own.

The downhill gate was abandoned, except for security traffic and the delivery of goods. In addition, Vivien dismissed the helicopter within hours of her arrival, as being too noisy and disorienting. So whenever she and Carl and Artie left the estate, they were forced to go on horseback. Down the steep and narrow trail on the canyon side, where there wasn't any road, then around the north end of the reservoir. It was about an hour's ride. When they reached Stone Canyon Road, a driver picked them up in the powder-blue Rolls and whisked them away through Bel-Air. The crowd at the gate was never the wiser. Vivien made the trek twice, to get out to dinner on Wednesday the fifth, and Thursday morning to shop for black.

It was just gone midnight Wednesday when she led the way uphill on Jasper's buff-and-spotted horse. Carl and Artie were fifty yards behind her, arguing what would have happened if. An hour ago, she'd sat with them in the Hamburger Hamlet in Beverly Hills. Rough and sweaty in her riding clothes and wearing mirror glasses, she listened while they blamed it all on Harry Dawes. The worst they could summon up to pin on Jasper was keeping Harry secret. Vivien wasn't buying their scenario, though she hadn't said a thing at dinner. If they were going to be strictly accurate, she thought, Jasper was more to blame for the boy than the boy was for Jasper.

She looked off across the ghostly outline of the bowl of hills that cupped the canyon. It looked like a mountain lake tonight, with the desert vegetation high and green around it. The sage was heavy in the April air, and something white beside the trail had broken into bloom. By the time she reached the top, she was far ahead of the others. She did not linger to watch the night. She ducked and clung to the horse's neck so they could shortcut, coming in through the moon gate and along the length of the Japanese garden. She called out Jasper's groom from the stables, gave over the horse impatiently, and fled inside. It was simpler to be alone.

Harry Dawes was not what he ought to have been, and Carl and Artie knew it. They made a show of his being a zero. They wanted him half whore, half messianic crazy, so they could put the whole thing down to Jasper under pressure. Vivien had seen the type herself, wandering openmouthed on the upper terrace by the pool, the morning after. She had no idea where Jasper ran across them. They seemed to understand they'd be wise to get a good look while they could. Sometimes, she'd almost wanted to give them coffee.

Then Artie would come and tap them on the arm and drive them off, while Jasper slept in until midafternoon. Ideally, Harry Dawes should have been that sort.

Vivien wasn't sure what she wanted him to be. From what she read, he was the Huck Finn of a small Wisconsin town that had lowered all its flags to half-staff and now stood waiting at the depot while the Willis Company shipped the body home, free of charge. The way it was being pitched in the tabloids, he'd announced to his widowed dad that he planned to spend his twenties finding out why the world didn't work. It was hard to see through shit like this, but Vivien had a built-in periscope from lifelong study of the pitch on her. He seemed quite nice, quite likable and real, this Harry Dawes of Turner's Falls, Wisconsin, son of a heavy-equipment man.

He only came to L.A., it seemed, to get to the harbor at Long Beach. He'd been on the road two years, and he thought it was time to sign on a freighter bound for the islands. But he got to L.A. and fell for the climate and the rootlessness, which matched his own exactly. He decided to give it a year—about seven months gone when he died.

Vivien didn't see how she could go along with the Steepside line, which made him sound like a sullen drifter. The kid loved animals. He lived on books. She decided he would have been good for Jasper Cokes. As the week rolled on, as she paced her bedroom and took no calls, she brooded more and more about the boy from Turner's Falls. It was as if Harry Dawes could have told her why. Could have told her who to blame.

Artie rode sidekick Thursday morning. They left the house just after seven and resumed the downhill trail as if they'd stopped the night at an inn. It had rained for an hour before dawn, and the bushes on either side of the trail swagged against their legs and wet them to the skin. The pewter sky was bruised in the east with white, where the sun was coming through. Artie had packed sweet rolls and a Thermos in his saddlebags. He pointed down to the grassy spot by the water's edge where they would stop for breakfast. He must have thought she needed cheering up, because he kept on reassuring her. He seemed to have gotten the tears out of his system.

In fact, she was holding up all right. Not feeling much of anything. A suicide got what he wanted, after all. Her anger had somehow disappeared, like jet lag. Maybe, now that she saw what a fine man Harry Dawes turned out to be, the rage had no place else to go but Jasper. And she didn't want to take it out on him. So she played it numb and glassy-eyed, and waited out the run of other people's tears. This feeling next to nothing was almost second nature. It was part of her breeding, like the love of high prices.

"Artie," she said, because she had to say *something*, "was Jasper scared of getting old?"

He was riding on the switchbacks just in front of her—burrheaded, musclebound, guileless, shy. He leaned forward and whispered into his horse's ear, and she thought at first he hadn't heard her. Then, when he straightened up and pranced ahead, she thought perhaps he didn't consider the question worth an answer. She decided she agreed. But then he turned around in his saddle and for a moment looked at her piercingly. It was just the way he used to look at Jasper on the set, as if to check out whether he had a part down pat.

"It was *being* old he would have hated," Artie said. "But he wasn't the type to feel it yet."

"That's not what Max is saying."

"He never even had a hangover. Not once in sixteen years I knew him. Jasper *liked* the way he felt."

"It's a funny way to kill yourself," she said.

They stopped by tacit consent on either side of a hairpin angle, so they faced away onto different hills. She was a couple of feet above him, and she saw him backed by the canyon and the wide and leaden water. In his black shirt yoked with yellow thread, he was surely the only substantial cowboy for miles around. The frontier verities clung about his person, glinting like a sheriff's badge. Vivien made do very nicely drawing a blank with everyone else, but Artie seemed to require that she be present and accounted for. It was mildness a person couldn't ignore.

"Max makes out like he saw it coming, does he?" His own directness made his voice a trifle halting. "Like it's there in Jasper's face. Like some disease. That's bullshit, Viv."

"But Artie, it *happened*."

The spotted horse beneath her shivered with impatience, as if to say this wasn't the right approach at all. She knew that if she'd looked at Jasper's face herself, she wouldn't have seen a thing. But she wondered if it didn't expose some fundamental failure in her vision. Some loss of nerve in the face of love.

"I mean, it didn't come out of nowhere, right? A thing like this takes years."

"It's this way," Artie said. "He finally got too stoned." Sounding, all of a sudden, as if it ought to be self-evident. Just two days since, he was choked and panicked to find out why. "I think they both got ripped and played it out like a fantasy. They probably thought they'd wake up after and be as good as new."

As if it was only a movie.

The horses seemed to sense a sudden impasse here. They started forward, all on their own, as if to resolve it in physical motion. They sashayed down an incline. From the sandy ditch on the uphill side of the trail, a canyon hen and her chicks went scurrying under a bush. Vivien hadn't ridden here in years, and she was shocked to see how little it had changed. Nothing was ruined. Nothing gone.

When Jasper was in a picture—that is, when he wasn't on

camera—he segued from one to another of the recreational drugs. It was as if he had to work up a state of reverie over the story he was starring in. An air of distraction went with him wherever he went, like a background instrumental. So you never knew, late at night when he talked nonstop and went out slumming, if he was playing some kind of game or only lost in the role of Jasper Cokes. Vivien saw what Artie meant. For a man wrapped up in a starring role, there was no telling where a game might lead when the night began to fight it out with the morning. You might get carried over it like a falls.

"When you went away, Viv, did you know you were coming back?"

"Of course," she said—dismissing it even before she took it in, imagining they had turned to lighter matters. They plodded ahead. If Artie was right, it was only an accident. Jasper hadn't planned a thing. She wondered if this made her feel any less betrayed.

"Because I missed you, Viv," he said. From the hunch of his overmuscled shoulders, she saw how it shied him to say it out straight. "See, I never would have stayed this long. Not for Jasper's sake. It got so he made me very sad. He didn't *mean* to, but like I told him, what's the point of protecting a man on the outside, if all the risks he takes are in his head?"

From the first, there were birds around them, lighting in the sagebrush whenever they stopped, and betting they'd break out the sweet rolls early. A few kept pace—a scatter of sparrows and a pair of jays—but now they bristled and squawked. They had to turn back. They were hilltop birds, and they had no range in the canyon.

"Did Jasper think I was gone for good?"

"It's the first time you ever left when he was shooting."

"You're not answering my question."

"I know. You're not answering mine."

Somehow, she'd never gone out of her way to see what it was between Jasper and Artie. She supposed they must have been lovers once, long ago in college in Vermont. At the time, they must have been equally matched. But as Jasper's name got brighter, till they knew him in every town on earth that had electric lights, Artie's scope got narrower and narrower. He was chief valet and dialogue coach, as well as the unofficial final word on Jasper's look in a given scene. At night, with his stash of whites and blues, he was Jasper's last connection.

"I would have said goodbye, you know, if I wasn't coming back."

Though she had no knack for friends, she and Artie were something close. By dint of their lives' geography, they'd passed eight years in the same house, and neither one with a job in the outside world. Of the four of them, they were the two who most often had nothing to do, and they tended to do it together. Over the years, they'd logged a thousand hours of ordinary things. Walking half the night in the streets of foreign capitals, while Carl and Jasper hustled distribution rights. Or sitting on hotel terraces, sipping the local water, saying whatever came into their heads. They'd done a lot of getting by, and in the end they lived by a kind of shorthand.

"I miss you, too, whenever I go away," she said. She saw she owed him proof of what had survived between them. "I used to want to take you with me, only Jasper always seemed to need you here. We should have done it anyway. It might have made you famous."

"No," he said reproachfully, "don't say that. Some people are better off left in the background." He had to keep his back to her to speak about himself. The horses were footing a tricky bit of slope, so all their eyes were on the trail. "You don't want to crowd the people up front," he went on in a rueful way. "You and I would never have talked the way we have. Not out there." He nodded down the canyon and over the dam. "I'm sorry, Viv."

"About what?"

"I just couldn't keep him from being alone."

They were coming up to a length of level ground. The horses would break to a trot for a hundred yards along the water, on a beach of broken stones. They had, perhaps, a couple of minutes more before they could not hear above the beat of hooves. Five minutes after that, they would lay out breakfast on a jut of land in the reservoir—shaded by an orange tree the rising water hadn't ever reached. They must have known there were certain things they would only say today, at this one moment. That is really all she needed—just to know there wasn't time to waste.

"You thought I left? Is that what you thought? Let me tell you something, Artie. This whole last year, I'd look at Jasper and start to think: *What if you stay and he pulls you down?* So I took off. I had to get away from it. But listen: I would have come back. Jasper knew that. God damn it, I was on my way."

Though she hoped it would answer the question he said she was avoiding, she couldn't be certain now she knew what the question was. When she spoke again, her voice was a good deal smaller.

"Did Jasper say I left him?"

"Yes. But I told him he was wrong."

They must have used up half their time, just letting that sink in. She supposed that Artie knew he was staying on at Steepside. He lived there, didn't he? Why, therefore, did they talk as if things between them were in the past tense? They acted as if it wouldn't work straight on. The pretext had been removed. Perhaps they'd gone on too long devoid of ulterior motive, without a word like *friend* or *lover* to neatly wrap them up. Perhaps they couldn't make it all alone.

"Well, maybe he was right," she said, as if Jasper's guess was as good as hers. "I suppose I never got used to his fans. They're too damn loyal. *Mine* don't love me at all."

"He used to love them back," said Artie. "But that stopped too. He didn't love anyone anymore."

They were two steps short of the straightaway. Artie's fat-assed mare slid down the last few feet and scrabbled forward. Vivien called out louder than she liked, for fear he would get away before she got it right.

"Except for Harry Dawes," she said.

"No, no," protested Artie, "not even him." The horse shot off along the stony track. The rest of what he said he had to shout out over his shoulder. "I already told you," Artie bellowed, sending an echo round the canyon, "Harry Dawes was just a fantasy." The name repeated again and again, till it didn't mean a thing. Just then, she reached the flats herself. She hurried along in Artie's wake. He shouted one last time: "There *was* no Harry Dawes."

And that was the way they left it.

It was eight years past that Jasper Cokes arrived in the town that made him, straight out of two years in the army. Passed out cold in the bed of the truck he'd driven east from Cleveland years before, when he left to go to college in Vermont. He woke up squinting at the morning sun, just as they made the downhill turn off the freeway and passed the Hollywood Bowl. Hung over on Napa red, he wasn't in much of a mood, but he liked the palms and the stucco right off. He rapped his knuckles on the rear window, as if to knock on wood.

Up front in the cab were his college pals—Carl Dana and Art Balducci, mismatched as a two-man stand-up team— and much too busy arguing maps to turn around just now. And anyway, Jasper's first impressions were not of any real consequence, not to what they were after. The master plan for this career had been in motion all the while Jasper was stationed in Thailand, refining his taste to higher and higher grades of hash. The three of them had made their deal the night they graduated college: They would make a star of Jasper Cokes. They had their contacts all set up. It seemed what Jasper mostly had to do was let it happen.

There were two things on their side. They had no contingency plan at all, in case they didn't strike gold. They'd left fate no alternative. And they weren't too proud to do shitwork, either, if that was the only way. The rest was purely matters of timing. You had Vietnam on the one side, the desireless life of the street on the other, and so, for a brief time, every displaced adolescent didn't burn to be a movie star. Jasper and his cronies were the sort of investors who meant to get rich quick in the classic way. With the market down, they bought in big.

They gave the people the same old thing, but more so. In a year that was frantic for any diversion, Jasper scored in a part nobody wanted. It was a werewolf picture unredeemed by fear. The monsters looked benign as pandas. But every fifteen minutes, Jasper Cokes took his shirt off. Just at the climax, water swamped his yellow rubber rescue craft. For half a minute, he wore a pair of khaki pants onscreen, all wringing wet and steamy. It was clear he hadn't a thing on underneath. You could practically tell he wasn't circumcised. A blushing nun with nothing to compare it to would have had to admit it was awfully big.

On the strength of bookings in Southern drive-ins alone, Carl got a foot in at every studio—billing Jasper as the athlete type, but neglecting to mention the sport. It didn't much matter. To put his first million in the bank, Jasper squirmed in and out of half a dozen uniforms. He was linebacker, shortstop, three-meter diver, and middleweight champ. With an obligatory scene in the showers every time he came off the field. Conventional wisdom had it that you could only get away with khaki pants the first time. After *Night of the Howling Teens*—which the industry privately called the first mass-distributed six-inch tool—nobody ever got another chance to check out Jasper's best equipment. From that point on, they kept the focus mainly on his face. The rest of him was more or less a dream.

For three days after he died, Jasper was all the local news that mattered. It was rumored that he left a hundred million —in itself a lot to reckon with—but what was more, the press had found out how it divvied up. By the terms of the ancient contract, twenty percent had always gone to Carl. Five more went to Artie. All the rest was Jasper's. It stayed that way through eight long years of paperwork. There were pitchmen who swore they could make him better money, if he'd only get rid of his old school ties. But the terms remained as immutable as the set of relations among them. The roles they played for the media seemed like they were written in according to the percentages. Any star worth his salt required a fast-talk front man, as well as a dumb palooka to shoulder the way through crowds. In any case, death didn't change the cut of the money. Carl and Artie got twenty and five of every dollar that Jasper left.

The human-interest angle, meanwhile, did not hesitate to go baroque. A has-been starlet, Jenny Sutton, swore she talked to Jasper just before he died. He was woozy with barbiturates, all right, but he didn't sound anywhere near the edge. She further seemed to intimate that she and Jasper were getting it on, but then, she hadn't had a part in years. In another late development, the Miami-based Legion of Fans was suing, though it wasn't certain whom. They had information that an unidentified wino was shipped from the city morgue to the crematorium—where he showed up a few hours later as Jasper Cokes's ashes. Jasper's body, the rumor went, had been removed to a secret place. He was only in a coma. A team of doctors had flown in from Houston to monitor all his vital signs.

Jasper would have loved it. As a man who came from nowhere, he applauded the drive of those who liked to tie themselves to a good story. It was only common sense to try to parlay one's connections. You got a name, you dropped it. Let them have their sliver of limelight, all those various types who swore they knew the real Jasper Cokes. His barber at Universal, second-string hit for the Jersey mob, dabbed at his swollen eyes with a hanky, telling how down-to-earth he was. Lou Messina, the owner-trainer at Union Gym, who once rubbed Jasper down—in a scene that must have ended up in a curl on the cutting room floor—talked as if he'd brought his man to competition form. Then a woman emerged who said she was his layer-on of hands. By some odd quirk of UPI, a picture of her surfaced in a hundred different papers —long-fingered like a witch, in yards and yards of black, the lace shawl at her shoulders very like a tablecloth. Vivien had never heard of her.

But frankly, who was counting? In all of these assurances of kinship, no one made a move to separate what was true from wishful thinking. The strangers and tradesmen and tellers of tales had only the nicest things to say when they remembered Jasper Cokes. Nicer things than anyone thought at Steepside anymore. In the press accounts, such sentiments were banked about the casket, rather after the manner of floral arrangements. All of which was fine, except they couldn't last.

Greg and Sid and Edna didn't know what to make of it. Whatever prior claim they might have had on Harry Dawes was rendered moot by a flood of eye-witness reports. In a day or so, there wasn't anyone who hadn't seen the short main street of Turner's Falls. The grocer where the kid had worked his high school summers reminisced at length. The track coach put his two cents in. The rector and the milkman. It seemed as if there were dozens who knew him better than Greg did. He couldn't think of a folksy detail he could peddle. The coverage swept right by him, stopping off at the Cherokee Nile just long enough to show it was a fleabag.

As it happened, they were most uneasy allies. They found they had to go back a step before they could even start. They were stuck with all the things they'd put off saying. Greg came up from Harry's place, the *Walden* in his pocket, and spilled the whole thing out as best he could—lapsing for half an hour into helpless despair. But it turned out Sid and Edna had some losses of their own. Though they'd never given the slightest hint, it turned out they'd been tight with Harry Dawes for weeks and weeks. He'd let them have the small-town treatment that made him so beloved in Turner's Falls. Doing them little favors. Never too busy to talk. He drew out all the story of their lives. You couldn't really blame them wanting to give him something in return.

Even so, they nearly didn't bring it up, so certain were they Greg would savage them for meddling. But they couldn't stand pretending anymore. In a halting way, they admitted as how it was they who set him up. *"There's a brainy guy on the eleventh floor, you ought to get to know him."* After that, they stood apart and waited. Edna kept up Harry's spirits, feeding him wedges of carrot cake with a side of herbal tea. He came back quite dispirited, it seemed, when he ran into Greg in the foyer by the mailbox. Till the very last minute, apparently, he was certain Greg had looked straight through him.

"When we saw it was finally going to happen," Edna said cautiously, "the two of us bowed out. It wasn't really our affair."

Whose was it, then? Just who had had the thing with whom? It looked like Harry wasn't innocent at all. Not if he

57

plotted Greg's seduction with the likes of Edna Temple, who thought of innocence in anyone over eighteen as a sort of emotional disorder. Any other time, the three of them would have surely broken off relations over something as big as this. That they worked out a truce instead was tribute to a passion for the fixing of priorities. To clear the name of Harry Dawes, they let their crossed connections bring them close. They didn't go to bed that night till they were all agreed what crime it was. If they meant to bring a murderer to earth, they had to stick together.

So he probably wondered what he was doing all alone, at the crack of dawn on Thursday morning, walking across the canyon in a charcoal three-piece suit. Sid and Edna had let him off at the western end of the reservoir. Then they streaked away in the rented car—no time to lose, at an hourly rate—and left him to his own devices. He felt like a lonely terrorist dropped behind enemy lines. He had not been provided with a ticket home. He scanned the top of the hills as he skirted along the water's edge, in case they had a lookout posted. He was enough of a fatalist to know they'd pin him down eventually, but he hoped to get inside, at least, before the hammer fell.

Because he kept one eye on Steepside, he saw the two figures on horseback the moment they came through the gate. He ducked in the bushes and waited them out—elbows and knees in the damp earth, and a colony of potato bugs bumping about in their armor not two inches from his nose. When at last the two riders crossed his path, he pulled in his head like a turtle and winced at the fall of every hoof. As they passed three feet from where he lay, he held there steady as a canyon snake. He was crouched at the bottom of the incline where the horses shifted gears and sped away. And he only heard the one remark he was doomed to misconstrue.

"There *was* no Harry Dawes," he heard the rider shout.

A moment later, he scrambled up out of the sage. He watched them put some distance down along the straightaway, as he flicked at the mud on the knees of his suit.

Then he turned once more to the uphill climb. In a matter of seconds, he was striding up the switchbacks. He was out of view from above by now, but knew he had to get off the trail. They used it as a getaway.

So that, he thought, was Vivien Willis Cokes. He wasn't sure when he first glimpsed her, high on the hill above him. Now that he'd watched her ride away, he realized she was smaller than they made her look in photographs. She had the looseness in her limbs of a girl ten years younger. As faultlessly dressed for a morning's ride as *Vogue* could ever wish. And something else: If they told her Harry Dawes didn't exist, if that was the way they solved it, then she must live in a sort of cocoon.

He stepped off the trail to the bare wet hillside. His feet went sliding, on account of his cordovan wingtips, and he had to grab hold of the sagebrush so as to scramble up to firmer ground. He hopped from rock to rock and clumped through patches of knee-high grass. He tried not to clutter his mind with too much thinking ahead. He had not climbed anything other than stairs since he was twelve years old. He just kept going, till he came up over a rise and saw the beams and cantilevered bays looming above him on the heights, where Steepside rode the hilltop like a ship.

He sat on a boulder and wiped his brow. From his left vest pocket he took out a Hershey bar. Edna had stocked him with energy, nuts and raisins and candy, so his spirits wouldn't flag halfway. He tore it open and bit it in two. Then he looked about at the great green crater of the canyon, as if to get his bearings. It only took a second to pick her out, far below on a jut of land beneath a shady tree. She was breaking bread with a cowboy. Behind them on the trail, the horses cropped at the hillside sweets.

He didn't know quite what to make of the other-world arrangements Vivien's set went in for. How could she possibly understand, this woman who slipped by crowds on horseback? She was used to the sealed-off upper floors of good hotels. She drove the streets with a motorcycle escort. How would he ever make her see that Jasper Cokes, the night he died, was utterly defenseless? She seemed to have a moat around her wide as all this empty space.

He smacked his fingers and pressed on. As he closed the gap between him and Steepside, he stayed clear of the plate-glass reaches and the outdoor stairs and decks. Looking out for something more modest, he made for a small-windowed room on the lowest level. He flattened his nose against the glass to check it out. It was sparely furnished and quite deserted—the last and least of the guest rooms, maybe, or else the minimal quarters of a chauffeur and a maid. He eased the window open, craned an ear till he heard no sound, and slipped inside like a stowaway.

Then straight to the bathroom to fix his tie and brush the canyon off his clothes. He put a comb through his hair, gargled with a dollop of Crest, and spot-checked the state of his winter complexion. He stopped short of using the after-shave on the sink. By the time he crossed the room and peered around the door along the hall, he was ready for a sit-down dinner.

"If anyone asks," Sid had coached him the night before, "you say you're with the funeral. You'll see. The pros steer clear of each other, once they got a death going."

He couldn't be sure exactly where things led, but he was game to try. He walked the length of the hall, to the foot of a circular stair. He half expected to look up into the barrel of a gun being trained on him over the banister. But there was nothing there, nor the sound of voices as he mounted. He came out into an emptiness that seemed to mirror the gray light rolling off the reservoir below. The room was long and narrow, open to the canyon—a set of bays glazed with floor-to-ceiling leaded panes, here and there shot through with a disk of blue or blood red. He'd seen it in a dozen glossy layouts over the years. This did not prevent his jaw from dropping open on the spot.

For Steepside was afflicted with a schizophrenic split, so that only this, the western half, had been done by Frank Lloyd Wright. In 1937, Abner Willis had put the hilltop site and a seven-figure trust at the architect's disposal. Then he went off to Europe where, carried away by all the bargains, he sent back odds and ends of things that he trusted Wright would incorporate into the grand design. A coffered medieval ceiling torn from a monks' refectory. A paneled room from Paris. Frescoes and flower-carved balconies, dolphin-linteled doors—all of which were going to require a master feat of engineering. All of which Wright took a dutiful look at, leafing it through like the day's junk mail, before he ordered it put into storage.

So when Abner returned, all dosed with the chic of the royal houses he'd bought up, he nearly had a stroke. The spaceship ranch house high on the hill, with its floating planes and Mayan iconography, was as hateful to him as the suburbs. The architect was summarily dismissed—indeed, came down from Abner's mountain swearing a blood oath never to work again for a man with too much money. Only four rooms were done right. All the molds for the hand-cast, Mayan-figured bricks were carted off. The chevron-patterned hardwood floors, alternating rows of oak and mahogany, stopped at the door to the dining room, which was Georgian. Abner finished the house with the buckboard carpenter who mended his fences in Orange County. The rest was built to wrap around his travel souvenirs. As a result of which, Steepside from the air was like a priestess locked in the arms of a landed duke.

The place was empty. He figured he must have misread the

papers. If they meant to bury him here at dusk today, there ought to have been a flurry of running back and forth. He wandered down the row of windows. Far below, the vertiginous slopes that swept around the canyon had no place to hide. He saw it all. The trail he'd walked was clear as the dotted line on a map. Perhaps the funeral was just a trick. The silence was as total here as it was in Harry Dawes's apartment, Monday night at nine.

He stood at the final window, looking out. Now was his chance to search the place for clues. He wouldn't have thought it possible, but he had it all to himself. And yet, perverse as ever, he suddenly wanted out of here. The silence seemed to sound a warning not to begin a search there could be no end to. For the first time, he saw the clash of Harry Dawes and Jasper Cokes in terms of their alien habitats. The tumbledown apartment at the Cherokee Nile was a world away from the wilds of Steepside. All the transitions had disappeared. From where he stood, the mountains roller-coastered at fearful angles to the desert plain. The desert sheered off at the ocean.

No wonder it ended in violence.

He turned abruptly and crossed the canyon room, determined to go deeper. In the high wall opposite the bank of windows, a row of stone arches opened off the nave. He could see through into the European rooms, set out like dioramas. One arch led to a library bound in leather. The next went into a Deco bar, all mirrored like a jewel box. Instinctively, Greg passed them by. Beyond the arcade, the Wright plan continued down a narrow corridor. It was skylit every ten or fifteen feet, but otherwise it seemed cut out of solid rock. He felt like he'd entered the hill. When the tunnel forked, he went right, as if trying to keep to the rim of the canyon.

But somehow he must have got turned around. He came out into a bedroom that hovered above the Japanese garden and, beyond it, the green of the glen. After the treeless slopes of the canyon, the hill seemed almost wooded. The grass-cloth walls were covered with masks, in rank on rank of straw, mahogany, bone. Haitian, East African, Eskimo. Greg could not have pinned them down, even as to continent. He only took them in at all for the light they threw on Jasper Cokes. And then he saw—beyond the big-limbed, mountain-cabin chairs—a trail of Hermès luggage leading, half unpacked, into a closet racked with women's clothes. He'd followed his nose to Vivien's room.

He slipped the paperback *Walden* out of his pocket. He went to the bed and placed it dead center on Vivien's Navajo blanket. He walked around it a moment, then put out a finger and moved it a couple of inches clockwise, so as to make it look carelessly tossed. It wasn't the same as the book he found in Harry Dawes's apartment. Edna bought this one late last night, off a paperback shelf at Pickwick. It wasn't a clue to anything yet, unless Vivien chose to make it one. Edna wanted to write some little squib on the flyleaf—*This book left by the friends of Harry Dawes*—but Sid and Greg had managed to outvote her. If *Walden* was part of the plot, it would simply have to do the work of surfacing itself. Chances were, there was no connection at all. Still, they had to start somewhere.

He stood in his old abstracted pose—arms folded, shoulders hunched—till he heard the murmur of voices trailing towards him down the tunnel. He fairly leapt for the sliding door that led out to Vivien's balcony. Sliding it shut behind, he sidled left so the building blocked him. An instant later he fell to his knees, when he saw what looked like an army grouped below him in the yard. Down on all fours, he crept across to the waist-high balcony wall. His heart knocked something terribly. But he rose up slowly and peered over, freezing the scene in a flash. Then he dropped to the floor again as if he'd gotten it all on microfilm.

No wonder the house was empty. Down below, in a ring of ivy, was the scene of the crime itself. A dozen men were grouped around it in a circle—in varying states of official dress, and talking most laconically. The funeral crew in pinstripe suits. A couple of grim patrolmen, on either side of a stout lieutenant. Steepside guards and hangers-on. They all stared into the water as if they were reading tea leaves. They took their cue from the man in deepest black—Carl Dana, pale and grim, who worried the bridge of his amber-tinted shades and stood there in a silence. The whole unlikely throng of men looked strangely weary and out of ideas. They'd have made a lousy posse. Slow and dim, they might have been here to drain this tub, or to move it somewhere else. They'd come to the point where Jasper's death assured them they would live forever—as long as they kept the erotics normal.

Or so it seemed to Greg, who crouched in the balcony corner, hidden from every eye. He wondered which of the men down there would have passed up a chance with Jasper Cokes. It was wrong to think that everything after Monday night was a cover-up. Greg could tell in a single glance that most of those who came up here to play out Jasper's scene were something close to morons. Why did it make him angry, though? Did it hurt to think that a fool could have masterminded Jasper's death? Would none but a criminal genius do? Carl was the only one who really filled the bill. And Carl had been out of town till Tuesday afternoon.

But now he was getting ahead of himself. There was nothing to do but wait till sunset, to see how the three of them looked together. Pictures culled from the past had appeared all week in the papers. Bodyguard, manager, wife—they were tied up tight as an entourage. Sitting in palmy nightclubs, all lined up in the sun on beach chairs, squeezed in the back of limos, they looked as arbitrary as high school kids, as tenuously matched. Carl very bookish and tense. Startling Vivien, hair in a chignon, thin and tan and insolent. Artie plain as day. Whatever had happened to Jasper Cokes, Greg was sure he would get his lead when he saw how the three survivors stood at the grave. He would know which one to implicate.

For the moment, he was safe. He arranged himself on the slick tile floor, in a lounging sort of way, then tugged his book from his right side pocket. This was the *Walden* Harry left. When he hiked up here this morning, he'd had one on either side, like ballast. He looked as pure as an Eagle Scout, the dotted silk tie and wingtips notwithstanding. Though he hadn't planned to read a word, though he'd been in a frenzy getting psyched for the Steepside caper, he'd picked it up in an idle hour, and now he couldn't stop.

The cabin at Walden Pond was built. The bean rows planted straight and true. On every other page, Thoreau had shaken his finger at the men still trapped in town. Greg had already gone four chapters, but he started now with his last night's underlinings. Curled up in his solitary corner, he ran his finger along these lines:

> I went to the woods because I wished to live delib-
> erately, to front only the essential facts of life, and
> see if I could not learn what it had to teach, and not,
> when I came to die, discover that I had not lived.

How absolutely right, he thought. He looked up into the leaden sky, to see if he could say it any better, and found to his delight that he could not. He'd been thinking something very like it ever since the day he quit writing scripts. No doubt he would have been hard put to say what life in the Concord woods had to do with forging autographs. For his part, all he knew was this: The truth about Harry and Jasper would have to come from him alone. Not including Sid and Edna, everyone else was satisfied that everything was fine. It was probably just a coincidence, but he had in hand the very last word on being self-reliant. He used to think he had to know precisely what he was looking for. The last two days, he'd begun to see that it might be better to find it as he went.

He finished his raisins and cashews, wishing he'd stopped for a swallow of water along the way. He read maybe thirty more pages—openly rooting now for the strange, intransigent loner who made his stand on the Concord shore. In half an hour, the sky had parted just a crack. The sun got a bit of a toehold. Before he knew it, his eyesight blurred as he squinted down at the page. So he put in a finger to mark his place and drowsed his lids for a moment's rest.

Just at the last, before he went under and let the book fall to the floor, a shiver of grief for Harry Dawes shot through him. As if he dared not let it cloud his waking life, but he had no law against dreaming. Sleep after sleep, he turned again to the love they'd barely made. For a man who prided himself on having no philosophy, he was awfully single-minded. Perhaps it was tied up with reading Thoreau. Perhaps it was leaving his safe apartment to wander the world alone. Whatever it was, that one brief night with Harry Dawes seemed more and more the only place where he could be himself.

Greg was still sound asleep when Vivien closed the door to her room, with orders not to be bothered. She hung up six hundred dollars' worth of widow's weeds in the closet. She peeled off all her riding clothes and dropped them in the hamper. And she had a hand on the sliding door, meaning to let in a breath of air, when the book on the bed caught her eye.

As she only read books she could leave on a plane or, spotted with oil, beside her deck chair, she knew it wasn't one of hers. Besides, Thoreau was not her type. She'd had it assigned in college, of course, but there she'd used a fly-by-night outline that did it in eighteen pages. The strident tone and the unwashed manners reminded her of her forebears, Jake and Abner both. She wasn't the likeliest person to pick up and head for the woods. When it came to cabins, she flew to Bermuda. She didn't need a book to tell her how to leave the world behind.

But her first thought, seeing it now, was just what the team from the Cherokee Nile had intended her to think. She thought: *Who put this here?* It could only have been Carl or Artie, but which one? There was no point trying to figure what she was meant to feel until she'd matched it with the giver. Artie would have left it more or less for spiritual reasons, after the manner in which he brought her shells and potted plants and bits of colored glass. Carl, if it was Carl, was probably bent on finding an image vague enough to swallow up the suicides. Perhaps Jasper Cokes was simply a man gone off on his own.

But there wasn't any clue in the book itself. Not a cold-eyed memo from Carl or a timid inscription in Artie's hand. She flipped the pages in a desultory way, preparatory to throwing it in a drawer. Someone would bring it up later, if someone had a proposal. There was nothing that had to get done right now. She fixed on a passage at random, but hardly took it in. It was just that she saw the word "love," and wondered what Thoreau had fallen for, with no one else around. She read the paragraph straight through before she stopped to think.

> I love a broad margin to my life. Sometimes, in a summer morning, having taken my accustomed bath, I sat in my sunny doorway from sunrise till noon, rapt in a revery, amidst the pines and hickories and sumachs, in undisturbed solitude and stillness, while the birds sang around or flitted noiseless through the house, until by the sun falling in at my west window, or the noise of some traveler's wagon on the distant highway, I was reminded of the lapse of time.

Clearly, what this needed was an editor. With all those commas and dovetail clauses, she lost the train of thought before she got the drift. But if she read him right, he was given to mooning in doorways, a whole day at a time. The mere idea made her edgy. With her, the problem wasn't sitting still so much as too much time to think. Though she had her pick of doors to prop, she preferred to spend her days in transit. If she stopped too long, she tended to find an agenda waiting.

Solitary places were capricious, after all. They forced her to relive love affairs she'd hardly thought of at the time. Or they lit her far too harshly—Mexico came to mind—so she wasted the day just finding shade and turning down her hat brims. She had no use for a man who was free from time like Thoreau at Walden. She preferred her schedule tight, with an overlap if possible. She was limp from the morning's double ride as she tucked the book beneath her pillow. She curled like a snail in the Navajo blanket. Frankly, she was tired of leaving home for cabins in the woods. She'd as soon stay here forever, now that—

She fell asleep before she said it, but what she almost said was: *now that Jasper's dead*. If anyone else had heard her, they'd have had their proof that she was heartless underneath. She didn't care about anything, right? They'd always said so, hadn't they? No wonder she was silent. She could not wring out a single tear to satisfy convention, and no one seemed to understand that her very resoluteness was her grief. She would not bullshit Jasper Cokes. She could no more put on faces for him now than ever in all their sudden years of being married.

With only the wall between them, they more or less slept together, she and Greg. If one of them had been awake and cupped an .ear and listened, he probably would have heard the other breathing. It may even have been that their dreams got crossed. They could not seem to keep to separate corners.

Harry Dawes and Jasper Cokes went back and forth between them, twined like double shadows in the fog. No borders hemmed them in. The dreamers groped in the tidal darkness, fugitive as those they'd lost. Harry Dawes was on a train, riding east to Turner's Falls. Jasper was tinned in a box of ashes, guarded by a mortician's gray-lipped apprentice down at the garden gate. But Greg and Vivien couldn't stop. They were drawn by the selfsame pin of light and caught at shapes they almost knew. Until the dead were in the ground, a glimmer of something stayed, it seemed.

When Greg woke up, he slipped his book in his pocket and went over the railing. He climbed down the side of the house and circled the redwood tub, where he spent a long moment brooding. The crowd of men had all dispersed. The tub reeked of death, though the water was clear as day. They ought to cover it up, he thought. There was no telling who might tumble in and drown.

He went in among the lemon trees, as far as the crest of the hill. He could hear the crowd on the boulevard below, though the hillside growth hid everything from sight. He felt the sense of violation more than ever: The people a man didn't know did not belong at his funeral. All afternoon, as he poked about—expecting any moment to be caught and shown the door—he was seized with a sense of trespass, every time he heard a wave of rumbling from below. He'd have liked to clear out all outsiders, not including him.

He watched the groom brush down the horses. He watched the gardener hose the driveway. He stood for a while in the little pool house, rifling through a drawer full of bathing suits. By midafternoon, he knew all the cracks in the tennis court, and he could have told you where they piled the trash. He was happy to sit on the low stone walls and take the mountain air. For it turned out Sid was right, that nobody paid him the slightest notice.

He didn't feel any different, though, when it came to splitting the man and the myth. Jasper Cokes was nothing to him. His star was artificial. All his pictures junk. At some quite visceral level, Greg reviewed his old resentments: If Jasper had made it, why didn't he? About once an hour, he took a break with a page or two of *Walden*. Just like a monk with his breviary—or a kid with big ideas, reading books in snatches on the bus. What his old friends used to call moody, in the days when he lived at a typewriter. Sid and Edna, not so subtle, called it weird.

When Vivien got up, she took a bath she didn't need, put on a robe, and went from room to room as if to oversee the plans. From the deck that led off the canyon room, she watched a workman dig the grave on the naked brow of the hill. She stood at the kitchen door a while. The cook was dicing lobster for a salad. In the study, Carl was up to his neck in telephone calls. Artie was on the roof with the mini-cam unit, setting up for the main event. It was all going swimmingly. From what she could gather, nothing was out of line except her life.

It was getting time for her and Greg to meet. They wandered away, between them, the whole of the afternoon, just waiting to catch sight of each other. She didn't think to venture outside. He didn't dare go in. Nobody talked to her because they didn't know what to say. Nobody talked to him because they didn't know who he was. They were still in different stories, really. Both unnerved by all the waiting, though he didn't get quite as bored as she did. Given the fact that boredom was the very thing she hid, however, they were more alike than not by four o'clock. Completely out of it, that is.

It looked as if they were made for each other. But it may have been that fate had put it off too long. Neither had ever known anyone else whose moods were in such constant swing. So as not to seem quite mad, they'd each perfected something close to reticence. They only revealed to others every third or fourth reversal. Their moods appeared to change a couple of times a day, from afternoon to evening wear. In fact, they had sometimes got it down to twice an hour—from black despair to trills of drunken laughter. With it all locked up inside like that, perhaps they no longer had it in their power to show how much alike they were. They were all disguised in moderation.

At 4:45, she left the house through the Spanish cloister. Artie and Carl were at either side. The dress she'd bought at Giorgio's was the palest lilac—sadder than black, in her view. Now they made their way through knots of English roses, between two hedges ten feet high. She came right out with it. "Hey," she whispered, "thanks for the book." She was staring straight ahead of her, peripheral vision finely tuned to catch the barest nod of recognition. But Artie and Carl kept walking as if she hadn't said a thing. It was either some mistake or one of them was lying.

Either way, she didn't care. She had no plans to read it. She avoided doing anything on recommendation, out of a dread of disagreeing. She already had a *Walden* of her own, should she ever be so inclined. It was bound in calfskin, stamped in gold, and sat on its proper shelf with several others of its kind. One of these days, she thought as they crossed from the garden onto the hill, she would have to go pick out a classic and read it cover to cover. The change of pace would do her good. But she had to do it on her own, with a book nobody bothered with. *Walden* was simply not her style.

They walked single file on the upper trail. The rose and yellow rockets of the setting sun were on the wane, bathing the whole of the canyon Arctic purple. Up ahead, a half-dozen men were clustered on the hilltop. They looked a bit like a scouting party. Most were only undertaker's men, but, seeing twice as many as she planned on, Vivien stopped to wonder what the union rules were. How many did you need to dig a simple grave? To put to rest one modest urn of ashes, she would have thought a single man with a shovel was enough. Somehow, this many meant trouble.

As the three from Steepside came along the ridge, the party at the grave cast their eyes down, glancing at the ground as if embarrassed. All but the perky minister, who pattered up to Vivien and took her by the hand. Closely followed by Maxim Brearley, red-eyed and just finished drinking, who clasped her other hand in both of his, as if he planned to play the devil's advocate. Together, they led her forward. They murmured a string of platitudes till she thought she was going to scream. They brought her up to the brink of the pit before they let her go.

She stared down in. It looked like someone planned to sink a fence post. Then she turned her eyes on all these strangers. For an instant, she thought she would turn and run, but Artie came up close behind and squeezed her by the shoulders. She let out her breath and relaxed a bit. As the minister started to speak, she focused across at Max, who stood on the opposite edge. She couldn't remember inviting him, but decided to let it pass. Since Jasper had no blood relations, Max could act the long-lost cousin. Besides, he'd directed Jasper first and last. If he hadn't had the brains to put his star in khaki pants, they never would have gotten past the werewolf stage. His presence here today was more or less inevitable.

But who the hell did the rector think he was? Did he think they were having auditions? Given as he was to a phony British clip, he was clearly schooled in a God that wore a coat and tie. And he gave it extra resonance today, since the death at hand was sorely lacking in decorum. He'd picked the wrong crowd to try it on. The more he gave it like a speech, the more did Vivien, Artie, and Carl look off and shift their feet. They probably couldn't have pooled among them a whole hour spent on their knees in the last ten years. By the time he asked them all to join him—"Brethren, let us pray"—he didn't stand a chance.

The violent gold and broken glow of the sky was dwindling down. All along the crater of the canyon, the brush and grasses deepened into gray, as if the source of the night was shadows rising out of the ground. One by one, as Vivien watched, the listeners looked away to the landscape. Two lines into the Lord's Prayer, the minister must have known he was fated to go it alone. Abruptly, the high-toned manner and Richard Burton rhythm dropped. His voice got very thin. The mourners and workers had banded together. They gazed in all directions, sweeping the hills in the falling twilight, a deaf ear turned to the pieties. It was better than hymns and the ringing of bells.

She was free at last. She could be as bored and tearless as she wished. Nobody here was out to pin her down. The class of officials who'd overrun her life, massed all week like cops at a car wreck, had no power now to make her take it hard. The busy crew from ABC, shooting it all from the roof, reduced her to three or four inches high and could not read her mood. The Cinemascope dimensions of the scene were on her side. Then too, she was the only woman. The others all had to act like men and keep their feelings private. And they didn't lock eyes with a woman like her, in any case—for fear of triggering coolness that would ice their very hearts.

She had come to say goodbye and nothing else, and so she said it. She didn't tart it up with proper feeling. She had managed, eight years running, not to care what Jasper did in bed, or wonder who he made it with. They were none of each other's business, Jasper Cokes and Vivien. And they owed it to the boundaries they'd fought for, somehow to keep things in their places. One goodbye was all the moment needed. That and a windy hillside.

Vivien looked up. At first, she thought she must have spoken it aloud. Though the rector droned along entirely unaware, a look of confusion had passed like a chill among the men around Jasper's grave. Everyone stared straight at her. They saw she was a renegade. Then, suddenly, Carl and Artie, standing beside her left and right, broke from the circle and ran. She realized what they'd all been looking at was going on behind her back. She spun around, thinking: *Let it be something grand.*

But it was nothing, really. There was someone there in the path, about twenty yards down the hill. A couple of Steepside guards had closed around him. Though they made a wall like a football huddle, she saw they were roughing him up a bit. It was all that pent-up guardsmanship. All week they'd been deprived of criminal trespass. None of the fans had climbed the fence, and the burglar class instinctively stayed clear of so much raw activity. Thus, this overcurious man, whoever he was, was the very first live one they'd tracked down.

Vivien ran to catch up with Carl and Artie. The cameras on the roof had pulled away from the crest of the hill, to train themselves on this new scene. All at once she understood—seeing the way it would be from here on in—that now, with Jasper dead, it was she alone being trespassed on. The show of force was in her name. As she came up level with the incident, she felt strangely helpless. Carl and Artie had joined the ring around the man inside. She couldn't see a thing. Luckily, she was only skin and bones. She saw a space and ducked between two fullbacks, worming in before they knew what hit them.

She came up into the midst of pushing and angry questions. A finger poked her in the side. She had to catch at the intruder, just to keep her balance. He was hunched in his charcoal suit, shielding his gonads, but he put out a hand and caught her. Suddenly, they were arm in arm. The oafish guards, a beat behind in reflex, watched it happen and shrank away, as if to make them room. After all, it was the boss who'd just popped in.

"Are you a friend of Jasper's?" Vivien asked. Dispensing with preliminary matters—how he got in and what he was after. He had the look of a loner.

"No," said Greg. "Harry Dawes."

"Oh," she replied, a trifle faintly. She hoped it sounded something like an apology.

"What do you want?" demanded Artie, grabbing him up by both lapels.

"I don't know," he answered truthfully. His plans had somehow slipped away. He told the truth for the hell of it. "I figured this was the only place where the whole thing might make sense." He fixed her with a penetrating look. "You know what I mean?"

"Artie, let him go."

She saw him struggle to give a name to something odd about her eyes. In fact, she hadn't a clue what he meant. For his part, he felt as if he'd been misinformed by the flat of a thousand photographs. He went on talking a moment more, but made no attempt to appease the men who threatened him. He let all present danger slip his mind, so drawn was he to the mischief playing in her glance. Could a person be that self-contained? Even at a time like this?

He said: "It's just two people dying, right? The same as anyone else." He tried not to put any pressure on her arm. He figured she'd been squeezed till she was black and blue. "All I'm trying to do is see it plain. Without the bullshit."

"You'll have to go," said Artie coldly.

The guards closed in a second time, still eager to do it by force. But Carl had had a chance to mull the implications over. He was ready as ever to turn the screw. "It's not that simple," he put in dryly, overruling Artie. "If we don't press charges now, this sort of thing will never end."

"Later," she said dismissively. "Now that he's here, he might as well wish Jasper luck."

And she led him away like an honored guest. She didn't agree at all that it was just two people dying, but she liked a man to generalize. This candor and right-mindedness were just the thing they needed here, to stand against the rain of hollow pieties. For the rest, she meant what she said about "later." He would have to talk his way out of it himself, once she left him again to his own devices. She had no room for someone new. Besides, she figured he must have an alibi, or friends who owed him a favor. A person took care of himself. That was her number one rule.

"You aren't, by any chance, the other widow, are you?"

She ventured this as gently as she could, but it must have come out pretty hard. She felt a sudden spasm twitching in his arm. It seemed he wouldn't answer. She had plainly overreached. It was only that she wanted someone feeling just as she was—nothing—and here she thought she'd found her man at last. A case of misreading the moody glint in his eye as a mirror image. For all she knew, he was something a good deal simpler—Harry's brother, or his agent even. Full of tears, if you scratched the surface. Not the same as her at all. And yet she wasn't sorry that she'd taken up his case. As they walked uphill to the grave again, the Steepside forces neutralized and trailing in their wake, she saw that the minister was most put out by the interruption. All around him, the funeral crew was visibly buoyed by the outcome of the scuffle. So at least she could console herself with this: She'd turned the mood of the moment on its head.

"Not exactly," Greg said slowly—at a loss to know why he was lying.."We were friends," he said. "Isn't that enough?"

"Of course," she said. They were only a few feet off from the grave. The minister lifted his prayer book and took a deep breath. Vivien let go of Greg's arm, but she leaned up close and whispered one last thing. "By the way," she said, "thanks for the book."

He was supposed to beg her pardon and pretend she'd mixed him up with someone else. He wasn't meant to show his cards just yet. If he blew it now, Sid and Edna would have his ass. He turned and looked in her eyes again. He heard the minister call on God. And he whispered back: "Don't mention it."

chapter 3

EDNA TEMPLE WAS FORTY-FIVE when she waitressed her last meal, in a bar and grill in Shiner, Texas. She woke one morning and decided it was Hollywood or bust. With nary a backward look, she hitched a ride west with a strawberry trucker who took out the fare in trade. Though she harbored no illusions of making a go as a movie star, she figured there was lots of room a little lower down. In any case, she'd wasted all the time she had for wasting.

Within a week of her arrival in L.A., she'd set up shop in the concrete court of Graumann's Chinese Theater, about a foot and a half from Lassie's paw print. She sold hand-drawn maps of the stars' homes—with actual X's, as if it were *Treasure Island*. The maps themselves were completely out of date, since nobody lived for long in any one place. She copied her information off the more commercial version sold in liquor stores along the Strip. But the crudeness of her handiwork had a certain air of authenticity about it. She looked like she had the latest dope. Besides—as she would have been first to tell you—in a thing like this, it was all in how you pitched it.

She understood exactly what the tourists traveled out here for. They wanted a personal nod—a glimpse of somebody very big or, failing that, a peek at where the famous hung their hats. The good people of Cedar Rapids were lost in Beverly Hills. They could not get a table for lunch, for love or money, and they couldn't so much as go to the cleaner's without being valet-parked. The way they kept their windows rolled, they acted as if it was breaking the law to drive up and down the boxwood streets. Which is why Edna manned her little booth in a down-home style, after the manner in which she sold brownies at the Shiner Baptist Fair. The out-of-towners knew right off whose side *she* was on.

In ten years, her maps grew more and more skilled—and even more eccentric. She took to listing certain houses with their pedigree of scandals, all done up in medallions. She sketched in palms and bathing beauties, to give the whole a bit more color. Between 1956 and 1969, her price hiked up from fifty cents to $3.98, the latter figure verbally discounted anywhere up to a dollar. She became such a fixture that the L.A.P.D. stopped turning her out.

In the end, she might have parlayed it into a proper job at Rand McNally, but she developed an allergy to the desert sun. She would blow up with hives and prickle and wheeze. Hats didn't do her a bit of good. At fifty-eight, she found herself banished to nights and early mornings. Her Marco Polo skit was over. She would have gone mad with cabin fever if it hadn't been for Sid.

Sid Sheehan was a spinner of yarns. In the beginning, out on the street in the thick of the Great Depression, he did odd jobs to get by. When Pittsburgh started to cramp his style, he packed his tools and rode the rails in search of the last frontier. At the end of the line, in Hollywood, he discovered there were people quite content to have a thing done slapdash, as long as they got the week's gossip thrown in.

From the wives of studio craftsmen to the actors waiting at home for the phone to ring, there was always someone who couldn't put up a shelf. Sid's stories never had any basis in fact. It was his casting that gave them the ring of truth. Somehow, a good bit of dirt about this or that star proved L.A. was just another town—as small as those his customers had safely left behind.

"What do you hear about Marion Davies?" one of his homebody types would ask as he squeegeed a plate-glass window. And he always knew where he left off, since the serial form was his specialty. He'd fashion a little scandal up at Hearst Castle—say, a midnight swim in the Neptune pool that got out of hand. He'd leave his tales unfinished—hints of incest, hints of drugs—to keep them coming back for more. He was plasterer, paperhanger, chimney sweep, pool boy. But it was cliffhanger endings that made Sid indispensable.

The bourbon finally took its toll in blood-blue thumbs and dizzy spells. Slapdash evolved into worse-off-fixed-than-broken. Though he had come to be as picturesque as a knife grinder out of Dickens, people stopped answering doors when he made his rounds of the neighborhood. They couldn't risk the mess. Besides, after a certain point, one didn't need a journeyman for gossip. By the end of the sixties, gossip was in the very air one breathed. The age of the tinker was past.

So he stumbled into cemetery work. He was standing at Tyrone Power's place, one winter afternoon at Hollywood Memorial, when a tourist asked him if he was related. "Oh, sure," he said, off the top of his head, "I was the one drove his car." And he followed it up with a patch of the great man's love affairs, his hunting trips and all-night drunks. At the end he asked for a small donation, to put a little green around the tomb. "He deserves a bit better than weeds and dried-up grass," Sid said reproachfully as they started to fish their pockets.

Though he tried them all from time to time, he seemed to do his most creative work with Ty. On a good day, he could take in fifty or sixty dollars. Unfortunately, he was scarcely three years into this new career when he started to suffer from tremors and spells. He lost the power to thread a proper narrative. People still cocked their ears and listened, but soon it became apparent he didn't know what he was talking about. For all his poignant details, this old man was an out-and-out liar.

Between them, Sid and Edna made Hollywood work for the little guy. Being as how they'd put out such good products, they should have been able to live off their residuals. Fate derailed them both too soon. There came the day when they couldn't afford a cup of coffee to get them going. Groggy and down for the count, they met by chance in the Cherokee Nile, at the door to the manager's office. Both had been drawn by a card in the window, announcing a cozy apartment that went for eighty dollars a month. A classic case of the "cute meet."

They couldn't agree who'd seen it first. They swapped some verbal abuse and finally roused the manager—who pegged them as a couple right away. Then they all trooped down to the basement, where they walked through a warren of rooms that was clustered about the boilers, all shot through with pipes. Cozy was putting it mildly. If they hadn't been so broke, they never would have agreed to it. But, having lived alone so long, they'd both forgotten how to shout and carry on. Edna could feel her sinuses clear. The buzz stopped buzzing in Sid's temples. It must have dawned on both of them how simple things could be, if only they had someone else to take it out on.

For the next ten years, they pooled their welfare checks.

They scrapped like kids, saw three or four movies a week, and never for a minute fell in love. Nothing much happened, one way or another, except they survived. Until, one summer day, with the blinds drawn against the midday dazzle, Edna Temple came across a minuscule notice, buried at the back of *Modern Screen*. Pictures for sale, it looked like. Hard to tell why anyone would want them for two dollars apiece, unless they were frontal nudes. What struck her was the return address: the corner of Franklin and Cherokee, apartment 11D.

She waited in the foyer, close by the mailboxes, all day long till Greg came down. She confronted him with the evidence, then stuck with him, talking nonstop, all the way back to his apartment. Greg could only nod and dumbly shake his head, so appalled was he to be confronted in the flesh by an actual fan. To gain time, he showed her the stacks and stacks of photographs in his dining room. Then he gave her a Cary Grant, by way of a little souvenir, and pushed her toward the door.

But Edna knew a break when she saw one. She took the stub of the pencil out of her apron pocket. She licked the end and wrote in big round letters across the heart of the picture: "All my love, Cary." Then handed it back to Greg with a defiant look, her tongue against her upper lip to steady her wobbly teeth. She saw the dawn of a great idea pass across his face. And then she said: "I bet a guy could charge five dollars for a thing like this. Wouldn't you say?"

In that one stroke, she showed him how to hit the big time. The United Fans of America was launched. Greg stopped selling dime-a-dozen studio shots and went full steam into personalizing. Soon he needed two assistants, just to handle the volume. And the hard-luck pair in the basement flat came into their own at last. Like Greg himself, they'd only lacked the proper vehicle. Now they raked it in.

But it wasn't any wonder, since they gave the world the better mousetrap it was always on the lookout for. They'd hit on a way to package dreams.

"Hold still!" gritted Edna between her teeth.

She sprayed a wide swath of instant disinfectant. Slumped in the chaise where she held him down, Greg choked as the mist caught him full in the face. He held out his chin till she daubed it clean and iodined the scratch. After that his poor left shoulder, where the scrape was deep, bright pink, and oozing freely. Then his knees, his shins, and two stubbed toes. He looked like he'd taken a bad fall off a skateboard.

"It's your own damn fault," she scolded him.

He lay there stinging in his jockey shorts and made as if to take a little sun. Grumbling, Edna packed her first-aid kit. She hitched up the tits of her great balloon of a bathing suit. She sank herself down on a rubber mattress just at the base of the sphinx. She wasn't done with him yet.

"Listen, honey. You clutch like that, you're gonna get screwed. It's as simple as that."

"I didn't clutch," he protested wearily, drawing the back of his hand across his forehead. "I got sick of skulking around, that's all. I thought I could sidle up to the grave and check out all their faces."

"It's Vivien's fault," said Sid, from behind his *Times*. He sat at the shady end of the terrace, under an awning propped by bamboo spears. His pants were rolled to his knees, and his feet were cooling in a kid-size pool, about four by six and plastic. A birthday gift from Sid and Edna when Greg turned thirty-two. He let the paper down a minute. "*She* could have got him out of there. All she had to do was walk him down to the gate and turn him loose. They wouldn't have called the cops if she hadn't let them."

"You can tell Sidney Sheehan to spare us the hindsight,"

she said as she put on a coat of lotion. "*I* was against it, right from the first. Didn't I tell you you'd end up in jail?"

"Yes, Edna."

"And I trust you don't have any weekend plans. We're four days behind as it is."

The week's mail was spread out on the terrace floor, in an arc around her mattress, fanned like some enormous deck of cards. She began to open those that looked as if they might have money inside. Slowly, little piles of checks and money orders grew beside her. Now and then—though all their advertising begged the people not to—she pulled out cash, smiling as if she'd got a prize.

"I'll tell you what I'd like to do," said Sid. "When they get the stone on, I'd like to see it."

"You mean the grave," she said, "is that it?"

"Well, why not? I'm something of an authority, after all."

"Gee, Sid," reflected Edna dryly, "maybe Vivien Cokes would hire you. You could sit up there and tell stories."

"She's jealous, Greg," said Sidney Sheehan. "On account of I'm so creative."

Reluctantly, as if pushed too far, she heaved herself to her feet. She padded across the terrace floor to talk some sense to him. She stepped in and joined him, ankle-deep in the little pool, while Sid put his paper aside and stood up proudly. They were forced a bit too close for a proper fight. To work up to a pitch of fury, with all the right gesticulations, they needed a fuller range. For the moment, however, they seemed to prefer to cool their feet on a hot spring afternoon.

"Listen, smart-ass," Edna growled, "when's the last time *you* did something right?"

"You know what pisses you off?" he said, unruffled and aloof. "You always got the yo-yos, down at Graumann's. Now, when I was in the cemeteries, I drew a higher class of people. Why don't you admit it?"

They let their feathers fly as if it were a cockfight. Each had a finger jabbed at the other's breastbone. Sid swayed back and forth on his blue-veined legs like a stork. Edna's dimpled thighs and meaty upper arms began to shake as she got going. Water splashed over the lip of the pool. From a distance, it looked like a native dance.

Greg winked an eye to see how they were making out. Convinced they were over the worst of it, he rolled away to a fetal crouch. The bumps and scrapes were minor enough, but he still had a lot of nursing of his ego to perform. It wasn't just that he'd never spent the night in jail. He'd never had a parking ticket, either, so assiduous was he not to cross swords with the law. It amazed him, in a way, that he'd survived it. All the same, as he swooned on the chaise in the midday sun, at a stage where things hurt worse before they started getting better, survival was small consolation.

The Steepside guards had led him down to the very room he'd broken into, there to wait for the L.A. police. When he asked for a lawyer, the bully in charge stomped on his toes. Later, a couple of beer-belly cops took him away in handcuffs. They tripped him hard as he got in the squad car, and he didn't remember another thing till they slapped him awake to be booked. His ears were ringing by the time they dumped him in a detention cell, but by then he'd begun to detect a pattern.

"You and that cocksucker movie star both," said the pasty-faced jailer. He sent Greg sprawling down a flight of stairs. "Who you fairies gonna cum in now?" the turnkey snarled as he locked Greg in.

They were all getting back at Jasper Cokes. They'd always thought he stood for something decent. His being a deviant underneath called into question every other tough guy's act. It meant they had to prove themselves, which they did by kicking ass. Though they hadn't a shred of evidence that Greg was one of Jasper's boys, they were partial to guilt by association. Any old fairy would do in a pinch. If they made a mistake and pummeled a man who was perfectly straight, well, that was life. Besides, a real man ought to act butch enough as to leave no doubt at all.

Quickly, word went round the cell that Greg had been at Steepside. He resigned himself to a multiple rape by drunks and vagrants. Sure enough, a mangy pickpocket—breath like the end of the earth—flattened Greg against the bars and ordered him to suck. At which point this doped-up gorilla came reeling up and put himself between them. He knocked the pickpocket over like a bowling pin. Then he gathered Greg in his arms and wept. It turned out that he'd had a thing with Jasper once himself. He fell into broken sobs that rang all over the jailhouse. When at last he went to sleep, he curled with Greg on the hard dank floor beneath the soapstone sink. All night long he whimpered in his dreams.

Greg was in too much pain to sleep. He lay there hugged in a bear hug, glad to be safe from injury, and used the time to puzzle out his evidence. At sunup, Sid and Edna having arrived with cash enough to spring him, he couldn't wake the gorilla to kiss him goodbye. He had nothing to leave behind as a souvenir. Then he noticed his one-night stand was barefoot. He took off his wingtips, knelt at the other's crusted feet, and tied them on. They were probably too tight to walk in, but maybe the guy could trade them for something he needed more. A quart of hooch or a couple of cartons of Camels.

The upshot of it all was this: He wanted to stop right here. Nobody really cared if Jasper Cokes had been killed or not. They seemed to prefer it the way it was, as being somehow seamier than pure and simple murder. Sid and Edna didn't see how indisposed the police would be to putting any effort in. They thought he got licked in a fight with a cellmate. They still believed the proper scrap of evidence would turn it all around. It didn't even seem to daunt them that Harry Dawes had left no trace beyond the three of them.

"Hey, Greg!" they chorused from the pool.

"Huh? What?" He rolled from left to right and squinted along the terrace, only to find their fighting posture had undergone a sea change. Sid sat crosslegged in the water. Edna, standing behind him, kept dipping a styrofoam cup and pouring it out across his naked shoulders. His face was all scrunched up, as if he had dunked in an icy mountain stream. He slapped his torso to bring the blood back up.

"Sid thinks we should wait till it all dies down. As soon as the killer believes he's home free, he'll make a mistake. He'll try to tidy something up, and he'll fall right into our hands. It's the stupidest piece of reasoning I've heard yet."

"What I *said*," corrected Sid imperiously, "was, why should *we* be the moving target? Let the other guy make the move. Then we go in as a team."

Oh, Jesus, he thought, *it's Nick and Nora Charles.*

He lifted himself from the chaise and hobbled across the gravel of the terrace. They didn't seem to understand there was nothing more to go on. The detective part was over. He made a clearing motion with his hands, to let them know he needed room. Edna bent over, grabbed Sid around the chest, and stepped back heavily two or three feet. Sid slid along on his bottom. Greg stepped in and straddled the corner seat, careful to keep his bloody shin out in the air, to guard against infection.

But where was he to begin? If they'd only seen the scene of the crime, they'd have understood in a minute. The mood was all wrong. Steepside might be a movie set, but the movie wasn't murder. No lingering air of blame, attached or unattached, appeared to mist the top of Jasper's mountain. Beside the chaos of Hollywood Boulevard, just a stone's throw from the Cherokee Nile, Steepside was completely in the clear.

"Listen, you guys," he said. "I've got a whole new theory." Elbows on his knees, hands in a steeple, he peered through the clouded water at the grinning figure of Mickey Mouse stenciled on the bottom. From where they watched at the other end, he looked like a kid in a sandbox. "What if Jasper did what they say? What if he killed himself?"

"I don't give two shits what Jasper did," said Edna. "The point is, somebody bumped off Harry."

"That's what I'm trying to *tell* you," Greg protested. He made it all up as he went along, just trying to keep it simple. "He finished his movie, right? He was on a real downer. He goes out to pick up a trick for an overnight, and he meets this terrific kid—coming out of Thrifty Drugs or something. They look at each other, and bingo, they connect."

Across the water, Sid and Edna had a hooded sort of look. She gripped Sid's shoulder, and it wasn't certain whether she was reassuring him, or holding on so she wouldn't keel over. Already it was two against one.

"So he takes him back to Steepside." Greg went on a little faster, hoping to pick up the pace. "They get it on all right, but Harry won't play it as rough as he likes. So Jasper goes bananas. He hits the kid too hard, and the kid goes into a coma, like. So he panics. He gets the blades, he gets the pills—"

The gathering silence mocked him. At the other end, Sid and Edna had retreated to an awful stillness. Arranged as they were, one above the other, they looked to Greg like South Seas royalty—set on a floating throne in a lagoon.

"Ick," said Edna, very unconvinced.

"What *you* need's a little R and R," Sid Sheehan observed, though not unkindly. "That's why I think we ought to wait. Our *off*ense is out of commission."

They didn't give his story the time of day, but they didn't call him a quitter, either. Greg was their legs and their bankroll both. They understood, rather more than he suspected, that the thriller they'd hitched a ride on was at a sudden standstill. Perhaps they'd known all along what a man like Greg was liable to say at the first big impasse: What was the use, since it wouldn't bring Harry back anyway. As for them, they had no heavy schedule to juggle. They were at an age where they liked to get a thing done before they went on. Loose ends was a young man's game.

"Put it this way," Edna said. "We aren't going to know a goddam thing till we know what the wife is hiding."

"That's absurd," he responded quickly, a bit as if he expected it. "Vivien has nothing to do with it. All she wants is to be alone, and frankly, I don't blame her."

"I'm sure she appreciates the vote of confidence," Edna threw back coldly. "Tell me, have you hooked up with the entourage officially? You think they'll put you on the payroll?"

At which point the phone rang. If this was a fight they were having, it seemed they had ended round one. Edna stepped out onto dry land. She trotted ten feet to the Bakelite black extension, catching it up on the second ring. The phone was fed through the amber casement window from Greg's bedroom. She answered briskly, echoing back the last four digits the caller had just dialed. Then a small pause, and then she turned, grinning as if she'd heard a marvelous joke.

"Vivien," she said triumphantly, and held the receiver out to Greg.

He couldn't let on how it made him feel, though of course he hardly knew. As he and Edna passed each other—at the canopy's edge, between bright sun and shadow—he tried to look as if he couldn't be more surprised. But Edna wouldn't give an inch. She was bursting to go have a whisper with Sid. By the time he picked the receiver up, Greg was pretty rattled. He thought he'd seen the last of Vivien Cokes when the night came down at Steepside.

"Greg Cannon here," he said—perhaps a shade too eagerly. *Ready-when-you-are-ma'am* was clearly not the right approach.

"It's not a fair match," she said by way of hello.

"What's that?"

"You and me. It turns out I know something you don't think I know."

"It's not my police record, is it?"

"Oh, I heard about that," she said, with evident disapproval. "You know, you're simply going to have to get yourself some names. I mean, so you can drop them. Why don't I start you out with a couple of mine? I never use them anyway."

Did the breeziness mean she agreed with Edna, that the way it turned out was his own damned fault? He wondered again, as he had all night, why he didn't blame *her*, like Sid did. It was as if they'd reached a tacit agreement the moment they met: They'd both take care of themselves.

"Where *I've* got the advantage," she went on cheerily, "is with this *Walden* business. You're still on page 106. I'm all the way up to—uh—167."

"You are?"

He thought perhaps he'd had an episode of memory loss, from being beaten about the head and neck. He had this impulse, every time she spoke, to ask her to repeat herself. He wasn't getting the point. When had they ever talked of *Walden*?

"How shall I get it back to you?"

"What?" he asked.

"Your *book*. Are you stoned or something?"

"Aha," retorted Greg, catching on at last. He'd left his *book* there. The lady was making a formal call, with a script a gentleman ought to know. "You could put it in the mail," he said helpfully.

"I've got an idea," she said, and he knew she had had it

before she called. "Why don't we meet at the studio? I have to go in on Monday, to have a look at Jasper's picture. You come too. I understand you've done some work in the industry."

"Sort of," he said vaguely. "Where do I go?"

"Artie will pick you up. Is noon too early?"

"No. That's fine."

"Good. See you then."

He could tell she was going to hang up as abruptly as she said hello. He hated to break the mood, but he called out: "Wait! He doesn't know where I live."

"Of course he does," said Vivien Cokes, severing connections.

He held the receiver to his ear a moment longer, to gather his wits before he turned around. Just what did she mean by "work"? In the field of unbought scripts, the grasses had long blown over his name. She couldn't mean the autographs—or could she? Anything but that. He prefered to be billed as unemployed, he thought as he put down the phone. He walked across the terrace, trying to look nonchalant.

"You won't believe it," he threw out lightly.

"Oh, don't worry," Edna reassured him. "We're going to give it everything we've got."

She leaned against the butt end of the sphinx. Sid was still under the canopy, patting his torso dry with a threadbare motel towel. They had all the time in the world.

"She's got my book," said Greg. "We have to get together, so she can give it back." He tried to leave it at that, but they wouldn't budge. They let the silence build. "At Universal," he added lamely. "Monday afternoon. She's sending a car to pick me up."

"I wonder what she wants," said Sid.

"I just told you," Greg replied quite evenly.

But Sid was not one to be threatened. He twitched his hips in a little hula and sauntered away to the terrace doors. "*I'll* tell you what you ask her," he said as he flung them wide. "What the fuck's she gonna do with all that money? Ask her that, why don't you?"

Irrelevant as it seemed, the question hung in the air as he disappeared inside. Edna knelt to the papers and started to gather them up. It seemed she too had had her fill of the great outdoors. *Well, let them go,* he thought. He looked away over the city, where the visibility was a bare two hundred feet. A savage veil of smog, the first of its kind this spring, had sorrowed down in the night, while he was stuck in jail. He wondered which was the real L.A.: the city in winter, clear to the ocean, or this today, the ruined air choked with the coming summer. It occurred to him that Steepside was above it.

"What *I'd* like to know," said Edna Temple, bristling slightly, "is, what did she go to Bermuda for?"

She plopped the mail in the basket, stood up heavily, and headed after Sid. Clearly, she saw no need to draw it out any further. She'd already raised the specter of collusion, after all. "You think they'll put you on the payroll?" she had asked, only moments before the call came through. The turn of events spoke volumes, all its own. Besides, he ought to know by now that what she said was the tip of the iceberg— especially when she was mad. She liked to savor being right. Words didn't always do it justice.

"Hey!" demanded Greg. She turned halfway as she passed inside. She poised mid-step to hear him out, but the forward motion never stopped. She was on her way, no matter what he said. "What's *with* you two? You trying to say she did it herself?"

"*Vivien?*" Edna asked, incredulous as he. "From what I hear, she don't do a goddam thing herself. What do you think she's got flunkies for?"

And she floated on through to the living room—leaving him more or less out in the cold, though the temperature hovered near eighty. If he'd followed them in just then, he'd have found them getting right to work. Industrious, cheerful, bustling about the dining room like Santa's elves, they would ground themselves in the only way they knew—by going into detail. "Getting *on* with it," as Sid would say. There were countless things to be put in their place. Debts to pay and parcels to send. A part of Greg longed to go inside and get lost in the stars like they did. He counted, day to day, on that feel for the concrete act. He'd learned it as much from them as anyone.

But not now. He stuck to his mood and went to the rail. He fell into his old position of repose—leaning over, staring down into the tops of trees. He saw he could no longer argue that events had shut them out of the case. They were in, all right. Sid and Edna, of course, didn't really believe it was Vivien Cokes behind it all. Some other brand of fear—abandonment by him, no doubt—had made them snipe at her. They would all get along like a house afire once they were introduced. They shared a common habit, after all, of saying what they pleased. And they seemed, all three, to labor under the same gross misapprehension—that they understood Greg Cannon better than he did himself.

It wasn't a mood that had a name. It was simply his. He was hobbled and bruised and throbbing, but he wouldn't give in to any of that. What he wished to be right now was an aimless man. He measured the shades of green in the gardens far below. He watched for rifts in the smog. He had no inclination to convince anyone of anything. The man in jail who'd wrapped him around like a coat, like a Saint Bernard in a blizzard, had fled irretrievably into the past. As far from here and now as Harry Dawes.

It must have been jail that brought this on. However it was, the rest would have to come to him. He had no desire to meet halfway. As to Vivien Cokes, he didn't care what she meant to do with all that money. Nor why she went to

Bermuda, either. What was on his mind was something quite specific: If she was going to read the book, then he didn't have to. Hard to say why it mattered, but the very fact that it did was why they didn't understand him half so well as they thought. It was doubtless all bound up with his perversity.

He followed the sway of the tall old palms that burst like so many fireworks just below his terrace. Whatever it was, he thought with a lilt of vagary, was not in any book. Till the day before, he'd been afraid to leave his own apartment. He couldn't travel half a mile from home without a sense of doom. But now he knew there were others besides himself, and it made him want to wander all around. From wood to wood. From notion to notion. He had no use for *Walden*, having been there now for two whole years. He would go instead where the spirit took him. Out of this world, if the right thing came along.

They all holed up for the weekend, trying to change the subject. Edna spent the lion's share of Friday just going over the Crawford file. The Crawford fans had to be handled carefully, since they had a way of asking for an autograph that made it seem like what they needed was a good caning. Sid did his stable of dancers, personalizing madly. "Hello to the boys back home," he scrawled across a glossy, sending Ann Miller's best regards. And Greg sat under a visor, off to himself, doing the names of the dead on faded bits of paper. Bogart and Monty Clift, to be precise.

When they'd done a whole day of it, going from this one to that one, they grouped together at five on Saturday afternoon—amply supplied with highballs. They stuffed the envelopes, licked the flaps, and stuck the stamps, in a kind of crude assembly line. They turned the local news up loud, and now and then, when an item was aired about Jasper Cokes, they found themselves turning strangely quiet. The portents were queer, all over the place. A story went out that the western branch of Jasper's fans had just convened in Reno, where various amateur mystics planned to raise his ghost for a last goodbye. Women with child stepped up to say that Jasper was the father. People still swore they'd seen him alive— as recently as this afternoon, in eight different states and several foreign capitals. So far there was no suggestion that he'd risen from the dead.

They processed it all in a flash, and saw how far ahead they were. Sid jiggered another round of Seven Crown. Greg fizzed the glasses with ginger ale. Edna laid out a bed of Wheat Thins, slathering each with half an inch of avocado dip. They worked on into the evening, till all their reserves were lowered and talk between them was loose again. Perhaps the instinct to compromise was stronger than their egos.

By the time Sid and Edna left, to go see *Shane* at the Tiffany, they both averred to be satisfied that Greg knew what he was doing. He'd secured a route direct to the widow, hadn't he? Just to get past the loonies and dime-store seers was something. They buttered him up outrageously. By Monday afternoon, they were sure, he'd have pried her deepest secrets out of her. Then they patted his arm approvingly and went off sloppy drunk to hail the bus at Highland.

He made no move to disabuse them. Maybe he'd be in the mood, come Monday, to do just what they said. For now, he sat on the arm of the sofa and played the channels with his portable eye. He kept flicking back to *How to Marry a Millionaire*, but only turned the volume up when Marilyn was on. He tried to remember just how far Thoreau had gotten to by page 106. Though he hadn't noticed the book was gone, the whole night through in the county jail, one thing stuck with him still. The curmudgeonly loner at Walden Pond had just described a season of visits from a dark-eyed Canadian woodcutter. A real hot number, he sounded like. In any case, Greg was convinced there was much more to it than Henry Thoreau was owning up to.

Everyone he met was wasting time. Men with one idea, he called them—"like a hen with one chicken, and that a duckling." All but the woodcutter, chopping away and stacking it up, four by four by eight. He was favored as being at one with the woods. More so, it almost seemed, than the writer himself, with his endless record of phenomena. Thoreau had found a man who was larger in his consciousness than what he said or understood. Regrettably, they never got to bed. Greg would have known, he read so close between the lines.

Professors and sellers of books would not have been amused. Greg didn't care. He had nothing he felt like saying about this book he refused to finish. Grudgingly, he did admit that Thoreau was a hell of a writer. He wrote out his days at the pond as if there could never be time enough to get it right. The hardest thing about writing, Greg had always thought, was having no excuse. When you couldn't do it, you blamed it on your income and your celibacy, or else it was the heat, the downstairs neighbor, or the phone. Yet Greg had toughed out days when the outside world did not intrude for an instant. Still he stared at his sea-green Hermes, looking as if he expected a scrap of teletype to rattle out onto the page. A career with a built-in gun at one's head. It got so a man could hardly think without thinking he would fail. Thoreau, he saw, had worked his way beyond all that.

By the time the Sunday paper arrived, the scope of Jasper's holdings had begun to be accounted. *Wanted!*, his last year's picture, grossed a hundred and twenty million, of which Jasper's cut was twelve cents on the dollar, starting at dollar one. His up-front fees had always been common knowledge, part of the hype that went with his deals. He made a couple of pictures a year, and they paid him a million six, a million eight, for two months' work, maybe three. After *Wanted!*, where his salary worked out to a flat two million for an eleven-day shoot, he suddenly had a new handle: the man who earned a million bucks a week.

But even so, no one was quite prepared for the fortune he was piling up in points. Well over a hundred million dollars in just eight years. With figures big as this, the verdict of the press was clear: A man this rich has forfeited the right to kill himself. Or at least he ought to have signed it all away to worthy causes. It would have been better, moneywise, to drop it in stacks from the wing of a plane. Anything not to surrender seventy-five per cent of it to Vivien, who already had too damn much for her own good.

The widow came in for harder knocks than Jasper. What kind of a wife was she to him that he had to go the route of sucking cock? The midnight press ran pictures of her meant to show she was good for nothing. Sunning topless on the deck of an oilman's yacht. At a supper club with a married man who had to be more than her lawyer. In a word, this woman was fallen. An exclusive interview, splashed across the vilest of the tabloids, quoted a shadowy source to the effect that Jasper thought Vivien *turned* him queer.

"I have nothing to say," said Vivien Cokes. And they printed it as if it were a signed confession.

It's none of their fucking business, Greg thought glumly, tying his tie in the mirror Monday morning. It was the second time he'd worn a tie in a week—in a year and a half, for that matter—and he didn't think it boded well at all. He would have preferred to go dressed down. But Sid and Edna, while he wasn't looking, sewed up the rips in his seams and pressed his charcoal suit back into shape. He didn't have the heart to leave it hanging in the closet. As for the tie, the long end came out shorter than the short, and he had to start all over.

He fumed at the generalized presumption that Jasper's being gay was the source of all his fuck-ups. He decided he ought to ask Vivien to change the public image before the plaster set. Why not go with the Romeo mood of the suicide note? Jasper had braved, as long as he could, the corner the world had painted him in. The tragic isolation of the lovers was the story with beginning, middle, and end. Greg could have written it in his sleep. It wasn't true, of course, but for now it would serve to cut the Satanic edge, at least till they found out something more. Greg had always run the other way when gay people fought for their rights—so much did he shrink from siding with groups. But now he was pissed at all this innuendo. He knotted his tie like a noose, till it looked as if he'd used it to strangle a sudden assailant.

He stood on the curb in the noonday sun, ducking back into the lobby three or four times to mop his brow. When the powder-blue Rolls glided up, he had just hung his jacket on the fire-alarm post. He was waving his arms like a bellows to dry the sweat in the pits of his shirt. Artie braked on a dime. He stared straight ahead through the windshield, waiting for Greg to pull himself together. At last Greg reached for the front-door handle. And just as suddenly froze. From high above him, he heard a noise of whistles and hoots.

Oh, no, he thought with a claustrophobic shiver, cupping a shady hand above his eyes and looking skyward. Sid and Edna were leaning perilously over his railing. They pointed and called, but he couldn't hear. It sounded like they were warning him of a bomb. He shrugged his shoulders and shook his head, sure it would wait till he came home later. Then the breezes seemed to shift, and he heard them loud and clear.

"In the back," they were shouting. "Ride in the back!"

"Go to hell!" he hollered up at them. He thumbed the handle pointedly, and the front door opened without a sound. He climbed in next to Artie and settled back, one hand pinching the putty-colored leather of the seat. The Mozart was so loud he felt like he was trapped in the belly of a cello. But he absolutely refused to be overawed. He searched the panel of gauges till he spotted the proper knob. He cut the volume to a whisper.

"It's pretty silly, isn't it?" said Greg. He tried to sound like a regular guy. "The last time we met, you got me arrested."

"You're lucky," Artie countered, without a trace of apology. "Most everyone she meets is a fool and a liar. She don't usually bother, if you know what I mean."

"Ah, well," he retorted vaguely as they sped away up Highland. He leaned back into the seat to regroup. Did they have to dispense with small talk quite so fast? He liked a bit more foreplay, somehow. "Tell me," he said, "have things sort of quieted down at the house?"

"I guess so," Artie said. "People don't bother us much." They were going about eighty. In a moment, the Rolls would connect with Route 101 and rocket them through to the other side of the mountains. "She told me you wanted to talk about Jasper. What do you want to know?"

It was all in the nature of a dare, Greg thought. Rooted in sex, like everything else. They had known it Thursday evening in the hills, when the course of things had put them face to face. They were both gay, and they both knew it. Vivien probably had her own reasons for asking Artie to open up, to do with the fact that Greg was Harry's lover. There were things he had a right to understand. It was obvious too that Artie had some use for the occasion—some kind of confrontation to enact.

"You were lovers?"

"Used to be," Artie said. "For a couple of months. We were kids."

"In college, you mean," Greg added, nodding. What's-its-name. The place where the three of them met, all snowbound in the mountains of Vermont. They had formed a little corporation, for the purpose of building a movie star. Greg had heard the· *yarn* of Jasper Cokes a hundred times. There was no need to start so far back. "Couple months," Greg said. "That's a long time. And nobody ever made a move to get it on again?"

"You mean, was I still in love with him?"

"Weren't you?"

"Not really," Artie replied. "Not at *all*, at the very end."

He smiled at the road ahead in a funny way, as if a private joke were about to pass. They crested the mountain, and Greg saw the white-smoke mist of the Valley. Then, like an afterthought, Artie went on—as if candor were one thing, the truth quite another. "You have no idea," he said, "how perfect he was when he was twenty."

A bodyguard, thought Greg, had all the opportunities. The very man you stationed in the hallway by your bathroom—so Norman Bates couldn't get you in the shower. It sounded to Greg as if Artie put a lot of stock in an old one-liner, to the effect that a man had to sell his soul to see his name in lights. Was it enough to make a long-lost lover slit your wrists, on the grounds that you're dead inside?

"Did he ever make it with Carl?" Greg asked. He was talking half to himself. Trying in his mind to see the whole trio—far far back, when they first met up.

"Of course not," Artie scoffed. "Carl was Jasper's *straight* man. Carl doesn't make it with anyone." And though clearly not a man who made witty remarks, he said the rest with an acid laugh that bubbled up in every line. "Actually, I don't either. There's this one part of Steepside we call 'the cloister.' Celibates only."

Imagine: The bodyguard turns and goes for the throat of the man he's meant to protect. Now, there was a paranoid's nightmare. It would be, Greg thought, a spur of the moment thing. Just double the dose of Quaaludes, and powder them up in the evening's Mai Tais. Then, when the two men are lolling at the edge of sleep, their heads on the rim of the redwood tub, you come lumbering through the garden, a single-edge blade in one hand. Hardly believing you're doing it, even as you cut.

"With me, it's because I don't try," continued Artie. "The other guy's gotta come to me. I don't know how to ask."

And Greg thought: *Wait a minute.*

The Rolls swung off on the exit ramp. For the whole long curve, nothing was said. Greg gripped the handle beside him and hugged the door close. Though Artie had only made the mildest pass, the centrifugal motion seemed to push the moment to a pitch. They were going so fast, he thought he'd fall over, right into Artie's lap. Or the Rolls would jump the divider and hurtle into a truck. He shut his eyes, waiting to go up in flames.

It would have been the perfect way for a moralist to go—one's virtue all intact, in the death seat of a Rolls. But Greg didn't get to die of it just yet. They reached the end of the ramp and came to a stop at the boulevard light, quite without incident. After all, it had only been a moment. A third party listening in on every word—say Vivien Cokes—would not have detected a shred of innuendo, or not the kind that dragged a man to bed. Perhaps it hadn't happened.

"And what about Vivien?" Greg said into the silence. "Does she get as much as they say?"

"Ask *her*," said Artie snappishly. "It's none of your goddam business, if you want to know what *I* think."

So there. It *had* just happened. Artie wanted to fuck, and Greg had turned him down. It had all been done without a word. And they were already into the phase of trying to live it down. Greg cast about for excuses, wondering if he should make a case that he was too stricken with grief to get it up. It wasn't so at all. It was just that Artie was not his type—had the same color hair, for Christ's sake.

At the studio gate, the guard waved them on without making them stop. They rode in past the black tower of executive offices—like a great computer dense with circuitry, or a Xerox machine half a block long. Then on down a row of buff-colored stages. Greg didn't want to count the times he'd moved the earth to get this far, whereupon he was usually shuffled through and out the other side. He refused to act like a tourist. Refused, after all this time, to be cowed and peasant-grateful.

Just behind the commissary, they came up against a wall of men—the crew of a starship heading in for lunch, with a gang of armored aliens in tow. As Artie slowed the Rolls, the group from outer space divided down the middle to let it through. Some in helmets, some in masks with saucer eyes, they turned to look at what brand of star was riding by. When they saw it was only Greg, they seemed to draw back like stars themselves. As if they couldn't bear to see a nobody acting big-shot.

They turned off into a narrow lane between two stages vast as hangars. Now the late-noon light was high above them, washing the upper walls as if someone had re-aimed a spot. Greg could hardly see in the sudden shade. Artie parked snug up to the building on the right, got out without a word, and came around to open the door. Greg felt banished. He stood up and paused, with the door between them like a shield. He made a move to salvage what he could.

"You think we can meet somewhere and talk?" he asked.

"I don't know," said Artie, clearly quite uncomfortable. "I mean, what's the point?"

"I'd like to tell you how it was with me and Harry Dawes."

For a moment, neither looked the other in the eye. Greg glanced up at the hard-edge line where the sand-colored stucco met the blue of the midday sky. He realized he and Artie had never been introduced.

"If you want," said Artie finally. "Why don't you give me a call when Viv takes off."

"Where's she going?"

"Away," he replied, with a rolling shrug of his massive shoulders. He walked across the alley. Taking hold of a rusty lever, he slid a dented metal door along a track. "You're late," he said. "You better hurry."

As Greg went in, with a sheepish smile, he gave a gentleman athlete's squeeze to the melon of Artie's upper arm. He entered the dark, and the door roared shut behind. The first thing he did was stretch the muscles of his face, to rid it of the bullshit throbbing in his smile. Every word he'd said getting out of the car was a rotten lie. He'd made his unavailability crystal clear, but only by tricking it up with a fine veneer of niceness. He hated the taste it left in his mouth. It was worse than if they'd had the sex and got it over and done with.

As he waited to let his eyes adjust to the sudden loss of light, he began to think it was only fair that Vivien make the next move. He'd expected a little theater carpeted in beige, with stand-up ashtrays full of sand and a cart of fruit and Perrier. He wasn't a rube when it came to industry aesthetics. He thought he had come to hobnob with studio brass. So where was the movie? What was he doing all alone in an empty warehouse? Vivien ought to take care of him. This wasn't a place where he was free to go where he liked. There were probably holes in the floor.

Then the emptiness started to clear. Up ahead, like a dream cohering, he made out a dimly lit sprawl of buildings. Spanish, it looked like. Huddled around a fern-choked fountain, all of it dead as a ghost town. He moved toward it stealthily. He thought he saw a man and a woman embracing beneath an arch, but the shadow fell all the way to their knees, so he couldn't be sure. Before he had a chance to wrap them up in a story, the woman broke into the open and walked across to meet him. As soon as he saw her face, he knew it wasn't love he'd interrupted. She looked too furious.

"Greg," she said wearily, "please forgive me. It's just not going to work."

So saying, she took his hands and held out a cheek to be cheeked. They touched like the glasses of wine in a toast. Then he moved to retreat, since he thought she had dismissed him. But she wouldn't let go. She tugged him back to the tile-roofed town, as if to bring him in from the desert sun. He struggled to think of a way to say goodbye. As they neared the fountain, she said: "The picture won't be ready for a week." And he saw it was not the two of *them* that had no chance. It was just a minor systems breakdown.

"Talk to Brearley," she murmured, just as a man stepped out of the shadows. "He can get you in."

"In where?"

"Oh, shut up," she said with some annoyance, as if he were being a spoilsport. Then, much louder: "Max, you haven't met Greg Cannon, have you?" They all came together beside the fountain. "He's a marvelous writer," she added, fairly beaming with assurance.

"Friend of Jasper's?" Maxim Brearley asked, on the point of handshake.

"No," Greg said. He suppressed the desire to throw in his lot with Harry Dawes, whenever that was asked. It was almost like a wedding, with the ushers inquiring: "Bride or groom?"

"What have you written?" asked the director, pleasantly enough. But Greg heard a harder version, echoing in from the past: *You got any credits?* That was the way it was usually put.

"Oh, I had a whole stack of screenplays once," said the writer lightly, shrugging it off. "But that was some time back."

"He's been doing a treatment of *Walden*," Vivien said, not one to be deterred. "We'll have to get you a copy."

"Do that," Max replied—looking all the while at Greg, and telegraphing word of his rejection in advance. Then he turned to her directly, lowering his voice by just enough to cut Greg out completely. "Viv, I'll get us a print. By the end of the week, I promise. We can screen it up at Steepside."

"But Max," she protested, "I'll be *gone*."

Greg couldn't understand why this news made him feel so lonely and so broke. He couldn't afford to go with her, even if she asked. Besides, why in a million years would he ever want to? He hated all this ritzy chitchat as to how the rich passed time. As much as he hated Brearley's pricey clothes— baggy khaki head to toe, like a Jerry Magnin mannequin. The butterscotch finish on his tassel shoes was the match of the briefcase under his arm.

"You'll see it before you go, Viv. You have my word on that."

Greg was startled. Did people still give their word out loud? It sounded almost quaint. Max threw his arms around her shoulders—a purely formal gesture, somehow, meant to make a show of comforting the bereaved. Greg could have been a footman here, for all the part he had to play. But he relished his silence like a good night's sleep. He stood there peering about at the set, still as the Spanish town the others broke the mood of. Let this gibbering asshole have the floor, he thought.

"Hey, give me a call," said Max, as he offered Greg a second shake. The message was plainly the other way. There were so many baffles set between Max and an idle phone call. Greg would be smart, he seemed to say, to give it up now before he got started. Brearley was far too big to be of any help. Besides, an untried talent came across as an omen of doom to men with power. A writer without a lot of credits might, without even knowing it, carry a dose of failure like a virus.

"About that other matter, Viv. I don't think it's up to Carl anymore. Tell him that, will you?"

Greg snapped back to attention. What were they saying about Suspect Number One? Was Max going to let him in on something? He'd either decided Greg was too low down to make a difference or far too hip to try to fool. Which was it?

"If it does come out," said Max, "then *all* of us ought to have a say in how we handle it. Me, I mean to protect my picture."

That was all. Dispensing with goodbyes as if they were unoriginal, the director walked away and through the arch. They could hear the click of his hand-sewn shoes receding into the distance even after the dark had swallowed him up. Greg took a breath to apologize for coming in too early. But when he turned to speak, he saw from the antic look on her face that the main conspirators here were the two of them. It was Max who was out in the cold.

"Pay no attention," she said, her voice gone normal again. "That type never gets over the junk they make to get a foot in the door. Don't worry—he'll read it. If he doesn't, I'll read it *to* him."

"Read what?"

"It doesn't have to be *Walden*. That was just off the top of my head. You give me whatever you've got."

Ah well. He stared down into the basin of the fountain. Now for the first time, he noticed the brown-edged fiddle-head ferns were potted. The stonework around them was papier-mâché. The moss on the rim was thickened paint. And just when he saw it was all a trick, he registered the sound he had taken for granted—a cricket, chirping away in the leaves. It must have got in by mistake, having hitched a ride on a fern. It thought it was safe in a twilit garden. Poor little bastard.

"Somebody's misinformed you," he said. "I've put away my Scripto and my Big Five pad."

He would have protested even more, except he was so relieved. Somehow, she hadn't stumbled on his current line of work.

"But that was a loss of nerve," she said. "This here is another chance."

She patted his cheek as if to pose his head and walked around him purposefully. Then she went stage left. He followed her with his eyes as she mounted a flight of broken steps. Yellow weeds grew out of the cracks. On the landing, ten feet above the floor, was an iron gate which seemed to lead to a rise above the town. But in fact, of course, it went nowhere. The whole of this village was just façades—with the empty sound stage all around. At the seventh stair, she stooped to retrieve what looked like saddlebags. She called the next bit over her shoulder.

"Does it violate your principles to use a connection?"

She stood and faced him, in a white silk shirt and belled black pants, the saddlebag over one arm. She looked as if she might be fancy with a gun. Her head was framed by the iron gate, on which a string of words was wreathed in rusty curlicues. It looked like it must have taken years to make, and a hundred more to get so old. He didn't see how it could have been faked.

"Where are we, exactly?"

"This? It's an old abandoned mission," she said. "They did the exteriors up near Santa Barbara. The problem was, the whole inside was a pile of rubble. So they did it here, with the odds and ends of other sets. It's the end of a trail, you see."

"And what's on the other side of the gate?"

"The graveyard."

"How do you know so much, if you haven't seen the picture?"

"I read the script," she replied with a shrug, as if to play down her privileges. "I'm sorry about the movie, by the way. Ingmar Brearley says he needs more time."

"Can you read what it says up there?" he asked, pointing above her head at the filigree line on the gate.

He already had the clearest picture of the graveyard. Fenced around with high adobe walls, the inner space cooled by a stand of eucalyptus. The mission, no doubt, would be high on a hill, so the summer grass sloped to the ocean half a mile away. The markers on the graves were made of local wood—bone-white crosses and two-foot slabs. One slept beneath the palomino trunks of eucalyptus, hearing the clatter of branches as the sea breeze swept the hilltop.

Vivien turned and looked along the gateway. In a halting high school accent, she read out the Spanish word by word. "*Quiero descansar,*" she recited, "*con los que tanto ame.*" When she spun around again, she was smiling with something like pride. "It's very pretty, isn't it?"

"How would *I* know? Say it in English."

"But it won't sound half as nice," she said. "Tell me first about Harry Dawes."

"There's nothing to tell," he said guardedly.

She came down a few steps and sat. Then she rummaged a bit in her leather pouch. When she pulled out a copy of *Walden*—same green cover, with the shore of the pond like the shadow across the face of a haunted man—it seemed like a rabbit come out of a hat. He'd managed yet again to let it slip his mind. Of course—this was the reason they were here. Clearly, the book was more determined to find its way to him than he to it.

"It's very beautiful, what he says here."

She flipped the cover and read out loud a fragment of Harry's inscription: " 'You can't pull up a single flower without the whole universe coming up with it.' Don't you think that says a lot about you both?"

He scrambled for words that would prove her wrong, but she lobbed the book to him underhand, and it was all he could do to catch it. It thumped against his chest and he held it clutched as she went on.

"Let me finish," she said, as if she understood what a low threshold he had for supportive remarks. "If I didn't believe it was good between you, I wouldn't have gone to the trouble to track you down. The moment I saw you, I knew who you were." She stopped to grope for a way to say it—to tell him how it was she saw right through him. "I mean, you were off on a cloud somewhere. Like you couldn't think straight."

"It's an endearing little habit of mine," he said with a snort of irony. "I get bored very easy. Before I know it, I've started to drift. Someday I'm going to have to wear a collar with my name and address on it."

"I didn't say bored. It was like you were hardly there at all. It reminded me of—me."

There was more of a trick to things between them than he thought. He'd been gearing up to disabuse her. Right from the first, she'd blown it all out of proportion about the bond between him and Harry. She gave them too much sentimental license—seemed to see them honeymooned in a cabin on Walden Pond. But he didn't really understand the reason until now. She wanted him in as deep as she was. In a marriage that ended up rotten with lies.

"I hate to be technical," he said, "but I think the nothing *I* was feeling wasn't quite the same as yours."

"Who's counting?" Vivien scoffed. "It *amounts* to the same. We were both of us left in the lurch."

"Well, but not *really*," Greg protested, stubborn in this if nothing else. "I hardly knew him. It was just one night." He held out his open palm as if there were water running through it. He couldn't think of another thing to say. He snapped his fingers once—but softly, as if they were numb from the cold. "Just like that," he said quietly.

All along, he'd kept a certain distance from her, in case she proved to be a simp. He was scared there might be a nasty streak of hearts-and-flowers in her. Now he saw it was quite the reverse—she took an even darker view than he did. He felt an urge to fly up the steps and take her hand and apologize. He'd misjudged her very badly. The third path didn't occur to him: to keep his distance all the same, lest her case of the bleaks was contagious. He moved to close the space between them, as if it were up to him to turn the tide of betrayal.

"Oh, Harry and I would have made it, I guess. But I'm very slow on the uptake. It comes from thinking I know all the lines. I'm always waiting for cues."

"Does it matter how many nights it was?" she asked, with an edge of real disdain. "You loved him, right?"

"Well . . . yes."

"Well, Jasper was fucking him too. Now doesn't that make you feel a little—I don't know—*preempted?*"

"It *would* have," he argued. "I'm sure it would have *killed* me, just thinking about it. But—that's not how it happened." He would have loved to add her nickname here, to gentle the bluntness of it. "You see, I don't think they ever met. I think somebody made it *look* that way."

He managed to get it said without actually saying the word, but murder hung in the air from that point on like a film of carbon gas. Vivien drew back. She raised her head and looked out levelly over the roofs of the mission. For that one moment, the feeling she spoke of was on her face—she was hardly there at all. Perhaps no feeling had the guts to rise to the occasion.

"Oh, do you think that's wise?" she asked in a vague and melancholy way. She made it seem like a matter of taste. "I mean, isn't it bad enough the way we have it now? At least we've gotten some of it behind us. Can't you go some other way?"

The truth's the only way, he thought, but luckily didn't say it. His earnestness could be quite oppressive.

"But don't you see," he demanded after a pause, pressing on with the greatest care, "if it was murder, then you didn't lose him. Not the way you thought."

"Really?"

She didn't sound convinced. Didn't sound remotely interested, in fact. When she brought her eyes back to his face again, he saw she'd left the whole idea behind. It didn't mean she wouldn't listen. She was more than glad to let him talk it out. But the concept didn't grab her.

"You know what? You need to get away," she said. "I know *I* do. Saturday morning, I leave for a month in Baja. Sailing." She didn't sound very interested in that, either. "I know you don't make very much, but I have an idea. You see—I left something behind in Bermuda. That's where I was when—"

She stopped, got up, and started down the stairs. He felt as if she hadn't completed a thought in several minutes. Still, she wasn't trying to get rid of him yet. She hadn't said he couldn't investigate around her. Even so, he was glad that Edna Temple wasn't here. She would have found all manner of unsolved crimes in everything Vivien said. He watched as the widow paused on the step above him. He trusted her, God knew why. Perhaps because she went out of her way to put them on equal footing.

"If you went and picked it up for me," she said, "I'd gladly pay your way. I'd pay you *twice* as much, if you thought it didn't violate your principles."

She stepped down onto the floor, and together they strolled across the square. In the cracked squat tower on the other side, he could see the green of a copper bell. He made out a wreath of leaves and berries, cast around the rim. *Real*, he thought—that is, not gum and paint and plaster of Paris. Real like the wrought-iron gate was real.

"I have an old house on the water," she said. "There's a lot of trees, and a field of lilies. In a way it's like Walden Pond—except it's ʈhe middle of the ocean."

"I have to find out all I can. I can't stop now."

"Well, that's up to you," she replied. She wasn't about to engage with him on the moral point. "*I'll* be away, so I can't help you. Maybe Carl and Artie will—unless, of course, they did it. I don't know what your theory is. But listen, Bermuda can wait. You can go when you're finished."

"When I'm finished, there's going to be hell to pay," said Greg in an even-tempered voice, for once not trying to hide the forties-gumshoe mimicry. He found he wasn't afraid to say goodbye. They'd had the talk required of them. Till now, he didn't see how he could ever proceed without her. He'd made her the ground of his inquiry. But here he found she was just another outsider like himself. She was better off out of the way.

"Do I have to say I'll do it," he asked, "before you tell me what it is?"

"Oh, just a diamond," she said lightly. "Sentimental value, mostly." But insured, she might have added, for a cool four hundred thou. She rummaged again in the leather bag, till she pulled from the tangle the copy of *Walden* he'd left on her bed last Thursday. With them both thus armed, it looked more and more like a seminar. "There's a map in here," she said, slipping an envelope out of the book. "The X is where I left it hanging. Also, money for the plane. I'm afraid it's cash, but I didn't know what else you took. You don't need a key. The house you'll figure out as you go. It's built to be very simple."

He took the envelope out of her hand, briefly weighed its heft, and tucked it in the middle of his book. There was a pause. There ought to have been a pause *before* he took the envelope, giving him time to struggle with the verities. But something had sent his mind racing ahead—the deserted mission itself, perhaps, with the air of a thousand stories buried just beyond the gate. Suddenly, Vivien's errand didn't seem terribly out of the ordinary. In any case, he shrugged the issue of where it all would end. More and more, he seemed to know he would solve this case for no one but himself. It didn't much matter what roundabout ways he took.

"How do you know I'll go?"

"Writers like to travel, don't they?"

As they came in under the shadow of the tower, she took his arm and turned them back the other way. It might have been nothing more than a walk around the courtyard. A couple of stately mission elders, making plans to spread the word. When they drew up close to the fountain again, as if to toss a final coin, Greg realized the cricket had stopped its dry-legged racket. It probably heard a scrap of him and Vivien, he thought—till it knew, with a sudden sinking in its heart, that somehow it was stranded on a set.

"I'll call you when I get back," she said. "We can meet in some dark alley to make the exchange. I think that's every-thing, isn't it? Let's go eat."

"But you haven't told me what it says."

"What?" she said, for the first time caught off guard. She followed the point of his finger. "Oh, you mean the *gate*. Well, all right. It'll only depress you, but you asked. *Lay me to rest*," she recited, her voice gone singsong, cool as a breeze, "*among those men I loved so much*."

She was absolutely right. It was almost more than they could take, such lonely types as they. The mission priests were lucky men, to give it all up so peacefully. They made it out to be something tender, mixing earth to earth with all the men of their kind.

"Sounds great," said Greg. "Maybe we should all go live in a mission."

"Or *die* in one, at least."

There was nothing left to do but go. Arm in arm, they

walked away without a backward glance. They seemed to feel the motto wrought in the gate as a sort of reproof. For living in fear of sentiment, perhaps—though here they might have retorted that it read a lot better than it lived. Besides, Greg thought with a dry-mouthed pout, the problem wasn't love. If the two of them had laid out their résumés, it would have been clear what a creditable job they did of loving well when occasion arose. The real trouble lay in *being* loved. With so many mirrors and mug shots hanging about on the walls, a person took care of *that* part all by himself.

"Is there still a Walden Pond?"

"Of course," he said as he disengaged his arm and reached for the dented metal door. They had to get out of here fast. They'd done enough lagging back and talking it out in the dark. "Why?"

"You mean they didn't pave it over? Well, that's a relief. Ever been there?"

"No."

The daylight broke upon them, and they froze. They'd have liked to keep their chitchat going like sixty, if only to show they'd each survived the other's grandstand play—he with his verdict of murder one, she with her all-expenses-paid. But they'd surfaced again in the real world now. For all they knew, the match of wits would not sustain in the light of day. Perhaps, like champagne left in the glass too long, they would flatten and go sour. To look at them then—in the glare of the studio sun, and neither one with a deal—they seemed as dwarfed as children. Still, they could not turn back.

She made a sudden beeline to the Rolls, where Artie was slumped in the driver's seat, reading the trades. She handed in her leather bag, retaining only the book. She wasn't the sort who needed liquid assets on her person. She leaned down and murmured some words about matters of scheduling, while Greg checked out the people who were walking

back and forth in the street outside the alley. He felt afraid
of everyone. Because things were so private now between
him and her, people would start to notice. Would doubtless
jump to conclusions he hadn't the power to reverse.

When she came his way again, they instinctively kept a
foot of space between them. Then they emerged from the
alley beside Stage Nine and fell in among the studio workers
hurrying back from lunch. Each with a bright green paperback, they looked as out of place as out-of-towners. Only the
unconnected needed guidebooks, after all. Greg tried to tell
himself it was just a bad attack of being oversensitive. Besides, they weren't looking at him. It was Vivien—strolling
along as if it were any old busy street, and she some clear-
eyed country girl, having a day in town. They gawked at her
from every side, and she didn't miss a step.

"I gather it's smaller than Tahoe," she said.

"Of course," he replied, looking into the face of a mogul
who tried to catch Vivien's eye as they passed. "It's really
very small. I think you can walk around it in an hour."

"The smaller the better," said Vivien resolutely. And Greg
had a horrible thought: She was going to start waving the
book in the air, like a redneck toting a Bible. "You get tired
of a view that goes on and on," she said, her mind on some
specific vista Greg could not hope to imagine. "Well, *I* do
anyway. Tell me, do you think it's still in private hands?"

"What? You mean Walden?"

She wanted to *buy* it?

He gave her a sidelong look. She honestly seemed to pay
no mind to the way they watched her. Unlike him, she didn't
come down with the woozies when she found herself in the
teeming mass. Perhaps because it parted automatically, just
to let her by. Whatever the explanation was—untouchable by
dint of royal blood, so rich she could buy and sell the crowds
she walked through ten times over—she seemed to have no
fear of being overwhelmed.

"'I think it's a national park or something," Greg informed her dryly. "Why don't you make them an offer? Nothing ventured, nothing gained."

What he'd always looked for before, he thought, was someone to lead him through the line of fire. He'd come across some fearless type, and right away he'd think: *This is the one.* As an agoraphobe, he tended to live with his back to the wall, armed for all-out war. But the longer he watched her, detached from the melee around her, the more did he wonder if, after all, he couldn't make it on his own. It was a matter of what one paid attention to, it seemed. The others didn't exist unless you let them.

"Well, something *like* it, then," she said, dismissing the thought of eminent domain. "There must be other ponds. All you need's a realtor with a little brains."

The heads kept turning, wherever they went. As they pushed through the glass doors into the commissary, three big men from the starship crew came out the other way, toothpicks in their teeth. They rolled their eyes at Vivien Cokes, and then they looked at him. He clearly didn't exist, except in terms of her. When they trailed behind the maître d', making their way to a corner table, he saw the room erupt and crane for a glimpse. It made him feel two things at once. On the one hand, quite invisible—no more than a kind of shadow that she cast. But terribly important, too, or else why would she eat with *him?* Altogether, he found himself strangely unthreatened. Ready to go to the ends of the earth.

As they ducked and slid into the booth, he had an awful urge—to come back at the end triumphant, the diamond in his hand and the killer's name on the tip of his tongue. All he had to do was tough it out alone. He bet he knew more about *that* than she did.

"You know," he said in a worldly way, taking a glance at the prices on the menu, "it's not supposed to *require* a pond. I mean, Walden is really nowhere. It's in your head."

"Well, it's not in *mine*," she protested smartly, scanning the list of specials with a rueful eye. "And I'll wager it's not in yours. But like I said, I'm ahead of you. You're only on 106. We'll talk about it later. I wouldn't want to spoil the plot."

"I'm not much of a reader," he said. No time for anything now but heroic isolation. "Don't hold your breath."

"What are you going to have?"

"Soup. Why did you go to Bermuda?"

"No reason. What kind?"

"*I* don't know," he said irritably, putting the menu aside. "Whatever they've got."

"You'll be sorry," she said. "Don't say I didn't warn you."

"Did you leave him?"

"Jasper? Oh, I suppose. At the time, I was sick of everything."

"And now?"

"Do you think I killed him?"

"Good God, no!"

"Well, *that's* a load off my mind, right there."

She snapped her fingers once in the air, as if to spirit them off. And the waiters came running from every side, falling all over each other to get there first.

chapter 4

"SAILING" WAS ONE WAY of putting it. In fact, it was two
hundred feet of oceangoing yacht, formerly in the hands of
the Aga Khan. Of eleven staterooms, Vivien would occupy
numbers 1 and 2—the latter set aside for her personal luggage, in her case enough to fill the belly of a 707. Erika and
Felix, who always cruised in the spring and fall, had moved
up the sailing date by a full two weeks, so that Vivien Cokes
could flee the tawdry aftermath of Jasper's death. In Erika's
set, the feel of unparalleled luxury was the only way they
knew to prove that life (though a vale of tears) went stum-
bling on.

Thus they kept on board such amenities as pastry chef,
hairdresser, and Sicilian masseur—the last of whom did a
double shift in the nightly round of musical beds. Viven,
needless to say, would not be required to do anything, beyond a minimal amount of keeping up appearances. Everything else would be done before she thought to ask. Besides,
Erika and Felix were a known quantity. She'd covered the
seven seas with them at the helm. The food would be three-
star all the way. At the backgammon board, the stakes would

be in five figures. This tub was not for nothing called *The Ritz*.

No matter if Erika got capricious, sometimes halving her lithium so as to get a little mad. Or that Felix was so dreadful with the locals—furious if no one spoke English—that he threatened to turn a day in port into an international episode. Vivien let a lot of things go by. Like the other guests, for instance. She had sat in the course of time at the right of every major power—all the Joint Chiefs of Staff, it seemed, and men who were on as many boards as she had pairs of shoes. There was always some fleetingly famous type who'd pitched a winning season. People she couldn't keep straight from year to year.

It meant maybe three or four hours a day of attending to other men's dreams. In Vivien's presence, they seemed to affect a slow and low-voiced version of the boys they must have been in high school. They didn't know what they wanted from her. She made a thousand little murmurs of assent, no matter what they said, and watched for a chance to break away. On balance, she knew that her brief appearances paid her way. She still had a dozen waking hours a day to stare out across the rail.

She'd only admitted it once, to Jasper: Travel of any sort made her feel as safe as a child again. She never remotely entertained the thought that anything would crash. She'd spent the summers of her youth rocketing through the landscape. She shuttled back and forth between one parent and the other, developing all the skills of a commuter. Her earliest recollection was a *Queen of Angels* Pullman bound for San Francisco, with Vivien tucked between a governess and a Spanish maid. The first of every October, she crossed on the *Queen Elizabeth*—once in the thrall of a tutor, Miss Wharton, who walked the decks reciting Byron, as if they'd put out to sea in Plato's Academy. Somehow, it always felt good to get moving again.

Though she'd learned in time to be moved by the sight of mountainous harbors, of coral-island chains not big enough for an airport, she never became a creature of destinations. A change of landscape didn't really strike her as much of a change. It was pure and simple journeying she loved. The feel of the open road. As a girl, she liked to imagine herself a wild horse or a migrant bird. It was never quite the same when she grew up, but still she traveled for good luck's sake, the way another woman might touch wood. As if death could not pin down a moving target.

This time, though, it wasn't going to work. She made up the usual lists and went about taking care of details, but with only half a heart. From Monday night till Wednesday afternoon, she oversaw the packing—tucking things one in the other, and minimizing wrinkles. From Carl she borrowed a smart-ass secretary, to help her clear the desk of the heaviest of the condolences. She knew all along it was mere diversionary tactics. She filled up a string of trunks, but like somebody throwing off excess baggage. As if she planned to put her past in the attic.

She betrayed nothing of this to Erika, though. As the day approached to cast away, Erika called her woman to woman, practically on the hour, to talk out matters of policy as to hemlines and porcelain nails. Vivien swore she couldn't wait to be out of sight of land. She affected to find it thrilling that Felix had signed up·a psychic to come along for the ride. As always, she called and arranged for two cases of Dom Perignon to be delivered right to the dock. She ordered pots of orchids placed in every stateroom. She even remembered to have made up a refill of her Lomotil. She found the acts of preparation bracing, in spite of the fact that she wasn't about to get stuck in a boat off Baja.

Not that she had any alternate plan. All she knew was this: She had to go off by herself, because everyone else was still tied up disposing of what was left of Jasper. She wouldn't have minded joining Greg for a couple of days in Bermuda, but that was out of the question now. She'd badly misread him. Somehow, she thought he'd had a thing with Harry Dawes that lasted years and years. That hangdog look, last Thursday at the grave—it seemed so unmistakably tied to the loss of one's other half.

Poor Greg. She could see that he needed some time in a place like the house on Harrington Sound. A walk on the cliffs would clear his head. What's more, he needed to have it all to himself. Before they talked on the mission set, she had more or less hoped they could have their *Walden* seminar moved to the limestone house in the cedar grove. She saw them sitting in lilies up to their ears, tossing off quotes and living, however briefly, off the land. But that was a lot of wishful thinking. For some reason, he couldn't bear Thoreau. Not even for Harry Dawes could he get past 106. He'd decided it was bullshit, though he wouldn't tell her why.

So who exactly was he, if he wasn't who she thought?

It would have to wait till they both got back. She packed and packed and got used to the fact that she had to travel solo. She'd done it enough before. It was what she was really good at. Thus, late Wednesday, after she heard what she happened to hear, she was just as glad she'd put it all off, deciding where to go. It was only then that she understood how far away it would have to be. Somewhere she'd never been to. Somewhere she wouldn't be seen. So far away, she might not even know it till she'd passed the last frontier.

Lucky for her, she had everything ready.

It was just after six, on Wednesday evening. She was propped up in bed, reading over the end of Chapter 10. "Earth's eye," Thoreau had just called the pond. Vivien gripped a spotty Bic and underlined five lines at a stretch. She'd grown so used to the prose, she no longer got tangled among the burrs. She read it straight through and saw what he meant:

> Men come tamely home at night from the next field or street, where their household echoes haunt, and their life pines because it breathes its own breath over again; their shadows, morning and evening, reach farther than their daily steps. We should come home from far, from adventures, and perils, and discoveries every day, with new experience and character.

How true, she thought contentedly. And she plopped an exclamation point in the margin just beside it.

She closed her eyes to let it sink in, more than glad to take it along on a nap. The farther she read, the odder it seemed that Thoreau had developed an audience. Surely, at any given time, there were only a few who felt this way. She could hardly believe they numbered enough to keep the book in print. As to why the colleges pushed it so, she couldn't really say. She assumed they all read it the way she had, in the crudest kind of outline. In any event, Thoreau wasn't like a college kid at all. He didn't want to be popular, for one thing. He didn't hate the little town he grew up in. And he wasn't after a girl.

She started up and turned her head, as if she'd heard a gun go off. In fact, it was quite the opposite. For the first time since returning here to Steepside, she missed the sound of water. She got up and opened the sliding door, but she wasn't thinking clearly. The angles of the house were such that she couldn't see west from this end. Could it be the water had not been on all week? She tried to recall, but she drew a blank. She'd been hearing it all her life. It was just as much a given as the view. The loss of it was something like the windows going dark.

She turned and hurried along the tunnel. She loped across the canyon room, then onto the deck on the steepest side. There didn't appear to be anyone anywhere, neither in nor out, and she wondered again if the emptiness was all they'd ever bought for living here. Somebody watching her make her way around the western end—one hand gliding along the railing, the other still holding her place in the book—would have thought she'd had a sudden need to ponder the dome of space that ranged about her house. Only those few who knew Steepside top to bottom could have second-guessed her destination. For this was the only route to Jasper's place.

At the farthest reach of the deck, she climbed a flight of white stone steps that angled up to the roof. At the top, the whole expanse was planted in ivy, so as to cool the house beneath—or at least Wright's half of it was. From the head of the stairs, a pebble path wound its circuitous way across the ivy field to the roof's far edge, where a kind of square stone shrine was perched above the canyon. This was where Jasper had lived. It used to be Jacob Willis's office—before that, Abner's—but Vivien always felt, as she walked the lush and well-kept ground that hovered above the surrounding hills like a flying carpet, that Wright had wanted a temple.

To a person approaching it up the path, it looked like a solid block of stone—a cube maybe fifteen feet on a side. The figures carved on the outer walls depicted, in the Mayan style, a flight of water birds on a pattern of scalloped waves. It looked like the winter view down the canyon, when flocks of northern birds were blanketed all across the water. Some few were frozen in stone up here, like fossils. As she came up close, she put out a finger and touched the outstretched wing of a crane. She hadn't been here in a long long time. It grew to be out of bounds between them, very early on. But the stonework friezed on the walls was in her blood. The Mayan birds still peopled the dreams she sometimes had, of places so wild they couldn't be owned.

She came around the corner, closer to the door. It wasn't going to be easy. She tried to focus on nothing but this, that the water had to be started up for Jasper's sake. There was sure to be death still hanging about inside—in his clothes, in his drawers, in the odds and ends of his everyday life. It was one thing, she knew, to look down on the redwood tub from the balcony off her room, for there it was just the dying that mocked and rang in the empty yard. Up here it was everything Jasper ever kept, and one of his quirks was souvenirs.

As she reached for the handle, she put her mind on the water's course and blocked the treehouse clutter that lay all about the room. The water was piped from deep in the house. It bubbled up into a shallow, half-moon pool in the room beyond. The farthest point of the moon cantilevered out through a plate-glass window. From there, it spilled a stream that fell and splashed in a second pool—down below in the garden, just outside the dining room. It flowed and played like mountain water. It pulsed all through, like the house's blood.

So do it, she thought. *Go in.*

"No!" bellowed Artie, fierce and grim from the other side of the door. She froze with the handle turned a quarter turn. "If you touch that stuff, I swear I'll kill you."

She released the handle slowly, clicking the door back into place. Then she hugged the wall and crept along to the edge of the roof. Since the big plate window in Jasper's room faced west—flush with the drop to the garden below—she couldn't see in or be seen. But the voices came to her clearly, filtering out the hole where the stream had dried. She gazed down blankly the length of the canyon, letting it all come out.

"You *do* that, baby," Carl replied with huge contempt. "Why don't you see if the cops would like it? Maybe you don't realize—they got questions you can't answer. All I'm doing is getting rid of stuff that's nobody's business."

"Business I don't give a shit about," said Artie coldly. "Just don't mess with the past."

"You planning an exhibition?"

"Half of it's mine. Leave it alone."

"But Artie, honey, it's *over*."

Fast. It went very fast. She couldn't imagine what anyone thought. It was all too raw.

"Oh, Carl," said Artie, "you think I don't know. But I *do*."

"And what might that be, Artie? You're real smart. I always said so."

A split second's pause, like a beat in timing. Then Artie, bitterly: "He was going to fire you. He told me so. That's what was over—you and him."

And the silence fell so thick and fast, she thought at first they must have blocked the window. Was *that* all they had to say? Had they both turned back to the drawer they were rifling, the argument safely behind them? She couldn't remember them hating each other out loud like this before. It was part of the ancient contract, somehow. No disagreements. No dirty laundry. No twisted arms or assigning of blame. Perhaps they always waited till they were alone, but how had she managed, eight years running, not to overhear a word?

"Go ahead," said Carl at last, very icy and under control. "That's all."

"It is like hell. What exactly did Jasper say?"

"Just what I said. Once this picture was out, he was breaking contract."

Curiously, she had no fear of being caught. She convinced herself she could have walked right in, except she didn't like to break their train of thought. No more would Carl have butted in on her and Artie. As she stood on the brink and listened, she seemed to go out of her way to protest that it wasn't really spying. She *knew* these men. They were what she had instead of a family. They might be saying things that she should know—things they had tried to protect her from, in case she couldn't take it. But she could. If either one had suddenly thrown the door wide, she would have remained quite calm and said: "What's this about the contract?" Indicating that any problem to do with Jasper took them all in, all three at once. She was included as much as they, by the nature of the survivorship they shared. The last thing on her mind was that they'd gone behind her back.

The room beyond the wall had grown so quiet, she knew it was time to go. Otherwise, she would try to guess their movements. Overhearing what she couldn't help but hear in the very air around her compromised her not at all. But now she was craning forward—trying to ascertain if it was papers being shuffled, or something more substantial. Wondering once again how Jasper could have died in a redwood tub, since they made him sick to his stomach.

"Carl?" asked Artie gently, and Vivien knew he was standing still and staring down at his shoes. It was Carl doing all the rustling. "Can't you tell me why?"

"Why didn't you ask *him?*"

"I did. He wouldn't say. I guess it was no one thing, huh?"

"Like fraud, you mean? No, it wasn't as simple as that. You know," he said, with a sudden throb of broken feeling, "he was like a brother to me."

Vivien heard him start to cry, except it wasn't exactly tears. He seemed to be trying to cry *out*. But nothing came. It was as if he'd lost his voice from the strain of saying "brother." The door flew open. She turned from the edge of the roof to face him, ready to say she was sorry. Corrupt as she'd always believed him to be, she had no other choice but to go with the living. She saw the situation clearly. It simply wouldn't be fair, to try to prove the contract null and void by reason of Jasper's final whim. Carl was a bastard, all right, but she had to admit that he'd earned his twenty percent. And he didn't have to profess a lot of brotherhood to get it. She took a step forward to tell him so. To say she was on his side, no matter how much she hated him.

But he strode out of Jasper's room and didn't wait to hear it. He took no notice of her at all, though she stood just a few feet off to his right. He lurched away along the pebble path. The moment's glimpse she had of his face showed all the pain of the thing he'd said. It was strange, how willing she was to take his part. It must have sprung from his having been abandoned. She knew that Jasper said things at the end of a shoot that he later regretted. She was sorry for Carl in the very way she was sorry for herself—that she'd talked to Jasper just before and heard no clue at all.

With a knock and a gurgle, the water went on in the room beside her. *Oh yes*, she thought with a pang, to think she had failed to reach the switches first. She took a couple of steps to the open door, uncertain how best to announce herself. She peered inside with a tentative smile, prepared to pass it all off as a joke. Artie was sitting where she would have been—on the low, tiled wall of the half-moon pool, trailing a hand in the ripple of water. He looked out onto the canyon, his back to her and to Jasper's pack-rat jumble of things.

"I beat you to it," he said quite mildly, not even turning his head.

How did he know she was there? She thought: *Will we keep on reading each other's mind—even now, with Jasper dead?* He must have heard the door go click, when she started in and stopped. In which case, he also knew she'd overheard them going at it.

"It's harder for him than us," he said.

"You think so?" Vivien asked as she came inside. The drawers in the old oak rolltop desk were closed. The papers and fan mags stacked on the shelves behind were undisturbed, or at least put back. There were cowboy hats in three different shades, hanging on hooks in the wall. A big green highway sign from Sweetwater, Kansas, was propped on the floor. In a tall gray milk can, stuck like pencils, were a hockey stick and a pearl-topped cane. It was all just props, from a hundred scenes. She let it all be and turned to the window. She stood not a foot from Artie and stared, like him, at the miles of view. She said: "I've been acting on the theory that we all feel about the same."

"Except Carl doesn't really go in for feelings, does he?"

"Well, he doesn't with *me*. But I gather it got pretty heated with Jasper."

"Oh, I don't know," said Artie vaguely. "Not that *I* ever heard."

What was this? He was acting as if she hadn't had a ringside seat throughout. Or more than that—as if it hadn't even happened. He seemed to imply there were things that were best forgotten. It struck her again what a curious widow she was, to have to share the loss in equal parts with the other two. Outside of the extra contract she and Jasper had signed and sealed to satisfy the state, she knew she had no special claim to having lost the most. So why shouldn't Artie improve the truth—pretending things had never changed—since who would it help, to break it all up this late in the game? She didn't blame him a bit. In his place, she would have done the same.

"I guess you're right," she said. "I don't suppose I've ever heard Carl overcome with emotion."

So the lie was agreed to. Nothing at all had taken place. She supposed she would never hear it spoken of again. She watched out the window quietly, fixing her eyes on the tip of the moon, where the water lipped over and fell. Just at the verge, the current had a thickness to it, swelling up like a bud about to flower. The moment was smooth as glass.

"Why do you always carry that book around?"

"Do I?"

"Since the funeral you have. You taking a correspondence course?"

"Not quite. I'm having a kind of debate. I guess you'd call this *my* side."

"It's that guy Cannon, right?" They hadn't said a word yet about Monday afternoon. Greg was not one of the things between them. Not till now, anyway. "Let me tell you something, Viv. He's a yo-yo. You're the biggest fish he ever caught. He's gonna rip you off."

"Don't be so protective," Vivien said with a little laugh she meant to end the matter. "All I'm trying to do is—I don't know—get out of myself for a while. Maybe do a little heavy thinking."

"Why him? He's a philosopher, is he?"

"Near enough," she replied with a shrug. "He's a writer who's given up books. I suppose he's gone beyond them."

"Well, he's also a star-struck faggot," Artie said in a cautionary way. "Remember that, will you?"

They looked each other in the eye. One on one, they had no suspicions and no desires. They had always brought out each other's best side. For a moment, though, they looked like childhood pals about to go off to college a thousand miles apart. They did not seem to know how far afield they'd gone from the safety of their former guilelessness. The sound of water played in their ears, and they had the high ground covered. No one else could approach unspied. The one lie wasn't so much. They could see they were quite all right.

"Should we go through Jasper's things?" she asked.

"You mean now?"

"Why not? Between the two of us, we ought to be able to figure what to keep and what to throw out."

She took two steps toward the desk. She crouched and pulled out a drawer at random. It was full of programs—concerts, plays, the circus, one-night runs and road shows. She'd never saved anything much herself. The point of it all escaped her. Just as surely, unlike Greg and his killer plots, she never assumed a force as vivid and particular as evil. She was much more conscious, in human affairs, of the blurred and imprecise. If people killed at all, she thought, they did it in bits and pieces, over a term of years.

"Can't we leave it the way it is?" he asked. He betrayed no special sentiment, or none she could put a finger on. It sounded as if he simply didn't have the energy.

"We don't want to have a museum, do we?"

"More like an attic," he said.

"Oh, I don't care," she retorted, sliding the drawer back in. "Whatever you like. You think there's anything hidden here?"

"You mean, like an outlaw's loot?"

"I guess. Or a diary, maybe?"

"Not a chance."

"He wasn't much of a romantic, was he?"

"He wasn't much of *any*thing," said Artie. "Do you miss him?"

"Not as much as you."

She turned around and watched him as he wept above the stream. The water was now a couple of inches deep—enough so it lost the look of being mechanized. They were perched at the top of a falls, at the moment where the water pitched and fell into smithereens.

"I thought we weren't comparing," Artie remarked in a brokenhearted voice.

"Well," she said gently, stroking his hair, "I lied."

*   *   *

By Thursday afternoon, with only two days to go, she had thirty-eight pieces packed, and the balcony end of her bedroom looked like an orchestra set to go on tour. The sketch of a plan was in her head. She would phone the apology in to Felix and Erika Friday night. Then she'd take the barest bones of the luggage and go to LAX and board the next available flight. To Rome, perhaps, or Amsterdam, for starters. In her present mood, the place was less important than the posh of this or that hotel. She imagined a room appointed in country French, with yards of eyelet embroidery fleecing the four-post bed.

She didn't think of what she was doing as anything quite so Garbo as going into hiding. The European press, so assiduous in pursuit of her, would find her in a minute. But if she stayed here, she'd start to keep out of the way in her own house. She knew now some kind of power struggle was taking place at Steepside. Let the balance settle where it might, she thought, while she was safely far away. She didn't really care how it ended. Whatever the outcome was, she'd be as strong as ever, no matter if Jasper's money was all dispersed to the poor and the Roman church. She couldn't be burned or cheated. The Willis clout went too deep. She could see it was all going to turn on which of those in Jasper's circle he'd told about his pulling free from Carl. It had gone beyond Artie. Max knew too. At least, she guessed that's what he was hinting at, the other day on the mission set.

She didn't want a bit of it. She was totally neutral, like the Swiss.

But then why, if she didn't care, if she meant to leave it behind and flee, did she skulk about looking for clues? It came on her Thursday night in the middle of dinner. She sat on a stool in front of the double-doored Amana, only a dozen steps from the bank of garages. She was crouching forward into the fridge, a thin little vermeil fork in her hand.

She picked at a leftover plate of bass and poached white grapes. There was a pony of Mumm's uncorked beside it, which she sipped from the bottle like Pepsi. And all of a sudden, she heard the Porsche pull out of its berth. She knew the sound of the 911 from all the other cars they owned. The 911 was Carl.

Yet she seemed unaware of any irony, as she slipped off the stool and made for the kitchen door. Before the noise had quite died away down the drive, she said to herself that maybe Carl and Artie would like a little supper too. She oughtn't to eat up all the fish before they had a bite. The fork was still in her hand, in the eating position, as she walked across the dining room to Carl and Artie's quarters. The fork to give her an alibi, it seemed. She hummed in a most distracted way as she closed the distance, step by careless step.

She rapped her knuckles on the studded oak door to Carl's room. Of course there was no answer. She pushed on through. "Carl?" she asked in a stagey way, peering around the door. Dead silence. Then, in a flash, she was all the way in, and her heart was pounding dreadfully. Nobody home, imagine that.

She didn't suppose she'd been here since she was married, though she'd had occasion to be in Artie's room across the hall a hundred different times. Abner Willis had done this wing in a kind of Bo-Peep chalet style, with rough-beamed ceiling and leaded diamond windows. The Wagnerian furniture, if she recalled, used to be Cardinal Richelieu's. The desk where she now sat down, laying her fork on the blotter beside the fountain pen, was grand enough for the signing of treaties.

She raised the manila edge of a folder square in front of her. At the sight of figures in columns, she drew the usual blank. She wasn't the Horatio Alger sort of heiress, with a longing to fill her father's shoes and double the family holdings. The up-and-coming types in the banks of Beverly Hills took care of that part for her. All she had to do was lunch three times a year in the penthouse suite with the president. The economics went right by her, the import being that the rich got rich.

She pulled out the drawers one by one, looking down in but not troubling to root around. She could see right off, from the general look of compulsive neatness, that she probably needed a CPA for sidekick, if she meant to clear a proper space to sneak about in.

She flattened herself against the back of the chair, to slide out the middle drawer. When she saw it was stocked with secretarial odds and ends, she slid it right back in. Then she stared up into the awful Alpine sunset framed in a cruddy engraving over the desk. She wondered idly if Greg might not have the requisite business training to crack these numbers. After all, he'd kept his organization in the black for two years running.

And then it hit her.

Her fingers, still wrapped around the drawer pulls, clenched as if she meant to start a fight. She slid the drawer out a second time. It was no big deal. Probably no one else would have even stopped to notice—except it was so odd. A narrow dark blue folder, of the kind that held an airline ticket. American Airlines, to be exact—which Vivien could be, since she traveled every other week and knew the props by heart. But Carl always used the private jet. It was his idea to buy it. Where could he possibly have to go by commercial service? On a package tour to Hawaii, maybe? Considering what a snob he was about perks—wherever possible steering clear of the masses—it delighted her to catch him out on the smallest incongruity.

She assumed it was quite beside the point. She didn't share Greg's sixth sense for clues. The case of Jasper Cokes, if there was a case at all, was buried in the inertia of accounts.

Money was where it began and ended. Thus, she picked this ticket up now from among the pencils and old receipts as if she'd found some respite from the headlong drive of the recent past. All the bad blood between Carl and Jasper had vanished from her mind. It was something minor here. Perhaps she could even tease him with it, she thought as she flipped it over. It might help break the tension for them both.

On the reverse side, a clerk had felt-tipped in the passenger's name: *WILLIS, J.*

It hadn't hit her at all, compared to how it hit her now. Her fingers went rigid. The paper shook. She had a horror of looking further, for fear of where this journey went. There had been no Willis with a J since Jacob, her father. There were no more Willises *anywhere*, outside of her. She counted herself the last of the line. The starkness of this had staked its ground in her long ago. It was some kind of high offense, therefore, to find somebody playing loose with the old ancestral name. No wonder she'd drifted in as soon as Carl drove off. She had picked up the trace of a rank impostor.

She opened it like a birthday card. She read the printout easily, as if it were a story in outline form. *NY/LA, Flight 509F, 3 April, 9:25 AM*. Then, on the line below, like a film being threaded in reverse: *LA/NY, Flight 14F, 3 April, 9:08 PM*. Two coast-to-coasts in a single day. *God, what a drag*, she thought dully, thrown for a moment by so much wasted time. It read as if this Willis, J. had flown out for something he couldn't face—and then chickened out at the last minute, and run the other way.

Except the ticket was all typed out in advance. No spur-of-the-moment changes written in. This trip was planned to the last detail. Perhaps there was some kind of document, which had to be signed and hand-delivered. She tried to make it sound, in the reasoning out, as dreary and stupefying as the papers stored in the drawers on either side of her. She could chalk up what she didn't understand to the lunacies of corporate life.

It was no use. Something was out to punish her for coming all this way and feeling nothing. She knew it down in her bones, just as she knew the third of April was the day Jasper died. One whole side of her mind had refused to countenance any intrigue, for no other reason than that Carl was three thousand miles away. That side suffered a sudden change, as if she'd had a minor stroke. Or as if she'd touched a socket with the tip of one wet finger.

Carl had come all the way home, just to kill the man he called his brother.

She thrust the ticket back in the drawer and ran. Banging down the halls as if the noise would bring her to earth again. She was all the way back in the kitchen, standing once more in the ghostly gray refrigerator light, when she recollected the fork. She ran back. She burst into his room and snatched it up. She kept her eyes averted from everything else, for fear of what she yet might see. She'd just closed the door behind her, going out for good, when Artie opened the facing door. Stark naked and half erect, and scratching his fuzzy head.

"What time is it?" he asked sleepily.

"Dinner," she said, without batting an eye, though her voice was half choked with horror. She held up the fork like a crucifix. "I divided up all the leftovers. I put out three plates, but Carl's not home."

"Is that why you've been crashing in and out? To tell him *dinner's* ready?"

"What do you mean? I've only come this once."

He smiled at her faintly and took his cue: "I guess I must have dreamed it, huh?"

"I've got things cooking," said Vivien, backing away, and he shrugged and let her go.

She knew he didn't believe her. She couldn't boil an egg. Didn't really think to eat unless something was put in front of her, sprigged with parsley and freshly peppered. They'd had another round of saying the most convenient thing. Perhaps they ought to have known that one evasion led to the next. They'd let in so much slack in the line, they might not put it straight again for months. But if it made them sad, they didn't betray it. If anything, Artie seemed faintly amused as he ducked back into his bedroom. Telling lies, she thought, was played like any other game. He would put down the terror he saw on her face to his having caught her spying at keyholes. Being caught was part of the game as well. It brought them closer together—letting them know just who they were, now that Jasper was dead and buried.

She dialed Greg's number on the kitchen phone, but he wasn't home. Then she made up the plates of food she'd lied about, feeling it as a point of pride that her alibi be watertight. She spooned things out of covered dishes, fast as a short-order cook. She slicked each plate with a skin of plastic wrap, laid them side by side on the refrigerator shelf, and retired at last to her room.

Lightheaded, by then. Not the least bit scared, once the shock wore off. There was all the more reason to run away. She had an enemy now, and wrongs to right. The problem with Greg was over, once she could follow it all the way to a murder charge. She could throw in her lot and help him decide where best to take it next. She dialed the number eight times in an hour. She counted.

In the meantime, she unpacked four of her suitcases off the pile. She found an empty overnighter, lifted the lid, and studied the inner space alertly. Then she filled it with just the barest minimum out of the other four. Her economy fairly made her hum a Broadway tune. As she tracked down a two-piece bathing suit, she spun out the number again on the phone, letting it ring and ring. In a little while, she'd put together one of everything she'd need. With a knee on the lid, she fastened the clasp, and then stood back admiringly. She felt like the Swiss Family Robinson.

After that, she called him every other minute, like clockwork, filling each interval between calls with a page of *Walden*. She paced around the bedroom, the book held up in front of her like a hymnal. At the end of the chapter called "Higher Laws," a farmer sat in his dooryard, watching the evening fall. Off in the distance, he heard the sound of someone playing a flute. He tried to ignore it. Tried to think only of his work. But Thoreau knew the music went deeper than all the farmer's desires to be bound by his forty acres. The flute was *Walden* itself. And the burden of the music floated on the dark, till the farmer could not deny the words it sang:

> Why do you stay here and live this mean moiling life, when a glorious existence is possible for you? Those same stars twinkle over other fields than these.

She let it ring thirty-two times, one for every year, and let it go at that. So what if she couldn't get through to Greg? Morning was soon enough. As she gathered up her final things, she had a fantasy of herself, arriving at his door at seven A.M. With a bag of croissants, berries and cream, and half a pound of *espresso* beans. As long as they had to talk murder, they might as well go first class.

For now, she changed for the road. She put on a sea-green sweater and a putty-colored suit, so as to look a bit like a lady banker—that is, deadly serious. Then she went into the bathroom. She dropped a dozen vials and bottles into a gauzy bag. On an impulse, she pressed the button that opened the wall at the back of the medicine chest. In the secret space behind, her jewels were ranked in dove-gray velvet boxes. She put out a hand for pearls and stopped. Too cold. Then she touched a box of dinner rings—but rings, of course, told tales. She settled at last on one thing only—a leopard-headed bracelet she bought herself at David Webb, once when she couldn't go on getting all her stones at the whim of sentimental men. She slipped it over her wrist and shut up the rest. She sailed through the bedroom, gathering up the overnighter in one hand, *Walden* in the other. Altogether, she went out clean.

She stowed her things beside her in the passenger's seat of the Rolls. The key was in the ignition. She turned it on, hoping Artie was nowhere about. The Rolls was really his, by virtue of all the miles he'd logged. She did not have the same kind of rights in the matter. None of the cars was hers—not the Cord, the Dino, the '55 T-Bird, the Morgan, or the Jeep, all of which she thought of as Jasper's toys. Vivien mostly drove cars picked up at the airport.

Backing out into the drive, she wondered if she should go in and pocket the airline ticket. But then, it would only tip him off. She put the car in neutral and headed down the hill. By the time she decided she ought to have it as evidence, risk or not, she had passed the point of her motor skills. No way could she back a car this big up a hill this steep. Only then, as she rounded the last long curve to the gate, did she stop to wonder where she meant to go.

She saw lights in the trees as she came around, but she didn't connect them up with a car till she suddenly flashed across its path. She shut her eyes and stood on the brake. She missed him by a hairsbreadth.

The bowels of the Rolls shrieked over a bed of stones. When the dust had cleared, she saw she'd run up against the hill and snapped an aspen in half. Through the rear-view mirror she saw the Porsche. Having swerved to the outer rim, it was one wheel over the edge of the drive, above the long embankment into the glen. Their windows went down, and they both leaned out to have a good yell.

"What do you think you're doing?" he shouted.

"Nothing," she said. "Just getting out for a breath of air. Don't panic."

"You're going to *kill* someone!"

"Oh? Who?"

He pulled his head back in and threw open his door. He leapt out. Stormed across the gravel. She rolled her window a third of the way and kept her hand on the handle.

"You can't *drive*," he said in a choke of rage, thumping the palms of his hands on the roof.

"Carl," she replied, and she sounded so bored it must have driven him crazy, "it isn't going to do us any good to discuss it. There's always two sides. Talk to my lawyer, why don't you?"

"And what's this shit about Saturday?"

What shit was that? She couldn't recall.

"Max just told me," he went on bitterly, seeming to let the accident go. "You're shipping out with Erika. Don't you see—his fans'll *lynch* you."

"You saw Max?"

"We just had dinner. Don't you understand, you've got to *be* here. You want to protect your interests, don't you?"

"I have no interests," Vivien said.

"Just remember, you can't trust everyone. Everyone's not like me and Artie."

"Where'd you have dinner?"

"*Where?*" he choked, dazed at the sudden irrelevance. He shrugged and looked around, as if he'd lost his way on the dark hillside. But after a moment, he seemed to understand it was a social question being asked—by a woman who was a fixture in all the hundred-dollar French cafés. The name of the place would tell her a lot. She would see right away what kind of time they'd had.

"Nowhere," Carl said flatly. "Just some two-bit diner. We had a *burger*, for Christ's sake. Why? You got a heavy date tonight?"

She stared at him fixedly, almost as if she hadn't heard a word. In fact, she had a very clear picture of it—him and Max, huddled in a booth in a fast-food joint. Max would have finally told him that he knew what Jasper meant to do. They probably made a deal, right on the spot. So the power was shifting quicker than she thought—quicker than she could make a move to leave. Already, it seemed she had to try so hard to pretend that things were the same as ever. They couldn't even get off a proper gasp of relief, to think they hadn't collided.

"I'm going out to get magazines," she said. "I just realized —I don't have any idea how I look this week."

"Wait a while, Viv. Don't leave town. We should have the money settled in a few months' time. Then maybe you and me and Artie can get away together. Why not, huh? We'll hire a boat of our own."

"But Carl—*why?* It seems like we've been together half our lives already. We haven't had a good time yet."

She remembered the night Jasper died. When they left the house, there was this same pitch of darkness. The shafts of their headlights swept the trees. And Carl had said: "I've been in New York these past five days." They were just as far out of the world as now, except here there were no lilies.

"It's irresponsible, that's what it is," said Carl in a truculent temper. "You're acting just like Jasper. You do what you damn well please, and the rest of us can go fuck ourselves."

"Is that what I want, do you think?" she asked. "A month on the coast of Mexico, with Erika and Felix?" She was angry now, but it came out sad. She couldn't seem to hate him. Crazy, huh? She'd never had the slightest trouble hating him before. "Why do I bother with magazines, when I've got you?"

She went into reverse and came away from the blasted tree. Then into first, with her foot very light on the brake and rolling forward. She glanced at him now to say goodbye. He looked as if he'd caught a chill.

"Remind me to tell you some day what I really want," she said. "It'll restore your faith in simple things."

"You know I'm right," he seethed in answer, hugging his arms against his chest as if he thought he would burst. "You won't go now. I'll bet you money."

"Bet your ass," she said with a smile. "It's cheaper."

She rolled away like somebody caught on a current, so she never caught the final look she left to twist his face. She swung the last loop to the Steepside gate, which opened automatically. On an impulse, feeling ornery, she hung a left at the boulevard and headed up instead of down.

She climbed a mile up into the mountains, as far as the light at Mulholland Drive. From there, she could see out onto the plain of lights that spread below in the Valley. She veered to the shoulder to take the view. Because the April night was clear, she saw to what seemed like ten or fifteen miles on either hand—as if the whole expanse were one vast printed circuit, or an endless airport where a thousand routes touched down. It was really nowhere at all, of course—just suburb on suburb, flung wide on the desert floor.

She started down the steep and hairpin route. A Willis, she thought, could spend a lifetime in the mountains high above L.A., without ever once descending here to the inland side. She couldn't recall the last time she had been this way—unless to hook up to Route 134, going out to Pasadena, but who knew anyone there anymore? She could have sworn she'd never passed this stretch of hillside lots before. Two bedrooms, two baths, and a carport, cheek by jowl the whole way down the mountain. Each one worth about as much as the powder-blue Rolls she rode in.

Who lives here? she thought dreamily, as if she'd found the cleft in a wall of solid rock, passing into a great lost city. She realized no one would ever think to look for her anywhere here. She felt an instant sense of relaxation, as if someone had laid a downer on her. She drove like a woman bent on winning, risking more at every curve. The Rolls was fleet as a racehorse. Never the slightest screech, and all the lights were green.

When at last she reached the level ground, she turned east on Ventura Boulevard, through the heart of Sherman Oaks. Hunching up to the wheel, she read the neon left and right. The chicken stands, the bargain banks and raw motels, the flash-on time and temp. She felt like getting lost in it, though she knew she had other things to do. She tried to focus on murder and nothing else. Like a drunk trying to walk a straight line, she affected a kind of inner squint and lasered in on Carl. She tried not to feel so happy to find herself free in a foreign clime.

Had Greg been right? He swore she'd have it easier, once she could pin it on someone else. Perhaps she was just perverse, she thought, but she wasn't a bit convinced. Between Carl and Jasper, killer and corpse, it struck her the deal was exclusive. No less so than the deal it seemed to supersede, between Jasper and Harry Dawes. Either way, she didn't see that she came into it at all.

It was no one else's business but the duellists'. She wasn't caught up by a rage of justice. She didn't think death was wandering loose to seek more victims. Whatever it was was over with. There was no one in any peril, was there? After all, it could have gone the other way, with Carl as dead as Jasper. Jasper would never have been so dumb as not to know a duel was on. He could have struck first.

She turned into the Tower of Pizza's parking lot. Needless to say, this whole line of argument wasn't allowed. The widow, she knew, didn't have the leeway to settle the matter out of court. She could see how the press would distort it, if they knew how she really felt. She sat staring in at the glare of fluorescent light, momentarily paralyzed. The hardness that had gripped her was as true to Jasper as all the decorous sentiments of his fans. But how could she ever explain it?

She slid out and locked the car and wished she didn't look so overdressed. Worst of all, she thought, she wasn't even sure that *Greg* would understand. Perhaps, from here on in, she'd better keep her feelings to herself—the way she'd always done before.

She knew she must have tried a pizza. Everyone had them all the time. But she honestly couldn't recall. She had no associations, to this or anything else, since the moment she started down the back side of the mountains. As she walked in now to a place that traded in nothing but, she shied at the blinding light reflecting off a dozen cuts of plastic. She'd figured on taking a hint from the people in line in front of her, but she saw she was quite alone. She tried to read a snatch of menu, painted in red on the upper wall, but the yellow-wigged woman in the turquoise smock did not appear to countenance indecision. Vivien stepped up to the counter.

"Pizza," she said succinctly, the one word coming off her tongue like a minor breakthrough.

"Suits me fine," said the waitress, giving a friendly crack of her gum by way of punctuation. She pulled a pencil out of her hair. "How do you like it?"

How will I know till I taste it? thought Vivien puckishly. "Oh, I don't know," she said. "Surprise me."

"Combination Florentine," retorted the other, writing it down. "I wouldn't warn you, honey, except you look so pretty in that red scarf—that's with the anchovy. Makes some people gag. You want me to hold it?"

"No, no," she said. The anchovy struck her as comforting.

"To drink?"

"Just coffee."

The scarf in question was, in fact, the color of highly polished saddle leather—russet, perhaps, with perhaps a touch of the tile roofs of Siena. In any case, it would have given Pucci hives to hear that it was red. Yet Vivien couldn't help but like this woman. The garish air about her hadn't got her down. The country cheer that she gave off was tied up with an urban case of irony.

"I'm Kay, I'm here to help you" was how the Tower of Pizza put it, on her plastic pizza badge.

When was the last time someone told Vivien she looked pretty? The press was always quick to tick off what she wore, but the point they were usually trying to make was that no one deserved a change of clothes for every day of the year. The people she knew wouldn't dream of liking a scarf out loud. It would have been unseemly, somehow, now that she was sainted in the Best-Dressed Hall of Fame. Of *course* it was a pretty scarf. Didn't that go without saying?

She strolled about the room, uncertain how to pass the time. She supposed it would be unmannerly to watch Kay work from too close up, though she dearly would have loved to see a pizza made from scratch. She loitered at the jukebox long enough to read the listings, but made no move to play. She had no flair for plucking the theme of her present mood from the ranks of the top forty. Still less could she summon up the English for a proper go at pinball. Thus, she made her way around the room, rejecting all machines.

At last she reached the raft of attractions clustered around the register. Devon mints and Jersey City taffy. A rack of postcards variously depicting all the Southland's flash points,

Griffith Park to Disneyland. Whistles and jars of preserves and dry cigars. But what caught her eye was the newspaper stand. Especially an inky rag called *Hollywood Midnite*, splashed with a foot-high picture of herself. She sat there weeping, head in hand, and the headline, sixty-point or better, shouted out: I LOST MY HUSBAND TO A HUNDRED MEN!

It had to be a trick. When had she ever cried on camera? Her hair hadn't been that straight in years, and the fur that wrapped her shoulders looked like housing insulation. *God, she thought as she squinted close, where am I?*

It came to her in a rush. This was the summer of her debut. Nineteen and totally out of it—here, at a ball in San Mateo, where someone had filled the living room with topiary shrubs. Well, she thought, at least there was visible proof that she could cry.

They took a line close to the bone, these scandal weeklies. The implication was that she let a man walk all over her. She'd ended up alone in bed, surrounded by an overload of things a normal person did without. Was any further proof required of what a rich girl came to? It seemed so oddly Puritan a view. But then, she probably wasn't the one to ask, considering she was the moral of the story.

She'd been staring back at herself for as long as she could remember. At a newsstand sometimes, she felt as if she were in a hall of mirrors. And the more she saw, the more it made no sense to her. Wasn't she dull? The whole thing should have petered out for want of real material. This part of her life they took pictures of was the dreary part. She wondered if she didn't affect her famous vacant smile to prove to the world there was nothing there.

But even nothing was news, if she was in it. *Hollywood Midnite* and its ilk were always prepared to say that she had cancer. They swore she broke up this one's marriage and aborted that one's child—both in a single week, sometimes. Clearly, it was easier to make it up than tie it to what she was doing in fact. *Oh, well,* she thought, with no more urge than usual to turn to page three for the gory details. They certainly had the goods on Steepside now. Perhaps, after all, they were smart to stick so close to her all these years. It meant they were there at the scene, so to speak, when the mine at last hit paydirt.

"Three eighty-five with the tax," said Kay.

Vivien looked up startled, to find they were barely a couple of feet apart. The pizza was boxed between them on the counter. Where was she supposed to eat it? In the car?

"All I have is a twenty," she said apologetically.

As the register digested it, she wondered if she ought to leave a tip. She didn't like to offend. She held the pizza cradled in one arm and brooded about it, as sixteen dollars and fifteen cents was counted out into her other hand.

"Listen, I wouldn't worry about the papers. Not if *I* was you."

"What?" asked Vivien vaguely. Just then, she was weighing the cash in the flat of her hand, undecided what to do. She came in a moment late. She saw that Kay was glancing down at *Hollywood Midnite.*

"Everyone knows it's lies, what they say about you. It don't matter. People don't believe a thing they read."

"They don't?" she murmured quietly, gazing at her weeping face like a picture in an album. So as not to seem so spooked, she raised her voice. "You think it's true, what they say about sticks and stones?"

"Listen, I'm real sorry about your husband. I lost somebody once."

Vivien thought: *Should I ask her who?* But she didn't really want to. It would only make her sad.

"It makes you numb for the longest time," said Kay. "Nobody knows."

Vivien looked her in the eye. There were no demands at all. She remembered the fans last week, on the boulevard by the gate. They were after a very specific thing—some single glimpse to take away, sharp as a Kodachrome snap. *She shook her finger at me. She tried to grab my camera. She pleaded with us to go.* They wanted a piece of her. This one didn't.

"But I feel nothing," Vivien said, with a hairline crack of irony. It came out like an answer to a question no one asked. But she had to give the acid test. Check this woman's existential fingerprints. Just as she had the other day, on the mission set with Greg.

Kay nodded briefly and looked away, transported for a moment by a nothing of her own. In any case, she seemed to pass the test. When they said goodbye, it was unadorned with the hope they would meet again. They didn't say anything cheery, not "Take care," not "Have a nice night." They left all that to the wheel of time. They stuck to the one word only. Just goodbye.

As Vivien walked away, she balled up the money and stuffed it in her bag. When she got to the car, she opened the box on the seat beside her. The suitcase served as her table. She sat and ate the pizza wedge by wedge, trying to distinguish what was what in the chaos of ingredients. Now and then, they glanced at each other through a double shield of windows. Never in phase, so they didn't lock eyes. For a moment, Vivien had a spell of thinking she ought to do more. She could have a color TV sent out: "To Kay at the Tower, with all my thanks." Maybe arrange to have her children put through college.

She let the moment pass. She downed her coffee and licked her fingers and readied herself to go. They were doubtless right to stick to the rules of brief encounter. A beat-up Dodge pulled in beside her. The backfield of a football team came tumbling out. They barreled across to the restaurant and shouldered in with great hurrah. As soon as Kay was busy, bantering back and forth, Vivien took the chance and fled. So they wouldn't have to endure that final glance—or worse, the first gleam of regret.

Once she was back on the boulevard, she turned again to the business at hand. As if she had film wound up in her head, she played it with Carl in the lead. He slipped them some kind of sleeping pill. Then he went round the tub, slitting one wrist after another. They probably didn't feel a thing. But that, she thought, was just what they said about people who died of attacks in the dead of night. It always struck her as wishful thinking. Surely the dying woke up in time to know the jig was up. And they clutched their chest and groped in the dark for the someone they couldn't bear to leave, lying there beside them in a dream.

Was it supposed to be some kind of comfort, to think that Jasper died easy? It seemed like a man had a right to a death that caught him at the pitch of conscious life. Jasper would have wanted to go out wide-eyed—feel it for all it was worth.

The thing about neon signs was this: The very thing you were looking for began to shine brighter than what was around it. Just as soon as you needed it, there it was. First it was food, and now it was places to sleep. She was on very tenuous ground, of course. She could say she'd had a pizza before, and assume it had slipped her mind. A motel was something else entirely. Perhaps it was only an accident that she'd never touched down in a place that lacked a good hotel. More likely, her life was programmed long ago to exclude all towns that were not equipped with suites of rooms in muted tones.

So how did a person choose? First, she cut out the names she knew, like Travelodge and Hojo's, as too reminiscent of airports. She'd be much better hidden in one of a kind. She went at a midnight clip, scanning the signs on either side. The traffic was light to moderate. She followed the foot of the mountains, all the way into Studio City. It had to be soon. In a minute, she'd hit the Hollywood Freeway—the route that would take her over the mountains, tomorrow morning at seven.

She pulled the Rolls over and went in under a sign about ten feet high: THE VAGABOND. *That's me*, she thought lightly, parking off in the dark end of the lot, so the car would not stick out. The name was scrawled in a bold blue hum of neon, meant to echo the script of a human hand. As she came across the gravel, it loomed above her, as if the god of the place had put out a lightning finger and penned it on the air. In smaller letters, stenciled on the office window, it said: *Motor Inn of the Stars.*

Because of who she was, she probably went in acting the way she did at the George V or the Royal Hawaiian. A bit high-pitched for the wall-to-wall industrial nylon, the kidney-shaped tables and maple-jug lamps. On the other hand, the blotchy man in green suspenders seemed to need all the help he could get. Fifty-five and fingerbitten, he wheezed his way from step to step, with a small amnesiac pause at every turn.

He filled in the name, *Mrs. Gregory Cannon*, and handed over the key to number 9. Yes, he would give her a wake-up call at a quarter after six. No, he didn't know where she could send out for croissants.

"You got any bags?" he asked anxiously.

"Oh, I can handle them," she said, quick to reassure him. "I travel very light. You think the traffic will keep me awake?"

"Soundproof," he said—tapping the wall to his left with his pencil. "We don't let *anything* bother the guests. Not even cops."

"Well, that's very thoughtful. I don't think the cops'll be asking for *me*."

"Sometimes it's cops. Sometimes it's somebody won't go away. Photographer, maybe."

Did she only imagine it, or had the glassiness cleared in his eyes?

"I keep the whole lot of 'em out," he said. "To me, it's invasion of privacy."

"I appreciate that," she answered pleasantly. Should she give *him* a tip? "It's all bullshit, right? You can't believe what you read anymore."

"It's true," he agreed with a magisterial nod. He seemed pleased to find her so savvy. "Promise me now. You need anything, you dial 'O.'"

"Thanks," she said.

And she picked up her key from the counter and turned away. She couldn't recall a like degree of chivalry—not at the George V, anyway. It was all a good deal cooler way up there.

"Oh, Mrs. Cannon?"

The first thing she noticed, turning back, was that he'd managed to button his shirt. That, and he'd brushed the fall of dandruff from his shoulders.

"I saw every picture he ever made."

She didn't have to ask him who he meant. With his index finger, he pushed the bridge of his glasses further up his nose.

"To me," he said, "they were all about doing the thing that was right. He was decent—you know what I mean?"

She nodded. There was a sermon, it seemed, in every stone she overturned. She saw that she wasn't required to· say a blessed thing in return. It was enough to hear these people out. Was that why she didn't mind it? She didn't mind it at all.

"Most of us disappear," he said. "We don't get to leave behind a record of what we believe in. *He* did."

Imagine: a combination of Pauline Kael and Heidegger, right in the middle of Studio City. With, now that she took a closer look, a certain vivid glow about the eyes. He didn't seem specially brilliant and doomed, so that you felt he ought to have been a doctor. Desk clerk suited him fine. He had twenty-eight units to oversee, full of people lost in transit. She could see that he'd come to perceive it as work that did the right thing. He was satisfied.

"I don't think Jasper *thought* about what he accomplished," she said. "Unless it was being a star. I suspect he was proud of that."

"A man that big doesn't dwell on what he's done. He just keeps going."

"Well," she replied in a neutral way, and let her voice trail off. She couldn't go as far as that. He made him sound like a hero, when all he was was a star. For a moment, she thought he was coming around the counter to take her hand. She could tell he felt none of the same mystique in her, since she'd never appeared in a movie. But he stopped himself and came no closer. He pulled in again like a turtle.

"I've talked out of turn," he said. "I'm sorry."

"No, no," she protested. "I'm glad you spoke up. It's just that I feel—I don't know—so many things at once."

Nothing was what she meant to say.

He nodded and took off his glasses and smiled. "Go to sleep now, Mrs. Cannon," he said. "You'll see. You'll sleep like a baby here."

And the funny thing was, she did. Though she had to laugh when she let herself in. The traffic out in the street was loud enough to be a joke—like sound effects in a sitcom. Every surface all over the room was rubberized, so a reeling drunk wouldn't get a concussion. The furniture was hodge-podge—knocked around and color-blind, full of fray and broken corners—but on the whole she found it pretty clean. The bed had sagged and softened to the point of no support. It cradled her like a cloud.

She turned the Aunt Jemima bedside lamp on low, and she read maybe fifteen pages. Thoreau introduced what he liked to call his "brute neighbors"—the mice, the phoebe, the woodcock, the loon. To her it was as otherworldly as the forest in *Snow White*. She knew no creatures herself. When she finally turned to go to sleep, with the susurrus of traffic in her ears, she thought of a weekend long ago, in the Florida keys with Jasper. He was shooting a two-bit thriller, on a salvage boat at Bahía Honda. He came home tired and sunburned every night, with a bucket of shrimp he bought in the harbor. They didn't eat anything else for four days solid.

Outside the cabin, they had these walking catfish, walking across the lawn. Whenever they came, she averted her eyes. Scared to face them because they were weird—too wild, somehow, too close to the edge. How stupid she'd been, she thought to herself, as she fell asleep in the Valley. She should have taken a good long look. There would be no second chance.

She woke up at 6:15 exactly, in the hair-trigger second before the phone rang. But she wasn't the least bit jumpy. She opened her eyes with the sweetest pang of expectation. Her book was still open beside her. She answered before the first ring was quite rung, and the desk clerk told her the time in an upbeat way, announcing that she had a package, just outside her door.

It was a white waxed-paper bag, with half a dozen croissants packed inside. Still warm, in fact. She ate one while she brushed her hair and wondered how he figured out she needed all this many. They tasted rather more like Pepperidge Farm than Ma Maison, but what the hell. She went and got a ginger ale from the bright blue machine at the end of the hall. She ate her second croissant sitting at the desk, while she wrote a note to Artie.

I'll be back. Don't worry.

When at last she came downstairs, at ten to seven, she had a twenty-dollar bill all folded up in the pocket of her skirt—to pay for the rolls, *et cetera*. She would make him keep the change. Alas, like somebody met at a crossroads, he was gone. The cold-eyed European who'd taken his place explained that the shift was structured to change at 6:30 sharp. Was something wrong? When he'd ascertained it was only money, he put out his palm discreetly and promised to pass it along.

But something made her change her mind and pay for the room and go. She didn't want to say goodbye in cash. Her night clerk must have felt the debt was paid, or he would have got through to her somehow. Goodbyes were maybe his weak suit. Same as hers.

She beat the rush hour over the pass. It was still quite early, not quite seven-thirty, when she pulled up in front of the Cherokee Nile. She hadn't stopped to buy the rest of breakfast, but figured a bachelor must keep butter and jam and freeze-dried. If he didn't, they could just go out on the terrace and eat them straight from the bag. And look out over the hush of the city, while all the shades of mist burned off the morning.

Anyone would have thought it was a romance she was casting. It was lucky for her that no one knew where she was right now. Ringing bells at eight A.M., like somebody serving a warrant. He didn't answer, but then who would, at the crack of dawn? She waited around till a groggy type came through the lobby door on the way to work. Then she slipped in quick before it shut. She tapped the eleven on the elevator panel, as if to knock on wood.

But no one came when she knocked on the door of 11D. She refused to accept that he was out, since she thought of him safe at home compared to her. He'd never told her in so many words that he was a budding agoraphobe, but she always had the feeling that he preferred things done on his own turf. She knocked in sets of three, ten seconds in between. For a while, she beat with the palm of one hand, keeping up a steady thud. But a minute could hardly have passed before she had quite let go. She pounded with both fists, drumming hard. To hell with 11A through C. There must be something wrong.

When the elevator door creaked open behind her, she spun around in a flash of terror. For that one instant, she was convinced someone had followed her all the way from Steepside. False alarm—it was only Edna Temple.

"Help me," Vivien pleaded. "I think he may be sick."

"No," said Edna flatly, padding forward. Very unsurprised. She might have been expecting it. "He's away on business. You want me to tell him you dropped by?"

"Do you have a number? I have to talk to him—right away."

"I'm not allowed to give out that information," Edna said —fiddling the keys to Greg's apartment, but not yet approaching the door. She made it clear she wasn't going in till Vivien had safely left the premises.

"I'm Vivien Cokes," she explained, wishing it didn't sound so pushy. She only meant to say she was his friend. She wasn't trying to act VIP.

"Really? You could have fooled me. You're thinner in pictures, huh?" And she bent to the door as if she meant to crack it like a safe. Using one key after another, she started releasing the locks. "Wait here," she said. "I'll get it for you. I'd ask you in, but I'm just a neighbor. He pays me to water his plants."

With that, she opened the door and pressed on through. She would have closed it tight behind her, not allowing so much as a look, if Vivien hadn't spoken up.

"You're Edna Temple, aren't you?"

Edna stopped with the door between them almost shut. A moment later, silent and grave as a footman, she opened it wide. The visitor's credentials were too good to argue. Vivien fell into step beside her, all the way through to the dining room. It wasn't a bit like she thought it would be. She'd expected a lot of silver frames, clustered about on blond-wood tables, with studio shots of faded stars. But in spite of the phony wall reliefs from Nineveh, and a pair of seated panthers holding up the mantel, it was just another single man's apartment. Haphazard chairs and things from people's attics.

"I would have thought you'd be the *first* to know where to find him," Edna said, laying the stress on the rank like mortar on a brick. She pulled the string on the dining-room light and threw the domed ceiling into Moorish shadows. She picked up a stack of paper slips and began to go through them, dealing them out in different piles like somebody playing solitaire. "I thought he was doing an errand for you."

"Is he?" Vivien asked, sitting down on the edge of a bentwood chair. "Already? I didn't expect him to leave so soon. It's not what you'd call an emergency."

"Nevertheless," said Edna crisply, "he was out of here at the crack of dawn on Tuesday. I remember, he put the number on one of these orders. But I didn't think we'd need it, see? We don't keep a phone ourselves."

She refused to identify Sid by name, because Vivien seemed to know this part already. Let her ask if she didn't get it. Vivien recognized the attitude right off. She'd used it for years with Carl.

"But there *is* no number," protested Vivien. "The house in Bermuda is half a mile from the nearest phone. He's totally out of touch."

"Bermuda?" Edna pulled up the collar of her housecoat as she squinted down her arm at a square of paper. "I wouldn't know about that. Vermont's what *I* heard." Pause. "Aha!"

She reached the memo across the table, as if she had no further use for it herself. Vivien took it between two fingers,

An order blank from the UFA, made out to a country inn at Hamilton Falls, Vermont.

"Vermont?" she echoed. Totally thrown.

"Why? You got another errand? Maybe he didn't tell you this, but we're up to our ass in business."

"What's he doing *there?*"

"Working for *you*, as I understand it," retorted Edna dryly, unconvinced by all this protestation. "For his usual fee of zip, I might add."

They stood on opposite sides of the table, the stuff of the UFA between them. They took stock. With Greg not here, they were on their own. And the longer the thing drew out, the more did they seem to feel they had nothing whatever to lose.

"It must be Carbon Mountain," Vivien said at last.

"There, now. I *thought* you'd remember, once you put your mind to it. Must be a bitch to keep track. You probably got an *army* out there, huh?"

"Maybe now you'll tell me what it is I've done."

"Done?" she asked. "Not a goddam thing."

"I mean, to make you so mad."

"You know," said Edna, leaving her place to pace about, "I was the one used to sell the maps in front of the *Chinese* theater. This was when you were a kid." She couldn't have been more amiable. Though she seemed to have let the barb go by, in fact she had changed completely. Vivien started to breathe again. "It was mostly the homes of the stars," said Edna. "But every now and then, I'd put a few people in who were very rich—like the Willises. And you know what happened? The stars moved every six months—I couldn't keep up with it. The rich men all stayed put. They'd build themselves a house, and that was that. I always thought there was a parable in there somewhere." She stopped at the end of a pace, spun round, and lobbed the last bit gently. "Maybe *you* can tell me," Edna said.

Vivien shook her head. She saw they were getting down to basics, but by the same token, the current stop was slightly out of her league. She dropped her eyes to the table, where a stack of glossies stood at her place. On top was Katharine Hepburn, a little over thirty. There were dozens more, from five or six different pictures, but in every one, she was just that certain age. Vivien sifted through them as she talked—as if she were trying to fill a part that required a bit more than a pretty face.

"Jasper's the only star I ever really knew," she said. "Beyond a certain point, I mean. Did you ever think maybe the rich men wanted their houses behind them? Then they could just go back to making money. That's what they're good at, isn't it? Houses are something else."

She paused at a still from *Adam's Rib*. Hepburn and Tracy nuzzling in a roadster, surrounded by the midtown traffic of a generation past. It all looked kind of pastoral, somehow. Vivien flashed on Jasper, doing it raw onscreen with a string of vapid women. She thought: *They just don't make 'em like they used to.*

"I don't know *why* I never moved," she said, going on from still to still. "It's not that I'm so in love with Steepside. To me, it feels like a waiting room."

"You want a cup of coffee?"

"Sure," she said. She held up the paper bag like she'd pulled it out of a hat. "You can help me eat my breakfast, so I won't get fat."

"Me, I've been on a diet since 1935," said Edna, as they threaded through the pantry, single file. The cream-colored kitchen was wall-to-wall with painted wooden cupboards. Edna knew just where everything was. "I make a lot of exceptions," she said.

What was it, Vivien wondered, that turned these things around? She washed away Tuesday's eggs from a delft-blue plate, then arranged the croissants in a ring. It was nothing she herself had done. Edna had simply finished up the agenda of private resentments. Partly it was jealousy, with a certain measure of bruised maternal pride on Greg's account. But it didn't matter now. Vivien wouldn't hold the grudge if Edna wasn't going to. Besides, it had been a bit of a lark, to have somebody treat her without kid gloves, as if she were no one at all.

"Do people ask for Jasper Cokes?" she wondered aloud, as she searched the fridge for jam.

"Not us they don't," said Edna. "Our cutoff date is the fifties."

She handed over a chipped white diner mug. Then she picked a croissant off the plate, put it between her teeth so she could take another, and led the way back to the dining room.

"It's not *my* idea," she protested as they both sat down— just at the places where they'd stood, five minutes since, in combat. "I think we ought to pick up on every overnight sensation. It's because he got burned when he tried to be a writer—he's put all his money on the good old days. I say you got to adjust to the times. It's bigger than just the movies now. There's stars in every walk of life." She gave a heavy shrug, as she talked around half a roll she gobbled up in a single bite. "He's the boss," she said. "Either we do it his way, or we go get another job. So we do it his way. Hell, I'd include someone like you in a minute."

"Oh, I don't think you'll ever get people *buying* pictures of me. They're everywhere."

"Don't be so sure," retorted Edna grandly, finger raised. "Depends on the picture."

"Without any clothes on, maybe."

"I should say not," she sniffed. She patted a hand against her breast, as if the mere idea made her queasy. "On the contrary—I'd have you just the way you are. Sitting down over a cup of coffee. Like you slept in your clothes. There's too much of you all dolled up."

"I see what you mean," said Vivien politely.

She thought: If only the *Hollywood Midnite* types were all like this. Perhaps she wasn't *meant* to take the whole thing personally. She could sit here, calm as you please, and discuss her image bloodlessly. With the same detachment she would have had if Edna had been a GYN, and they'd gotten together to talk about her body.

"But Edna," she said, "would it make me seem any *nicer?* How do you make a regular guy out of somebody rich?"

Edna shook her head. "Money's not the issue," she said. "All stars have too much. *Your* bad press has to do with you and Jasper. People hate what they don't understand—you must know that."

Vivien saw she was being invited to talk about her marriage. Dared to, almost. Too bad for her, she had nothing to say. If she and Jasper had been, hands down, the loneliest people they'd ever met, at least they were the only ones who knew. It had been clear to them both from the start that they had no private lives. In all those years together, they never got a whit less lonely. All they achieved was this: to know there was someone else who felt it about the same. Now, with Jasper gone, it seemed she'd inherited *his* half.

"But listen," she answered with some authority, "nobody really believes the things they read. Do they?"

"Maybe so," said Edna, nodding slowly, "maybe so. But it's not so much what's printed—all the affairs you're supposed to have had, or the money you throw away. It's that the two of you survived. You never seemed to want a thing from him—and him vice versa. It makes people mad, because they want something all the time."

"What is it they want?" she asked, though without much hope of an answer.

"Attention," said Edna, prompt and cheerful. She dipped her hand in a shoebox full of orders, pulled up a handful, and fanned them out on the table like a hand of gin. *"That's* what they can't get enough of."

But if you're so smart, thought Vivien, heartsick all of a sudden, *then why are you poor and old like this?*

"What am I going to do?" she asked, as practically as she could. How was it she hadn't a clue what people wanted? Hadn't she ever asked?

Clearly, this was the perfect time to change her image. She had a head start, what with all the allowances made for the lot of the grieving widow. Here she was, on her own again.

Edna dabbed a fingertip in the pastry crumbs on the table, transferring them bit by bit to her tongue. She let go by a little digestive pause, and then said, with a tinge of disapproval: "Well, I guess you're going to Vermont, though I can't imagine why. If Greg said he'll do it, he'll do it. You'll just be in the way."

"But this is something else," said Vivien, trying to play it all down. Then the rest came blurting out, because she couldn't keep up with who knew what. "See, that's where they went to college. It must have to do with—you know— the killing."

"Oh I see," said Edna, as if to say: *So he told you all about that.* "I didn't know. I thought that part was over with."

Without another word, she bent her head at a swanlike tilt and studied her fan of orders like a fortune teller. From the look of things, the prospects weren't auspicious. She gathered it all in a pile again, as if to wipe the image out.

"If you know who it is," she said with dangerous calm, "you better not tell me. He'd be dead by noon. I'm one of those redneck nuts, you know. I think the law's too slow."

"It's the strangest thing," said Vivien. "I suppose I'm the only one who knows. I'm not even scared. I feel—"

She couldn't think what she felt. She looked across at Edna, woman to woman. There, in the puffs and crisscross lines of those great exhausted eyes, she saw it did no good to talk too much of feelings. One thing was sure: Her fear of death had dwindled to a breeze. But it struck her now—as she sat with a finger curled at her empty cup, her sentence broken off—that another edge of fear began where the old one drew its border. Like a longing for things she used to think she'd give anything to lose. She was scared that she couldn't go back to her loneliness in peace. Scared that she wasn't a star anymore. They would no longer save up the days of her life, investing her every gesture with the weight of instant replay.

"But I never make plans," she said. "How do you know where I'm going, if *I* don't."

"Looks to me like you're out to prove yourself. Why,"— she shrugged—"I couldn't say."

She took a deep breath. Gathering up her pile of orders in one hand, she stood as if it were time to get to work at last. She went to the stand-up card file by the window and leaned on one big hip as she opened a drawer. She flipped from folder to folder, pulling out this one and that one. "*You* want the killer punished," she said. "Him, I don't think he cares. Why is all he ever wants to know."

It was true, she thought, as she watched this clear-eyed, solid woman elide into daily life. She knew now just how justice ought to be: inexorable. She couldn't say when it had changed for her, but she had the taste for blood. She shrank from none of the scenes that waited up ahead. When they came for Carl, she'd be holding the door wide open as they muscled him off to jail. She would go to court day after day, and gladly fight through a crowd of reporters, till the jury asked no mercy. Thus would the world be put to rights, like a mended vase.

She knew, if she plannned to be somebody else at the other

end, she would have to be very deliberate. None of the details left to chance. So she picked up both their cups and bussed them back to the kitchen. She rinsed and stacked them neatly in the drainer. Then she went through half a dozen drawers. When she found the aluminum foil, she tore off a good three feet and covered the last two croissants tightly. Every act, however small, drew her that much closer toward control.

"Goodbye," she said airily, passing through. She had learned the business of moving on in the course of a starless night beyond the mountains.

"Tell Greg to bring us a box of maple sugar," Edna said, as she looked up briefly from her deskwork. "Whatever it is they're selling."

"We'll get you one of everything," she shouted over her shoulder, flying out the door.

The elevator hadn't moved. She swept inside and punched the *1* and capered about in a space no bigger than a closet. As they sank the eleven floors, she thought: *I can fly.* By which she meant she had to catch a plane. New York or Boston, whichever left first. Say Boston. Then a short hop to the northern woods, in a little two-engine Cessna. Couldn't be simpler. She could do it blindfolded.

She breezed outside to the waiting Rolls, where she picked a ticket from under the wiper and flung it into the street. She got inside and did a U and pointed west-southwest. The silver-wingèd zephyr butterflied on the hood was aquiver with expectation. Now that they were bound for LAX, the portal of all her dreams, there was nothing could stop them. She knew, as she sailed down La Cienega—half a hundred street-front shows, mile after mile of the marginal life, the oil fields, the cat's-cradle freeways, the raw sea air—she was rid of all but the smallest pull of the old life, up on the hill.

Goodbye, she thought over and over, *goodbye*.

With a twinge of something sad, like seasons.

chapter 5

Oh, it's all my fault, he thought ruefully, as he inched the minuscule Dodge from Hertz up the muddy road to the inn. But he simply couldn't help it. He hated this gray and lunar weather. He'd probably been in the sun too long. For all he knew, he'd developed a toothy grin as well, like an overage surfer.

If only the clouds would be done with it and rain. They'd settled in so low, they threatened any moment to sweep down like a plague. The bare black limbs of wintered trees were hung with drops of condensation. They would have looked terrific with the light refracted through them, but there was no light to speak of. The night came down a little after five—the regulation time—yet the day had made so little headway, the gesture hardly mattered.

He had in his head, he realized now, what amounted to a coffee-table book. He passed the main lodge, in its oaken gloom, and went through a tunnel of graveyard trees. He'd always thought Vermont was a mix of covered bridges and barns in pastures, with the forest floored in red and yellow leaves. The Vermont of the national anthem. But now he was here for real, he hated it. It was cold as Eastern Europe, and

Appalachian-poor. Dotted with mingy local markets that stocked the meanest, drabbest goods. He was practically sprouting moss from two straight days of lowering skies. Still, he grew faint from thirst for want of a little Perrier.

He turned off at the one-lane track that led to his peak-roofed cabin. He parked on a bed of wet brown needles. A sign on a stake beside his porch read: *Old Mill Stream.* It took its name from the swollen water that coursed through the black-grass meadow behind the house. The mill was nowhere in evidence.

He kicked the car door shut behind him, registering a blow that seemed to go straight to the Dodge's heart. He got a lot of satisfaction out of the fact that the car was coming apart before it had gone two hundred miles. He had worked at banging the newness out, whenever he had the chance. Besides, he hated to drive at the best of times. He only got in a car when he'd exhausted every public means of transport. Thus, it usually required both Sid and Edna riding shotgun—one with a map, the other calling out landmarks—to get him from A to B.

He let himself in and drew the drapes against the desolate woodland view. He had nothing at all to look forward to. Dinner was served in the lodge from seven to nine, but he couldn't get too excited over that, since the dozen other guests had all become fast friends before he came. They traded snapshots and recipes with a vengeance, till he felt like David Niven in *Separate Tables.* Even now, they were crossing back and forth along the ridge, having drinks in one another's cutely nicknamed cabins.

All Greg had was a bottle of rye and his tooth glass. He'd forgotten to stop for ice. His head still swirled with jet lag, four days after he left L.A. His two-suiter had disappeared between Bermuda and New York, so he only had what little was packed in his carry-on bag. Luckily, he'd been able to buy some farmer clothes at the general store in Hamilton

Falls—stiff new overalls, red-checked shirt. He supposed he looked like the worst sort of weekend hayseed.

He poured his Four Roses neat, two fingers' worth, and sat on the end of the bed. At least he'd got this far without an attack of the horrors. Considering that he teetered close to blackout standing in line for a movie, he was some kind of study in courage. It happened the trip just fell in his lap, the very day he decided the answer lay at Carbon Mountain. Normally, that would not have been enough to get him to fly five thousand miles, but he'd had a sort of breakthrough. He wasn't sent into a panic to think he wouldn't make it back to the Cherokee Nile before dark.

He crouched to the fireplace. Every day the inn supplied him with packaged sawdust logs. He struck a match against the brick and lit the balled-up paper down among the ashes. He had a modest pile of real wood stacked on his porch, which he'd foraged himself on the banks of the stream. It was too wet to burn, but he figured to bring in a couple of logs and prop them on the hearth to dry. Later on, when he lay in bed reading, he'd be able to hear a truer crackle and smell the musk of a deeper smoke.

What a lot of trouble it was to be rural and safe from rain.

Still, once he was safe inside, he was fine. He liked the up-country rough of the dark pine paneling. The old New England furniture sat by the fire like a clutch of crones. The spring wind whistled beneath the eaves, as if it would freeze the very blood of a man out walking. As long as he had a room to himself, he was high and dry and cut off from all the threats of wildness. He'd discovered it didn't have to be the specific room he'd retreated to, when he gave up the hustle two years ago. The southwest quarter of the eleventh floor at Cherokee and Franklin wasn't magic after all. Any old room would do in a pinch.

His grasp of the whole psychology was very rudimentary.

It was as if, in turning thirty, he'd gotten too old to work the street, and opted instead for a desk job. Like a hooker, perhaps, or a Bible salesman. He wasn't afraid of open spaces. The true agoraphobe, as he understood it, was always strangling for a breath of air, no matter how sweet the scenery. In his case, the realization had come on him gradually that he simply felt like staying home. It got so he had to work up the courage just to go to the market.

So he dealt wherever possible with stores that delivered, preferably round the clock. He cajoled Sid and Edna to buy him things he was running out of—razor blades and dental floss, dreck like that. His main foray into the world outside came down to Friday morning, when he wheeled the grocery cart to the post office over on Highland.

And now, without any warning, he was suddenly transcontinental again. He had an international layover to his credit, as well as a day and a half on a coral-island shelf. Pretty posh, considering where he'd come from. He wondered now if he hadn't snapped out of it altruistically, for the sake of Harry Dawes. He'd heard of amnesiacs doing that—coming out of it just in time to save their dearest friend, when a speeding car required diverting. He felt as if he'd emerged from a fog, and the sky above was blinding clear. Was it possible? Could craziness break like a fever?

Maybe so, as Edna would say, twice in a row for good measure, *maybe so*.

The heat from the fire had flushed his face and made him drowsy. He stretched on his side along the hearth and pillowed his head in the crook of his arm. If he *was* cured, he thought, then he had the last laugh on a string of shrinks. Those winterized, rational types he'd gone to when he was young and scared, in college and just after. Three or four sessions apiece, and he'd had enough.

More than once in the last two years, he thought he'd have to go back. He didn't see how he'd ever come out the other end alone. But he put it off and put it off, in the hope that the thing would pass.

And now it had. What's more, he knew deep down it was gone for good. It didn't make him cocky, though. He had the good sense to take none of the credit. It was one of those things that just happened.

As he hovered at the edge of a twilight sleep, he thought of the yellow diamond, buried in a jar of Vaseline in the drawer of his bedside table. Probably worth a hundred times what Vivien told him. The moment he found it hanging off the jut of rock above the sound, right at the point where the map said X, he saw the screw was turning ever tighter. After all, he couldn't simply plop it in among his cufflinks. For all he knew, it would crack if he dropped it. This was the sort of rock they frisked the miners for. The sort that left a trail of bodies stewn up the coast of Africa.

He had knelt at the edge of Vivien's cliff for two hours Wednesday morning. The water, radiant blue, stretched away in a measureless calm. The catch was in his hand. He realized, now that he'd crossed the border out of madness, just how little time he had. There was no more room for detour. He had to get to Vermont and get it settled which one did it. He probably wouldn't recognize the clue until he saw it. It wouldn't hold up in a court of law. But he wasn't out for something hard as a diamond. What he hoped to find was a kind of lens, to bring it all into his field of vision. Like a sight on a high-powered rifle.

So he stood and slipped the diamond in the pocket of his jeans, patting it like a charm as he turned away up the cedar path. She was right, of course. It was just like Walden Pond. A man could go barefoot for weeks on end, subsisting on berries and clams. For him, it could have turned into the first vacation he'd ever had. The lilies breezed in the air like music. The old stone sill at the cottage door was hollowed with three hundred years of going in and out. But for once he preferred to be on the move. He felt no particular need to protest the cant and pageant of civilized life by making a stand in the boonies. Thank God there were more immediate matters.

His fireside sleep was a jigsaw of mismatched pieces. He made out a body of water as deep as a grown man's mind, with a house beside it built from scratch. *Walden*, he thought at first. But he changed his mind when he saw the bougainvillea flaming all around it. It was Vivien's house above the sound. Yet the water was too far off, and he seemed to look down from an eagle's perch on a mountain. *Of course*, he thought—it was Steepside. Even then, before he could be absolutely sure, the mountain beneath him went dead and wet. He was wandering out in a driving storm, trying to get back to *Old Mill Stream*. Remaining calm at all costs, of course. He'd just sniffed the faintest trace of wood smoke. He knew he was on the right track, when he woke with a start.

I'm not going out, he thought quite calmly.

He wasn't hungry anyway. He'd make do with his cache of salted nuts and Oreos. He got up from the hearth, and the heat held on like a sunburn on one side. He felt a little woozy, mixing drinks and sleep. So he opened the drawer beside his bed to grab for the Anacin Plus.

He effected a kind of miracle cure in the process. His head went naked and clear, as he quivered with sudden adrenaline. He crouched like a wrestler, out for a fight. For though the Anacin tin was there—loyal as ever, between the Tums and the Ocusol—somebody'd pinched the Vaseline. *It's not your fault*, he thought, putting first things first. So maybe a jar of salve was an old cliché—the first thing a crook checked out, like the safe behind the painting. Well, Vivien should have thought of that beforehand. There were couriers out for hire who'd handcuff a thing to their wrist and swallow the key. She shouldn't have tried to get out of it cheap.

He didn't for a moment think he was being followed. His paranoia wasn't tuned in that direction. To him, it was a very abstract thief who'd broken in and ripped him off. He didn't connect it up with anything else. He hardly saw the book at the back of the drawer. He noticed it seemed a little fancy to be a Gideon Bible. But after all, at a country inn in mid-Vermont, they probably did the phone books up in antique cowhide. What drew him to it, perhaps, was a sense of *déjà vu*. He'd begun it all a long time ago with a book about this size.

He lifted it out. The robbery slipped his mind as he weighed it now in the palm of one hand. It might have been the log of the journey he'd taken from there to here. He opened the scarred and spill-stained cover, his mind on Harry Dawes. The inscription in the old book's flyleaf didn't register at first. He must have stared at the water-marked page with the one-word title for five or six seconds before he read the handwritten script. In sherry-colored ink, it said:

RWE from HDT, on this tenth of May in 1855.
This one particular sunny day, with the lilacs out.
Some things a man can't put in a book.

On the facing page, a washed-out bookplate. Very spare: a chestnut tree and a pinch of Latin. *Ex libris* above, and then the name: *Ralph Waldo Emerson.*

Greg took it in, if a little numbly. A first edition of *Walden*, from one Concord thinker to another. He was sure it was all a coincidence. Somehow, it didn't seem unreasonable that the inn should supply each guest with a period volume of contemplations. The way things happened lately, it was only to be expected that the book that set him up went with the territory.

He thumbed his way into the middle, to page 160, but the numbers didn't match with the paperback. The print was bigger here, the margins much more leisurely. He flipped ahead another quarter inch. Page after page was marked to the edges with notes and arrows. He tried to remember the last thing he'd been reading. How to build a chimney, maybe. Though he'd put the book down for good, on account of its vast irrelevance, he wanted to find the place where he'd left off, just to see what Emerson scrawled in the near vicinity.

A square of paper fell out like an autumn leaf and lilted to the floor. Not old like the book, so he nearly let it lie, supposing it to be a former tenant's bookmark. Then he saw there was writing on it. He bent down and grabbed it and read it through. Right off, he understood why she wrote on a separate sheet. She didn't like to jockey for space on the flyleaf, Thoreau having beaten her to it. More than that, she didn't want to upstage Harry Dawes. She made it sound as little like an inscription as she could.

> *Since you won't take money, I had to find you something you wouldn't dare give back. Come to my cabin for drinks? Say at six? I'm in number 4— the one they call "Riverbend."*

Greg looked down at his wrist: 5:38 exactly. He wasn't a bit surprised that she was here, but how could she be so sure he'd find the note by six? He didn't like to be quite such an open book, to anyone. He scanned the map of the inn and grounds that was tacked to the closet door—plotting out the shortest walk through the woods to number 4. It was farthest off from the lodge, and it looked to be the biggest too. Leave it to her, he thought, to book the royal suite. As with the old mill, there didn't appear to be a river for it to be at the bend of. It was simply off in the woods, like everything else.

He could always sit tight and wait, he thought, and by and by she'd have to come to him. But what was the use? The diamond was Vivien's caper. Let her play out the final scene at "Riverbend," if she liked. Finish it off with a shot of cognac. In point of fact, he was lucky to have the diamond safely out of his hands. With this loose end tied up, perhaps she'd hear him out about the killer.

He set off at a trot through the meadow and up the hill, not stopping to change his clothes or comb his hair. It was next to amazing, how willing he was to go with the turn of events. But he'd come to see that the momentum of the investigation depended on what he could hold in his head at any given moment. The truth was no one final thing. The bits that sprang up in the way were more and more the key to it all. You couldn't seek them, or even deduce them. All you could do was keep up your speed and cover ground, going over and over the paths you made.

The trees at the top of the rise were evergreen. The pad of needles beneath his feet soaked up the wet of the mud, so he lost the dread of sinking. The ruthless view of blasted hills—fungus gray as far as the eye could see—gave way in the heart of the woods to a season of mists. He looked up as he jogged along. The pines were blue and motionless above him, as if listening still for the coming on of rain, even now after two days' false alarm. The moss was full. The ferns were finger-high. So far did the whole thing take him in, he forgot for a moment where he was headed. To reach her clearing, he had to pass two forks, a left and right. He wasn't aware of either.

But he must have got it right by a sort of natural radar—because there it was, across a field of waist-high grass. Its shingles had bleached to white, so it glowed in the mountain dusk. A curl of smoke floated out of a fieldstone chimney, powder-gray on the lead of the sky. As he entered the meadow along the winding path, the feather ends of the grass rushed against him. How long, he wondered, since he'd been entirely in the open, without so much as a surfaced road or a visible neighbor? Perhaps never. He knew it was just this kind of place that Harry would have led him to, if they'd only had the time.

He could tell the dark would fall as he reached her door. Already the night poured over the woods. There was no going back without a light. He broke through the last of the grass and leapt up the steps to her porch. He realized even the dark was safe enough, so long as he wasn't lost. The night had a thousand reasons all its own. It wasn't out for him.

She opened the door before he could lift a hand to knock, and the firelight glowed behind her so that he craned his neck to see.

"You were running so fast," said Vivien lightly, taking his arm, "I thought there was somebody chasing you."

She guided him forward toward the hearth, as if she sensed he needed warming up. He fixed his eyes on the crackling fire till he stood so close he could feel the heat on his overalls. Then he looked all around—at the high barn ceiling, the cushy chairs, the cocktail table decked with canapés. Then he looked at her. Hair tied back, in a putty silk dress to the floor, she might have spent the day on skis in St. Moritz. No detail here to connect this place to a public inn. It was more like somebody's private chalet. Even a good hotel seemed slightly vulgar by comparison.

"Nice layout," Greg remarked. He still hadn't said hello. "But if *I* had money, I'd never put it down for a thing like this. It's like restaurants—the prices are way out of line. When it's over, you don't have shit to show for it."

"A good hotel is always worth it," Vivien answered evenly, as she busied herself with drinks. Greg sat down on the hearth stool. "It takes people out of themselves for a while."

"That's the worst reason I ever heard."

"Is it?" she said, passing over a vodka gimlet. "Sounds like you're all caught up in your reading. How do you like the book?"

She meant the rare one. He held it tight in his hand, like something saved from a fire.

"I'd just as soon read it in paperback, frankly. Then I don't have to be so careful."

"Who says you have to be careful?"

The diamond hung around her neck, paler against the gray of the dress than it had seemed in the bright Bermuda sun. He wouldn't give her an inch—wouldn't ask how she tracked him down or found his cache. As for the leather-bound Thoreau, if she really meant it as payment for services, he shouldn't have to be grateful.

"I don't get it," he said. "If you didn't mind coming this far, why not go all the way." He loved the rapid-fire investigative mode, where you asked a slew of questions all at once. "Come to think of it," he went on, "aren't you supposed to be stuck on a yacht? Bored out of your mind?"

"I canceled," she said, though of course she hadn't. "It's just—I know who did it."

He stared back at her politely, without any change of expression. She didn't know what she'd expected—"I told you so," perhaps—but she wondered now if he didn't resent the intrusion. She probably should have waited.

"Who?" he said at last.

"Uh—Carl."

"Wrong," he retorted, shaking his head.

"Well, *who?*"

"Artie."

"Bullshit."

They took a little break and sipped their gimlets. Greg stared into the fire, and Vivien fiddled at the antipasto. They probably both should have waited. After all, it had less to do with who than how they ought to proceed.

"What did you think you'd find up here?" she asked, not so much to change the subject as to start on firmer ground.

"They closed the place, did you know that?"

"No," she said. It struck her she'd never heard of Carbon Mountain College, except for the fact that Jasper went there. That was its one distinction, somehow. "It's all boarded up, is it?"

"Not exactly. It's crawling with monks."

"Catholics?"

"Crazies, more than likely. I didn't ask them what they were into, beliefwise. I guess they keep a few bees. Mostly, they pray for us worldly types."

He sounded very tired. Clearly, she thought, he'd hit a dead end. But no wonder—the past always covered its tracks. He ought to have known there wouldn't be any concrete data left behind. No relics, no husks, and no abandoned campsites. Time didn't have any patience for the leaving of human artifacts. Everything simply came and went.

"They don't suspect a thing," she said.

By "they," she meant to ,diffuse the issue of who was guilty, parceling it out to Carl and Artie both, as if it were a conspiracy. She went to the mantel and stood above him. The fire made light of the silk.

"You couldn't know there was nothing here till you came and found out for yourself," she said.

Which was really quite expansive of her, but all he had to do was pick up the phone and call ahead, and they would have told him they weren't in the education business anymore. Vivien persevered on the bright side. She didn't like to see him full of second thoughts.

"Did I say I failed?" he asked in some surprise. "I guess I must project a lousy attitude. You don't have to fret over *me*, you know. I got what I came for."

Not a word about the cost. How they put him through half a day's runaround, yesterday in the bitter cold. A slack-jawed second-rank priest had grilled him a full two hours to discover if he was worthy to see the joker who ran the show.

Greg said he was Jasper Cokes's brother—which elicited several pieties about the wages of dissipation. When at last he was ushered in, the man at the top turned out to be a jelly-eyed fanatic, who talked as if he were training a band of terrorists. Luckily, Greg had learned to filter out the nutcake gods, through years of walking among the messiahs of Hollywood Boulevard.

All for what? An hour and a half in the musty attic where the college records were locked away. Watched by a postulant booby, who picked his nose and sifted through a trunk full of academic hoods. In the end, Greg could come up with nothing more germane than Jasper's transcript. A 2.8 overall average, with remedial work required in French and mathematics. Disciplinary action taken only once, to do with a snowman built on the desk of the freshman dean. Probable career: undecided.

"Like what?" she asked. A little too pugnacious.

"Artie was home that night," said Greg. "Isn't that right?"

She nodded—for the sake of argument only, since that was what everyone thought. In fact, of course, he'd been miles away, but she was the only one who knew.

"He says he heard Jasper and Harry come in," said Greg in a methodological way. He stood and put his gimlet down on the mantel next to hers. She saw they were both quite even, having drunk them two-thirds down. "It seems they were falling all over each other to get to bed. Artie let them alone and went away to his room. He never saw Harry before, he says. About two hours later, he went for a walk, and there they were." These were the barest facts as reported in the papers, minus the tears and hysterics. Greg droned over it now with no editorial comment. "So Artie's the only one who ever saw them together. Nobody else—not even Carl."

"Maybe they used to meet at Harry's place," she offered. "Jasper didn't always bring them home."

This wouldn't do at all, she thought. She was coaxing him farther and farther in, as if she meant to go along. She simply had to tell him. Artie had made it all up about them coming in drunk and horny—to cover the fact that he was somewhere else. What held her back from saying so was wishing not to win.

"Anyway," Greg continued after a moment, "this is the key, right here."

When she looked toward him, not entirely sure she'd heard him right, she saw he was tossing an actual prop. A filigreed key, about four inches long. It must have weighed half a pound. He tossed it and caught it, over and over, like somebody bent on a dose of self-hypnosis.

"I'll take you in tomorrow," he said. "Unless you've got other plans." For all he knew, she had leads of her own that needed following up.

"Whenever you say."

She understood the subject to be closed for now. She would have to hold off springing the news of the airline ticket. Still, she couldn't figure why, if he'd broken the case wide open, he seemed so sorry underneath.

"There's all this food," she said. "You hungry?"

"Sure," he said gently, and turned with her toward the groaning board.

Where, in these godforsaken mountains, had she found a wedge of brie? She had fifteen kinds of vegetables, razor-thin and raw, circling a bowl of sour cream and curry. He decided she probably had a deal. Some market in Beverly Hills sent along, at a dollar a radish, a chest of dainties wherever she went, packed in a fog of dry ice. He chewed on a couple of pea pods, smiling across at her benignly. Thinking: *I bet we look like quite a pair.* Him in his baggy overalls. Her in her Marc Bohan.

"You still feel nothing?" he asked.

She shrugged, as if to say, *Who knew?* "The last few days," she said, "I haven't had the time to notice. That usually means it's passed. What about you? You still a loser?"

"Depends on what I'm losing," he replied. He dipped a carrot and passed it across, since she made no move to feed herself. "Tell me, when did it change for you and Jasper? Did you *used* to get it on? Or was it always to each his own?"

Could they really ask each other questions no one else had ever been allowed? Artie wouldn't have dreamed of putting it to her straight. Even assuming the light was green, could they talk this way without attendant rancor? Perhaps if they had no ulterior motives. None whatsoever. Though how could they ever be sure?

"Never. Not once," she said precisely, without any trace of regret. "We'd had it with acting out, before we ever met. We didn't have the stomach for charades. How is it you got to know Harry Dawes so *well?* Without sleeping with him, I mean."

He plucked up a handful of vegetable bits and cut off a two-inch slice of cheese. He bore these back to his seat by the fire, like so many winter provisions.

"You mean, because gay men usually do their fucking first."

"Oh, I wouldn't say gay," she said. "These days, *everyone* fucks before they say hello."

She walked to the hearth, where she reached down into a wide-mouthed basket. She brought up two birch logs. Deftly, she slung them onto the fire, first one and then the other. From a hook in the stone, she produced a crude straw broom and swept the hearth of ashes. Greg took note of her charwoman's skills. No ersatz sawdust firewood in the royal suite, he thought.

"He came on so subtle, it went right by me," Greg said finally. "I'm used to more explicit propositions."

"But you see my point," she said, and though he nodded, he didn't see at all. The nodding was more like a wave of sleep. It took him the whole of the speech she spoke to figure this was the thing she'd been getting at all along. "Officially, we're the two widows," she said. "Isn't it strange? We never got to first base with either one of them. I don't know how many men *you've* had. Probably more than I, but then, they don't put yours in the papers. Still, it's safe to say we're not exactly virgins. So how is it we've come all this way for the sake of these men we couldn't love?"

Couldn't?

The way *she* put it, it sounded strange enough. She said "widow" the night they met, he remembered, on the hillside by the grave. He'd bridled at it then, and he didn't much care for it now. Why did the woman insist on finding parallels in him and Harry? There was no particular story behind his missed connection. Not the way there was with Vivien and Jasper. It was as if she'd found out only now, with Jasper dead, that she couldn't live with what they added up to. Nothing to show for the last eight years but a lot of coverage. Greg didn't blame her a bit. He'd have felt the same himself, in her position. Which he wasn't.

"See, if it was someone I really loved," he said, "I'd *never* have come this far. I'd just quietly fall apart. I'd starve to death in my own apartment. If he was really my other half, I wouldn't have gotten over it at all."

"You ever *have* a man like that?"

He heaved a deep shrug, as if to say that was a very tall order. Then he took a deep breath and answered: "No."

No, he thought suddenly, *don't get pissed at her. It isn't to do with her at all.*

"Me neither," she admitted. "Maybe there's no such thing."

"That's what I always tell myself, whenever I'm near a mirror. Doesn't help. I'm always looking."

"Like waiting for a break, huh?"

She meant the Hollywood kind.

He nodded: "After a while, it drives you crazy. You get so you'll take almost anything."

On that note, as if to test him, the sky broke open. With a long moan of release, it flung down on the woodland lodge the storm it had been holding for the past two days. It probably started by degrees. While they talked by the hissing fire, there were probably spattered drops and gusts of icy wind. Doubtless, it overtook the land mountain by mountain. But somehow, they didn't hear a peep till it fell in full Wagnerian force on top of them.

The water came in sheets and hit the barn like a tidal wave. They turned to the door to listen, though it pelted all over the roof like a drum of stones. The gods, it seemed, had had enough of moods. If they wanted to talk their feelings out, then let them take their cue from the seethe of nature. You didn't come to Vermont to sit inside and castle the air with what you thought of love. You came to thrill to the wilderness. To throw your civilization off.

When they eyed each other again, it was with a certain measure of relief, she thought. They'd about used up their stock of naked questions. Drawing each other out like this, divulging all they could, they'd cut to the heart of things in record time. The rest was just a list of names.

Why bother? They had no use for chapter and verse. What they had to get to the bottom of was the whole idea of it all. Unless, she thought, it was only something *she* was partial to. She froze with a sudden pang of doubt, as they grinned at each other about the rain. Could it be that he had no theory of love?

"You want to go for a walk?" she asked.

"We'll get wet," he said, but as if the prospect were delightful. He only wished he had a change of overalls. He didn't want to go back just yet to the pants he wore at home.

"Oh no we won't," exclaimed Vivien, laughing openly now. She took his hand and tugged him along to the bedroom end of the room. She flung open a closet door and gestured proudly. "Compliments of the management."

She had enough rain gear hung inside to outfit a dory of fishermen. Hip boots and bright yellow slickers. Rain hats brimmed like firemen's helmets. Amenities not included with *his* room, Greg thought, prickling slightly. It seemed like only the rich were allowed to go out in the rain.

He kicked off his field hand's mud-warped shoes and pulled down a high black-rubber boot. Out of the corner of one eye, he could see her worming the gray silk over her head. She dropped it in a heap on the quilted bed. Naked, she went to the dresser and rifled a drawer for jeans and a sweater. He knew enough not to watch her. She'd gone ahead assuming it was no big deal, whether or not they closed the door to strip. He wouldn't have tried the same with her, he thought as he wrestled the boot—in case he would seem to mock her with the specter of his indifference. She did right, he thought, to act so freely. They didn't always have to think.

He hadn't put on galoshes since he was a kid. The raincoat slumped about him like a tent, till only his fingertips showed at the sleeves. He felt like an astronaut crossed with a scarecrow. He squeaked across the floor, rubber against rubber, and laughed to get her attention. She stood at the mirror, pinning up her hair.

"Captain," he said, "I'm going out on deck to batten down the hatches."

And he tramped away to the door and threw it open. She begged him to wait. So he ventured only as far as the porch, while she threw on her outer gear. The force of the rain was loud as Niagara, though even as close as this, he couldn't see six inches into the night. He put out the flat of one hand beyond the shelter of the eaves. The storm, alert to the least impertinence, slapped it so hard that he drew it right back in again and held it against his cheek.

How did the seedlings stand it? Of course, they were built to bend with things, he thought. Go with the flow. Do not go counter. He flipped his hand sideways and knifed it into the rain. It held steady. He stood there a moment, mesmerized by the icy cold.

When did they say, without stretching the point, that winter was done around here? Was the cold so deep in the land that it never let one year alone before it came round the next? If Vivien hadn't bounded out toward him, leaping into the thick of it, he probably would have chickened out and rushed back in to the fire.

"Put on your hat!" she shouted out of the dark. "I'll race you to the trees!"

He wasn't in competition form, but he clamped the rain hat on his head and marched out into the whirlwind. He couldn't run out on her now. The rain set in to pummel him fiercely, as he staggered forward toward her. Surely, he reasoned, they wouldn't be out two minutes before they'd had their fill. Then they could brew up a proper toddy and talk about simpler matters—huddled close by the birchwood fire.

When he reached her side, they propped each other up as they crept ahead through the beaten grass. They couldn't see what was the path and what wasn't. One or the other slipped at every second step. But somehow, they didn't go both at once, so no one fell. They kept a precarious balance and made a little headway. He had to admit he was bone dry, in his neat cocoon of waterproof stuff. Perhaps if he'd been alone he would have turned back by now, but going arm in arm was something else again. They shared it half and half. Though the mud was now up to their ankles, they slogged ahead.

Somehow, it got them started laughing. They probably couldn't have said what the funny thing was, but it had to do with their expectations. They'd come a long, long way to front nature face to face. If they'd had any picture at all, it was sitting pensively on a rock, the view in all directions fifty miles, fixing a dreamy look on a daisy in their hands. What could they possibly contemplate here, stunned and giddy like this? They might have been in interplanetary space.

Dimly, up ahead, they could see the line of spruces bordering the woods. They ducked their heads against the sudden whip of the wind. With a tangible goal so near at hand, they made their way more resolutely—laughing all the way. They weren't going to have to talk about it, for one thing. Rain was rain. It didn't allow for a lot of contradictory theories.

Greg was beginning to tire. He had a sudden sense that this was how it went when one was drowning. He'd gotten so used to the buffeting wind and beat of the rain that, somewhere along the way, he'd started to drift. He no longer seemed to know how far afield they'd gone. Didn't even, after a certain point, open his eyes to the little he could see. It was rather like being asleep, he thought. He gripped her closer around the waist and lurched ahead again. Like being asleep, he thought, in someone's arms.

Then they bumped into the tree, hard.

His head and his knee cracked against it, both at once. Vivien struck one shoulder, wrenched to the side, and felt the pain root in her back. The situation was suddenly stood on its head. If they'd been alone here, and not so arm-in-arm, they might have stayed on their feet. As it was, they went down in a tangle.

The mud was so thick they couldn't get a foothold. They slopped around like pigs for a bit, then pulled themselves up by the bark of the tree. Greg lost his hat. By the time he retrieved it out of a puddle and stood erect again, he could feel the soak of the shirt against his skin. He looked over. Vivien's poncho was turned so the hood was up around her face. He twisted it till it was right again.

They looked each other straight in the eye. Even now, with the aches and chills, there was something close to glee in the way they smiled. It was on his lips to say they ought to go back. Yet the rain was a good deal muted beneath the tree. Having made it as far as this, they might as well have a walk in the woods for their trouble.

Which course they agreed on without a word. They nodded and bowed and stepped around the offending tree. Meeting up on the other side, they walked along on a sponge of needles.

"Have you ever picked up a guy," he called through the rain, "and a minute later you're sorry? You just want to be alone, all of a sudden. But by then it's too late. You have to go through with it."

"What?" she bellowed back.

"I said, I met this *boy* this morning," Greg sang out. Maybe loud like this was the only way. He told it statement by simple statement, coloring things as little as he could. "I was walking around the college," he called. "He was some kind of student monk. Somebody must have told him I was Jasper's brother."

For a moment she seemed to miss a step, as if she'd sunk into a soft spot.

"That's my *cover*," Greg hastened to clarify. "He says he knows the place I'm looking for. Which throws me a bit, because *I* don't. But see,"—and a throb came into his voice, like a trill in an aria—"I sort of had to lead him on. That's how I got him to take me there."

Was that the way it was? he thought. How could he get it across that a thing like this could happen without his choosing? Sometimes you met a man who'd held it in from the moment he broke through to puberty. There was this terrible need to try the darkness. You felt an obligation to it—like it needed space to thrive. So he flexed a little, as they sood and talked on the chapel steps, and hitched his pants and rubbed himself till they both were close to frantic. What he didn't know how to tell Vivien was who the poor guy looked like.

Harry Dawes.

"It's a crazy place," said Greg, with a small jump forward in time and a change of scene. "Like a little Greek temple. Off by itself, way up in the hills. Some kind of fraternity."

They stopped in a circle of firs. The evergreen boughs high above them were flung like the spokes of a great umbrella. Close around them, there grew a strain of pine much thicker in the branches. Each of these was tall as a man and seemed the perfect size for hauling in at Christmas. Even now, in a crashing storm, a certain stillness held.

"Well?" she said. "Did you fuck him?"

"Yes, but—"

Yes but nothing. So what if the thing was done in fifteen minutes flat? So what if the kid ran off, with a look on his face like he'd killed a man? The act was all that counted in the matter of sealing fate. The night trees stood stock still in the tempest. Next to them, the riddle of guilt and remorse was the merest phantom. In lieu of moods, the forest stuck to seasons. Cold and slow and furious, but at least they came and went without a second look.

Greg looked down at the ground, as if he were puzzling out what more to say. For no reason at all, he bent and fetched a pine cone. Perhaps he needed a souvenir before he could turn back.

"I still don't know how it happened," Vivien said.

For a moment, he thought she wanted a bit more dirt, as to what led to what this afternoon. But just when he turned to tell her more, she went on talking herself. This "it" she couldn't figure out was something to do with her, not him.

"I suppose it was all that time on the road," she said. "The first two years we were married, Jasper did all those secret-agent pictures. We were gone two months at a time. Late at night—didn't matter where we were—Jasper would go out hunting. Artie usually drove him. That left me and Carl. I don't know how it happened," she said, squinting like someone whose mind plays tricks, "but I think it went on a couple of years."

How was it, he wondered, that no one had ever said this in the press? There had always been an unwritten rule that barred a reporter from letting it out that Jasper Cokes was queer. Were Vivien and Carl accorded a kind of contiguous protection? God, it must have been awful. Worse, there was no way to get rid of him, once it was over. They still had to live as before, all together, four in a house and bound by a labyrinthine deal.

Was this supposed to be the motive? Did Carl still love her, and did he kill Jasper to clear the field? Or was Vivien merely trying to tell him why she wanted it pinned on Carl?

Greg didn't say what he thought. He let what she said suffice, just as she had with him. He watched her now, in her slick and faintly luminous yellow canvas, running her hand along a branch. She snapped off a sprig of needles and brought them up under the hood to sniff them. There was something to be said for rural inertia. One puttered about the landscape, picking up feathers and fallen fruit, telling the truth for the hell of it.

The rain was only raining now, as if somebody'd turned the volume down. They were five or six yards apart. It was ten minutes after seven. But it felt like the deep of the night, with no one awake but them for miles. They'd each let out a secret, here at the end of the earth. As to the likelihood of miraculous recovery, now that their hearts were bare, it was not a throw of the dice they were given to.

Did they solve these things, Greg wondered, by shouting them into the rain?

Not likely. The moon didn't elbow out from behind the clouds and make their faces shine. Putting it as they had in the form of a confession, it wasn't even certain that they'd got their stories straight. In fact, he thought, they were probably both a bit let down to discover how shallow the darkness was that opened off their unrepentant souls. With killers in their midst, their sins were very little.

Looking down, he saw he was square in the path again, though he'd stumbled on it aimlessly enough. The sight of it trailing away through the trees reminded him of the fire he planned to lay. The rain grew lighter and lighter. He had to get back to his place, he thought, before it let up and made the night too gentle. He couldn't wait to get into bed.

"We'll have breakfast up at the inn," he said. "I'll meet you there at eight."

"Say seven," she countered. "Morning's the nicest time of all. You want to come get your book?"

"Tomorrow," he said. "I'm reading something else right now. Good night."

"Good night."

And they tipped their hats like kinsmen met on a forest trail. It was the ideal way to see your friends, Greg thought as he headed down the path. For backdrop, you had the crackling air and the various face of the woodland slope. When you took up your journey again, you went with the memory of one irreducible face, which quickened your heart like a thumbnail sketch in a locket. All the while, you were drinking in the enormous world of the perfectly real.

Last year's leaves in silken piles. The blue-black gleam of rain on rocks. Nothing got saved and nothing spent. People could meet in the middle of things without treading on anyone's property. He walked downhill through the overarching trees, and he thought how the breeze that followed a storm was light as the breathing that came with sleep. The longer he stayed outside, in fact, the plainer did all things seem. Was it only two or three hours ago that he cursed this raw and sunless country? Well, so what. He admitted the inconsistency quite gladly. Took a certain pride in it, almost.

He came out of the woods and saw his cabin at the foot of the hill, a single lamp at a single window. Another time, he might have asked what good it was all going to do him in *real* life—that is, the far-off corner of Cherokee and Franklin. For once in his life, he didn't care. The first star clicked in the clearing sky like a flashbulb. The crickets skirled in the hillside grass. All across the mountains, there was no straight line discernible between any one thing and any other. The world was nothing but arcs and whorls and random clusters.

She's right, he thought as he trotted zigzag down the slope. She was just like him.

chapter 6

" 'THE CARBON MOUNTAIN PLAYERS present *A Midsummer Night's Dream*, a play by William Shakespeare.' In case you're not up on your authors," said Greg. He tossed the flyer to Vivien. "With Artie Balducci as Puck, you'll notice. That's the fall of their freshman year. In the winter, he did *The Country Wife*. In the spring, a very racy *Glass Menagerie*. I have the reviews, if you'd like to see them," he said, holding up a sheaf of documents.

They sat on the marble steps in the sun, the mountains spread before them like a postcard. Dotting the distance here and there, they could see the red of a barn or the skyward thrust of a village steeple. Mostly, they noticed the first faint green like a mist in the wintry trees. The April sun had drawn the sap, till the buds glowed greenish-gold. The morning was warm as California, though the buds did not yet dare to break and send out leaves. There was still a month of drift and savage changes coming—still a blizzard waiting in the wings, and a couple of killing frosts. Today was just an article of faith.

"So what?" she threw back with a shrug. "So Artie used to be an actor too."

"Not *too*," corrected Greg, as he stood up and put his arm around a fluted white stone column. He swung on it like a lamppost. "Jasper never acted once," he said, and waited a beat before he went on with the résumé. "*Sophomore* year," he announced. "Artie Balducci in *West Side Story*—very big hit up here. Then a one-man cabaret, the whole of it written by him, with original music. Right after that, a season of summer stock in the Adirondacks. Junior year: They let him drop all his courses, so he could stage the *Oedipus* cycle."

Vivien had to give him credit. If all of this was news to her, it was probable nobody knew. The thing itself was not as startling as the fact that no reporter ever turned it up. She could hardly see why Artie's past should have to be kept a secret. But then, this whole approach was the last thing she expected. Having hiked for an hour straight up these untracked hills, she supposed the signs would be a bit more mystical.

"He was some kind of regional theater, all to himself," concluded Greg. "Twenty-four hours a day—except for the time he spent up here."

"Here," as far as Greg had been able to ascertain, was a kind of honor society. In the midst of the Great Depression, a beer-baron alumnus had funded the carting of eighteen tons of yellow-veined marble halfway up the mountainside. The membership convened every Thursday and Sunday evening, where it underwent a form of group interaction somewhere between a cocktail hour and a seance. Though the story of Jasper Cokes had always had the three of them backslapping pals from the day they arrived on campus, in fact they never even met till they got elected into this, in the fall of their junior year. Only then, maybe six months later, did they further decide to share a room.

"How do you figure it?"

"Well," she said, as she hefted the documentation, "it looks from this like Artie ought to have been the star. By *rights*, that is. By rights, it seems like Jasper should have been parking Artie's car. But Jesus, Greg. What is it with you? You still think cream's the thing that rises? No wonder you can't sell a script."

It irritated her mightily, if only because he made her feel like such a cynic next to him. And she wasn't that way at all. She was only fifty pages shy of finishing *Walden*, damn it— thus refused to come across as anything less than pure of heart. But she couldn't sit by and let him go off on a tangent as to how it might have been. What was the point? There wasn't enough for murder in any of *this*.

"Mm," said Greg, with a sudden squint in his eye. He might have been reading the wind on a weather vane, far in the valley below. He went on, half to himself. "But that's the way it must have been. It was *Artie* they planned to make a star."

"Listen," she pleaded, slapping down on the step beside her all his stack of evidence, "this is all *my* fault. I should have told you. There's proof. Carl flew all the way back to L.A., the Monday Jasper died. Fictitious name and everything." Then, by way of apology, she tacked on a bit of a motive. She said: "See, Jasper was just about to fire him."

"I thought we'd agreed to hear *my* side first."

"But it's more than that," she protested. The sharpness had fled from her voice, as if she longed to apologize for knowing more than her share. She spoke it gently, like somebody breaking terrible news. "Artie wasn't there that night. Not till he came in later and found them dead. He's got fifty different witnesses could tell you where he was from five to seven. Honest."

"Are you done?"

"Now don't get mad."

"What you don't seem to understand," he said, pointing a finger at her like the barrel of a gun, "is that we have reached an impasse." He cocked his thumb as if to click the hammer. "This part's over, Viv. We got no choice. You have it out with *your* killer. I'll have it out with *mine*. I heard you, all right? Now you listen."

He went to the wooden box he'd hauled to the porch from deep within the airless marble room. He'd planned on bringing her in, so they could sit in the faded wing chairs, hard by the dusty fireplace. The only light would be what fell through the open door. She would see what it was to be surrounded by the aimless memorabilia of men who assumed the future cared.

But Vivien, once she'd seen it, wouldn't cross the threshold. It was more of a tomb than she bargained for. She'd had her fill of death, not two weeks since. She saw now how it got them off on the wrong foot. How could he ever begin to sustain his atmosphere, working against the morning sun and the reach of the mountain vista? She'd fucked around with his staging.

"All right," he said, pulling out Exhibit A.

She knew it from Steepside: Jasper's yearbook. He thumbed to the place he'd marked and passed it over. She looked at a gray group photograph she was sure she'd looked at time and again.

"There are sixteen men in the club at any given time," he said. "Eight from the graduating class. Eight from the class below."

She nodded and stared along the line, automatically picking out *her* three. Carl was third from the left, the only one in a tie. Jasper, last on the right, grinned as he held two fingers up like rabbit ears behind Artie's head. She felt the raw edge of grief well up, at so much innocence all in a row. Eight men stood on this very porch where she now sat in silence. They looked out over the photographer's shoulder and saw the world was at their feet. Nothing could touch them.

"This one," Greg said, crouched at her ear. He reached around with a felt-tip pen and drew a circle round the face of the man on the left of.Artie. He lowered the pen to the string of names that made up the caption. "Gary Barlow," he said, laying a line of ink beneath the words.

"Never heard of him," she said.

"Right," he nodded—not a bit surprised. He flipped to the back impatiently. "See, here's the graduation. Here—you've got all your societies marching, every one with a banner. Notice the letters."

He touched the tip of the pen to what looked like a square of satin, held aloft on a pole. Under it bobbed a wave of caps and gowns. Three Greek letters she couldn't begin to decipher were blazoned on the banner. Greg might have read them out like a line of Homer, except his Greek was as bad as hers. Instead, he tapped her shoulder and pointed up, at the pediment over the door. The letters cut in the stone were a perfect match.

"Now," he said, as if the trick were all in place at last, "I want you to count. How many men in the group?"

Seven.

"All right," she said. "What happened to Gary Barlow?"

She hoped she didn't sound bored, but somebody had to pick up the pace. Having gathered speed so recently herself, she began to think that fast was the safest way. If he'd only state his evidence succinctly. Why did they have to have separate suspects? Couldn't they narrow it down right here? Either he had the goods or he didn't.

"Died," said Greg. "Five weeks before commencement. The third of April, to be precise."

"How?" she demanded sharply, like she wanted it over and done with.

"Exposure, I think they call it," he said. He sounded uncertain. He reached in his conjurer's box again and brought up a yellow clipping. "It's very hard to say without an autopsy. But they wanted the matter buried quick, so they couldn't be bothered with all the fine points. There isn't a paper in twenty miles of here. We've only got the campus rag to go on. From what I can gather, it started out as a Boy Scout trip."

She read the brittle account in snatches, while Greg spun the story out in more detail. They had eight men in four canoes. They paddled down the Connecticut River, from close to the source high up in the mountains, as far as the Massachusetts border. Very uneventful. The country wasn't especially wild, the water hardly ever white. When they came ashore at night, they always managed to reconnoiter a liquor store at a close remove. After six days in the bush, they were met at a prearranged spot, where Vermont Route 2 crossed the water. A couple of pledges drove down in vans. They lashed the canoes to the roof and stowed the gear. They piled in, five in a van, and—

"That's when they had the idea," said Greg, as he paced the columned porch. "I don't know who it was, but somebody says 'Hey, I'm gonna *walk* home. Anyone want to join me?'" Pause. "You have to be twenty-two to understand the moment. There's a ripple of laughter. Then one steps out— then two and three. You got four altogether." He ticked them off on his fingertips. "Jasper, Artie, Barlow, and another guy. They get out their packs and sleeping bags. The only map they can find is a Texaco road map. Doesn't matter. Once you start a thing like this, you don't turn back—for anything."

She could see the kind of day it must have been. Late afternoon, with a pale, banana-yellow April sun. Chilly as hell. A day not so different from what today would soon turn into, once the sun was past its peak. The four men set out overland. She could see them, whistling "The Colonel Bogie

March"—as if the rolling hills of Vermont led all the way to Katmandu.

"Every now and then, they'd cross a country road," said Greg. "They'd take a break in a small-town bar. The mud was up to their ears, of course, but say it was warm for the end of winter. They probably froze their ass at night, but the tougher it got, the better they liked it. There was really no danger. They could always follow a valley and find a road. They were only six miles south of Carbon Mountain when it hit."

She had no idea what a blizzard was like. It had never so much as crossed her mind.

"If they'd only kept going north," he said, "they would have made it easy."

He was standing between two pillars, holding on and leaning out as if to get a bird's eye view. Vivien sat on the step below and narrowed her eyes to picture it. Knowing half the people made it twice as hard. If they'd never seen fit to mention it, what made it any business of hers? She tried to see it at one remove, shooting it like a movie, with anyone else in the lead but Jasper. She looked along the placid range, where the near edge of spring had taken hold, and measured six miles as the crow flew.

Greg now built to the climax. Snow was driving down. The four men staggered forward, blind before the first inch fell. The wind or the hill's steep slope threw them off course in a flash. Still Greg seemed to hold out hope. For a moment more, he appeared to cling to the notion of change implicit in all things not complete. Somebody might yet pull out a compass. Somebody might see flares.

"They did the worst thing they could do," he said, with obvious disapproval. "They stopped to wait it out."

He shrugged and sighed, and his hands fell numbly to his sides. He appeared to have lost all interest, now that his men had failed him so.

"They got fourteen inches in nine hours. By the time they were spotted, Barlow was dead and Jasper had gone into shock. The other guy lost four toes."

"And Artie?" she asked, when he didn't go on.

"Not a scratch. He walked away from it."

For the rest, he said, he couldn't begin to guess why Artie took the blame. Perhaps he felt guilty, lucking out. With the others laid up in bed or dead, it devolved on him to make the explanations. Artie had the status of a star at Carbon Mountain. His was the most conspicuous lapel to pin it on. Deep down, he may have had a will to fail. Perhaps he'd been waiting all along for a precipice he could topple off.

"But there must be something *else*," insisted Vivien. "A man doesn't throw his future away. That would be too perverse."

In fact, of course, there were men who did just that. She had to admit, the scene of him taking the guilt for everyone else wasn't hard to imagine at all. Sweet-tempered Artie, gentle to a fault, would go that far instinctively. Just as he always had at Steepside, taking care of the errands, the clamorous fans and broken toys.

It must have been Carl who'd intervened. His plan for an empire built on Artie's star had gone awry, and it probably made him furious. He would have put it to Artie just when Artie was too upset to object. How a man who had a past to hide never made it to the top without it all coming out. He'd be pitched to the ground before he ever closed his hand around the prize. He was already in up to his ears with the deans and the slow-witted local police. There was only one way to cut their losses. Jasper was clean, by reason of being hospitalized. They would have to play the scapegoat up and the victim down. This entailed a minor renegotiation of the future.

"If he had to kill somebody," Vivien said, "I don't see why he didn't kill Carl."

"You're forgetting something. Artie was still in love with Jasper at the time. I don't know what it was like during all those years between, but lately that love got turned around. How do you think it made him feel, coming up on ten years later? He took the heat and fucked his career—and for what? So Jasper could piss it away on drugs and street meat? What does a man like Artie think, when he wakes on the morning of April third?"

"When we first got married," Vivien said, in a most abstracted way, "it was all so strange. Artie loved him more than I did."

"I almost wish I didn't have to drag the whole thing up again. He's worked so hard to become the forgotten man."

"But I still don't buy the murder," Vivien protested—even if the story moved her more than she could say.

"Of course not," Greg assured her, as he turned to stow his papers in the box. "That's what I mean. We got two different crimes. We have to make separate arrests."

He turned to the temple proper and pulled the double bronze doors toward him. From the pocket of his bright red hunter's shirt, he took the heavy key and fitted it into the lock. The bolt shot like a .38, as if to say no one was getting in for ten more years at least.

"May the better man win," he said with heavy irony. "Or I guess I mean the right one."

There was nothing left to do now but go. They each grabbed a flap of the cardboard box and stepped out onto the hillside trail. They had so far to backtrack now, it must have crossed their minds they hadn't a moment to lose. Besides, they couldn't guess how much of the journey home would be in tandem. They might hit a fork that would split them up before they got to the foot of the mountain. They could only take it step by step. But they went without a backward glance, though they'd puffed an hour uphill to get there. It was as if they realized, both at once, that they had to get good at giving up backward looks entirely.

"What'll you do with the key?" she asked. "You have to give it back to your baby monk?"

"It's out of the dead file. Nobody's going to miss it."

He clearly didn't want to talk any more about his assignation. That was all right with her. She'd come around to his way of thinking. She wanted no advice on Carl, and she figured she owed the same hands-off to Greg as regarded Artie. They shouldn't give up their separate tracks till one of them got a confession. If the one with the weaker case should give up now without a fight, he'd end up being the other's badly armed assistant. They'd probably never get over it, whether or not they got their man. Besides, the idea of a race appealed to her—not least because she knew she'd win.

They kept their downhill remarks to a bare minimum. They praised the cloudless weather, pointed out all the early flowers, and remarked on the pungent smell of rain from the night before. They might have been two naturalists with a box of specimens between them. After a while, the college came into view below, in a sheltered valley beside an oval ice-blue lake. Built of a pinkish local brick, with its towers and courts and long arcades, it was a college right out of a movie. Without any bad ideas, or the ravening after professions. It looked the perfect place for a man without worldly airs.

No wonder Artie got to be a hero here, she thought. He was made for a cloistered world. Even given the chance he lost to the freak of fate, she doubted he ever would have made it big like Jasper. He didn't have the flair for being a regular guy. He'd kept his pride instead.

Her hiking shoes were fat with mud, her wool slacks soaked from the trailside grass. The unthawed ground sent a chill to the pit of her stomach. The sun beat down on the rest of her, roasting her good. None of it seemed to bother her. She just kept striding forward.

They tramped to the foot of the mountain in twenty minutes flat. As they made their way across the college quad, a bell was ringing for midday prayers, or perhaps it was only lunch. The monks were coming by in twos and threes. Greg flinched at first, to think someone would ask to know their business. But as he cast a colder eye over all these misfit types, he realized they didn't have the balls to approach a man and woman. There was too much eunuch introversion in the way they glanced aside. There was one, of course, who would have known instantly where they'd been and what they'd pinched, but Greg didn't see him about just now. He was probably lighting candles somewhere, strangling with remorse.

Then he became aware of the strangest thing. Though the robed and close-cropped members of the order probably banned the media from their midst, they all knew just who Vivien was. He could tell from the furtive, sidelong looks—the whispered tones with which they passed her name, like a relic from group to group. *She* was the reason no one made them stop. He felt like he was crossing enemy country on the arm of a wizard. The ground on every side was simply inviolate.

What he never could have predicted was how much he would like it. They seemed to charge the world they walked through with a vivid, low-voltage field of force. And though Vivien alone was the object of desire, Greg possessed the equivalent power, by reason of proximity. It made him feel terrific.

"I thought they were going to kneel and strew your path with palms," he observed as they passed out under the arch to Vivien's rented car.

Since she didn't answer and didn't laugh, he could only assume it happened all the time. From where she sat, he thought, everyone else must seem like zombies. He felt a proper pang of sympathy at all her isolation, but he also thought to wonder how she used the fact that people went into trances when she passed.

"I'm driving right through to New York," she said. "Are you?"

"Uh-huh."

"You could turn in your car up here," she proposed. "We could share the driving."

He watched a row of cathedral elms go by at the side of the road. If he had his choice, he'd go by train. With his forehead pressed against the window, and a three-course lunch as they skimmed among the Berkshire Hills. He scarcely remembered how it used to be—locked in at the top of the Cherokee Nile, without a breath of air. Perhaps he'd done such a turnabout that he suffered now from an opposite condition. Maybe he'd have to live outside. Pitch a tent on his terrace, or out in Griffith Park.

"As long as we split the expenses," he said.

"Sure," she allowed, turning left at the gate to the inn. "Think of all the money we'll save. Enough to buy a Rembrandt."

It was certainly cause to marvel, Vivien Cokes with a little extra cash. She laughed out loud at the thought of it. To Greg in the other seat, just then, she didn't look widowed and thirty-two at all. She was simply young and free.

"I'll leave you off at the mill," she said, "and then go up and pack. We'll meet at the lodge in half an hour."

"No, no—go right on up to your place. I'll walk back."

He supposed he took the same care she did not to get sentimental over people. The woods were something else again. He wanted one more episode, entirely to himself. So he grew quite silent as she drove the narrow lane between the trees—with the underbrush so close on either side, it scraped the car like nails across a blackboard. Half a mile later, they came out into the clearing and whooshed through the two-foot grass. She parked in a weedy patch of dirt beside her cottage. And when she turned to make another point, he was already out and gone.

He capered across the meadow as if it really were a race. He gained the trees in a matter of seconds. Then he dropped his speed to snail's pace, plunged his hands in his overall pockets, and breathed a little sigh. This place was his. And, though it was only a public path connecting up the units of a swank motel, it possessed him as if he'd cut it out of the virgin bush himself.

What did he need with *Walden*, as long as he had this?

He would probably never be here again. But now that he'd had it all to himself three times—in twilight, torrent, and midday sun—it seemed like nothing could take it away. He'd always thought he could only possess what little he kept around him, the closer the better. Now he was pretty sure it went the other way. He most nearly owned the bits of life that came in flashes and were gone. Like a length of northern forest, or a boy like Harry Dawes.

He came out of the trees and headed down the long hill toward his cabin. Less and less, he realized, was he troubled by the circuitous route the investigation took. He hadn't really begun with the thought of defying all convention. Two weeks ago, in Harry's room, when he stood robbed of the chance to fall in love, he must have longed for the straightest line to lead him to the killer. Only it turned out there was too much else to uncover along the way. If the god of vengeance wanted his sentences merciless and swift, he had picked the wrong detective to exact them.

There was no other car but his on the gravel beside his porch, so it wasn't until he got quite close that he noticed something wrong. The door was ajar. It must be the maid, he thought at first, though he knew she didn't come till late in the afternoon. Perhaps he'd left it open himself. But really, try to convince an agoraphobe that he hadn't locked up before he went out. There wasn't a neighborhood on earth folksy enough for unlocked doors.

He did a quick cut to the left and ducked behind the cabin. He hugged the rear wall and inched to the corner, peeking before he turned. Then he crept down under the window and came up slow, like a periscope.

He must have known he wouldn't get out without a second meeting. The gray-eyed monk from Carbon Mountain sat in the Windsor chair by the hearth, reading what looked like his breviary. Greg would rather have found him going through the luggage. He supposed they were meant to have the morning-after weighing of souls. The boy would doubtless tell him he wasn't really gay. He might even, given the sanctimony that presently bathed his face, plead with Greg to turn from the darkness while he yet had time.

It was the very reason Greg hadn't bothered to look at Harry twice. Twenty-five and under, men were kids. They did up their sex with guilt and self-absorption—anything not to grow up. They secretly feared there was certain death on the other side of the carnal act. They hemmed and hawed and didn't know what the fuck they wanted.

Greg was hopping mad. He didn't owe the time of day to other men's illusions. Having gone so far for Harry, thousands of miles in a single week, he'd paid his debt to nice ideals and pipe dreams, once and for all. It had taken him half his life to believe he could go get laid like anyone else. Who did this dreary think he was, obsessing about a minor brief encounter? Who *cared* if it made him sad?

If the kid had only looked up then, he would have seen Greg not two paces off, framed in the window, scowling. They might have come together and had it out, setting the record straight as to who did what to whom. Greg didn't wait to see. He dropped to a crouch and vanished out of the other's line of sight. Then he waddled along to the corner, rose to his feet, and made a break for the way he'd come, uphill and into the sun. Damn it all, he thought as he reached the trees again, it wasn't his affair.

So here he was, back in the woods already. It went to show the things one truly loved were never gone for good. Conversely, Greg couldn't think of a single thing in his cabin he couldn't happily leave behind. It amounted to half a bag of tropical clothes that made him look like a duped tourist. As for the Dodge, somebody up at the inn would sooner or later get it back to Hertz. He wasn't remotely interested just now in the trouble a man got into, ignoring the orthodox methods. Screw all that.

"But where's your stuff?" she asked in some confusion, when he loped across the field again. She was putting her own bag in the trunk.

"This is all I really need," he said, hunching the woolen shoulders of his shirt.

"Gee, and I thought *I* was a light packer. What about your car?"

"Could we just get out of here?"

Of course. She beckoned him in without another word, then backed and turned and headed out. They stopped at the inn, where they dropped their keys and paid in full. Greg owed ninety dollars for three nights running, Vivien a hundred and thirty for one. It gave him a rough idea what it cost to have birchwood logs on the fire and rain gear hung in the closet. Coming out to the car again, they flipped a coin to see who'd drive. Vivien won the toss. He made a mental note not to bet with her at cards.

She did without maps entirely, while he, who loved them all—from bus routes to folio atlas—had left his own in the Dodge. Worse still, she had no apparent route. She seemed to make do with any road that came to hand and headed south. He tried to put it out of his mind till it came around to *his* turn. At which point, he would stop at the very first service station and get all the data he needed. For now, he rested his head against the window and looked across three counties.

They ran for half an hour through a north-south valley hollowed out by a glacier, with a perfectly beveled slope on either side. He was getting a cosmic picture of the ice, as it shouldered its way between two ranges, when he caught a glimpse of coursing water beyond the roadside brush. *So that's what it is*, he thought: *The river*. The same as bore the eight men down to a fatal crossroads ten years past. How little he really understood the flow of forces. If he couldn't tell, in the valleys he traversed, an ice cut from a river cut, how did he ever expect to follow out the trails of vanished men?

"How far do you think it is?" she asked.

"New York? About four hours."

"No—Walden Pond."

He looked at her sidelong, to get some clue in the squint of her eye. She had a finger pointed at his lap—where, much to his chagrin, he found he was cradling Thoreau, flipping the pages aimlessly. He hadn't been conscious of slipping it out of his pocket. Now he was caught in the act. He laid it down between them on the seat and edged it closer to her.

"Who knows?" he answered, bored at the mere idea. But the words were scarcely out of his mouth before he was hit with an opposite whim, to show what he knew of the lay of the land. "Say an hour south and three hours east."

"Really? As close as that? It's almost worth a detour."

All this got her was half a mile of silence.

"Wouldn't you like to see it?" she asked.

"Not especially."

"You'd rather I didn't talk about it, right?"

"*I* don't care," he said wearily, wishing he had a map to see how far the road kept pace with the river.

"Yes, you do. We'll change the subject. Tell me about your movies."

"You must be thinking of someone else. *I* never did a movie."

"Well, your scripts, then."

"Oh, them," he scoffed. "Didn't you know—there's an epidemic. The girl at the dry cleaner's got three scripts. The bag boys at Ralph's spend half their money on their Xerox bill."

"Didn't you write some comedy?" she asked. "Didn't somebody option it?"

He exploded: "Why don't *you* tell *me?* I gather it's part of my file."

"Listen, honey," Vivien said, "I'm sorry you never made it. Don't let it turn you into a prick. Okay?"

Okay. He counted to ten, or thereabouts. Relieved to be rid of this whiny brand of sensitive that made him cringe when he saw it in anyone else. She'd gotten too close for comfort. Seemed to know how he got to sleep on sleepless nights: still fashioning scenes and great locations, adding fresh snippets of dialogue, though he hadn't had them out of the drawer in two and a half years. It wasn't that he was afraid of Vivien's bad opinion. She'd probably love them. Then what? Why undo his two good years of getting slowly better every day?

"Option is far too grand," he said. He kept an eye on the trees outside, to cover his line of retreat if he found his confession getting out of hand. "Guy paid me twenty-five thousand to rewrite one of my scripts. Make it funny, he says. What the hell, I was broke. I would have made it a *western*, to pull in that kind of money." And he shrugged in such a way that his shoulders stayed up till he finished speaking. "Didn't matter. By the time I was done, he had a better deal, and I got shelved. End of story."

"But don't you see," she said, who had all the deals she needed, "that's what I want to hear. Tell me the story."

She didn't see, did she? Telling his stories to people who

found them not quite right had been the very thing that made him stop. Too odd, they told him. What was he doing, changing the plot in the middle? His people went off on so many detours, they ended up in a whole new story before they were done. You either did it straight or not at all.

"*Last Wish*," he said, "by R. Greg Cannon."

"What's the R stand for?"

"Ronald," he said, "and don't you dare ever say it. These two drunks meet in a bar and get to talking. One of them's just been writing his will, and he has to have it witnessed. He's left all his money so people can have a party when he dies. They're bums, you know? It's late at night. They get some men to sign it. This one guy, Chuck, agrees to be named executor. Everyone thinks it's a big joke."

"They're gay?"

"No—why?"

"I don't know. They sound it."

"Anyway—a couple years 'go by, and the guy gets cancer and dies in the poorhouse. You don't see any of that. Turns out he's got six hundred thousand bucks in the bank. Every cent of it's earmarked for the party. Chuck's got to put it on."

"It'd never hold up in court," she said.

"Look, why don't you write your own fucking movie?" Greg retorted, lapsing into silence.

She suddenly saw that he might be telling the truth—he was glad he wasn't a writer anymore. She had lived so long with wild ambition, in the upper reaches of Steepside, she never gave much thought to the setting of modest sights. Perhaps he preferred his three-man operation. What if he wasn't a failure at all? She hadn't ever held a job herself, so could only guess what made a person work and like it. What if he'd found a job that fit him exactly right? Perhaps it never crossed his mind to guess how well he was doing.

"Now you," he said abruptly, turning the tables. "What's it like, being a star?"

"It's not like anything, really," Vivien replied evasively. She gathered she'd had as much synopsis as she was likely to get. "You want me to say I like it? I like it okay."

"Does it make you feel invulnerable?"

"Hmm," she considered, slowing to forty-five for a moment. "Not exactly. I know I'll get a good table, of course, but that's just money. You think it really gets me anywhere? I can't buy time, you know."

"Didn't you ever decide you ought to earn your keep? Why don't you run the March of Dimes?"

"I thought we'd agreed about what it is I do," she said, ignoring the dose of guilt. "I'm a star."

There was enough of an edge of irony to show she thought it an outrage—even she. Crazier, in its way, than the overpaid work of Jasper Cokes, at a million bucks a week— because in her case neither craft nor talent was required. Greg had always refused to take the broader view that Edna pushed, whereby one went with the stars the age provided, no matter who they were. He was fired, just now, with a burst of his oldest loyalty. A star, he thought, was something quite particular. It had to do with movies.

"I wouldn't be you for anything," he said.

It wasn't as if he'd been asked.

"Noble of you, I'm sure. You're right, of course—I don't do a hell of a lot. But you keep confusing me with *her*. This Vivien woman doesn't exist, except in photographs. It's a lot of bullshit, just like everything else in Hollywood."

"Some of them made some fabulous pictures."

"Unlike us good-for-nothing types. You're such a purist, aren't you? It's such a funny place for a virgin."

They'd had enough for a while. The next hour passed in silence, while they crossed the border and into the Berkshires. Here, the trees were much advanced. It wasn't the dream of green, as it was high up at Carbon Mountain, but green itself, completely grown.

When it got to be time to switch, she stopped at a roadside stand. She nosed the car in among Sunday drivers and went to root in the bins of country goods. Greg trailed along behind for a while, as she filled a market basket full of dubious homemade stuffs. Pepper relish and candied pumpkin. Jugs of maple cream. A burlap pouch full of pine needles, meant to be a sachet. This was not a down-home girl, he thought, perplexed and slightly annoyed. She didn't need to buy condiments to make her dinners vivid. The help did all of that.

He broke away and loped across Route 7, to a blank-eyed gas pump standing all alone in front of a tin-roofed shed. The dozing mechanic had given away his last free map a few years back, but he jerked his thumb toward the wall above his workbench, where he had one pinned, so old it looked pre-Revolutionary. Greg got up close and traced their route for the next two hours—south to the Mass. Pike, west to the New York Thruway. He noted the names of the towns they'd pass. Checked out the peaks and bodies of water. By the time he sauntered back, he had the territory fixed. He couldn't get tricked off course, no matter how the weather turned.

She'd meanwhile rung up forty-six dollars in crafts and folkways. They were stowing it all in a shopping bag when Greg appeared at the wooden counter. He was struck right off by the turmoil that attended her, even here. The hillbilly granny who kept the cash box was visibly shaken and couldn't make change. Her wizened sister, bagging it up, went on and on about canning. The browsing tourists were openmouthed and mute. Greg wanted to pound the counter with his fist. Did they have to act quite so much as if it were an appearance by Our Lady? What were they doing reading *People*, when they had these ripening fields and virgin hills to look out on?

"Do you always have to have souvenirs?" he asked with some contempt, as he set the bag on the back seat.

"It's just a few things for Edna," she said lightly. "After all, everyone can't have the same taste, can they?"

Oh, it was insupportable. Here was Vivien, calling him a snob for implying her rural goods were tacky. A total misrepresentation. She was the one who shrank from the crap that littered the world at large. Still, it was only the mildest sort of sniping, so far. They had so much ammunition about each other now, they could have hit every shot below the belt.

"What's with you and Edna?" Greg asked bluntly.

She'd explained how Edna had put her onto him. The Vermont address had passed between them. It wasn't clear what else. Just now, he made it sound like she'd been trying to hire away his second-in-command.

"Nothing," she said, with an air of reassurance. "I just like her. Things seem to please her. The people I meet are usually so displeased."

"She's got a hell of a temper," said Greg, not really to contradict her. "But she loves life most obscenely. Not one of your biggest fans, I might add."

"I know," she replied resignedly. Was nothing ever news to her, he wondered. "You can hardly blame her, though. I'm disapproved of so. Princess Margaret doesn't get the heat I get."

"Don't worry," he said, relenting some. "With Edna, a lot of it's just hot air. Actually, we're all very live-and-let-live."

"Oh, so are we," she said. "It's every man for himself at Steepside."

Once they got to the highway, you couldn't any longer call it country life—even with all the miles of spring in the forested hills on either side. They were clearly going back. Already, the moment of stasis out in the rain must have seemed all but irretrievable. Yet, if it made them sorry to go, they didn't say as much to one another. It would have tipped them over into the sort of excess sentiment they dreaded. Thus, they began to brood about their suspects.

Vivien already had the table set for lunch, next day at Ma Maison. All she had to do was make the reservation. She wanted to put it to Carl in public, so as to keep them out of a shouting match. She'd permit no refuge in hysterics. It happened that nowhere in all the world assured her better treatment. She was one of the trends that made it trendy. She could see herself sitting across from Carl, alone at last in the middle of things, with all the power on her side.

Greg, meanwhile, had decided not to have his confrontation by appointment. He planned to walk in unexpected. Let Artie discover him with his feet up, smoking a dollar cigar. This would be in the nature of reparations, paying Steepside back for the night they muscled him out of there. He meant to tell the tale to Artie's face, with a most deliberate slowness.

"I made us reservations," she said, when they were about an hour north of New York. He didn't bother to ask what time the flight took off, or how she knew they'd make it, because he seemed to understand she was an expert in these matters. "I forgot to ask what the movie is," she said.

"It doesn't matter. They're all shit."

"Perhaps," she said, "we could get them to show *Birth of a Nation.*"

As the city grew, they crossed a lot of bridges, slung low above iron-dark waters. The expressways, routing them through the peripheries, then on out to Kennedy, skirted mile after cratered mile of bombed-out neighborhoods. The shells of long-abandoned industries stood fast in vacant lots. Spring had gained a good deal of ground as they traveled south, but it vanished as if behind a curtain, now they were in the arteries of New York. Thoreau, she thought, would have shaken his fist at the shell-shocked war zone of city life. She and Greg, at heart two Angelenos used to greener pastures, reacted instead in a purely provincial way: *Thank God I don't live here.* One could not stay forever at Walden, of course. In the end, one had to return dead center. But really, there were limits.

"It's two weeks tomorrow," she said.

"Yeah, right," he nodded, and flexed his hands on the steering wheel. "I think Lew Archer gets it all done in one."

He meant the time it took to bring the killer in. She was referring to the stage they'd reached in being widowed. Just now, out of nowhere, she recalled how Jasper never flew till he knew the movie. He preferred to go up with one of his own, to watch the people watch it. He wanted to know what went over best, so as to give them more the next time round. Today, this struck her as somehow rather endearing.

She used to tell him he gave up far too much to the man onscreen, who was after all not real. But who was she to say? He was happier being Jasper Cokes, boyish redneck sexpot, than he ever was in street clothes. Contrary to Hollywood form, he went into raptures over his public image. And he took on a vast enthusiastic grace, like an athlete striking matches wherever he went. Shadowboxing, half the time, if that was the only game in town.

"I wonder if Harry was Jasper's type," she said.

"Did he like them young?"

"I don't know. They always seemed to me, the few I saw, like men with lousy jobs. Like they worked in a liquor store."

"I'm sure he would have found Harry too romantic."

"Talk about him," Vivien said, though here she was pretty sure he'd refuse.

"Well, he was always out collecting up experience," said Greg, so easily she wondered why she'd never asked before.

"That's the reason he probably went with Artie—he thought he could find out Jasper Cokes' story. He'd practically stop a person in the street. You'd think they'd take offense, but I guess they didn't. He was so earnest, you couldn't turn him down." He paused for a moment, to catch his breath, and felt this stupid lump across his throat, as if someone had just delivered a blow to his windpipe. He said: "It was like he was writing a book. And all of us were the evidence."

"Well, if he got *you* to talk," she said, "he must have been something. He must have been a goddam hypnotist."

"But that's the irony, you see. I was the one he didn't ask. Because of how he felt, I guess. I made him very shy. Everything I just told you—that's from Sid and Edna. Like I said, I hardly knew him. We only spent one night together."

"Really?" she said. "I thought you never touched him."

"Yes, I know," replied Greg quietly. He hoped this part didn't sound too much like a bad apology. He willed himself to leave it at that, then blurted out one thing more. "It was just that once," he said.

"Well, that's once more than me and Jasper," Vivien said.

She hardly knew what she felt anymore. Three days ago, she'd have said it was nothing at all. But ever since she left L.A., there was something there—some phantom pain that cast about for a hollow spot to root in. Grief? Remorse? She couldn't say. Perhaps she saw that, if she always fled in the face of death, she would never get the hang of hating it on sight. It fed off her indifference, somehow.

They were almost there. He parked in an empty bay at Hertz and waited outside in the chilly wind while she went in and settled her account. They'd divvy it up later on. He knew he would have to be the one to bring it up, but that was part of the clumsy bargain rich men struck with poor. The reason he didn't go in, though his poor teeth chattered like a teletype, was because he couldn't stand to watch another clerk go limp with awe. It did no good to put the blame on Vivien herself.

He wasn't sure she didn't lead them on, but then, they fell for it all on their own.

The air was thick with the shriek of jets. The sky was shot with a shade of gray that glimmered now with the risk of snow. He was suddenly full of doom and feeling all alone. He wished he could tell her that what he feared most just now was finishing up this case. Because then he would have no more excuse.

It would have to wait till they got on the plane. They couldn't talk right now. The Hertz girl drove them, three in the front, through the loop-the-loop to TWA. She chatted as if they were all just folks, but Greg could tell she was secretly crazed with fascination. He knew he was being ornery, of course. What were people supposed to do with Vivien, if they couldn't affect stunned silence and couldn't chitchat either? He acted as if there were some third path that he alone had mapped. He sat between them and looked out at the exit ramps and hangars, on across a plain of cars, and thought with an air of resignation: *What the hell, it's all the same*.

"You know what I left in my room?" he asked, very *sotto voce*, cutting the Hertz girl out.

"No, what?" she asked. As far as she could tell, he'd left the sum of his worldly goods. She'd decided, though, that it wasn't her affair to ask. At least they had the diamond and the leather-bound Thoreau. The rest was probably expendable.

"It's this perfume, made out of lilies," he said. "I picked it up on the island. It's just junk—only cost a buck and a half. I wasn't planning to *wear* it," he insisted, mocking himself with the queerness of the thought. "I got it to prove how far I went. Like Columbus, bringing a load of spices back to Spain."

"Mid-Ocean," she replied.

She meant the brand. She wasn't plotting coordinates. In

fact, she knew the very shop he must have gone to, half a mile down the St. George's road from the house. The lilies were out of her very own field.

They came in under the swooping wing of the terminal. Now he saw they were going public with a vengeance. Vivien got out first. As he followed, he planned to call to the trio of skycaps standing by. But before he could draw the breath to do it, he saw they were already zombie-eyed. They'd seen her in a flash. One now came to greet her. The second went round to the trunk, to fetch the luggage. The third picked up the phone and called ahead. It was all in all like a princess making an entrance. The skycaps even dressed the part of footmen.

Greg got very tongue-tied, feeling so left out. He brought up the rear as best he could, while she walked on ahead, flanked by bearers left and right. One had her overnighter. The other, her bag of country goods. Greg fished his pocket for a proper tip. He'd carried his own bags, unassisted, through all the terminals of his life. He would no more have hired a bearer here than he would have let another man shine his shoes. Certain things a person did himself, if only to keep two feet in the real world.

The skycaps could probably spot the type a mile away. It was doubtful they chalked up the dollar lost to higher principles. All Greg had was eighty cents in change and a crinkled five. He was heavily armed with traveler's checks and credit cards, but so what? As they reached the check-in counter and the porters wished her well, he knew he would have to lay out the fin, for want of a couple of singles.

The two men turned in a friendly way. He palmed the bill to the older one—discreetly, so he wouldn't have to watch them trade an antic look. The five, he thought, would have bought him a shot of Bristol Cream, as well as the headphones for the movie. *For Christ's sake, let it go,* he thought.

As he sidled into place beside her, he saw that Vivien—huddled in league with the airline clerk—was already plotting their transcontinental phase. She put out a hand and rested it on Greg's arm, then spoke his name for the second reservation. Greg smiled wanly at the lanky clerk. He didn't begrudge the two guys their tip. For all he knew, a five was peanuts nowadays. Jasper probably tipped in twenties.

"Yes, Mr. Cannon, here you are," said the clerk. A bit like Henry Fonda, way back when.

What was it in his voice that alerted Greg to something fishy? Some note of gravity had crept in—as if they all had better things to do. He peered over Vivien's shoulder at the code thrown up by the IBM. His boarding pass was clearly marked with an F—like he'd flunked the final in English Lit.

"Excuse me," he said. "I believe I'm flying coach."

"What? But I thought you were going out together," the clerk threw back defensively. He looked to Vivien for support.

"Greg," she said evenly, putting an arm across his shoulder like a quarterback, "I appreciate your attitude—the simple life and all. I'm sure the whole of TWA would appreciate it if they knew. But I'm not free like you are. If I travel coach, the press will pick it up. Do it my way, will you?"

"Sounds a little paranoid, if you ask me," said Greg.

Of course he knew exactly what she meant. But he'd had enough of being eyed and treated VIP. The longer he stuck around, the more he found himself preempted. People were much too nice when they got within her orbit. They seemed, like stiffly mannered kids, to keep mum unless they had something good to say. If he once agreed to fly first class, they'd stuff him like a Strasbourg goose.

"I think we better call it a draw for a while," he said.

The road had forked at last. He smiled so wide it hurt, so

eager was he to show there were no hard feelings. He didn't for a moment think she ought to change the class she flew for *him*. It wasn't a case of right and wrong. After all, he thought, the irony was no greater in their flying separate fares than it was in a hundred other things, from their household goods to their bank accounts. They'd have plenty of time to sort each other out when all of this was done. For now, they simply had to go the way they came. Not like a couple in *Vogue*.

"As long as it's not the money," she said.

"Money? What's that?" he retorted. "Didn't you know? I carry a bag of cloves and gold dust. I barter my way from place to place."

"But why do you go in steerage?"

"To keep a low profile, of course. I don't want anyone wondering who I am."

"But I thought you *liked* celebrity. Haven't you got a franchise?"

Somehow, she hadn't realized—not till now—how much of their time together had passed in private. If he'd been her lover instead, they'd have surfaced in a dozen places where cameras clicked and the walls had ears. Because that was the nature of love. And this was something else.

"We're both so cute when we're mad," he said. "We ought to do it more often."

His manner, just then, was so easy, it seemed he ought to be signing on, not off. But that was the catch, she thought. Since they weren't together to fall in love, since they had no deals in effect between them, their freedom was what they shared. They were free to break off, whenever they wished—for however long. Mid-sentence, if need be.

"I'll think of you," she said dryly, "while I'm picking at my lobster." She opened her lizard bag and drew out Emerson's old Thoreau. "This is yours," she said, as she handed it over. "I don't suppose you're insured for a thing like this."

"Not a penny," he said, as he tucked it under his arm and stepped up close to the counter. He handed the clerk his original ticket.

"Wouldn't do you a bit of good," she said. "There isn't but just this one. How could you put a price on it? It's just what it is."

This was begging the question some, since she'd dropped a little over seven thousand for it, Friday afternoon on the way to the airport. She'd started to write out the check before the dealer could say the price. But she probably would have defended the casual nature of it all. For a woman with money to burn, what difference did it make? Freely given away like this, it meant the one particular *Walden* could go back to what it ought to be. Worth what it said inside.

While the clerk put Greg through the computer, he turned and smiled serenely at her. If he hadn't măde the first move, she thought, she'd have never guessed how relieved she'd be to be left alone—just her and the public. Nobody understood, not even Greg, what care she took to give them something back. Some minimal return for all that humanness.

"I'll see you at the other end," he said, for his papers were all in order.

He sounded chipper, like they were going off to battle and mightn't make it through. He fluttered one hand in a cheery wave and sauntered off to the gate. The hunting shirt was so bright, she followed him like a cardinal, darting away in the woods.

"Who's that?" asked the clerk conspiratorially. He seemed to mean that anyone walking in with Vivien Cokes ought to be some big shot.

"That," she said, "is the last of a breed. I don't think it answers to a name."

"How come he has no luggage?"

"Oh, but he does," she said, as her face flowered open in a sudden smile. She threw down a credit card, *slap* on the counter, to bring them back to business. "With him," she said, "it's all in his head."

chapter 7

"OH, ARTIE," SHE SAID, as the Rolls swung over and pulled to the curb to let her out. "I forgot—it's Monday. You got a show tonight."

"*Two* shows," Artie answered automatically, smiling wanly in the rear-view mirror.

"You think we can have a drink after?" she asked.

She sounded as if she'd only thought of it now. Already the kid who valeted the cars had come to hold her door, so the moment couldn't last. They had to get the date down fast. Her entrance was in progress.

"Sure," he said, "why not? You'll wait up for me?"

"Of course. What time should I expect you?"

"One, one-thirty," he said, but as if to apologize for the lateness of the hour.

"Fine," she smiled.

She was out of the car so fast that he had no time to ask her why. He was amenable, of course. After all, she'd been away three days, and he hadn't dreamt of asking where. Saturday morning, when Erika called hysterical from the dock, he'd produced all the proper excuses. The fielding of other people's outrage came to him second nature. Sudden had always been Vivien's way. He'd learned to keep his remarks to a brief hello when she finally got back from the places she went. Just as he had this morning, when he came in the kitchen and found her frying bacon, like she'd been there all along. It was Artie's perfect feel for accommodation—ready to pick up where they left off—that let him drive away now and leave her be. They had an understanding.

Vivien walked across the parking lot to Ma Maison, steeling herself for the weather ahead. Here in the forecourt, the costliest cars were lined up, L.A. style, like guardian figures before a temple. The garden room of the restaurant proper was screened from the street—like a one-ring circus, under canvas. Thus, no one ever got distracted looking out a window. All the sights that needed seeing were gathered on the inside, wall to wall like a diorama.

The best place to glimpse a star was coming up the trellised alley that ran along the garden room's right side. This is where all eyes turned as Vivien entered now from the world outside. She moved with an air of strolling down a boulevard, counting cracks in the pavement. To them, she must have seemed like an ivory queen gliding over a chessboard. For one split second of perfect silence, the whole room held its breath.

It was the first time she'd been here since she was widowed. No—since she left L.A. two months ago, the day they started shooting. *Everyone's still here,* she thought. Ma's hadn't folded its tents on account of her. Its number stood unlisted. Still, between twelve-thirty and two, its quota of who was hot was the highest in the city. All the same, it seemed to heave a sigh when she walked in. The canvas walls belled out, as if a sea breeze had blown through.

She drifted up to the maître d'. He gave her the barest nod and led her in. He was trained, in fact, to effuse in roughly inverse proportion to the degree of a client's celebrity. They walked down three steps into the garden proper. Every eye was riveted. This crowd was full of pros, of course—more in the taking of lunch, perhaps, than anything. They managed to watch transfixed and keep the drone of conversation steady. Kept an eye on Vivien the way they kept one on the clock.

Though she was prone as anyone else to checking out the clientele, passing recognition on some interstellar few, today she fell back on all her prerogatives—staring into the air as if she were miles away. She noticed, though, as they came to the table, that Carl was the only one who pretended not to see her. He made a big show of reading two thick documents, one in either hand, with a look of vague dismay that meant that neither side could win.

When she got so close as to cast a shadow, he looked up startled and said: "Aha." His attendant tight-lipped smile, his bowing her into her chair, may have hid his fury from the others, all of whom were fixed on her. She saw, well enough.

"Campari-Perrier?" asked the maître d' respectfully—addressing this to Vivien as if it were her royal title. She wondered, as she nodded, if she couldn't go the whole way through a meal not saying a word out loud, counting on everyone knowing what she liked. Sometimes it made her feel caged. Today, she was glad of any power she might command.

"I wouldn't have known you were back," said Carl, opting to start in a wounded tone, "if I hadn't got the message to meet you here."

"But that's why we're here," she said, "So you'll know."

"What about when you left? Did you leave a message then? If you did, I didn't get it."

"But Carl, you *saw* me leave, remember? We had that nice little chat in the driveway. You told me not to go sailing with Erika and Felix. And I didn't."

Her drink arrived. Carl asked for another vodka-tonic, snappishly. Her coyness drove him mad, but as he'd never had any luck in stopping it before, he wasn't likely to make much progress now. Still, he ought to have known her long enough to know how best to disarm her. He did the same old thing that always got him nowhere: lost his temper.

"Where the fuck were you?" Low and ugly.

"None of your business," Vivien said, darting a look at a laughing starlet just beside them.

"You know, we almost called the cops," he said. "Wouldn't that have been peachy, two weeks after Jasper?"

"You suspected foul play, did you?" she asked in a mocking way. She could see him sitting rigid by the phone while he waited for the ransom call. But she couldn't send him up as high as she was used to. Not today. She made a lateral move instead. "Tell me," she said, "how much money do we have?"

Carl drew back offended. "I don't think anyone knows," he said, with enormous condescension. "Not exactly, anyway."

And not including him, of course. There was no question but that Carl would know to the penny—projected into the next two quarters, with allowance made for inflation. There was always chaos, with movie money. For months at a time, the cash fairly rained from the sky. It was often difficult to see, in the general melee, who got fat and who got screwed. Due to the prodigies of studio accounting, profit points were eaten into everywhere. An army of clerks and specialists endlessly rearranged the figures.

The money Jasper had made was like a treasure house, she thought, hip deep in gold. You couldn't even see beneath the surface. After a certain point, you could only imagine.

"I daresay it's more than I can spend," said Vivien dryly.

"You better not let *that* out, honey. You wouldn't want to cause a panic."

"I never had Jasper's range," she said. "He used to say that if he were me, he'd buy himself a tanker. Or was it the Plaza? Some great *thing*."

"You want to hear what the specials are?" the waiter asked rhetorically.

As far back as she could remember, her money was all in the hands of managers and brokers. Jacob Willis believed his only daughter ought to grow up careless and capricious, letting button-down types do the paperwork. Long ago, she thought—tuning out the waiter's list of butter-and-cream confections—when they all first came together, Carl had tried to make her more demanding of her money men. At the time, she told him she couldn't be bothered. Until she was twenty-five, she'd rarely had occasion to carry around the movables of power. Not cash, nor credit cards—not even a checkbook. Her credit was on a much higher level. It was always left in such a way that the world should send her a bill for everything she got.

"Cold bass, white wine," she ordered, when the waiter was done with his list.

"Steak sandwich," said Carl. "Hold the bread, okay? And another vodka-tonic."

The waiter went away wounded. He felt it as a personal failure, not to be able to get them to opt for the serious stuff. The drift at lunch was toward a side of asparagus vinaigrette, with perhaps a sliver of brie. Though they charged an arm and a leg for these, it wasn't the same as veal.

"Last night," she said, "I was up in his study, looking around. I couldn't find his yearbook."

"Oh?" he retorted, bored to tears. "Well, you can have a look at mine—or Artie's."

"I already checked in both your rooms—this morning. They're gone."

"They're around somewhere," he said. There was a warning there, but she could have sworn he didn't know what he was warning her against.

"They've closed it," she said. "Did you know that? It's overrun with monks."

"Who cares?" he snarled. "It was *always* a place that barely made ends meet. Marginal—you know? There isn't room anymore for things like that."

You either had a big deal, she thought, or else you were lost in the shuffle. There was no third route by way of Walden Pond—not in this dogged world, at least.

"He used to tell me about this secret club," she said, as she unwrapped a pat of butter for a roll she wouldn't eat.

"Who did? Jasper?"

She nodded. "I gather it met in a sort of temple, way up in the mountains. No road up except a goat path. Meadows," she said, "as far as the eye could see."

She thought she'd described it rather well. Yet Carl shook his head the whole while she was speaking—rhythmically, side to side. It only made her want to say more, since how could he deny what she knew for a fact?

"I remember, he said it was very exclusive," she persisted. "You used to meet and tell each other the story of your life."

Still he shook his head—so finally and grimly, people all around them must have seen. It *looked* like he was calling her a liar. What did he want—some password? She wished she could pull out some crumb of a clue, to show she'd been there only yesterday. Because the mountain temple was Greg's preserve, along with the snowed-in expedition, she hadn't expected to bring up Vermont at all. She didn't know why she had, in fact, except that she'd crossed swords with this man's past. It wanted connecting up, somehow.

"He never would have mentioned it," said Carl. "We're bound by oath. Just what are you after?"

Something broke. She wasn't afraid anymore.

"You," she said coldly. "I'm after you, you bastard."

The look that passed between them then was the stuff of spells and curses. For half a minute, they sat there locked in combat, wrestling eye to eye like a couple of enemy hypnotists. The waiter poured them water, lined up a vodkatonic beside the one Carl gripped in his hand, and generally put their silence down to keeping mum in front of the servants. It wasn't clear whose move it was, but at least, she thought, he knew she knew. Let *him* think of something to say.

"Well, look at this—" said a sudden voice close behind her. "The principals have ventured into camera range."

She knew it was Maxim Brearley, but she didn't turn. She almost would have cut him—knowing he would have tablehopped to his next acquaintance, scarcely missing a beat. It was Carl who wavered and looked away.

"She decided to drop back in," he announced, grinning up at Max. "We didn't have to send a posse, after all."

"Oh, she's not so hard to find," replied the director ripely. "Most days, all you have to do is pick up the papers. There she is, plain as day. Viv, darling, how come you never return my calls?"

"Nothing personal, Max," she said. "I don't return anyone's."

"Now you see what we're up against," bantered Carl in mock despair. Turning it all to a joke, though she'd meant to be quite blunt. She didn't care if she never saw Max again.

"Not so fast," he said. He rested the tips of his fingers on the back of her hand, as it lay on the table. "When can I bring up the film?"

"How about Friday?" Carl suggested, looking from one to the other brightly. A press agent, of which there were several dotted about the room, couldn't have been more cheerfully disposed.

"I'd really rather not," she said, with only the barest flicker of apology. "It's not—I'm just not ready."

"Listen, you bitch," breathed Carl in a low fury, "it doesn't matter what you'd rather do."

Max laid a hand on his shoulder, to make him yield the floor. Now he was touching both of them. She thought: *It must look like we're having a seance.*

"You have to see the rough cut, Viv," said Max with forceful calm. "It's a keg of dynamite, whether we like it or not. The media's going to be on top of it like a pack of dogs. We better decide real early how we want to pitch it."

He dropped his voice to an intimate level she didn't want any part of. Everyone sounded rehearsed, she thought. Everyone but she.

"You do understand, I hope—he's not a pretty sight. He's sad and tired and out of focus. He's got death all over his face."

"Friday," she said, "will be fine."

If only to make him stop his gallows portrait. It sounded like he might go on for several minutes. But it wasn't just delicate feelings that made her agree to it here. It struck her she might have grounds to prevent release of the picture altogether. Perhaps the untold millions she'd come into would come in handy after all. Jasper may have left enough to stop this final marketing. She'd better see it right away.

"Till then, dear Viv," said Maxim Brearley.

He glanced off over the crowd and broke into a boyish grin. He looked as if he'd been seized with a marvelous idea. But all it was was a face he knew, a couple of tables away. Suddenly, there was business to attend to. Now that he'd got what he wanted here, he was off. He made his rounds like a country parson. Frantic to get his movie out before the legend died, she thought, as he bent and kissed her rigid cheek.

"Bright guy," said Carl with a certain fondness, as the director sailed away.

"Asshole," she retorted dully.

The food arrived. Off to one side, she saw Max kiss the gloss-lipped starlet. She cut a flake of pearly fish and dabbed it in capered mayonnaise. One thing puzzled her: What made Max and Carl so chummy? Carl treated everyone like a hack, because hacks were what he worked with most. He liked his movies grainy, shabby, and amateurish, knowing they'd find an audience just like him. So why was he coming on slick with Brearley—treating a cheap-shot drone as if he were Jean Renoir? There must be something not yet settled. She wondered again how big the deal between them was.

"Did you talk to Jasper the day he died?"

"Yes," Carl volunteered, as he snipped his steak into bite-size bits. "I called him that morning. I was at the Pierre."

By which he meant there was proof of it. The call would appear on his bill, with the time noted down to the minute.

"Did he sound—ravaged?"

"He sounded pissed, as a matter of fact. It seems I woke him up."

"And what did he say?"

"Not much," he assured her in a garbled way, talking around the meat in his mouth like an agent in a deli. "We just talked business, same as always."

He gobbled up his kiddie cubes of steak, filling his cheeks like a squirrel. He wasn't about to expatiate as to Jasper's degree of dissolution. He probably figured the movie would do all that part for him. Vivien noticed that he seemed to take the greatest care to paint his own relations as financial. Nothing more. It was a little late in the game, she thought, for innocence of *that* sort.

"But Carl—what kind of business? Was he giving you a raise? Did he want a new toy?"

"I don't remember," Carl said stiffly. "I suppose we discussed the picture. What does it matter now?"

"Bullshit, honey. I happen to know—you talked about unemployment."

The silence struck like lightning. Just five seconds, maybe ten at most. It seemed like half an hour. She studied the one pale rose in the bud vase, pinning it down like a botanist, naming the sum of its parts. Then:

"You have no case, I hope you know," he said. His voice was hard and tearless, dry like the tinder hills at the end of summer. To her it was like a song. She liked him mean. It made him real. "Sure, we fought," he said. "We always did, at the end of a shoot. What the fuck does *that* prove? Listen, bitch—I got twenty cents on the dollar coming to me. Don't try to get in my way."

"But I have your ticket," she said. Though perhaps it was only another brand of cruelty, she sounded almost sorry.

He darted a hand to his inside jacket pocket, as if she'd just held out to him the billfold or the fountain pen that never left his side.

"What ticket would that be?"

"You know—April third."

He stopped. The fork fell to the plate with a clatter, like he'd just had a minor stroke on the right. As if on cue, she picked up her own fork, broke off another flake of bass, and ate it, dainty as hell. She'd had about sixty calories. All the same, she felt quite full. The silence here in this one corner was absolute as a mountaintop. At the level where they were fighting it out, the fact of other people ceased to register.

He spoke at last, a bit too loud. "It was just between him and me," he said with a jittery smile. "He wouldn't let me talk till he finished the picture. When he finally did—well, it just wouldn't wait."

She didn't say anything back, but sipped her drink in a languid way. She wasn't trying to be clever. She simply couldn't think what she ought to ask.

"You know what he was like when he was working, Viv. You ran away yourself."

He reasoned this so swiftly that he managed to graze her with a dart of guilt. The accusation hung in the air, as if there were no end to the ways they had betrayed him. *Touché*, she thought.

"By the final week of the shoot," he said, "it wasn't even Jasper. He was just some cowboy drunk, like the guy he played in the picture. The rest of the world could fuck itself."

But wait, she thought, *which was it?*

Did he fall apart in fact, or was it just a spell of method acting? There were altogether too many versions of Jasper's crack-up. Not that she'd gotten hers across. Because she had not said murder—not in so many words—he was pleading guilty now to a lesser crime. His only sin was keeping that final meeting secret. In a second, of course, she could have turned the whole thing round. All she had to do was say it. But, though the power cried to be used, she couldn't bear the intimacy of it. Now they'd arrived at the moment itself, she felt as if she'd pointed a gun and pulled the trigger—and nothing happened.

"What about Harry Dawes?" she asked, as if it were all much clearer over on Greg's side.

"What about him?"

"How did he get from nowhere all the way to Steepside?"

She could have asked the same of Jasper.

"I already told you," he said with a cold dismissive shrug, "I never met him. He must have come in later."

Really, she thought, she just didn't have the energy. She knew that if she asked for details—what went on that day and what they said—he'd give her a script that made them look like princes, him and Jasper both. Carl could always come up with a lie on a moment's notice. He had them drafted and filed away for all eventualities. Which is why he was so good at marketing, she thought. She wondered how she had ever supposed she would have the upper hand. She sipped her drink and tried to recall what she used to think the ticket proved.

She decided she must be as shallow as everyone said. It was doubtless a flaw that came of being rich. Once again, it struck her that Jasper's dying was so bound up with these other men—with Carl, with Artie, with the dozens who came and went. In the end, it came down to a duel—in the old style, where somebody won and somebody lost, and the dead were buried with honor. It wasn't her affair. Just now, she had a yearning to be out in the open air. This garden beneath the tent was muggy and close as a funeral.

She wouldn't have minded him saying it was none of her affair. Then, though she might well dash a glass of water in his face and storm away in a photogenic rage, at least she would be relieved of this awful moral posture. It didn't mean she wouldn't turn him in. The moment she reached a phone, she'd get hold of someone official—someone preferably armed. She just couldn't say it herself.

That's what cops were for.

"Would you like me to tell you how much I loved him?"

She looked up startled. He had tears in his eyes, like an ethnic father. Fountaining up out of nowhere.

"God, no," she pleaded, squirming slightly. *Jesus*, she thought, *what an asshole*.

"He was the loneliest man I ever knew."

There were limits to how far down she'd let this sink. He was starting to sound like an Irish wake. She'd always wanted to scream when Carl let loose with sentiments. They came out neatly packaged, like half a minute of advertising. Very seamy stuff.

"Look," she said, "it isn't anyone's fault—he just didn't love us back. Love wasn't one of his talents. He never pretended it was."

At that, the waiter came and whisked away their plates, as if some phase of the ritual was done. She didn't mean to say there was nothing there at all in Jasper. Love simply didn't come into it. They were rather more like a family business. Not, she thought, so very unlike the mail-order thing that Greg oversaw in his dining room—except, at Steepside, it was Jasper that they sold.

They stared at the tablecloth while the crumbs were cleared away. They both seemed vaguely sheepish. They didn't look up till the waiter asked—pessimistically, it sounded like—if they would have dessert. Of course not. Coffee, then? Well, half a cup.

They sat with nothing to say and waited. Oddly enough, they had come full circle. Neither could even count the times they'd found themselves talked out in public places. Together with Artie and Jasper, on junkets and tours or on location, they'd eaten a thousand meals, no more aware of each other than if they'd sat at a counter in a diner. Some things got to be habit. With four lives going at different speeds, they met like folks in a boardinghouse, to feed.

"It's about a treasure, is it?"

"The movie? Yeah," said Carl. "This bandit, see—he hid a whole shitload of gold."

"Well," she said, when he didn't go on, "where'd he put it?"

"Buried it in a graveyard."

"Behind a mission—right?"

"Yup."

"And Jasper finds it?"

"Yes and no," he answered coyly—and she felt a wave of *déjà vu*. For this was just what he'd said before, the night he picked her up at the house on the sound. "Just when he's digging it up," Carl said, "the cops arrive. He tries to run, and he's shot."

"Dead?"

"Dead."

"But *he's* done nothing, has he? I thought the guy died a hundred years ago."

"You're forgetting something. He had to escape from *prison*, before he could pick up the trail. He's an outlaw, just like the other guy."

Now she got the picture. She thought she'd read this script, but it must have been some other. She'd imagined Jasper astride a horse, in a Stetson and black yoked shirt. It was a western, after all. He'd made a couple a few years back, very law-and-order and Texas flat, with a shootout on the quarter hour. She'd assumed *The Broken Trail* was fashioned from the mold.

But here she came to find out Jasper Cokes did not survive. She wondered who slipped *that* in. How did they ever get Jasper to okay it? He might not always get the girl. The money would sometimes fall just out of reach. But he sure as hell never failed to walk away in the final scene. No one rode into the sunset quite like Jasper.

They'd simply have to change the ending.

"Have you seen it?" she asked. "Is it any good?"

"I've been waiting till you got back."

"Who else is going to be there?"

"You know me better than that," he said. "This is just for us—just you and me and Artie."

"I'll be bringing a friend of mine," she announced—cutting through all the sanctimony, as if it hung like vines across the path.

"Whatever you say," he replied with a starchy primness. "I give up."

By then, their cups were empty. The coffee part was so painless, in fact, they allowed themselves another half as they sent the waiter off to do his sums. The movie talk had braced them, as if it were the only ground they both could stand on.

Here they were, in the one place in all the world where film was the actual currency. After all, no *cash* changed hands at Ma Maison—except, of course, in the parking lot, where fives and tens were lavished on the valets. Vivien usually didn't get the hang of picture talk. When they used to be four at table, she tuned it out.

But she saw that the power this picture brought about was up for grabs. She had slipped right into negotiations. She was the only one Jasper could count on. It was up to her to keep his image from going out of kilter. She would not leave it to his killer to resolve.

The waiter laid the bill face down and vanished. She plucked up the square of cardboard, flipping it over like a hand of blackjack. Forty-four dollars even. Carl made no move. He was still as a deer in a gunsight, trying to blend with the background. He always let Vivien pay, from time immemorial. They'd have saved more money in the end, no doubt, if he'd kept the stub from a lunch like this and put it down on the books as business, to take out of Jasper's taxes. But he didn't think at a time like this. He flinched.

She did a vague calculation, added fifteen dollars for the tip, and signed her name like an autograph. They would send the bill to the bank or something. Then she got up without a word and turned and walked away. She would have stopped if he'd called her name. If she thought he had something else to say, she'd have stayed all afternoon. If not, she wanted out of here, pronto.

She passed between two rows of tables, making for the stairs. She had no purse or packages. For all they knew in the garden room, she could have been casting about for a near acquaintance. She probably knew a dozen people well enough to kiss. As she made her way along, each place she passed, the volume was lowered a notch or two. By the time she reached the end of the room and climbed the stairs, she could feel herself starting to hurry. She turned around to see if Carl was following, but no. He was just now crossing over to where Max stood, hand to shoulder with a rabid agent who would have sold his mother to clinch a deal.

She retraced her steps in the trellised alley and gave them a hasty exit. She came out into the forecourt, passed between a regular Rolls and a Silver Shadow, and faced the empty, sunlit street. In the rush to make the date with Artie later, she'd forgotten to tell him when to pick her up. No doubt he assumed that Carl would take her home. Since Jasper died, she was out of practice, arranging services door to door. She hadn't a penny on her. Hadn't a dime to call a cab. Whatever else it was, it was a moment fraught with bankruptcy.

She jaywalked the street through two-way traffic, hurrying out of sight. She had no particular plan, except to be all alone. She turned off Melrose up a side street. Right away, she was walking in the shade of high-frilled palms, with bungalows on either side. She knew she wouldn't be walking far on three-inch heels, but all the same, for the hell of it, she made a rough attempt to figure out the distance home.

Offhand, it had to be six or eight miles to the top of Steepside. How long would it take? Three hours? Four? What with being driven about so long, she'd never been required to be very good at distances. Besides, no one in L.A. ever walked, except perhaps the mailman. People who didn't keep up the automotive pace were by definition vagrants.

She had finished *Walden* the night before, and couldn't get it out of her mind. Thoreau traversed the mile between the pond and Concord one last time. Somehow, she'd always supposed he stayed in the woods forever. What was he doing going home? He didn't even wrestle with it. One September afternoon, he shrugged his shoulders, closed the cabin door behind him, and headed back to town. It made her want to know what a mile was all about. There was no indication he ever went back to the house on the pebbled shore. If he passed that way on the path to other fields, he never said so.

By the time she had traveled north to Santa Monica Boulevard, the heel of one of her shoes had commenced to wobble and she to sway. She could feel the bud of a blister between two toes. Clearly, she had to rethink her equipment, but first she had to call Greg. She limped a hundred yards along the storefronts, holing up at last in a phone booth on the curb. It made no sense, since the dime she didn't have to call the cab was the same as the one that eluded her here, but she had a certain faith in the force of circumstance. She pulled at the coin return—empty. She banged the side and heard the jiggle of dimes, but nothing gave.

Discreetly, she stood against the accordion door of the booth and watched the people pass. Since she knew she didn't have the guts to ask it twice, she had to be very choosy. Because she kept her eyes down and her shoulders kind of hunched, nobody took much notice of her. Even Vivien didn't get recognized unless she really felt like it.

She let dozens go by for the simple reason they were younger. She didn't consider the men at all. The women her age were only one in ten, but she needed someone close to a mirror image—who would understand instinctively how a woman might get caught without resources. She had it narrowed down to a matronly type in nurse's whites, reading a magazine as she walked, and a woman with a Vuitton purse the size of a suitcase, stopped in front of a window. Then, out of nowhere, a girl appeared from around the corner and made a beeline to Vivien's phone. She stopped a couple of feet away, as if to wait till Vivien was done, and rummaged in a ratty bag.

"You want to make a call?" asked Vivien mildly.

"Huh?" the girl replied, still fishing among her things. "No, thanks. I'm waiting for the bus."

Suddenly, Vivien noticed slatted benches and a bus-stop sign on the curb beside the booth—as if they'd just materialized. With every day that passed, it seemed, she filled in more of the city's details.

The girl straightened up, having scavenged the proper change, and smiled through a row of off-color teeth. Her red hair sprang from her head like a fright wig. Not a girl at all, of course, except she seemed so careless. Over thirty, Vivien thought—just how far, she couldn't say. As to the clothes, it looked as if the cat had dragged them in, but on her they weren't half bad. She gave off a certain blowsy cheer, like the star of a traveling show. She was someone who clearly sang for her supper.

"Excuse me," Vivien said, "I don't have any money."

They exchanged a neutral glance, perhaps half a moment long—enough so Vivien knew there was no connection made to who she was. Even so, she felt as if she had price tags all about her person, in amounts she couldn't begin to hide. Yet the girl held out her open palm without a second thought. Vivien had her choice of a quarter, a dime, and three dull nickels. She took up the dime with a little thrill of victory. She said a quick thanks and ducked inside.

Once she'd dialed the number, she turned to shut the door. They both smiled broadly a second time, but already, she thought, they'd begun the retreat to their private lives. As it rang in Greg's apartment, Vivien wondered if she would have moved to help as quickly as the redhead did. Probably not. Though she wrote her share of checks to worthy causes, she couldn't recall that she'd ever been asked for a dime. Perhaps she looked too tight.

"Sid Sheehan here," came the voice from the other end.

"Hi," she said. "It's Vivien."

"Well, well, well—speak of the devil. You lookin' to buy an autograph?"

"Me? Oh, I don't think so, Sid. I'm not a *fan* of anyone. Is Greg home?"

"Yup. Doin' a full day's work for a change. Can Edna and me come over and see your house?"

"Of course," she said. "Whenever you like."

A scuffle ensued at his end of the phone. They fought for control at the Cherokee Nile, and while they did, she watched the bus come lumbering up the boulevard, bearing down on the corner where they stood. The motley woman was frantic, as she rooted through her purse to find another dime. The bus hissed to a stop. She sat on the edge of the bench and dumped the whole thing in her lap. The bus door opened with a sucking sound. A kid with a book bag darted down the stairs and sprinted off.

Though Vivien heard Greg say hello, she couldn't speak till she saw how things resolved themselves. For an agonized moment more, the bus doors stayed wide open. The redhead picked out pennies from the litter in her lap. This round could have been won as easily as lost—except it wasn't. The door shut tight as a vacuum seal, and the bus wheeled away into traffic. By the time the woman had gathered the coins to ride, she was doomed to wait a second time. With a slump of her shoulders, she stuffed the purse with her odds and ends. Vivien could not see her face.

"Vivien, are you all right?"

"I'm all right," she assured him, as if there had been some accident that only a few survived.

"Don't pay any mind to Sid, okay? He says whatever comes into his head."

"It doesn't matter," Vivien replied.

Inside, she quivered with rage. She'd missed a dozen planes in her life, but there was always a clerk on hand to fix her up with another. She vowed somehow to reverse this thing. A person shouldn't miss connections just for doing something nice.

"We're screening Jasper's movie," she said. "Up at the house, on Friday. You'll bring them with you—all right?"

"Okay. But don't blame me if he pockets the flatware. You talk to Carl?"

"Um—yes and no."

"What does *that* mean? He try to deny it or something?"

She watched as the woman examined her nails, buffing them up on her rumpled trousers. Clearly, Greg was in fighting trim. She had no wish to interfere. Perhaps he could bring off the scene with Artie that had just evaporated in her hand. For herself, she felt a sudden longing for life on a smaller scale. She preferred to attend to matters that crossed her path—like the redhead there on the bench, who stared out now at the passing cars as if they were on TV. Vivien hoped the next bus wouldn't come till they had a chance to have a word alone.

"Mostly," she said, "we just hinted around. I'm a lousy private eye. We better call the cops."

"Bullshit," he countered. "I haven't seen *my* man yet. Fact is, I can't find him. Where the hell did he go?"

"I can tell you where he'll be tonight," she said. "The Cock Tail. Studio City. You'll have to look it up."

"When will I see you?"

"When you're done, I guess. You know what?"

"What?"

"He was only at Walden Pond two years. I always thought it was longer."

"Well," said Greg, "at least he got a book out of it."

"I always thought it was years and years," she said, not sure why it made any difference now. "He was thirty when he went back home."

"Thirty," said Greg, "was older then."

She couldn't help thinking, all the same, that if Thoreau could leave the pond, then who could stick to anything? The firmest resolve had a definite term. Perhaps she should count herself lucky to know it now, so she wouldn't get all tied up, making fruitless promises too many years ahead. She'd do better to double her bets on what was on the table now, since she had no way of knowing how much time she had. It seemed she would wake one morning and simply turn around.

"Your three minutes are up," the recording said. "Signal when through."

"Where are you, Viv?" he asked, as if public phones were a private joke. After all, she had a line in the car.

"I've gone for a walk," she replied, with a certain cool belligerence.

She hadn't, like Greg, begun to think in aphorisms, quite —or not that took the form of *Life is thus and so*. Still, she was feeling Harry Truman sensible and Kansas plain. Everyone else but she had started out in the midwest—Jasper and Greg, Artie and Carl, even Harry Dawes. Not a coast among them, east or west. But she felt, just now, more wry and unencumbered, more bound up in the earth, than any of them had ever been.

"You know," she said, "I probably have a thousand invitations, waiting up at Steepside."

"You bragging?" he asked pugnaciously. "Because if you are, you ought to see the orders on my desk. Admit it, Viv—you don't miss real life at all."

"Well, neither do you!"

All of a sudden, a whir of static blew up like a whirlwind, cutting them off. The call, of course, was terminated deep within the circuit. Nothing to do with them *per se*. And yet she wondered, hanging up, if they weren't being warned to watch it, all the same. Perhaps they had to be careful not to get overspecific. She walked out onto the sidewalk, trying to think what one did if everything didn't get put into words.

"I don't know how to thank you," she said, breaking into the woman's reverie. "Here I've made you miss your ride."

241

"Oh, I don't mind," replied the redhead, placid as could be. "It gives me time to think."

"But I wish I could pay you back."

"A *dime?*" she exclaimed. She enjoyed herself immensely —though not, it seemed, at anyone's expense. She sidled left to make room on the bench.

"I mean, I wish there was something you needed—somethink that *I* had."

She didn't press it any further, seeing as the woman needed things she had no business prying into. Cash was the tip of the iceberg, clearly. Even as she closed the gap and took a seat on the bench, Vivien kept a little distance. She flashed for a moment on the desert west, where she was born and raised. She wondered how it must have been when the women got to talking—come to a brute, relentless land where half the men were wildcatters, rustlers, and snake-oil dealers. All that open space, and not a tree-lined street in sight.

"It goes in ripples," the woman said, like she'd thought it all out long since. "I do for you—you do for someone else."

"I'll have to remember to carry an extra dime. In case somebody asks."

"Whatever," the other shrugged. "It doesn't have to be money."

She seemed accustomed to start things out in the open. Vivien usually wore a mask, but she saw they had no room to put on airs. When the redhead turned and craned her neck, one eye peeled for the bus, Vivien felt the tug of time, giving them both fair warning. Now was all they had.

She must have wondered a little why Vivien bothered to wait, lacking as she did the wherewithal to ride the bus. But neither made any special claim, asking where the other meant to go. They were strangers quite deliberately. They meant to keep it that way—with nothing in common, particularly, but the crossroads where they met. That said, they were no less ready to speak their minds.

This, thought Vivien suddenly, was the place to talk philosophy: in passing.

"The only other thing a dime'll buy you is a parking place," the woman observed. "You can't even get a candy bar."

"Nothing's worth what you pay for it," Vivien said with a sturdy nod. "Not anymore, at least."

"There's always love," the other said, as if Vivien had set her a riddle. "But that's a special case. Depends if you're in or out."

She turned and cast a second glance at the oncoming traffic, rising slightly out of her seat to get a better view.

"I guess," said Vivien, smiling now. "But once you're in, it's a little like playing craps. You can't get out till you're broke."

"What they call inflation," the redhead said, making no economic sense at all. No wonder she was poor.

"With me," said Vivien, "once I'm in, I *don't* get out."

Just then, the woman spotted her bus. She stood up straight and stepped to the curb. She turned and smiled at Vivien. There was no last thing to say, it seemed. "Goodbye" would be as superfluous as "hello" would have been to begin with. She opened her hand and looked at the coins, as if she might have lost one in the meantime.

Vivien leaned forward and said: "See, that's why I don't get *in*. I never learned how to leave."

"There's always hope," said the redhead dryly. The irony seemed to impart to the word all of its old pre-Christian hunger.

The bus came at them out of the current, riding toward the curb. The woman looked up expectantly. Her hand hung limp at her side, and the rag doll's purse sagged open. She held it so loose, she might have been taking bids for the picking of her pocket. Vivien, still on the bench, put her hands to the back of her neck. She flicked the catch on the thin gold chain. She lifted the diamond off her throat, where it hung in the folds of a Bendel's blouse. It had hardly caught the first shiver of light before she scooped it in her hand. She had no time, so she wasted none. She reached across and dropped it, chain and all, in the unzipped purse.

It demanded a conjurer's sleight-of-hand. The last sensation she had of it was the warmth of the stone against her palm. Nobody saw a thing. The whole queer moment went unnoticed, in the general commotion attending the bus's docking at the curb. The brakes shrieked murder. The doors flapped open. A line of urban types came filing out.

"It's like they say," called the redhead over her shoulder, one hand gripped on the tubular bar in the doorway. "You might as well spend what you got. It's not going to do you a bit of good when you're pushing up daisies—right?"

With that she was gone. She leapt offstage like a harlequin. Vivien waved in a dreamy way, though the other couldn't see her now, as she made her way up the aisle. The bus let out a squeal. It veered off into the stream again. Vivien sat for a moment more of sun as she watched it go, her arms outstretched on the shoulder of the bench. The street breeze fanned her face, like a whiff of Paris.

She didn't appear to have any lingering worry as to who she might be taken for. She cast a glance at the crazy-quilt of shop signs, far across the boulevard. She read them one by one like a line of print, seeming to search out something quite specific. For the moment, she had the strangest sense that no one would ever know her on sight again—but that was her way of saying she didn't care. She was no longer modeling life for the camera, as she left her bench abruptly, running to cross at the crosswalk.

The diamond didn't surprise her, really. She'd felt the moment coming, ever since she got it back. It didn't set right anymore. As if ten days' hanging off a jut of rock in the mid-Atlantic—the round of its yellow light revolving with the sun—had sent it back to something like a natural state. Perhaps she would have done better to toss it off a pier. If she'd thought about it at all, she probably would have decided she had no right to shrug it off. After all, if you cashed it in, say at Sotheby's, you could keep the poor in oranges for weeks.

Lucky for her, she wasn't thinking.

She strode along the boulevard as if she'd never run an errand on her own before. She passed a florist whose plants spilled out the door to the sidewalk. She took a deep breath of pure spring green. After that was a shop stocked to the gills with vitamins—manned by a spare and haunted clerk who exuded a Zen-like certainty. Pet shop, button shop—Vivien let it all go by, indifferent to the sum of goods. She was after one particular thing.

She'd spent the last ten years shopping on impulse, going from window to window till something struck her fancy. Today she gave up browsing. Turning into Whitworth's Sporting Goods, she felt as cocky as Abner Willis, out to trade horses in a lemon grove. She wasn't in any mood to take no for an answer.

"You must be Whitworth," she said, sauntering up to the counter. "Am I right?"

He was a very medium man, was Whitworth. Medium build and medium income. Right away, she knew he'd worked this spot for twenty years. He looked as if he could afford a bit of a caper. For the present, however, all he did was nod.

"There's something I'm trying to solve," she said, forth-rightly as she could. Behind him were shelves of shorts and jerseys, gaudy as orchids. Next to the counter, a heaping bin of basketballs. "I need hiking shoes," she explained—holding out her hands in a gesture meant to indicate the size. It seemed she wanted shoes to fit a polar bear.

"Just where are you planning to hike, exactly?"

He sounded as if the jungle began in earnest in the alley behind his store. In a word, professional.

"Oh, up there," she said. "In the hills."

She pointed behind her in such a way that she looked to be thumbing a ride.

"What surface?"

"I don't know," she replied. She tried to think what kind of surfaces there were. "You know—sidewalks. Roads."

"You want a walking shoe," he corrected, somewhat tartly. Now he had the picture.

"Whatever you say." She was already three steps ahead, and making her plans as she went. "I'm not fussy," she said.

"Well, you ought to be."

He loped to the end of the counter, to where one wall was stacked with shoes in boxes. He must have been forty-five, but he was trim as a high school track coach. Used to dealing with runners, who liked to consider the niceties of heel support and lacing. Vivien saw she was doomed to disappoint him.

Though the issue here was money, he bore such a stack of boxes toward her that she felt she owed him a proper show of respect. She let him lay out half a dozen styles, heard the pitch about uppers and lowers, and generally murmured signs of fascination. In the end, she was inclined to a watertight model, where the leather was thick as a saddle. He patted the toe approvingly, as if pleased to see how quickly she learned.

"What size?"

"Wait," she said. "We got a small problem."

Since he was as familiar with the euphemism as she, he faced the cold hard fact of money. She didn't overburden him with reasons. She left her money home, she said. She had no credit with her. He shrugged and sagged his shoulders, as if to say they'd reached an impasse. Though he saw she was a woman of means, what was a man whose accounts were in black and white supposed to do? She saw what he meant, but she forged ahead. She lifted one foot up across her knee, teetering there like a stork as she unhooked the tiny strap that held her three-inch heel.

"I do have these," she offered, holding one up like a freshly landed fish. She plunked it down so it faced the others—hardly a shoe at all, compared. "I know they aren't any use to *you*, but I thought if I left them here, you'd trust me to come and claim them."

They looked down now at two sides of a bargain. The gray suede Right Bank shoe was flimsy as a slipper in a fairy tale. Surrounding it on three sides, the heavy leather Whitworth shoes were grouped like mongrels around a cat.

"Let me get this straight—you want to pawn these shoes for a pair of ours."

"I'll pay you tomorrow," she said brightly, in the deadbeat's classic play for time.

They appraised each other nakedly. She thought perhaps she ought to swear to be back by five P.M., but she saw it wasn't her promptness that was being weighed in this decision. After all, she could have told him outright that they cost two-forty new—this in spite of their looking stitched together out of scraps. But it wasn't the money either. It came down to just one thing, she thought. Could he see she was in the middle of something? Did he know what it meant to be out of time?

"I have to go measure this distance," she said, and she sounded so vague, it seemed there must be a gold mine at the end.

"Hell, you can do that in a car," he argued. "You'd have your odometer right there with you."

"I don't really care how far it is. I want to know how long it takes."

To him, she thought, she was just another idle B.H. lady, filling up the time between expenses. Who could say? Perhaps she was only *playing* at being Thoreau. If you meant to do it for real, perhaps you had to take a double vow of poverty and strict anonymity. That's what she'd always thought, at least, till she found out that even Thoreau himself went through it like a phase. As if it had to do with intensity, rather than time.

"You'll need some socks," he said.

"What?" she asked, not sure she'd heard him right.

"You don't want to get all blistered, do you?"

She shook her head dumbly. She held out her open palm for the balled-up pair of cotton socks he passed across the counter. She slipped the pewter suede off the other foot. She sat on a bench that connected up to a set of barbells at one end. As she worked her feet into the socks, Whitworth came around the counter. When he handed over the squat and rugged shoes, one at a time, she realized she was used to being kneeled to in a shoe store.

She threaded the laces, slipped the shoes on, and stood up like a fighter. Whitworth made a twirling motion with his finger. She tramped around in a little circle, so he could check the fit. He beamed like an impresario.

"Do you know who I am?" she asked, in a bantering sort of way.

"No," he said. "Who are you?"

"Nobody special," Vivien answered, letting loose a careless laugh. She floated around in her Whitworth shoes, ready to walk to Seattle. "It's just—why are you letting me do it?"

He shrugged off the implication of largesse. "Putting it

simply," he said, "I'm a nut. If I had things my way, there wouldn't be cars out there at all."

He gestured at the boulevard, as if they stood by a woodland stream that the traffic had turned to an open sewer. He was plain as a tinker in *Heidi*.

"I look like a convert, do I?"

"Lady," he said, "you look like the sort who'd drive from here to that barrel. But you got a walker's build. You might get bit by the bug."

She didn't know quite how she'd done it. Who would have thought she'd stumble across a philosopher, just when she needed a little creative input? Though he ran this store and kept it solvent, underneath he was pure and daft and two feet off the ground.

"You grew up here, did you?"

"Corner of Fountain and Citrus," he said, not so much nodding as taking a bow.

"Stone Canyon," Vivien volunteered, tapping herself on the breastbone.

"Pretty country up there."

He little suspected how deep the canyon ran between their lives. But they shared a particular brand of paradise lost: Half the desert city was wilderness still when they were ten years old. No matter that the Willises were in the forefront of the subdividers. You couldn't pin L.A. down as anybody's fault. It was too many people and not enough time that had done the old world in. Still, she didn't risk it one step further and own up to what she was heir to. Willises might be his sore spot.

They walked to the door together, quiet and lost in thought. They seemed to want to get out in the open, carbon monoxide or not. It was the kind of day they'd grown up in, after all—the afternoon sun grown long and dusty in the hills above the boulevard.

"Good luck," said Whitworth cheerfully, leaning in his doorway. He raised a cautionary finger one last time. "Remember—pedestrian's got the right of way."

"Hey, Whitworth—thanks."

"No matter what you do," he said, "don't ask directions. You can't get *very* lost. Besides, you might turn up on the edge of a view that goes all the way to Hawaii."

They gave each other a kind of salute, with the better part of a wink thrown in, and then she started off. She stuck to the heavy traffic of the boulevard, all the way through West Hollywood. She resisted the impulse to climb uphill to Sunset. For a while at least, she wanted to walk a purely city street, so she'd have it to leave behind.

Did she still believe it was just a bookish thing she had embarked on? If so, then she should have been hearing echoes of Thoreau in the clamorous street, sounding like the murmurs of a long-forgotten dream. Yet before she had clocked her first half mile, the checklist she'd been making up—as to whether L.A. was deep as Walden Pond—had slipped her mind entirely. Walking here in the midst of a thousand daily lives, she began to understand that, for all his talk of foxes, loons, and morning fog, Thoreau did not go walking with his mind on the woods around him. Probably the reverse. The woods were there to let his mind run free.

And where the freedom took her was back to Jasper Cokes. She was so surprised to see his face rise up at the edge of consciousness that she went two blocks repeating his name, as if to reacquaint herself. She put it down to the randomness of memory, assuming he would vanish now as quickly as he came. She tried to fix on the street's pop trail of unrelated matters—the car wash next to the pillared bank, the boutiques on the brink of receivership. She hoped the course of ordinary life would break upon her, the way it had in the Valley, the night she fled from Steepside.

Odd to think she could live eight years in Hollywood and not see there were no repeat performances.

So this was grief, she thought, as she batted back the tears and picked up speed. She gave it the coldest welcome she could summon. But once it had a grip, it took everything in its path—advancing now like a wall of fire, till there was no place to turn. She resisted the darker light of the past, even as it gleamed in the road ahead. *Why go into it now?* she thought. Far better the tale that had grown up around them over the years. At least she could close it like a book. She had a right to be left in peace—for having survived him, if nothing else.

There *were* things here and there, of course—things not even Carl and Artie knew. How, maybe once a year, she and Jasper would draw an evening out till they were all alone. Splitting a snifter of B & B, they would settle down to have it out, propped on the pillows in one or the other's bed. They reeled off all their recent items, couched in the innuendo of the gossip-monger's trade. The nonsense put out about them struck them so funny, they wept with laughter. Reveling in their comic-book personae, they laughed off, petal by petal, the artificial flower of public life.

Till the one who was meant to leave would contrive to stay on a moment longer. Something clicked. They climbed in under the covers, tittering like schoolgirls. Thus did they defy the ironies that crowded them. With the lights all out, they were safe as kids in a cubbyhole. Talked and talked till they fell asleep. But they knew when enough was enough, as well. Some time before dawn, like Cupid in flight, the one whose room was across the house got up and crept away. As if morning were much too much of a risk, and breakfast a curse of fate reserved for the disillusioned.

Strange, she thought, how even grief was a thing you got used to fast. She didn't double up with pain, the way she'd always supposed she would. The effect was more like fever. These were the stinging sort of tears. They ached and burned, but they didn't blur the vision. Rather, they seemed to enhance it, like the morning after rain. Nothing got in the way of the hard-edged outside world she walked through. She took it all in as never before.

When she reached the border of Beverly Hills, she crossed through a fountained park that made it seem the weather had changed—as if this part of town were climate-controlled to seventy-two degrees. There were trees of every sort, like an arboretum. Beds of roses and creeping vines. Flowers to cut by the basketful. The blooming shrubs were on fire with color. The rocks on the lawns looked to be imported, the moss applied by hand.

She hung a right at the next corner and felt an uphill slant to the land. She was having to do more work to keep the pace—a thing she didn't know she had, till she felt she must maintain it. The houses on this street, she thought, must go as high as five or six. The old tall palms trailed up the sidewalks into the distance. The vivid gardens were ripe with April growth. Though some front yards were sculpted so as to look like holes of miniature golf, the flowers were no less bright and perfect. One had to learn to cultivate a double focus—so as not to overlook a single blossom, even as one avoided all the overblown bouquet.

She saw it was going to be hours before she got home, if she meant to start as far back as the day she and Jasper met. She trotted along the grassy line between the sidewalk and the street, for all the world like an overdressed jogger. She scanned the front of each house she passed. She could have been looking out for a place she'd left behind—say, in another life. She appraised each property, plot for plot, just as she'd been taught to at her father's knee. Figures rolled in her head like dice. She squinted like a bookie, doing up odds on his greensheet.

"You know what L.A. *really* is?" Jasper used to ask, whenever the city was eaten up by fires and quakes and mudslides. "It's Atlantis—that's what it is. You wait. Someday, we're all gonna go to the bottom."

She had a flash of him lifting a bottle of beer to toast the moment, grinning from ear to ear. It was one of Jasper's stubborn notions that people shouldn't get so worked up over owning land, when the land paid no attention. No mention ever made of his own baronial holdings. If he didn't exactly wish for calamitous times, still, he went into a state of alert whenever they came to pass. Word of a flood or brush fire sharpened his grasp of the world around him. He'd watch the night sky and keep an ear cocked, as if to wait for the aftershock. Vivien didn't pretend to understand, but she saw now just how well it suited the haunted edge he walked. After all, he had slipped away as he swore he would, to the bottom of the ocean.

The fans outside the gates had missed him more than she, those first few days. This was because she was busy coming down out of thin air. As long as there was someone else to play at it with, stardom was the perfect place to live. Safe as a bulletproof dome, it rode out fires and slides and all the shifts of the earth but fashion. An open ticket went with it, booked to the ends of the earth. But then, at a single stroke —or two or three, whatever it took to slit the wrists—she had no mirror image up there with her anymore. For days she battled the sense of having arrived from outer space. Like somebody cursed with highborn blood in a country torn apart by revolution, trying to pass unnoticed in a peasant skirt and shawl.

Still, the more she walked, the more she saw that grief was not just tears. It was more like a series of explorations, having to do with everyone else and how they all got by. She must have passed a hundred houses, looking in vain for signs of life, before she caught on to the way they were built.

Turned in on themselves like sleeping dogs and shut of the street entirely. Vivien had always thought that only the *really* rich could live in a fortified camp. Now she saw that everyone put up walls who could afford it. They locked themselves in to live as they pleased.

And the reason she knew it was this: A widow was a spy.

She crossed Sunset, but not at a corner, bringing three cars to a halt. Then she made her way into the hills, where the shadows were later still and the green grown deep as ink. A fondness for desert islands notwithstanding, she knew she wasn't the type to simply chuck it. She wasn't out to find a lonely pond to live by. What she needed to ascertain was how much of the world she walked in she could bring home. Was there some sort of quota, like at customs? The road ahead was not just clumps of roses, after all, nor anything so specific as a load of blood-red berries she could tie up in a scarf. It was everything else but the self out here, and nothing to keep it straight but the way one walked.

She had Greg to deal with too, of course. She couldn't pinpoint when it was she knew for sure, but early on, before Vermont. By some fortuitous cross of planets, she'd found another mirror image before the week was out, just when she'd begun to see she had to live without it.

She'd gone after Greg, from the start, on the hunch that he liked to breeze around as much as she. She guessed he had a secret yen to discover what else was out there. They might have turned out to be perfectly matched. More than anything else, she longed to have someone along when she took off for places unknown. She needed the sort who had a higher calling than going to frivolous cities and powder-white beaches. They would go after things off the normal route: Angkor Wat, Stonehenge, Walden. Turreted, whitewashed monasteries high on the sides of cliffs, accessible only by donkey. Painted caves. Mosques.

As if there could be no boundaries. They had more money to get them there than the world had ways to make things inaccessible.

In the end, she'd had to stop herself. She had no right to take him over. It began to seem the only way to keep them equal was apart. Without a thing like the murder spinning out between them, they'd be lost. They were too much alike, too full of opinions, to be satisfied having each other to tea. They weren't the sort who could be seen just twice a year. Better to break it clean, without any sop like Christmas cards, or the invitation now and again to parties on the lawn. If it turned out even Greg was something of a phase—bound to be gotten through, hell or high water—then it had to be said that he read like *Walden*, no less vast for the time allowed.

Out of nowhere, she came to an overgrown fork. There weren't any smartly lettered signs to label the dead-end streets at either hand. They were all full of last year's leaves and the ruck of storms. The shrubbery twisting up on every side grew twice as tall as she, so thick with growth it could have been made of stone. She'd stumbled into a cul-de-sac where three estates backed up. A narrow little warren of service roads that had fallen into disuse with the rise of the new breed of servants, who arrived by the front door.

The gardeners didn't bother tidying it up, treating it rightly as no-man's-land. The city's spiffy street machine, with its four-foot brushes and vacuum ducts, couldn't make it this far into the bush. It was the Beverly Hills equivalent of an alley. Though the amber light of the westering sun still tipped the tops of the trees with gold, it had no further say down here in the deeply shadowed lane. An evening chill had started up. A mountain breeze went riffling through and stirred little twisters among the leaves. There wasn't a human sound.

All right, she was lost.

She did not have far to go to get found. It wasn't as if the trail behind her couldn't be traced right back to the canyon road from which it split. She was only four blocks north of Sunset. But that was all beside the point. She was in a most didactic frame of mind, such that it pleased her to think she was heeding Whitworth's best advice about getting off the beaten track. She sat on an egg-shaped rock to take the measure of the place. Wrapping her arms about her knees, she sniffed the forest air. A bird she couldn't see was singing in the hedges.

She realized that if she tunneled through to the close-clipped yards on the other side, there was better than half a chance she'd know these houses instantly. It only made the moment more delicious. If the fantasy that went with fame was the thought of hiding out in the open—under the public's noses—this took it one step further. A person could still get lost in the places he knew too well.

She studied the bed of leaves about her feet—all coral, russet, here and there shredded as fine as tobacco. A half-eaten orange lay gutted a few feet off, with two bees combing it over. Close by that, someone had flattened a Coors can with his heel, as if to let her see she was not the first. She spied all this with a neutral eye—an eye gone neutral just today, from an overload of seeing. Nothing here wanted the slightest anticipation, human or otherwise.

Things simply happened. A fox-red squirrel ran out of the bushes, saw her, screeched to a halt, and turned tail. He was gone in a moment, absorbed once more by the scenery. Yet she knew more then about squirrels, just from that, than she'd managed to pick up in thirty-two years. She didn't doubt they had them by the hundreds, roaming the hills round Steepside. But who ever got right down and saw them, with all those windows looking out to China?

She knew what people were going to say. When they saw her starting over, venturing out once more to the main event of the week, they'd assume the convenient thing right off: Vivien Cokes was herself again. A little sadder about the eyes—a fraction less inclined, perhaps, to turn toward the camera. She was the only one who'd ever know there'd been any change at all.

Or to put it another way, the only change they'd look out for now was the one they would hold against her: the business of getting old. Her public image served as a kind of camouflage for all that had befallen her. Her going home would be a snap, compared to how it was for poor Thoreau. The townsmen of Concord, seeing him in their midst again, would have spread the word like lightning: The experiment had failed. They must have been lightheaded with relief, to find that a man couldn't last forever in a cabin on Walden Pond.

But the cabin on Walden Pond, she thought, could last forever in him. It was more or less what Greg had tried to tell her. Walden wasn't a place so much as a thing you carried in your head. Well, yes and no. You could look at it that way, certainly, but only once you'd done it. You couldn't get it out of a book. It had to be *gone* through, start to finish. Dead of night to midday.

She decided to wait for dark before going on any farther. She hadn't sat to rest like this in months. Could it be it was just two weeks ago—it seemed a hundred years—that she took a last swim in the waters off Bermuda, late at night? From there to here was a lifetime. After all, she hadn't planned on bumping into that old bucket on the wall. Hadn't meant to go back to the house, nor to ride away with Carl. She would only own up to it now, in the twilight hush that filled this minuscule square of wilderness, that what she planned to do that night was not come back at all.

She'd crossed the earth to the last safe place she knew, the coral sea at Harrington Sound, with the thought of swimming out to the open water. One way only. Something drew her back—she felt it—some small detail unimportant as the taste for a feast of clams.

When she found out Jasper beat her to it—*drowned*, for God's sake—she no longer had the heart. Once the story swept her up and sent her home to widow, she could not seem to recover the one still point in time She began to make these judgments, moving forward, staring at life with a kind of second sight. She assigned the world its qualities as she saw them, on the spot. There was no end to what she noticed.

The hedges were tight as a tapestry. The sky was still a certain blue, though now, as the day cooled down, grown milky as a pearl. A pair of crickets had started up, and they swept each other like radar. A palm frond lay like a plume on a nearby pile of leaves. The dusky breeze was winter dry, and it seemed so light as to hardly be able to blow the hair across her face.

One hand trailed about in the dirt beside the rock. She sifted and brought up close a couple of brackish seed pods— full of chance like a pair of dice. She bit into a seed and did not wince when it juiced out sour and slimy. She smacked her lips and tried to place it. Classed it among the fruits and nuts. Then wondered what it cured.

As if stuff like this—the merest shit in the road—could bring the dead to life again.

chapter 8

ALL THE WAY HOME from the airport, jouncing around in the back of a ruined taxi, Greg planned to spend the evening up to his eyeballs in junk. He'd had his fill of nuance for a while. Though he knew there would be a week's mail waiting in a pile, he meant to pick it over quickly, looking out for the tawdriest magazine in the bunch. He would leaf it through till a scandal caught his fancy, then prop it up on the kitchen counter and read it as he ate his way through a stack of jelly sandwiches.

By way of weightier matter, he had the semiliterate memoirs of a starlet tramp on his night stand. He'd already gotten up to World War II before he left. He would doze over that till eleven, whereupon he would flick through the late-night movies, going with the lowliest feature he could find. He sent up a silent prayer for the likes of Veronica Lake.

But, as it turned out, he only got as far as smearing currant jelly edge to edge on a slice of bread when the doorbell rang. It did no good to wait it out. He'd let them take the spare key, so they could go on working while he was away. They'd be damned if they weren't going to use it one last time. The bell was only a warning, really, rather as if a play were about to start. *The Man Who Came to Dinner*, say.

"We had a feeling you were home," said Edna Temple, swinging through the kitchen door. "Didn't I say so, Sidney?"

Sid was only a beat of the swinging door behind her. He said nothing at first, but made a beeline across the kitchen, where he put the light on under the kettle to make himself some tea.

"We didn't do shit, the last few days," he said with a measure of pride. "Mostly, we sat by the pool and got drunk. Did we get a nice tan, do you think?"

"Oh, Sid," she said, "can't you tell he's not impressed? *He's* been swimming off yachts."

He'd been gone a whole week, he realized, without once being spoken of in the third person. Or not in this particular way, while he was right there in the room.

"He'll refuse to go out on the roof with us," predicted Edna, nudging Sid. "Now that he's seen the real thing, he's never gonna be satisfied with Mickey Mouse again"

Perhaps, Greg thought as he chewed his bread and jelly, it wasn't the packaged brand of junk he needed—scandal sheets and best-seller trash. The normal run of disconnections trailing in Sid and Edna's wake was more the ticket here.

"Come on," he said, "we'll go out and eat. We'll charge it up to the company."

"But I'm not dressed," protested Edna, hugging her peachy wrapper close about her.

"We already ate four times today," said Sid, as he took a medicinal slurp of his tea.

"She caught up with you, did she?" Edna asked, getting right down to business.

Greg could sense the glimmer of something separate here, as between two women alone. He understood that Vivien Cokes wasn't his exclusive preserve, nor a secret he need keep. He should have been glad to be off the hook, but he wasn't. He was too tied up with making sure nobody got the wrong idea.

"She met me at Carbon Mountain," he said, as though it were under the chapel clock. Perhaps he was being too cautious. These two were surely the last to wonder where it was all going to lead between him and Vivien. *They* knew the way the wind blew. Yet he felt an edge of caution creeping in. "We did research," he added lamely.

"Well—who did it?" Sid asked bluntly, cutting through all the red tape.

"It's got to be one or the other," Greg replied, as he rooted through a drawer to find an opener. He had a bottle of Dr. Pepper in one hand. He wasn't remotely thirsty, but it gave him something to do. "It's either Carl or Artie," he announced.

"Well, of *course* it is," retorted Sid. They didn't need a mission halfway round the world to tell them what any dope could have figured out. "Which one?"

"Actually, we're split," he said, as if it were something admirable, like divvying up the spoils. "I say it's Artie. She says Carl."

Sid and Edna gave each other a long significant look. It showed what they thought of amateur gumshoes altogether.

"You plan to flip a coin?" asked Edna mildly.

"For now, we're just going to talk to them," he said.

"Gee, maybe you ought to give them a week's vacation," Sid remarked facetiously. "Let 'em rest up before it goes to the cops. Or will you turn 'em loose with a reprimand? Maybe you think they've suffered enough."

"Don't you see," snapped Greg, "the whole thing's closed.

Nobody cares who did it anymore. It's not like a TV show, you know. Things aren't always *wrapped* at the end."

"Excuse *me*," retorted Edna, waving a hand as if she'd burnt it. "That's a lot of bull. Somebody did it—somebody's got to pay."

He looked from one to the other, as they stood there cold and adamant. Apropos of nothing at all, he thought: There were two ways to die by violence. At the end of a long and twisted cave, the way Jasper did—or like Harry, caught in crossfire.

"What would you do? Shoot him?"

"*Sure* I'd shoot him," Edna said defiantly.

"Me too," Sid piped in. "Let's shoot 'em both. They both look crooked as hell."

Greg strode off. He batted the swing door back on its hinges. He entered the dome of the dining room like a big shot taking cover in his office. The two-voice chorus followed close at his heels, but at least it lost the feel of a backstairs plot. Besides, they were used to shouting here. They threw out fifteen half-cooked theories all at once. Nobody lowered his voice for an hour. Long before they ever teamed up, the three of them had learned to keep their contacts temporary, lest they get preempted. Now they were in cahoots, they had to renegotiate their rights from time to time.

They accused him of going astray of the main idea. Swift, they said, was the only kind of justice that could kill the rage that ate you up. When he tried to tell them the story he'd smuggled out of the temple, he kept having to stop and go back, till he lost them.

And one by one—it was almost imperceptible at first—they picked up the thread of their work. Shrilling and ranting, Greg tore through a pile of mail. He split things into first and second, forgetting to set aside gossip to chew over dinner. Edna stood shouting across from him, calling for blood. Not missing a beat, she pulled over a stack of Merle Oberon, fished in her apron pocket for a pen, and started signing. Sid, meanwhile, did a lot of footwork, back and forth to the filing cabinet.

They stayed at it till half past ten. There was no one moment when they could have sworn the argument was over, but after a while the fighting got sporadic. It didn't die out entirely. Squalls blew up out of nowhere. Accusations flew. "Who broke the stapler?" "Who's got Marilyn?" All along, they logged a little nine-to-five and got a bit ahead. The last whole hour was more or less business as usual. They processed all their intervening orders, till their tongues hung out like hounds from so much licking envelopes.

Finally, they'd worked up such an appetite they could have eaten brussels sprouts. Greg didn't even have to ask. They were mad to get out on the town. They dropped by Sid and Edna's on the way so the two of them could put on street clothes. Then they went gingerly down the steep part of Cherokee—arm in arm, with Greg in the middle. As the incline leveled off, they broke free into three different strides and sallied along the avenue to Hollywood Boulevard.

Though they had their pick of gritty, late-night ethnic fare, in the end they settled on burgers, for reasons of decor. Burger Satori had a big plate window on the street. The counter was built at the windowsill, with eight red swivel stools that faced the traffic. They sat in a row, their burgers wrapped in butcher paper, sharing a bucket of fries. They witnessed a coke sale, a coke bust, and a sudden escape—all in the space of thirty seconds. A pimp and a hooker leaned on a mailbox by the curb, working through a jealous spell. There were teen-age boys in earrings. Girls with green and yellow flashes in their hair.

"I bet she's never been *here*," said Edna, crunching ice from a paper cup of Pepsi.

"Who?" he asked, though of course he knew.

"Vivien Cokes. She's been everywhere you can think of.

Even when she was a kid—she'd been more places then than any of us'll ever see."

"So?"

"So nothing," she said. "It was just a thought."

At the window, as if he were on a screen, a man in overalls made faces at them. He gobbled a pantomime dinner like a pig, to see if he could crack them up. They glanced at him, mute and chilly, like they thought he was a bug. He hastened on dejectedly.

"Edna honey," Sid remarked, waving a string potato in the air, "we know what you're trying to say. With all that money, she's miserable—right? She never gets a chance to go out and buy a hot dog. Well, I'll tell you something—I'd still move in tomorrow."

"Oh, she's *happy* enough," replied Edna archly, following it up with a one-note snort, to think how little he understood. "As far as that goes," she added with great disdain.

"By the way," said Greg, "she sent you the bag of stuff you wanted "

"Who did?"

"She did. We stopped at this stand, by the side of the road."

"You mean the syrup? That was supposed to be *your* errand."

Greg didn't see that it made much difference. But as it seemed to get her fretful, he told her they had done it as a team. He painted it Norman Rockwell for her—filling the air with the cider smell of harvest, sweeping the floor with chips of pine. She perked up right away. She could hardly wait to get home and pore it over. As if to celebrate, she turned to the counterman and ordered up three hunks of custard pie. Sid and Greg protested that they couldn't eat another thing, but once they'd got it in front of them, they managed after all. They called for a round of Sanka, just to wash it down.

"Tomorrow we go on a diet," Edna resolved between bites.

"Tomorrow," Sid swore, "I don't give a damn what the plans are. *I'm* getting up at noon."

Greg didn't make any promises.

Next morning he rented a car—briefly wondering, as he signed, if the Dodge he left in Hamilton Falls had gone onto the computer yet as being out of bounds. For all he knew, the scanner that Avis put his papers through might trigger a squad of cops to come pouring in and goon him. Once, he thought, was quite enough.

He drove away without incident. He headed out to Steepside, not really thinking to call ahead. He had some fuzzy notion of arriving just at lunch, when he figured they'd all be gathered round the glass-top table by the pool. There he would make his formal request, grave as an old inspector, to speak to Artie privately. Then they would walk down the garden, as far as the redwood tub, to have it out. It all had a certain symmetry that appealed to his sense of things in place.

A housemaid sprang the gate and let him in without a hitch. He drove uphill and parked along the shoulder by the garages. The gardener looked him over briefly, shrugged off all the questions put in English, and left him in the living room, staring down the canyon. He couldn't believe security had grown so lax. Somehow, it made his own ordeal two weeks ago seem pointless. He would have felt more at home being grilled through a hole in the door. Then, at least, he could have presented his impeccable credentials.

He called out all their names and went from room to room. There wasn't a sign of life—except the great outdoors, which opened out at every view with its old and vast abandon. The door to Artie's room stopped him cold. He could tell—from the swirl of clothes on the bed, all drab and washed to death, the whole room overlaid with a detritus of magazines and ticket stubs—that a failure was in residence, waiting out the end. But, though he'd tracked the wolf to its lair, he didn't so much as cross the doorsill. Evidence wasn't his way—or anyway, not the sort that people hid under the mattress.

He traced his steps through the soundless house and drove home feeling cheated. For an hour and a half before Vivien called, he bossed Sid and Edna around like a brutish foreman —though without any notable success. They quickly slowed their pace to a crawl, to show him where he could put it. When Vivien finally gave him the clue to proceed, he should have been bloody relieved. But he felt a curious thrill of annoyance, having to ask directions to his suspect. He threw her a curve for sheer cussedness' sake.

"You don't miss real life at all," he told her—though who the hell was he to say? He didn't blame her a bit for hanging up.

Now it was well after dark. He drove the valley floor, reading off numbers five digits long. He probably would have found it faster, just scanning the line of the roofs against the sky, till he saw the name in lights. Yet he didn't want too much truck with neon, if he could avoid it. Neon signs were too eager to please. All the same, when he got to 44601 Ventura, he couldn't help but see the lit-up rooster, rising into the night. Perhaps because he'd heard the name as one word only when she spoke it—*cocktail*, as in liquor—he'd half expected a giant martini in profile. Instead, a ten-foot rooster twitched its ass in a one-two blink of ice-blue light.

What was Artie? The bouncer?

He went round and parked in the lot in back, which was all but empty at this hour. Then he crunched across the gravel to the door. Inside, it was standard issue—the room the size of a boxing ring, he thought, though he'd never been near one. Eight men stood at the bar, dressed down and just alike, working on Coors and cigarettes. The gauzy air was still as a third-stage health alert. A split-rail fence ran around two walls. The juke box had a country bent. In one corner was a makeshift stage, maybe two feet high, that didn't look too sturdy.

Greg sauntered up to the bar. No one turned to watch him. At this hour, he would have had to swagger.

"You got a Lite?" he asked

The barman, stripped to the waist, turned away without a nod, as if to ignore him. He was muscled like a discus thrower—so his every move played a rhythm across his flesh. He pulled open a heavy old ice-chest door in the wall and reached out a bottle. He swung around and set it on the bar. The other hand came up to grab the neck. Greg saw he carried the opener with him always, ready to flick off a cap in a flash. The Lite cap shot across the room, with a ricochet off the wall.

"I'm looking for Artie," Greg said, very low and neutral.

They locked eyes briefly and sized each other up. It was such a conventional scene, Greg could have rattled the next part off himself. "Who wants to know?" the barman would ask, to gain time. Or else he'd nod in the right direction, if Artie was at the bar—which he wasn't. Too much time went by for Greg to believe the name meant nothing.

"He's down the hall," the barman said at last. "I'd knock, if I was you."

The hall was lit by dark-red bulbs, as if it could not help but end in sin. At fifteen paces, it jogged to the right, so that even the music seemed to recede in the final lap. He put out a blood-red hand against the wall to guide him. When he came to the end, he found two doors, one on either side. GUYS on one, LADIES on the other—the stenciling blunt, the spray-paint furred around the letters.

He doubted a woman ever got this far.

He turned the knob on the men's-room door, slipped in, and saw it was empty. Claustrophobically small. The light on his digital watch was a positive beacon, here in the two-watt dim recesses. The whole place stunk so bad of old urine that he wondered if the plumbing was hooked up at all. Still, the power of suggestion being what it was, he stepped to the butt-clogged urinal, pulled out his pecker, and went.

He heard voices out in the hall—Artie and someone else. They must have come out of the ladies' room.

"Don't even think about it," said the other one. He recognized the voice, but couldn't place it. "It'll be years before you see a penny of it."

"Doesn't matter," said Artie. "I don't *want* it."

"Yes, you do. You need a place of your own. You can't live there forever."

"As long as I want," said Artie, full of a strange belligerence. "Viv said so."

"Please, I just ate," the other sniffed. "Don't you know the widow Cokes is crazy? You'd do well to get as far from her as you can."

One set of footsteps walked away. Greg shook the last few drops with a meditative air, put it back in his pants, and zipped up fast. He stepped out into the red-lit hall—and flashed to the day he walked on the set at Universal. The figure back in the shadows, under the mission clock. It was the only time he'd ever heard Maxim Brearley speak, but he had no doubt it was that same man who'd just retreated into the night. He rapped on the ladies' door.

"Don't come in," said a voice inside. "Not unless you got a J and B and soda."

Greg was at a loss. He tried to think of a clever riposte, by way of announcing himself. He failed.

"Just kidding," Artie called. "Come in—I can't stand suspense."

What Greg saw first, when he pushed the door and went on in, was a woman's face in the mirror, staring back at him. Of course it was Artie too. He knew that right away. But it almost worked. No matter that the elements, one by one—

the ash-blond fall, the sable lashes, hoops at the ears, the lips hot-pink—were frankly overblown. He knew the effect was meant for whiter lights than these, with a no-man's-land laid down between the audience and the act. He was too close in to see it right.

"My dear," said Artie, leaning into the mirror to draw the line along one eye. "You'll never guess who's walked in."

It was like he was speaking to someone just across the table—only here, it was himself.

"You're busy, huh?" said Greg apologetically.

"Oh, I don't know about that. The show doesn't start for twenty minutes yet. You got something in mind takes longer than that?"

The room was about six by twelve, with a makeup table wedged between a toilet and a sink. Not grisly like the room across the hall. Just blank and rather seedy. On the wall were blown-up photographs, of Bernhardt's *Hamlet* and the Lunts. Then a cracked and smutty poster that must have weathered a season on Shubert Alley: "Katharine Cornell and Brian Aherne in *The Barretts of Wimpole Street*," SOLD OUT THROUGH APRIL plastered across it. The Bakelite phone on the makeup stand was the twin to the one in Greg's apartment. Artie was in his underpants, with a towel at his shoulders. The bentwood hatrack just behind him was loaded with boas and sequined gowns.

"It's Jasper," Greg began.

"It always is," said Artie dryly.

"What I mean is," Greg went on—too haltingly, somehow. He came off so slow that his charge got watered down with pauses. "See—I figure it had to be you."

"*What* had to be me?"

"Killed him," Greg replied politely.

"Is that so?" said the other vaguely, lifting up the phone. "Greg dear, you'd like a J and B and soda, wouldn't you?"

"Sure."

"You're a real sport."

He dialed a single digit and ordered up two from the barman. Then he stood up, turned to the hatrack, and started to sift through his evening clothes. He kept his gestures quiet, as if to make it clear he wasn't setting up diversionary moves. Greg should go on talking—get it all out on the table, so to speak. This may have been nothing but acting. Now was the time, if it ever was.

"Well, now," Artie said, as if to get things straight, "you went to Vermont. How was it?"

"Muddy," said Greg. "The whole place smelled of rotten grass. Lots of rain."

"Hideous, isn't it? The people die the day they're born. You found some relics, did you?"

Greg, who was bundled up in a fleece-lined flight jacket, was getting woozier by the minute. He reached right away for his inside pocket—where a flyer would keep his charts. He brought out a yellowed handbill, smoothed the creases out, and dropped it on the table. "*A Midsummer Night's Dream*—Saturdays through October, no admission." In the role of Puck, the freshman whiz Balducci.

Artie heard the paper rustle among his things, unavoidable as a subpoena. He pulled out an ink-green velvet dress, slung it over one arm, and bent to the table to take a look.

"My, my," he declared, "you *are* thorough."

He stared in the mirror again, as he held the green dress up against him. He winced with sudden displeasure. He balled it up in a pettish way and heaved it in a corner. A woman, thought Greg, would not have done it quite that way. For all his flash and artifice, Artie looked just then like nothing more than a man with dirty laundry, putting his gym gear out to wash. He turned and grabbed at a jersey gown—this in a pretty salmon color, which did a lot more for the white of his skin.

"Listen, honey," he said, "I think the quickest way is for you to tell me what you know."

In other words, tell it straight through from start to finish. Greg had to bridge the last ten years with a rope as thin as a spider's web. It wasn't that he couldn't *do* it. Having told it over and over in his head, he could lay it all out in a narrative in ten minutes flat. He didn't object to the suspect's getting dressed while he was speaking, even. But he had the strangest sense that he'd dropped through a hole in time, and come up playing the writer again. As if, after all these years, he was about to pitch a plot for a feature to an agent who hated everything.

The door knocked once, and Artie called the barman in. The latter was much more raw and violent here than he seemed a few minutes back—with a string of rawhide tied around one bicep, and the Levi's riding low against his hips. He set down an improbable linen-draped tray, with the Scotch in shots and a silver-aluminum bucket of ice. It looked like the Beverly Hilton.

"Hey, Artie—this guy giving you problems?"

"It's okay, Roy. Just an old admirer."

The drinks were mixed, the soda splashed, and Roy retreated most discreetly. The moment the door was shut behind him, Artie stripped out of his T-shirt. He pulled open the center drawer in the table, lifted out a padded bra, and slipped his arms into the straps. He wasn't going to utter another word till Greg had said his piece.

With a voice gone suddenly thin, Greg sketched the other's long-ago career, with snippets out of reviews and bits of Carbon Mountain lore. Through it all, Artie betrayed no special surprise. He smiled a quarter smile as he fastened the hooks of his bra in back. Then he dropped his shorts without any fanfare, revealing a perfectly good-sized tool—but only for a moment. He shimmied right into a dance belt, tucking the extra equipment out of sight.

He turned his back and asked to be zipped, just as Greg began the account of the winter trip downriver. Greg slid the zipper a couple of feet, but his aim was off because he was talking. It caught on a curl of fabric halfway up. He bent very near to pull it loose, but found it could only be done a millimeter at a time. It was lucky he had a proper feel for close work, having stuffed a thousand envelopes and fixed a thousand stamps. In any case, it didn't stop him talking. All the while he unraveled the dress, he brought the canoe trip down to its fatal hour.

". . . then somebody says, 'Hey, I don't know about you guys—I'm gonna *walk* home.' Like he was daring everyone else to follow. Four men started off—you and Jasper, a guy named Barlow, and somebody else. Sixty miles cross-country."

"It was Jasper said it," Artie volunteered in a shaky voice.

Just then, the zipper broke free of the snag and sailed all the way to the neckline. Artie took a step forward to the table. He put out a hand to a cardboard box, brim-full of costume jewelry. He snatched up several thin gold bracelets and forced them over his wrist. Greg couldn't say, though he darted a look in the mirror to check their faces, just what Artie felt right now. The transformation from tough guy to showgirl was so far advanced, he couldn't see his way back to Artie all alone.

"Okay," said Artie, "you've made your point. Could we stop right there, do you think? I already took the heat for that. Go on to Jasper. Why did I kill him?"

The phone rang out, as if it couldn't bear to hear. Artie picked it up, throwing back the long bleached hair to put the receiver to his ear. He listened, then snapped out:

"I know what time it is. Announce me."

He hung up, slid open the bra drawer one more time, and brought out opera gloves. As he drew them on, Greg could see the fingertips were smudged.

"The show is half an hour," said Artie. "I'd prefer if you waited here. Do you mind? There's magazines. You got a little fridge in the closet, if you're hungry."

He took a last look in the mirror—cool, objective, frank— and seemed content with the whole effect. As he crossed in front of Greg, he went into a kind of glide, like a dancer.

"I'll tell you what," he said, relenting some, "I'll let you come to the late show. By then, I'll be too drunk to notice."

With that, he opened the door and hurried away along the hall—leaving Greg with the smoking pistol. The room was suddenly deadly quiet, the mirror empty of even the barest transformation. Greg sat down at the table and picked up his drink. Far away through the walls, he could hear a scattered round of applause as Artie took the stage. He had no idea what the act involved. Bawdy songs, he supposed, tied up with a string of one-liners. The give-and-take with the audience was doubtless very heavy. It was safe to say there wasn't much in the way of Shakespeare.

This, then, was the alibi that Vivien had alluded to. On the night of the third, his man was all dolled up and doing a show when Jasper Cokes was killed. Greg had imagined all these scenes. Artie picking up Harry off the street to go meet Jasper Cokes—spooning the ground-up pills in the wine— slitting their wrists to ribbons. Moments that had come to seem so actual, they had the same authority as moments Greg remembered out of life.

Now he watched his whole case slip away.

He drained the J & B, picked up the one that Artie hadn't touched, and made for the door. He only wanted a glimpse. He'd gladly wait till later for the show, but he had to see what it was like. Rounding the bend in the long red hall, he heard a noisy melody, half drowned out by catcalls. He stopped just shy of the doorway, keeping back in the shad- ows. He couldn't see round to the stage—it was off to the left—but he noticed the place had filled in the twenty minutes since he'd arrived. There must have been thirty or forty now, at the bar and just in front. It seemed they came for the show alone. From the way they hooted and grinned, it seemed they never missed a night.

The song was taped. Artie sang along like someone with the radio turned up. Though the mixer had left no room for a human voice, Artie had gone through too many summer-stock heroes, doing Lerner and Loewe in tents, to be drowned out by a lush arrangement. He had his own way with a lyric—down in the throat like Peggy Lee, every word freighted with time gone by.

> *Give a girl a chance*
> *And she'll learn to dance—-*
> *All it takes to be gay is a man.*

All full of smoke and whiskey. When he drew the last line out a second time, he quavered over it ripely till he drained it of all its sap.

Awful, really. But how could you argue with what went over? They hollered for more at the end as if it were Vegas itself up there.

"Reminds me of a cruise I went on once," said Artie, right up close to the mike. "We had a little trouble, see? This sailor, he runs up to me screaming, 'Women and children first!' So *I* say, 'Okay, honey, but I'm *second*.'"

A roar of laughter swept the room, right on the edge of the joke—like they would have laughed no matter what, or they knew the punch line all along. The voice that Artie opted for had a certain basso root to it, rather like Tallulah. Not so much female as feline. Greg leaned into the room and peeked. What he saw was a white and smoky light shining around the up-lit star. The dress glowed orange. The hair was all platinum flash.

"I'll tell you something, honey," Artie said. "You never shake the past. When you get to be *my* age, you can't go out without you meet a man who's fucked you over. This guy says, 'I know *you.* Remember? New Year's Eve at the Golden Bowl?' I mean, puh-*leeze!* The whole thing's such a blur!"

It didn't make the slightest bit of difference, not to Greg, how Artie dressed for after dark. The people of the night were always Chaplinesque. He did, however, stop to wonder where a man's profession had a right to lead him. Was it worth it to be an actor and end up here? Perhaps it wasn't so bad, given the choices. Money aside, Artie was no worse off than Jasper Cokes, with his string of cheap-shot comic strips. At least a thing like this was theater.

Besides, he thought, a man like Artie wasn't in it for the money, what with Jasper's five per cent coming in like a gusher. He probably didn't give two shits about fame, either, having served so many years as handmaid to it. He acted up a storm on the stage of a two-bit bar. It wasn't the storm in *Lear*, perhaps, but so what? In the end, it all came down to having a little work to do.

"Did you ever get lost in a blizzard?" Artie asked. "If you do, you better bring a marine along—'cause honey, it gets *cold!*"

They even laughed at that. It didn't appear to matter that it wasn't especially funny.

"I double-dated in a blizzard once," said Artie. "It's just like anything else, believe me. You always think the other two are getting more than you are."

In a monologue, thought Greg, you don't stick with anything long, or you lose them. A digression is never more than three beats, start to finish. Artie was already deep in the middle of another story—a smutty bit about a politician, caught going down on a butch little page in the Senate cloakroom. Greg didn't stay to hear the upshot. He pivoted round and felt his way to the dressing room, trying to decide if what he'd heard was as good as a signed confession. He wandered into the windowless room and stood by the hat-rack, dazed and fretful. He sat at the mirror drinking, weighing what it meant. From the other room he could hear a bellow of laughter every ten seconds, like clockwork.

The phone rang, loud enough to wake the dead. Greg started. It wasn't for him, he was pretty sure, but if it proved to be, the only one who knew he was here was Vivien. If he'd thought about it, he would have realized—she was getting to be the only one who ever called him anymore.

"Hello," he said. "Stage Door Canteen."

"Oh—it's you," she answered, a bit off balance.

"Who did you expect?"

"Greg, listen—the police are on their way."

"Here?"

"No—*here*," she said emphatically. He caught for the first time all the drained emotion in her voice. Before he knew what was going on, he knew it was out of their hands.

"They're coming for Carl?" he asked.

"That's right."

It was as if she wanted to talk but couldn't. If he didn't pull it out of her with questions, they might not get to it otherwise for hours.

"Has he called his lawyer?"

"Greg—he's dead."

And now it was he who couldn't speak. The shock was sharper here, perhaps, than what he had felt two weeks ago, though the loss was nothing to him. It had to do with hearing it person to person. The phone brought him in at the level of things that needed attending to. He thought: *Tell her you'll be right there.* Not that he wanted to, not at all, but he had no choice. In a way, it was all his fault that she was in this deep.

"I got home about eight," she said. His eyes glanced right. It was 9:36 by the digital clock on the dressing table. "I didn't expect there'd be anyone here. The servants are gone by six. But it got so quiet, I couldn't sit still. I went through the whole house, room by room. Like I had to turn on every light and check the doors and windows. Greg, I never do that. I'm not the type."

"Where is he?"

"Well, that's the funny thing," she said. "I was satisfied. Everything looked the same as ever. I started back to my room, and then—I don't know why—I decided to come up here."

When she paused again, he realized what it was: She was trying to fill up the empty space before the cops took over.

"You mean Jasper's room?"

"That's it!" she replied excitedly, as if he'd guessed a riddle. "Shot himself in the head. The gun's right here in front of me."

"Look—why don't you wait downstairs?"

"Oh, it's all right—there's no blood. He fell in the water and floated out. He's right on the edge of the falls, like he's just about to go over."

"You want me to come?"

"No, no," she said. "If I'm all alone, they'll go to a lot of trouble to make it easy. It's one of the perks, you know."

In the silence now, he saw her staring down the stream to where the rag-doll figure of the dead man poised at the lip of the stream. Beyond it, the dark bowl of the canyon. Somehow, this was the plainest talk they'd ever had.

"What about Artie? You want me to break it to him?"

"I guess so,". she said vaguely—as if, in half a minute, she'd forgotten it was Artie she had just been trying to reach. That Greg was only an accident, coming in on the line this way. "Be good about it, will you, Greg? He hated Carl like crazy, but they go back a long way."

He ended it with promises to be there later on. She protested gamely, but he overrode her. With one last bit of
advice: "Hey, Viv, don't let them take a thing except the
body. As far as you know, he died of grief."

It was only when he hung up that he realized she and
Artie might just want to be alone. After all, they were two
out of four and counting down. As he drained his second J &
B and rolled an ice cube round his mouth, he realized something harder still—he was glad it was over and glad she'd
won. He was sick of thinking in overdrive.

There was no need to let this business out. Who could it
possibly profit to have the tale told straight? The storm of
Jasper's headlines had only just died down, till a reader had
to flip through fifteen pages to get to the day's terse update.
Justice—or some more rabid force—had already done its
damnedest over Carl. The wider proclamation of the charges
laid against him had no appeal to Greg, though here he could
be overruled by Vivien and Artie. They had the prior claim.

But how would it make things better to say that Carl was
the culprit? Jasper would never again be restored to his
former larky prominence as macho man-about-town.

What about Harry Dawes? Wasn't he reason enough to
trumpet the facts abroad? If only to clear his name in Turner's Falls, Wisconsin—where in one fell swoop they'd lost
their Eagle Scout, as well as their very own Candide. Greg
had a moment of pure and unspecific sentiment, in which he
waffled back and forth. As it happened, he also had a mirror
not two feet off, in which he watched a veil of sorrow gauze
across his eyes.

As if from an aerial view, he saw the whole Midwest as a
string of towns where men had names their whole lives long
and sought to keep them clean. It was nothing but a fantasy,
of course. What did a boy from the Near North reaches of
Chicago know of the real Midwest? Yet he wondered now if
there wasn't something deep in the land that explained the

furies that blew up here. They had all come such a long, long way. By the thousands, they couldn't go home. They would not say who they used to be, and time wasn't on their side.

He was struck so sad, he gasped. The crack inside him widened. He was only moments short of sobs—when the door flew open and the star sailed in.

"You peeked—I saw you," Artie swore, flinging a white silk scarf at him. It swirled and streamed and fell in a pool on the makeup table. Greg was lightning quick. He had his mask in place in half a second. He smiled in a sleepy way, like he'd had too much to drink.

"What shall it be tonight?" asked the man in the salmon jersey, sweeping back and forth. " 'Mad About the Boy'? 'Satin Doll'?"

"I beg your pardon?"

"My *encore*, dummy!"

Greg could hear the clamor from the bar as it rose another notch. They clearly wanted more.

"How would *I* know?"

"It's settled, then—we'll do 'April in Paris.' Order me up some oysters, won't you, darling? I'm feeling a little mad tonight."

He pulled the door wide and vanished.

Greg, who was still not finished processing Vivien's call, realized he was half a step behind, the whole way through the scene. He'd become convinced that he had in hand the missing piece of the bigger picture. He was just about to set it in place, when Artie came and went like a false alarm. It was something to do with the pairing-up at Carbon Mountain long ago. He'd lost it now. He would have called Vivien back to ask, except he was pretty sure it was nothing she said.

He wondered if this new death would cancel Friday night. Could they get a body in the ground that fast? Would the mourning up at Steepside be sufficiently low-key to let the screening go on as planned? There was something here that would not fit—not till they'd connected up with Jasper once again. If they could only get to him, just to see the way he moved in the days before he died, the rest would surely fall in place.

Okay, so it was over. The last gun had been fired. Greg wasn't out to beat a dead horse, just because he'd been one-upped in the pinning down of the killer. But really, he thought, this story had no passion. So what if Carl had been cracking at the seams, from living out his life in Jasper's shadow? What had all of that to do with Jasper? For two weeks now, Greg had been digging for a concrete act that could trigger a murder ten years down the line. He figured it must be something completely specific, to leave a welt so deep on somebody else's heart.

Perhaps he fell wide of the mark because he never had a good look at Jasper Cokes. He'd avoided all his cruddy movies automatically. Never liked his look, somehow. It was just such a hard and antic manner, sleek with lust and effortless charm, that proved to Greg he was less a man himself, way back in the jungle of high school. Jasper's pitch—the sneering kiss and the one-way rush, the locker-room swagger of a tennis jock—was more than a delicate sort could bear. Greg wouldn't play ball with the enemy. He'd stick to *Laverne and Shirley* before he'd pay four-fifty to have his cock teased.

Now all of that had changed. In part, it was knowing that Jasper was gay, so the whole of his macho stance washed off like so much makeup. Among the clones and anorexics of the new breed here in Hollywood, Jasper Cokes was suddenly more than just another cipher in the toxic sky above L.A. Still, Greg had no clear picture of him. Everyone kept insisting Jasper wasn't quite himself. He was drugged, they said, till he floated two feet off the ground. He coasted from one anonymous fuck to the next. He wasn't *there*.

But if that was so, then what was the self that he left

behind to *get* that way? What did he used to be like before? Nobody ever said. Though all Greg had were the old haphazard snaps from Carbon Mountain, he thought perhaps he had a better idea than they. As with any dream too much told and retold, everyone else had ceased to see Jasper at all. They just saw what they made him into.

He picked up the phone and peered at the dial, trying to figure how to ring the bar. Before he had time to guess, there was a click. The barman came on the line.

"Yeah, what?"

"Send in a dozen oysters, will you?" he asked. His stomach followed up with a sudden roll, as if to beg for the lunch he'd missed and the dinner he'd spurned in the heat of pursuit. "On second thought, make it two."

"Listen—all we got back here is Fritos."

Greg could hear the dusky, plaintive lyric of *April in Paris* riding behind the barman's voice. What now? He was not a man given to giving orders. He avoided clerks in stores with a second sight, just when they longed to help him most. He'd never used room service ever, not once in his life. He preferred to starve.

"I don't care where you get 'em—just *get* 'em," he said. "Send someone out to a restaurant. Say you got somebody sick."

"With what?"

"The vapors."

He could hear the barman serving beers, the bottle caps bulleting off when he brought up his church key. The ricochet made it sound as if Artie were singing in a bunker somewhere, in the midst of a pitched battle.

"Never heard of it," said the barman after a pause.

"Disease of the heart. You get so dizzy you can't keep anything down but oysters and good champagne. You'll do it?"

"It'll cost you an arm and a leg. A buck apiece, I bet."

"Money's no object," Greg assured him, squinting into the mirror to see how pale the East had left him.

"Yeah, I'll do it. But only because it's for Artie, see?"

Greg thought that was the end of it. He'd have hung up first, but stayed to hear as much of the song as he could. Distorted and strangely hollow-eyed, it crackled through the line, faint as an Edison cylinder full of the voice of Caruso. The bottles went on being opened, and Greg assumed the barman was momentarily stuck, without a free hand to hang up. He didn't suppose they had anything more to say. Then:

"Listen—if you're so loaded, do me a favor. Slip him a little cash, why don't you? He doesn't have nothing. You want champagne with that?"

"Of course," said Greg, dazzled at how elaborate Artie's lies turned out to be.

"We don't got French," said the barman, "but I guarantee it's good and cold."

He made it sound like ginger ale.

The connection broke abruptly, and Greg was left to ponder the notion of having come off as stinking rich. The big tycoon who appeared by chance in the leading lady's dressing room, lighting his fat cigars with twenty-dollar bills. The irony was compounded by the fact that Artie had six million socked away. As for being taken for a long-lost love come back for old times' sake, Greg didn't mind in the least. It was his kind of story, after all.

He rose from the chair and stood back to see what they saw in him. He was just beside the rack of gowns, and he picked up the end of a tawny boa and draped it across his shoulders. It made him feel vaguely threatened. He shrugged it off, not a moment too soon. The door swung in, as if someone meant to catch him in the act. In fact, it was only Artie, back as big as life.

He dragged the wig from his head and plopped it on the table. His short and sandy hair, all plastered with sweat

against his scalp, looked more than ever like a football play-
er's. The jersey dress was soaked at the pits and belly—
though not at the tits, where the falsies absorbed the heat. He
made no further move to cross back over now, neither strip-
ping out of the dress nor diving for the cold cream. The hair,
it seemed, was quite enough concession to the real.

"You were saying?" Artie asked, without benefit of backtrack.

"What?"

"No—*why*. You were going to tell me why."

"Look, I know you didn't do it," Greg began.

"Then why did you say I did? For kicks?"

"Because"—he had no notion what he meant to say till it
tumbled out—"I don't know how you stood it, frankly."

If what he was after was a moment's pause, he suddenly
got it in spades. Artie stood still and waited to see what
further twist was coming. From the neck up, he was just
another man, with a thin veneer of makeup on—like a kid at
Halloween. Neck down, the illusion held, especially as he
stood with his hands on his hips, a shimmer of bangles at
either wrist. The moment grew. The two faced off so nakedly
they even seemed to blink as one. Greg began to understand
that Artie might prefer to come across half and half like
this—like a man at a woman's window. As if one could have
things butch and pretty both at once.

"Say on, Macduff," said Artie dryly.

Greg took a deep breath, ready as he'd ever be: "Well," he
said, "you must have felt real fucked over, right? Like somebody stole your life right out from under you."

"What life would you be referring to?"

"Why, the theater, of course."

"Oh," he exclaimed, like the light had dawned, "you mean
them!" And he pointed across the room at the Lunts.

"Well, yes."

"This is all before my time," said Artie, walking across to

stand in front of *The Barretts of Wimpole Street.* He smiled as if it were the play itself spread out in front of him—third-act curtain just gone up. "I used to hear all these stories," he said, "about how it was in the thirties. The streets were paved with gold. The lilacs bloomed all over Times Square. And everything good was a hit."

"Didn't you want a piece of that?"

"Of course," he said. "Who doesn't?"

He spoke without trace of sarcasm. Turning away from the poster, he smiled a smile that seemed to mean it didn't matter. It was all the same to him how fate was broken down. He stepped up to Greg, put a hand on his arm, and leaned over as if to tell a secret. He said: "Things haven't turned out so bad—believe me."

"What about *Hamlet?*"

"What *about Hamlet?*"

"Wouldn't you like to try it?"

"Goodness," said Artie, "aren't we grand?"

He sat sidesaddle on the bentwood chair and turned at last to the mirror. He studied his face in a purely technical way, as if to see what needed touching up for the late show at eleven.

"What *I* like to do," he said dreamily, more to himself than Greg, "is go to the market. Or the dry cleaner's. I love it when things break down, because then I can run and get them fixed. I figure, if I keep my gear shipshape, it'll last me all my life."

Greg remembered something Vivien said—that Artie did everyone's errands. It seemed, when she said it, like part of a larger put-down, as if, six million or no, he was mostly a glorified valet. His bodyguarding duties, aside from muscling through the occasional crowd, more often than not involved his going out on rainy nights to score a bottle of aspirin. It had never occurred to Greg he might enjoy it.

"Besides," said Artie, "you never know where you'll be when the snow starts falling. You gotta be ready."

They were more alike than not, these two. It was just that Greg preferred to do his errands inside, as he made a circuit of his apartment. Recalling now his endless puttering—day in, day out—he felt the most delicious pang for the way he once got by, before all of this began.

"Carl's dead," he stated quietly.

"Yes, I know," the other replied.

But of course he did. Why else was Maxim Brearley here?

The wheels had wheels, and they turned like crazy. Greg leaned a shoulder against the gowns. He knew he had reached this point by sheer deduction. Everything fit. The rightness of it all was such that he literally would have staggered if he'd had to walk away. Yet he couldn't have told you when he'd puzzled it out in a conscious way—or what were the two and two that added up to four.

"I just remembered what I came to ask."

"What's that?"

"About Max," said Greg. It was all a lie to act as if he'd known it all along. It was only now, this very minute.

"Well, what?"

"This is going to sound funny," he said, "but—how many toes does he have?"

chapter 9

ARTIE PICKED THE THREE OF THEM UP at the Cherokee Nile, at a few minutes after seven. Sid and Edna, quite beside themselves since Monday, had on the sly alerted half the tenants. Dozens leaned out the windows as they left, to try for a glimpse of the powder-blue Rolls. The effect, thought Greg, was rather like a tenement in Naples. He ought to have known Sid and Edna couldn't be trusted to be discreet.

He wedged himself between them on the seat and launched into a course of manners appropriate to a stately home. They nodded and gave their solemn word. They swore they wouldn't speak unless spoken to first. But all the while, they checked out the car—running their fingers over the wood veneers and the calfskin soft as butter. As the sun set far down Sunset, filling the air with the twilight smell of jasmine, Greg could tell he was mostly talking to himself.

"And don't ask to see the hot tub, whatever you do. In general, try to act like bored aristocrats."

"I'll be the Duchess of Windsor, shall I?" Edna asked, stretching her feet to the built-in footstool. "Sid, can you do a duke?"

"I can do a maharaja," boasted Sid, by which he seemed to mean he could do them both at once.

"No, no," insisted Greg. "Just be yourselves. What I'm trying to say is keep it down."

"Don't worry, Greg," she said. "We'll dodder around like the Ancient of Days. You can even cut up our food in little pieces if you want."

At the end of Beverly Hills, they turned off Sunset and made their way up the pass. Greg wasn't sure what made him so fastidious of Steepside, all of a sudden. It certainly wasn't for Vivien's sake, though she probably turned out dinners as finely tuned as Mozart. He knew he could talk till he turned quite blue, warning them not to act overawed, but that was a losing battle. He stood a better chance, just now at least, of turning down the volume.

They had gone about half a mile when Artie called over his shoulder to point out a half-moon rock by the side of the road—the border stone of the ancient·Willis parcel.

"He had a whole square mile at one time," Artie said.

That was all the prodding Sid and Edna needed. In a flash, they asked him twenty questions, doubling up like a pair of overeager journalists. Greg was struck dumb. They knew so much already, with their facts and figures flying, it was a wonder they had anything left to ask. Artie managed to keep up his end, but just barely. Since most of it was news to him, Greg had no choice but to sit it out and listen.

At last they left the winding boulevard and snaked their way up Willis's hill, as far as the high wire fence that trailed away across the chaparral. With hardly a break in speed, Artie snatched up his electric eye and aimed it at the gates. They parted soundlessly and let the Rolls pass through. The silence fell in the first class lounge as the newcomers took in the reaches of Steepside. Greg, for all his cautionary pose, was happy as a kid for a moment there, to feel them on either side of him grow openmouthed and still.

They reached the gravel turnaround in front of the garages. Greg hadn't said a single word to Artie yet—not so much as hello when he first got in. It was as if he meant to hide whatever bond there was between them. Silly of him, maybe, since Sid and Edna were already wise to what was going on, but in fact, he wasn't the only one who was acting so discreet. They were all quite formal, in their way. They played to type, like a carful of character actors waiting out a plot.

When they came inside, they found the canyon room lit up with firelight and candles only. Vivien seemed to be making sure that the rose of dusk in the bowl of hills would not be lost upon them. Artie left them alone and wandered off to the kitchen. Sid and Edna lost no time. They slipped out onto the narrow balcony, gripped the rail, and gawked at the view. Greg slumped down in a leather sling chair and flipped the pages of a magazine devoted to endangered species.

After a moment, he heard her voice trail in from a few rooms off, giving a final order as to the imminence of dinner. Then the noise of footsteps as she came across the slate-stone floor. He turned to beckon in his fellow musketeers—only to find they'd vanished. Had they leaned out over the rail too far?

"Uh—I don't know where they went," he said as Vivien reached him. "I probably should have brought a leash."

"Doesn't matter," she said. "Saves me having to give a tour."

"You holding up all right?"

"Oh, sure. It's over now."

She'd sent the body back to Kansas City, where Carl had a younger sister. If the sister had her doubts about the details, she apparently put them to rest for the sake of the millions she fell heir to. Money didn't talk half so much as it worked to keep things quiet.

"Max here?"

"He's downstairs setting up," she said, smiling over his shoulder.

A Ping-Pong of voices just behind him told him who was back. Vivien moved to greet them. They flushed with pride to be taken up like guests from out of town. They'd been up to the roof and had a tour of Jasper's private room. They made as if to apologize, but who would have thought they'd find it open?

Open or not, Greg almost said, they didn't have to go in. But he held his temper and left the matter of reprimand to Vivien. From the smile on her face, he knew she didn't mind where they poked about. He wandered off into the bar and poured an amber liquid just as old as he was into a hollowed-out rock of deep-cut crystal. The room was paneled blond, the bar itself a sandstone slab pocked here and there with the print of fossil shells. Above the row of bottles along the wall, twenty feet of Chinese screen accordioned out, in an ink-brown silk overrun by storks.

He'd been in this house just twice before, and then like a common sneak thief. Tonight, like the prince and the pauper, he was due to sit at the head table. For sheer drama, it was more of a movie than any movie *he'd* ever thought of writing. But he dared not moon about any of that. The bar was an empty set just now. Greg turned and beat a hasty retreat, bumping into Artie as the latter came around the corner with a tray of hot hors d'oeuvres. Greg plucked up a puff of pastry, then stepped back to let Artie pass. This moment, he thought, was clearly not an accident.

"You want a drink?" asked Greg, stepping around behind the bar and reaching for the private stock.

"No, thanks," said Artie patiently, as he took a seat on one of the stools and spun around once. "I never drink at home."

"I see. Has it started snowing yet?"

"Uh-huh."

"How much?"

"Oh, it's very hard to say," said Artie, a trifle disapprovingly. He offered the tray of canapés again, and Greg took a chicken liver wrapped in bacon. "Three, four inches maybe," Artie went on nonchalantly.

"That much, eh?"

Greg buried his face in a gulp of Scotch, less struck by the fact they were talking in code than he was to hear that "eh." He sounded like he took his cues from the cutting-room floors of the forties. It was irony made him talk that way—or perhaps it was only nerves. Why else would he walk out saying what he did? With a pat to Artie's shoulder, he said: "Carry on, old boy." Like a British officer up to his ass in restless natives.

He snatched a mushroom stuffed with crab and exited back to the canyon room.

Vivien, Sid, and Edna huddled on hassocks drawn up close to the great stone fireplace. Vivien poked the roaring logs with an iron bar. Hell, he thought as he walked across towards them, all they needed now was weenies. It was very hard to maintain his Trevor Howard steeliness in the face of so much woodsy comradeship. But he made his way down to within ten feet, which he thought was near enough to strike a balance. He stood at a long bay window and stared across the ridge. There was still no marker on Jasper's grave, and the dark was so far advanced as to blur the fall of the slope. Yet he seemed to know precisely where it was, by a kind of instinct.

"Okay," Edna said, cozying closer still to Viv, "but that's just you and the masses. What's it like to be recognized by somebody else as *big* as you?"

Oh, shit, he thought, they were at it already. Still, he made no move to get out of earshot.

"Well, like who?" asked Vivien curiously.

"Oh, I don't know—Picasso or something. You're walking down the street, and all of a sudden he pops around the corner. You've looked at each other in magazines for years. What happens?"

Vivien paused to think. The fire smacked its teeth in the silence. Greg could no longer see ten feet into the dark. And then she said: "I suppose we'd say hello."

"I *knew* it," said Edna fervently. "It's like a little private club. You get to the top, and everyone's got this secret."

"What secret is that?"

"How would *I* know? I'm not famous."

Greg recognized the Edna mode of argument, where all roads went in circles. Vivien didn't seem to mind. In fact, she sounded ready to pursue it, as if it were some breakthrough notion. Sid, meanwhile, was ominously silent. Once he and Edna were off and running, they scarcely paid attention to what each other said. When he threw in his two cents, it tended to come from out of left field—as now, for instance.

"Tell me," he said to Vivien, very confidential, "how much you figure this place is worth?"

"The house?"

"Course, I know it's not for sale. But say it was."

"Hmm," she said, as she paused to give it a quick compute.

Greg, who had not asked the price of anything private since he was twelve years old, so as not to get a caning in reply, blushed like the Northern Lights.

"Well," she said at last, "you have to remember, there's twenty-six acres. Then you've got the view. Ten or twelve million, wouldn't you say?"

"Sounds about right," Sid allowed, as if he did a fair amount of speculative buying.

And Edna again, without a break: "Who did you used to play with, way up here?"

"When I was little?"

"We *know* who you play with now."

Greg looked over his shoulder to see what she would say. He'd totally blown his cover—all that studied indifference, as he brooded on the night outside. But he felt the strangest pang of fascination. It wasn't that he thought she had much to add to what he already knew. He'd already got her early life's itinerary down. But of course she hadn't played, in the sense that Edna meant. Her childhood hours had been taken up with skis and sloops and horses. It was all part of a tradition. Zillionaire heiresses darting about the marble halls of stately homes were solo for the first twelve years. Raised on a single fairy tale—themselves.

"Nobody, really," Vivien said, as if she'd had the cue from him. "I wandered all over, all on my own." And, lest it seem too lonely, fenced on every side with swirls of raw barbed wire, she went on to talk it up as a desert island. "Oh, but I loved it," she said. "I poked around the canyon till there wasn't a rock I didn't know. I could tell you the name of every bird that lives out there. It's just—well, nobody ever asks."

I bet Sid and Edna will, he thought.

He couldn't think of a thing he'd rather hear just now than a list of all the mockingbirds and swallows. He hoped she'd go on to the wilder game—the jackrabbits, quail, and white-tail deer. But other commitments got in the way. A hand came down on his shoulder, full of a nervous comradeship. He knew it wasn't Artie. Artie never touched.

"I thought you were going to send me one of your screen-plays," Maxim Brearley said. It was the Hollywood form of offensive serve, whereby you accused your opponent of minor lapses right away, to get the guilt in motion.

"All my stuff is two years old," Greg said, as he turned to greet the director. "There's nothing that would interest you."

"Well, if you change your mind," he retorted moistly, "don't forget who asked first."

He grinned to show he meant it, rather like a man with a suitcase full of Bibles. Greg could hear the trumped-up energy in the most offhand proposal. This was the sort of deal that was never meant to go through. Still, it was thrown out on the table all the same, since you never knew what might catch a fish. Besides, a man like Max had nothing else to say. If there wasn't a movie in it, what was the point in being here?

"The film's all set to go, is it?" Greg said, making talk.

"Oh, yes," said the other somberly, as he looked off into the night. "Show time, nine P.M. I don't think you and your friends appreciate just how lucky you are."

"Really?"

"We got *studio* people haven't seen it yet. If I had it my way, Viv and I would screen it by ourselves. Not even Carl and Artie. But what the hell," he shrugged, "she said you guys had to be here."

"We'll try real hard to be worthy."

"You always got a chip on your shoulder?"

"Me?" Greg wondered aloud. "I hadn't really looked."

"Nothing people hate, you know, like a failure with opinions."

"Actually," Greg went on, "it's not a chip." And he pointed at his shoulder like he had something funny perched there. "It's gotten a good deal bigger lately. It's almost half a cord."

And he walked away like a man who had no further time for small talk. It had taken him ten long years to come to a place like this—where he had the clout to cut a bigwig dead in his tracks, just for the hell of it. A bit like pissing on someone's shoes. Yet now the moment was finally his, he found he didn't care. Max was nothing to him at all. He'd practically forgotten what they'd all been summoned here for. To decide if *The Broken Trail* should be released? Well, who the fuck cared? As he crossed to the bar for another round, he didn't give a good goddam if the last big deal of Jasper Cokes hit big. Himself, he didn't expect to see but the first few minutes of it.

He had another engagement, shortly after nine.

The bell for dinner rang loud and clear, dark as the stroke of a final countdown. They gathered in Abner Willis's flawless Sheraton dining room, six at a table that could have sat twenty. Vivien had ordered up a full-course 18th-century service—china from China, the Bateman silver, and Abigail Adams's goblets, thin as a linnet's wing. She hadn't bothered doing up a seating plan, however. It was no use hoping she could fix them up with proper dinner partners. She let them gravitate where inclination led them. So Max ended up at the head, with Sid and Edna on either side. Vivien and Greg sat midway down, across from each other, and Artie brought up the foot.

Two men in tight black tie weaved in and out, serving without a sound. She'd kept the menu high and saucy, each thing more elaborate than the last, to keep them all as busy as she could. But even with the knotty task of lobster tails to crack, the dolloping-on of mayonnaise, Sid and Edna between them managed to keep up a barrage of questions. Max didn't stand a chance. He was used to the kind of coddling that begged him for opinions on the fine points of his art. Therefore, what the hell was this? With all that white-hot power, he found himself fielding questions as to what it was like to direct a *dog*. Or what did he do when it rained? Who was his favorite star?

Vivien let him stew in it. She'd been struck by the unmistakable sense—his calling three times a day was something of a clue—that Max was out to confide in her. Over and over, he maundered that he'd come to a fork in his breathless career. She let him go on, attending with half an ear, for the sake of seeing the film tonight. She guessed he was getting pressure from the studio to shelve it, on the theory that a darksome quest—especially one which starred a corpse—would prove too much of a down in a culture hooked on uppers. Max was out to move her, preferably to tears. He needed her on his side. So he kept on telling her what a tragic grandeur lit those jaded eyes. As if, this time around and quite by chance, he and Jasper had stumbled into art.

But the longer she thought about it, the more she became convinced they put poor Jasper through it in a trance. They squeezed out another ounce of product even as the vein paid out. Once she'd seen it, she would talk it over with Artie and Greg, till they came to some sort of consensus. Unfortunately, as far as late developments in *that* quarter went, she was spinning in air like a fifth wheel. Between Carl's being zipped in a body bag and the next day's flood of mortal details, Greg and Artie had somehow got it on. That is, she couldn't prove it, but —they *must* have.

In the last three days, it had been one clandestine meeting after another. Endless late-night calls that Artie picked up on the first ring. Greg's rented car was a semipermanent fixture in the driveway. Between Tuesday and today, he must have spent as much time here as he did at the Cherokee Nile.

Of course, it was always nice to watch one's dearest friends make contact. She had no doubt the two of them were good for one another. She just wished they'd tell her. It wasn't as if they'd neglected her, even. Greg called two or three times about the screening—with a running account of Sid and Edna's getting ready, as if for a season at Deauville. Artie went out of his way all week to clear out Carl's effects. She liked to think she wasn't the type to feel jealous. Still, she was alone at last—there was no denying that. She was the only widow left.

"It says in the paper," Greg remarked, in a stiff and din-nerish way, "you're about to go around the world."

She started. Stared at an untouched veal bird on her plate. She looked up puzzled, saying nothing. What the hell was he talking about?

"Three months on the *QE2*, I think it said. When do you sail, exactly?"

"Lies," she retorted dryly, as she watched him knit at the veal with fork and knife. "The Cunard people plant that rumor every spring. They think it sells tickets."

"Probably does. They ought to give you a freebie."

"I've already *seen* the world, thank you," she said.

She couldn't even catch his eye to make it funny. Now why did it have to be so awkward? Did they think she disapproved? She knew, the same as anyone else—a good fuck was the only way to shake the life back into you.

"*I* wouldn't go if you paid me," Artie observed laconically. He cut his roll crosswise, opening it up like an English muffin. He looked around for the marmalade. "It's much too long to be gone, for one thing. How would you ever get back to normal afterwards?"

"I think it's mostly for people with fatal diseases," Vivien said. "They're out to have a last look at things."

"The reason I wouldn't go," said Greg, "is, I don't like the idea of seeing everything once. I mean—you're in Bora Bora for twenty minutes. You come to this beautiful temple. The jungle's almost buried it. There's all these monkeys screeching in your ear. You think: 'Well, there it is. I'll never see it again.'"

"But that's what you have a camera for," she insisted, squinting down the table at the others.

"Well, I'd just as soon stay home," Greg said with some belligerence, rather as if she'd tried to ship him out.

She was damned if she'd go on this way, forcing a lot of chitchat, only to have it thrown back in her face. If they wanted to keep it all private, that was fine with her, but she was bailing out. She took up her glass and swallowed a gulp of wine. She stood with a murmured pardon and made her way to the raucous upper reaches of the table—where Sid, not one to waste good food, was spearing one by one the braised white grapes off Max's plate. Edna must have had her fill, for she sat back contentedly. She folded and fluffed her napkin, glad to take a breather. Max looked as if he'd given up eating for Lent—or as if he planned to stop by Chasen's later on.

"You giving them all the inside dope?" she asked him, standing firm at Edna's side.

"It was a bit more general, actually," the director said with a straight-edged smile.

"We ought to make *us* a movie, Sid," said Edna. "We'll call it *Close Quarters*—a story of modern love among the elderly."

"Not me," Sid shot back, fork suspended in the air. "My life's more of a western."

"Oh yeah? Well, who am I, then—Tonto?"

Vivien had to cut the visit short, as the endive salad was being brought on. Reluctantly, she resumed her place between the sudden lovers. Sid and Edna sparred at the other end like Fibber McGee and Molly. Otherwise, silence reigned.

As she looked around the table, Vivien saw them all for what they were—a room full of realists. Widowed or not, she thought, they knew they were all alone. So what if Greg and Artie had a momentary liaison in progress? That wouldn't last three weeks. Sid and Edna, after all, had gone so far as to live as partners, half and half, and yet one felt an air of separate bedrooms even there.

They were six of a kind, this makeshift party. None believed that things were made to last. They probably couldn't produce a sustaining illusion among them. And yet, she thought with dizzy irony, they still looked forward to sitting in ones and twos in a drafty theater. They kept their faith in movies.

All she really wanted, she thought, was a house on Walden Pond.

It was time to start. She promised them tart and coffee after and stood to lead the way. They rose as one, worn out with all these dinner-table notions. They followed her, lost in thought. One would have supposed the walking might revive them, but the lines of communication had all gone underground. Nothing could break the silence now but *The Broken Trail* itself.

As she swept across the canyon room and down the spiral stair, Vivien, up at the head of the line, felt like the others were ranked in single file behind her, rather like an expedition. Down on the lower floor, the corridor arced in a constant curve to the left, so it tended to straggle them out in a line, as if they were queuing up. Something to do with the curvature threw off their sense of level ground. They seemed —this band of loners, met by chance—to be winding deeper down, and deeper into the hill. By the time they got to the end, where a double door opened in, they must have thought the screening room was buried under a mountain.

But here the house had tricked them. As they crowded in, they found that one whole wall was a sheet of glass. They looked out, as if from a hovering airship, down the starlit canyon. They made their way to the triple ring of seats, while Maxim Brearley fumbled for the light. There was just enough nightshine to see by. They sat down as if to witness a dream. When he snapped the switch and lit them up, they squinted like sleepers shaken. The planetarium vanished.

In its place was the pebbled, snow-white screen—looming now at the end of the room like a window on some purely abstract region, polar as the limits of a sphere. Max went off to the minuscule projection booth. The room was walled with Mayan-figured blocks, plushly appointed in leather chairs that accommodated an audience of twenty. Sid and Edna sat side by side. Greg and Artie sat apart, with a row between them. Perhaps because she stood so undecided, just within the door, Greg beckoned Vivien over to sit by him. She went because she had no better offers.

"Tell me how it used to be," he whispered when she settled in. "Did you used to show movies every night?"

"We never came down here, really," she said. "Not when I was a kid. I hardly knew we had a screening room, till after I was married."

"See? They always meant for you to hook up with a movie star. This room's part of the dowry."

"Jesus, you've gotten weird," she said.

"Listen," he continued, without a shift of gears. "The minute the picture starts, you walk out with me."

"What?"

"He'll probably try to stop you," Greg went on, in a toneless way. "Just keep moving—don't look back."

"What?" she asked, a bit louder now. She was still a couple of steps behind. But he would not stop to repeat—would not accept that she hadn't heard. She had the impression he didn't have time.

"Just hold my hand," he instructed her matter-of-factly. "I'll tell you when."

She stared at him hard, like he'd just gone mad, but he chose that particular moment to duck, bending double to tie his shoe. So she craned around to Artie, just behind and to the left. He looked right through her, like she wasn't there. Sid and Edna, just beyond, were tight-lipped as village locals, eyes on the blank white screen. They were all in the grip of a common spell, and wholly self-contained.

Vivien saw it all in a flash: They were meant to act as a team. They had to avoid all contact till the moment was at hand. She understood that she mustn't try to catch anyone's eye, lest she appear to be in collusion. She faced around again to get her bearings. She looked at the screen herself, the better to clear her mind. In the past, she'd have given

some thought as to whether she'd left her senses. Not anymore. It came down to just one thing: They'd let her in at
last.

You had to know when to act alone and when it did no
good. She wondered if anyone ever guessed what a sudden
test the years came down to. The crisis came like a coronary.
There wasn't the time to moralize. Your people had to *be*
there—right there with you, all along. Mostly, you ended up
with acquaintances. The point of it all was this: Who could
you count on to stay the night?

Well, now she knew.

Besides herself, exactly four. They sat around her in the
screening room like crack commandos, fighting ready. She
did not know yet what the mission was, but she trusted
things would happen just when they were meant to. Her part
must come later.

"I don't know what I should tell you," said Max, sauntering up the room as if in search of a podium. "I've still got to
cut five minutes," he said, "and I don't know where to start.
It's down to the bones already. You tell me."

By which he didn't mean to imply that he valued their
opinions. He was trying to say the film was perfect, just the
way it was.

"Are there any questions?"

There were not.

"An audience after my own heart," he said with a gelid
smile. "A man's art speaks for itself—right?"

He headed back now to start it rolling. She didn't dare
turn to watch him go, but as he passed, she took in the
briefest glimpse of him from the corner of one eye. She saw,
as if on a single frame of footage, his pale patrician features
in repose. He had the slightly parted lips of a man forever
lost in speculation. *Don't*, she scolded herself, *don't think of
him*. She locked eyes front, on the square of white, till she
shut him out entirely.

The overhead light snapped off. The projector began to purr. A splatter of film went on the screen—dark flashes and bits of gray, like rain. It shook and fluttered, and then came clear. It opened on a long shot, down into an empty prison yard. For a moment, they were there as much as here.

And then they made a break for it. Greg took her hand as he leapt up. She saw the first title come on—A MAXIM BREARLEY FILM—as he pulled her to her feet. She could feel the film's light ripple across them both the moment she stood to follow. They lit up like sitting ducks.

"Viv—what's wrong?" called out the director.

She and Greg were already at the door. They pushed it hard and swung it back. She couldn't stand the sound of Brearley whining. She thought she'd scream if she heard another before they were safe outside.

"Hey," Max shouted, "are you sick or something?"

They flung the door shut behind and ran. The running was all their own idea, since nobody else came bursting out. They weren't being trailed at all. But the sped-up pace must have made them think they would save some time at the other end. As if they needed every second they could get. They flew back down the corridor and thundered up the stairs. Then across to the leather-bound study and out the French doors into the night. The Japanese plums were all in bloom as they streaked along the garden alley that led to the red-wood tub.

They'd arrived at the scene of the crime at last.

No doubt they would have been quick to deny they'd done so by design—though there wasn't a soul still left in the story who'd have let it go at that. They panted and leaned against the trees to recover. The night made not the slightest move to rush them along or hunt them down. They had more right to be here now than anyone. If the irony proved to be more than they could bear, they could always say the convenient thing, that the other had taken the lead and tricked them into coming out. But it wasn't so at all. They'd agreed, somehow, without saying a word, to follow this circle end to end. The deal was fifty-fifty.

"Max," he gasped, as he sat on the rim of the tub to gulp in air. "It's Max."

She was just as out of breath as he, but she knew she couldn't let it go without a fight. She slumped down beside him, demanding shrilly: "But what about *Carl?*"

"Him too. Max killed them all."

"But *how?*" she cried—reaching over to grip his arm, as if to keep from falling back.

It wasn't a cool detective's question. She didn't care what the weapons and tricks and setups were, nor how the thing was masterminded. She was saying "How?" to something more—to the whole chaotic round of fate that dogged these men till they tore themselves to bits. She'd always supposed she lived at the center of Jasper's life. All the high-strung apparatus of his dream, and everyone who crossed along it, came within the borders of a country she owned half of. Till now, there were some few things she was sure of.

So how could this be? Maxim Brearley was nobody, wasn't he? Just an oily man they worked with—neither here nor there. She couldn't think where he and Jasper had ever found the time to work up so much violence and passion. How did it ever get started, and she not know it at all?

"There were *four* men lost in the blizzard," said Greg. He ticked them off on his fingers. "Jasper. Artie. Gary Barlow. And one other guy who got frostbite. Remember? The guy who lost four toes? That's *him.*"

"Max?" she asked, as if she kept forgetting. "*Max* was at Carbon Mountain?"

"Goddam right," he said forcefully. It was all old-hat to him, it seemed, who'd been over this ground with Artie inch by inch since Monday night. "The reason we never turned him up is he was a year behind. He wasn't even in the club.

But Barlow, see, was his lover—which is probably why they let him go on the river trip. It's just a guess. Artie can't remember how he happened to be there."

She realized he didn't know half what he wanted. He had only the barest bones of the truth.

"I still don't see what it's got to do with killing Jasper now," she said.

"He always thought it was Jasper's fault," he replied, as he trailed a hand in the water. He gazed down in as if he meant to read the depths like tea leaves. "In *his* mind, Barlow was murdered."

How, they couldn't say. Perhaps Max saw Jasper steal an extra ration. Or Jasper worked it out so Barlow got the thinnest bag to sleep in. Who could say, in the snow and dark, what minor shift in the huddle—four men clinging to keep from freezing—might send one of them over the edge? Artie swore they were all shut up in a kind of coma the whole night through. He didn't see how anyone could have noticed much of anything. But Max must have got it into his head that Jasper had placed himself above the group. In a word, he had oversurvived—and killed the man beside him in the process.

"The thing is," Greg went on, "he never said a thing—not then or ever."

He simply let them take his toes off, gritted his teeth, and came out of the hospital barely limping. Tough in a way that boys admired, so the others all figured he'd put the pain behind him. He nursed it all these years, till it went off like a bomb.

"But how do you *know?*" she persisted. It sounded, for all the world, like a lousy movie.

"Figured it out," said Greg with a shrug.

Artie and Carl had suspected something for months—throughout the shoot of *The Broken Trail*. They saw that Max and Jasper were on the edge of something irreversible.

That once they went ahead and jumped, they'd never make it out alive—not both of them, at any rate. But neither one would speak of it. Whenever Artie tried to bring it up, Jasper dropped a deeper drug and swam away to sea. As the last day loomed for *The Broken Trail*, Artie could almost feel the air go chill, as before a storm. The duel was only hours away.

So he summoned Carl home from New York, and they tried one final time. On April third, from one to five, they begged the boss to get out of town. The horror was plain in his face. He shook like someone who couldn't get warm. But still he denied there was anything there. He fired them both summarily and swore to call his lawyer. Ordered them off the grounds, in fact, though the house was practically theirs as much as his. Then he slammed the door to his room on the roof and placed a call to Bermuda.

Vivien listened soberly, fixing her eyes on a yellowish star that gleamed quite low in the southern sky. She could not name it, for love or money.

"What about all those stories?" she asked quietly—though she harbored little hope that the version *she* knew had survived. It was so indelibly etched in her mind, she could have sworn there were photographs. Jasper and Artie and Carl, arriving in a pickup fresh from nowhere. The frontal assault on Hollywood, and the lucky break that struck them rich. The story told over and over, till it had the effect of historical truth.

"That was just *hype*," Greg said with a certain force, as he shook his hand dry in the cool night air.

Well, of course it was. How odd that she, who had heard every lie in the book embroidered with her name, should have ever believed a word of it.

"The first thing they *did* when they got out here was call up Max," Greg said. "He'd already put in two years waiting around, and he finally had a foot in the door. Some bullshit job at Fox, where he followed this goof around and kissed his ass. But at least he had a few connections." He looked her in the eye with an irony whose roots went deeper than the case at hand. "They couldn't have done it alone, you know. Nobody ever does."

So the four of them worked together, at first. How was it, she thought, that none of them brought up the past? It was as if they thought it would be unmanly to cry over all their losses in Vermont. They pooled their assets and hustled in relays till they clinched the deal for the werewolf picture. But they kept their distance otherwise. Max wasn't part of the magic circle.

It may have been just a fluke of luck, but overnight they were launched. Suddenly, Max and Jasper had no further need for each other. By the time they started granting interviews, they'd each come up with a separate yarn to explain their arrival at the top. By Jasper's account, he and his trusty pals hit Hollywood like sailors on a shore leave. And because they stuck together, all for one and one for all, they won their way to their wildest dreams. Maxim Brearley—scion of a humidification engineer in Tulsa—let it be thought that he grew up riding after foxes. Max had a thing for gentry. Once he got rich, he lived with a checklist, building sets to wander through.

"I *know* that part," said Vivien, as if to cut Greg off. She stood up abruptly and put a few feet between them. She'd always known that Max was just a pocketbook aristocrat. He'd made himself up out of whole cloth. Yet somehow, that was the very thing she found redeeming. Like Jasper, he shaped the world as he went.

"Go on to Harry Dawes," she said.

"Ah well," replied Greg, in a voice that was weary of ambiguities, "that was just bad timing. He hitched a ride down Sunset, and he got picked up by a guy who was out to cast a part. He needed a kid who was new in town." He shrugged at the rigs of fate. "There's thousands of them out there. They all get screwed, before they're through."

It seemed she had nothing to add. She set off down the garden as if she could no longer abide these games of chance. Or perhaps she saw no need to linger at a death scene that was done with. However it was, Greg had to scramble to catch up. As he fell into step, he could tell she was suffering no excess of sentiment. Anger, perhaps, but nothing more. She turned and blurted out, as if to let him know how hard the road she traveled was:

"It's not *enough.*"

"What do you want?"

"Why would he want to kill Carl?" she demanded. This was a mere for-instance. She had a hundred more.

"Well, as it turns out," he said, "that's *your* fault."

One almost would have thought he meant to make her flinch. To see if the harder edge was real.

"Artie and Carl would have dropped it," he said. "Jasper knew what was coming, didn't he? He could have shot *first.* When Max dropped by with his hitchhiker friend, he should never have asked them in. A duel's a duel—you let the enemy pour the wine, you better plan on a long night's sleep."

She started walking again, but not so fast as to shut him out. She let him keep pace on the mossy path, as she willed herself to be satisfied. She had no other option. At the canyon end of the garden, they reached the moon gate. They waited a moment more before going on. The intricate lattice of the double door glimmered like a hieroglyph. Flanked by a night-bloom jasmine left and right, it stood like a final boundary, with the bottomless well of the night beyond.

"Now, it happens I don't agree," said Greg. "You got an innocent victim here—Harry Dawes. The laws of the duel no longer apply."

Men's rules, she thought. Women did not play games like

this. Yet she understood, deep down, that Jasper must have done the thing that Max believed him guilty of. Ten winters ago, in the teeth of a northeast wind, Jasper went too far. Whatever it was—a sliver of greed, a single word—it had cankered inside him like a crime. There was never a question of his getting off free. In the end, he must have listened for Max's step on the stair behind.

She knew all this without ever asking. Jasper had lived with a sin in his blood, like a taint of tropical fever that made him weak from time to time. Out of focus and half asleep, as if he were under water. Vivien felt it the day she met him. He gave you the sense that he longed to beg your pardon—to break away from the moment at hand and hurry back to something still unfinished. It lived in a windowless room, where he never let anyone in.

"Why me?" she asked, in a neutral tone. "What did *I* do?"

"You went and pinned the murder on him," Greg replied. Then he rattled the next part off like moves on a chessboard. "Carl goes straight to Max, of course. And Max sees right away how to lock up his alibi. If Carl should die by his own hand, it only goes to prove the widow Cokes's case."

At "widow," he pointed a finger at her. He held it steady and cocked his thumb.

"Bang," he said. "Carl's dead."

"What are they doing down there?" she asked.

"In the screening room? Well, I guess you could call it murder one."

"But *how*?"

"Okay—it's got to look like a heart attack, right?" This part wasn't as hard as he expected, not at all. Just tell it step by step, he thought. "First, Artie saps him and knocks him out. There'll be a bruise, but you can't have everything. Artie says he can make it look like he cracked his head when he fell. Then a pillow across his face—like this—and you press down hard. Six minutes, I think we decided. A simple asphyxiation. Nothing grand."

She put a hand up to the gate, lifted the dolphin latch, and pushed back half the moon. She stepped over the foot-high threshold, holding the door as she went, so he could follow. As he came out onto the wilder slope, he was shocked by the whip of the wind, blowing ten miles in from the sea like the motive force of another story. The garden hedge had kept the weather moderate and still.

But what was more than that, there was nothing between them, all of a sudden. He found they had to walk single file as she set off up the zigzag path. So he had no clue what she thought of it all. It wouldn't do her a bit of good to protest the act itself. Six minutes was so far gone as to be the distant past. Maxim Brearley was over with. Greg braced himself for a cry of disapproval, even so. In the last few weeks, he'd gotten used to Vivien Cokes the humanist, who lived in a cloud of high ideals. She could afford to, after all.

Yet he had to give her this: She appeared to be a more persistent moralist than he. A force like justice, one could argue, wasn't something done in the dark like a bloody mugging. In theory Greg agreed. But the hunger for revenge was too far gone to settle here for reason. Vivien's air of civilization was doubtless high as ancient Greece. The lilac dress she wore tonight billowed about her like a dream. When she turned to speak, on the spine of the hill, he expected a dose of principles Euclidean in shape.

"Why?" she accused him fiercely. "Why didn't you include me?"

The sting of betrayal was in her voice. He saw with a pang of hindsight how it must have seemed. It was all a complete misunderstanding—but so what? There was nobody giving points for good intentions. Not this late in the game.

"But don't you see," Greg pleaded, calling through the wind without a word prepared, "we wanted you to be innocent."

"Why?"

"I don't know," he said helplessly. Oh, shit, there must be a reason. "I suppose we wanted to do it *for* you."

"Well, I won't be treated like that," she bellowed angrily, coming close. She beat with the flat of one hand against his chest, like somebody knocking on a door. He didn't try to duck. The ache was deeper down than all this surface tension. He knew she wasn't out to pitch him off the mountain.

"Like what?" he shouted, when the last blow landed.

"Like a fucking princess!"

Hollering this like a curse, she turned and strode away. He sprinted along in her wake and tried to backtrack all at once—glad for the chance to storm about, but reeling with a sense of vast miscalculation. He had only tried to protect her from the blood-cold will of the others. She didn't have any idea what the nicest people were capable of.

But he saw what she meant, that he had no right. It wouldn't happen again. He'd treat her the same as the rest, if she liked. He stuck close to her heels as they climbed the ridge. For a moment, he seemed about to seize her—as if he would make her stop to hear a proper apology. Except— couldn't she see that a fortune big as a minor Rothschild's led to a certain set of assumptions? The cover of every magazine in the free world didn't pick you up for being the same as everyone else.

It was all well and good to read Thoreau. A man like that was a genuine creature of equals—democratic in all his commerce. Two feet on the ground when he made a deal, and two feet off when he looked at sunsets. But could you really get away with it in the back seat of a Rolls? Where did Vivien ever get the idea she was *plain?*

By the time they crested the next rise, they were going so

fast it was almost a chase. Then all of a sudden she stopped without warning, right in the path. He collided against her and stepped back shaken. When he saw they'd arrived at the grave, a few feet off on the bare hillside, he felt strangely dizzy and turned around. He hadn't assumed they were *going* somewhere.

It was more of a grave than ever, in fact, on account of the limestone slab. Salt-white, shaped in the classic way—an inverted U—it glowed on the brow of the night country. Poignant by virtue of having been fashioned by hand. Three feet high and half as wide, with lettering etched across it. If it hadn't been set so straight in the earth, if an end had sunken in and pitched it at a tilt, it would have looked as dead and gone as the naked west itself—like a grave in an old churchyard in Yuma. He wondered if she'd ordered it before or since the trip back east. How did she get it up so quick?

"Everyone's always *dying*," Vivien said. Even here, the oddest sort of irony still played about the edges of her voice.

Greg could see that he wasn't keeping up. The statement he'd struggled to find the words for, about who had excluded whom, was already over and done with. She wasn't mad at him anymore. Now that they'd taken to roaming the night, the stakes were a good deal higher. This was death itself out here, black-hearted as a thief. It stood in command of the heights as it always had—cold as ice, its eyes the whole horizon.

"But everyone loses people," Greg retorted. As if to say the whole world understood a thing like this, because they'd been there.

"No—some don't," she noted with some dispassion.

Perhaps he had never met up with the type—who wouldn't allow a living soul within ten feet, so as not to have to risk the ending.

"Can you see what it says?" she asked.

"Not from here," he said. But he made no move to crouch and have a look, assuming she wanted to say it aloud.

" 'Jasper Cokes,' " she recited dryly, " 'Cut down in his 33rd year.' The rest's a quote, but you have to see it written."

She realized then—with an eye on the wind that riffled the chaparral, the piercing curves of the quiet hills against the ink-dark sky—how the world was perfect in its way. The Buddhist said that happiness was nothing. What you felt was the feel of absence: The engine of human suffering stopped to catch its breath sometimes.

What Vivien felt was nothing so precarious as that. The silence had fallen at last in the upstairs rooms of the clamorous heart. The killer was killed. The curse was off. The hundred different pains that kept a body down—tics, chills, toothache, twinges, gouges, strain—seemed to have vanished on the spot.

In a word, she thought, she was happy. In the Buddhist sense, at least.

Greg leaned forward, peered at the stone, and blocked it with his shadow. He dropped to one knee and squinted close. His pace from word to word, as he read it aloud, was slow. " 'The sun is but a morning star,' " he said. Then he drew back, stood with a sigh, and turned and cocked his head.

"What the hell is *that* supposed to mean?"

"I thought I'd lost you all," she said, like she hadn't even heard.

"You what?"

"I thought—you might have other things to do."

Okay, okay. Couldn't she see how sorry he was? He stood between her and the grave and shrugged it off, as if to say he never had much to do. But he saw that he must have left her out of it on purpose. Wanted to get to the killer first. Show who the real Lew Archer was.

"You'll be sorry," he said to reassure her. "You probably

hadn't heard, but once we take somebody up, from that point on they're family. You'll see—we'll buy you stuff for your birthday. We'll borrow all your records. You won't be alone on a Saturday night from now till doomsday."

"Well, that's a relief," she replied, and lowered her eyes to the stone.

The silence was not tense. She thought about Sid and Edna, and the way he kept them going. It was wholly unacknowledged, which is why it worked at all, but she heard the sharpened focus in his voice whenever he linked their names. She meant to do much the same for Artie. The difference was, she and Artie had enough to live on coke and caviar. Once they were settled in separate quarters, she planned to keep a watchful eye on the state of his affairs. Make sure he ate three times a day.

"It's from Thoreau," she said.

"I gathered as much."

Now she was back on the gravestone—as if she talked mostly in loops and parabolas, rather than straight in a line. Yet he found he had no trouble following her. Perhaps it was purely a matter of acclimation.

"I can't explain it," Vivien said, and he had the idea she was being honest, with herself as much as anyone. "At least it's not about going to heaven. I mean, you have to do what you can, right here."

"Did anyone ever tell you you make an improbable mystic?"

Pain in the ass, he might have said. He'd put in ten long years as a writer, after all. Failed or otherwise, he had twenty-six hundred pages of dialogue to prove it. So he ought to know, if anyone did, that a book was just a book. It didn't have to get up in the morning and make the coffee and drive to work, so what could it possibly know about getting along in *this* world? Still, he'd grown accustomed to Vivien's sounding off like a smart-ass Ph.D. He supposed it was little enough to take, next to what she put up with in him, with his endless grumps and privacies.

If you wanted a friend, you took the whole package.

"Don't worry," she said. "I've put the book away."

This wasn't entirely true, in fact. It was right on the table by her bed, not three feet away from where she'd found it fifteen days before. What she meant was, she was done reading.

"You mean you're not moving to Concord?"

"Steepside's near enough," she said.

They acted as if they had no clue what the normal scene might be beside a dead man's grave. There was something queer at the level of impulse, which urged them to go against the grain of whatever was going on. Before all else, they hated to be predictable. It made her wonder how they would ever get together, when all of this was done. That is, would the borders be open? She supposed they'd both be wary of assuming too much freedom. She saw that he kept no calendar at all. If he never made any plans, who did he ever get to see?

"What you've got to do," he said, "is call the ambulance when it's time. Nobody's going to hassle you—we're counting on that. Now, this is the story. We're all watching the movie. When it's over, the lights come up, and we find Max slumped in the projection booth. We try to revive him, but it does no good. You got five witnesses."

He snapped his fingers as if to say the rest was all downhill. Yet he seemed to feel some further self-assurance was required. He stepped down onto the path again and gripped her shoulders to buck her up.

"It shouldn't be hard to bring off," he said. "He's overweight. He's got lousy nerves. Besides, people die in the middle of things all the time."

"What if somebody gets suspicious? What if they want an autopsy?"

He shrugged, and his hands fell back to his sides again. "Then I guess we go to jail," he said, with a curious air of whimsy playing about the apology. "We'll have to pass notes through the guards. We'll get a good lawyer." He shrugged again.

At first she said nothing at all. She surveyed the surrounding night for signs of life. Perhaps, he thought, as he watched her look off down the canyon, dreamy-eyed and still, a Rolls was as good a place as any to act out Walden Pond. Or to put the matter in landed terms, twenty-six acres of desert green within the city limits was vast enough that its confines didn't show. The Concord original, after all, in the far-off specimen days of 1847, was something close to a staged event itself. Thoreau would doubtless spin in his grave to hear him speak of it quite this way—but then, with one thing and another, Thoreau had probably not stopped spinning in over a hundred years.

"Poor Jasper," Vivien said at last. "I hardly knew him at all."

He took it to mean she saw no problem in getting rid of Max. She'd probably thought of a doctor already—someone so greedy for status he'd sign the certificate happily. With the merest flip of the corpse's lids, and without so much as mussing a button on Max's shirt. As for this last remark, about Jasper, he found the sudden surge of melancholy most disarming. If they had to talk death, if that was the breakthrough these last weeks had brought them to, why couldn't they keep it roundabout, and curse the whole condition? The individual dead were too upsetting—thieves and cheats, to leave one so alone. Too much a mirror of who one used to be.

"You mean, because he had a secret?"

"I suppose that's it," she said.

He noticed the wind had died by the stillness of the lilac dress. She was staring straight at the western sky, but he knew she was looking at something far away in time.

"Is that what it means to survive?" she asked. "You lose everyone twice over?"

Once when they died. Then a second time, when the truth came out.

"But *everyone* doesn't have a secret."

"Really?" she wondered aloud. She wasn't convinced at all.

"I think it's time we headed back," he said. The demands of the schedule were more to his taste than the upper reaches of life-and-death. "They only allowed me half an hour to brief you. They don't want you to miss the movie."

He turned downhill, where the lights of Steepside made it hover above the bowl of slopes like a spaceship. All at once, as he made his way in the dark, the narrow track reminded him of coming down the mountain in Vermont. Yet there it had been wide enough for two to walk abreast. This was like a tightrope.

Still, it suited his present mood just fine, to walk down single file. He'd only start getting curmudgeonly if they kept on talking on mountaintops. He didn't mean to freeze her out. She could be his friend forever if she liked. But in matters of philosophy, they simply had to agree to disagree.

The journey was almost done that demanded all their like-nesses. If it meant to stick, this friendship had to go by way of seasons, till it grew like something out in the woods—untended except by the scheme of things, and tough by reason of what it stood. If it needed too much caring for, one or the other was bound to run away.

He must have been twenty steps down the trail when he realized she wasn't behind him. He glanced around and saw her, brooding still beside the grave. He shouted her down. She looked up sharp.

"Hey, Greg," she bellowed—gaily, it almost seemed, but she did not move till she said her piece. "If one of us dies—"

"Us?" he demanded. "You mean you and me?"

"Whoever's left," she declared, "has to promise not to go out looking. As far as I'm concerned, you know it all now. There's nothing else. You promise?"

The smallest pause took hold, while he did a quick fix on her motives. She didn't seem to mean she was sorry to know the truth about her husband. She wasn't so blind as to think she kept no secrets of her own. It wasn't a dare, or an accusation. What she hoped to do was absolve them both of the sort of quest they'd just completed—at least as far as it might pertain to the matter of each other. So neither one would ever be indicted by the past.

"Promise!" he shouted back.

She walked toward him along the ridge, and she knew it would never be quite the same again. Not the way it had been these last two weeks, here at the core of spring. Strangely enough, she could live with that, and with nary a pang of regret or attendant loss of nerve. She reached the spot where he waited, his mild unhidden smile the mirror of her own. He turned and started down again.

No one led, and no one followed. They both went on their own. Not ten minutes since, the uphill climb had afforded her the long view of the world, untrammeled by a single human step. Here, on the down side, things were reversed. Greg had the world to look at. She had him.

They could both lay claim to Walden Pond, or something very like it. But hers, she saw, was a good deal more external —vivid as the opalescent surface of the reservoir, glimmering far below them now in the belly of the canyon. Hers was the dream of summer that brought the blood up in every tree. Greg's was a few miles farther off, at Cherokee and Franklin. As if the glacier that decreed such things had dug in its heels not once but twice, and made two lakes before it fled these mountains.

His was not even waterbound. The raw terrain, the rock-strewn shore, the wind in the alders—with him, it was not just all in his head, but something he wasn't terribly keen on owning up to. He lived it after a fashion, of course, but not by the book by any means. So they occupied two poles. Two couldn't live in either place, at least not two of a kind. Only those who were rare and endangered—Sid and Edna and Artie—had the right to settle on their borders.

They came off the spine of the hill and crossed the tilted desert meadow toward the house. One had to know when a thing was done, she thought, snapping off a sprig of fennel as she passed. The trick was not to mistake for done what was only gone on to another phase. What tended to complicate matters most was learning all the rhythms out of love affairs gone sour. She'd probably been through half a dozen men at two weeks start to finish. They were all of a piece. They lacked the feel of the quick of time and, ten days after she met them, seemed as good as dead. None of them ever taught her how to let a thing go and keep it by. She supposed she bolted before they had the chance.

Greg pulled open the gate's other half, and the whole full moon of the garden shone dark green beyond it. He stepped through and stopped to catch his breath. When she joined him, they each reached out to one of the gates and swung them shut, like a pair of footmen. Greg secured the dolphin latch. The sudden quiet was twice what it was before. The jasmine scent was overwhelming. After the desert hills, the moss and ferns and fruit trees were the portal of a dream.

They walked on the pebbled garden path, and each step crunched with the gravity of all their going forward.

"Remember what I used to say?" she asked, as if it were years ago. "How it felt like nothing?"

"Of course."

"Well, that is no longer the case."

He looked at her sidelong. Please, he thought, no sudden conversions. Let her get all rosy on her *own* time.

"What is it you feel?" he asked quite briskly. "Hot flashes?"

They skirted the redwood tub—indifferent now to its clouded depths. Then down the alley of plums again, more sure of their footing the second time through. As they pulled the French doors open, he said:

"You ought to get the whole thing down on paper. Inspiration's very hot these days."

"Listen, honey," she shot back, though without a break in stride. "I'm not the only one got cured of being out of it. When I met you, you couldn't leave the house."

"Lies!" he bellowed, as they swept across the library like kids who couldn't read. "You know what your problem is? You keep imagining I'm like you."

"And you keep thinking you're not."

The canyon room. The spiral stair. They raced along, but they didn't tire. They rollicked down the corridor, trading remarks like a couple of standup comics.

"What's the best friend you ever had?"

"Are you counting Sid and Edna?"

"No."

"In that case," he retorted, "none that I can think of. Why?"

"Not even a dog, or *anything?*"

He shook his head with a drunken smile, as if this thing were a point of pride. They'd come to the double doors again. Each put a hand forth, gripped a doorknob, paused on the brink of breaking in. The music from the screening room was lonely as a desert trail. They glanced in one another's eyes without the faintest trace of caution.

"Right," she said. "Me neither."

Now they pushed, and the doors opened. They wasted not a moment's pang about the thousand doors they'd had to go through just to be none other than themselves. Though the dark hit hard against their unaccustomed eyes, they didn't wait. They groped their way across to the empty row of seats. Sid and Edna shushed and hissed them. They shrank to get under the beam of light, so as not to ruin the picture. They made a great show of getting sat, and when at last they looked—

"Let me tell you something, man," said Jasper Cokes, as big as life, in a pitiless stare straight at them.

He wore a red bandanna round his neck, gritty and bunched with sweat from so much dusty riding. Needless to say, he had no shirt on. Not an ounce of flab. His tan as deep as the summer sun.

"What if that treasure's not out there?" Jasper said.

He paused, and the camera lingered on him. Whoever he was talking to had the same view of him they did, here in the hill room. The pause was full of his polished skin and the raw unruly magic in his eyes.

"Wouldn't *that* be something?" Jasper scoffed with a thin-lipped laugh. He pointed a finger into the distance. "Three more days—that's as far as I go. If I don't find it by then, I'm gonna go someplace else. Back east, maybe."

"Come on—I'll show you," said a young man's voice, and the camera turned an eye on him.

A kid about twenty. They were out in the yard of a wooden house, on a bluff above the Pacific. The film rolled down the beach as the two men walked. The winter sun was yellow in a deep blue sky.

What scene is this? she wondered idly.

The only thing she knew was the end—where the sheriff's men come creeping up to the walls of the mission graveyard. This was still early on. They must be on their way to one of the bandits' hideouts.

"*Sst,*" said Edna Temple, crouching at Vivien's ear. "Are you okay? You think we're crazy?"

Vivien turned to the older woman, whose face was soft in the silver light. Close up, she was old as the hills and her eyes were dancing. Vivien thought: *I want to be just like this someday.*

"It's the strangest *wake* I've ever been to," she whispered behind her hand. She wasn't sure whose she meant—whether Max or Jasper. "You like the movie?"

"It's crap," said Edna. "I love it. Me, I could watch him eat a sandwich."

She toddled back to her seat.

"There's nothing here," said Jasper, casting a practiced eye up the muddy slopes of the wash. "The soil's too thin. You couldn't *bury* something in it."

What the hell was this? She leaned a little forward and took a bead on the landscape. It seemed to be some sort of runoff. The winter rains from one of the canyons fed through a wide-mouthed cleft in the bluff, and thus back into the sea.

"If he left his strongbox here," said the kid, "you're out of luck. The tides have probably taken it to China."

"He wouldn't have made a mistake like that," Jasper replied emphatically. "Wherever he's left it, it's safe. I *know* it."

So he *did* still believe it was out there somewhere. He's a better actor than people say, thought Vivien, cool as a critic. He gave off an air of endless yearning. It would have been almost tawdry if he hadn't been so hot. Vivien leaned around in her chair. She was wild with delight to see Jasper alive, and she wanted to share it with Artie. Who sat curled up in the row behind—shy around Jasper as always, even here in the dark.

"What's all this shit," she demanded, "about him looking ravaged?"

"Hey, I'm with you," he whispered back. "He's gorgeous."

"You think we ought to release it?"

"Sure."

That took care of the board of directors meeting.

"How are you?" Vivien asked, still twisted so she faced him. What she was thinking was: How did it feel to have blood on his hands?

"Me?" asked Artie, a bit surprised. "The same. Didn't you know? I always come out of these blizzards alive."

"So I've heard."

"Sh!" Greg said.

She swung around. He was leaning forward, as if he couldn't bear to miss a word. At first she thought there must be something crucial going on. But no—it was just the two men shaking hands, on the beach below the bluff. No violence. No sex. Not a major scene at all.

"You *like* this picture?" she asked him, slightly taken aback. "I thought you stopped at the fifties."

"We're expanding," he said. "*Sh!*"

Well, all right. She gave it her full attention. Jasper clambered up the bank to the top of the bluff, while the kid ran loose-limbed into the surf. He dived in, swam out past the waves, and turned to the north to free-style home. He waved to Jasper once. And high on the bluff, Jasper nodded and let the moment go. He turned and loped away. The scene dissolved.

"This is *boring*," called Sid from the back of the room.

"Be quiet," Edna snapped at him. "It's supposed to be symbolic."

"Well, it's boring."

If only it weren't so badly *written*, Greg was thinking. It wasn't a half-bad story. Whoever wrote it had seen too many movies and not enough life at large. The very mistake he'd made in a dozen scripts of his own. If this were really happening, he thought, Jasper would never have left it at a handshake. He would have asked the kid to be his sidekick. He would have thrown over his quest and dived in after.

Real life had to do with dropping everything. As near as he could tell, one never made it to the mission yard. There were better dreams closer to hand—more vital, more awake. The gold was only there to get you started.

He cupped a hand over his mouth and whispered left: "Was he really this beautiful?"

So much so, he made you want to stay as close as you possibly could, on the off chance he would drop it all and take you in his arms.

"I guess so," Vivien said.

It didn't depress her at all, to know the man up there was the real Jasper Cokes. Driving alone, as now, in a beat-up Cadillac—eating a pizza, wedge by wedge, off a cardboard tray beside him. The radio blared. The desert sun beat down on a land as blank as the skin of the moon. And the look on his face, as he readied himself for the next big scene, was rapturous with the certainty that here-and-now was all the world there was.

"The rest of us don't stand a chance," said Greg. "It's like he's the only one who's left a shred of evidence."

Vivien nodded in the dark. The time one lost, she thought, was never past redeeming. Here she'd managed to make it home to watch her husband die. It was coming right up in about an hour. She was glad to see that Greg did not exclude her. Technically, after all, he could have lumped her with the stars. How could she ever begin to fathom what it meant to leave behind no image and no name? He talked as if, for the moment at least, she were every bit as anonymous as they. As free to come and go.

"Can you bear it?" she asked him lightly.

"Doesn't much matter," he said with a shrug. "It's the way things are."

"But *can* you?" she insisted—grinning now in the ghostly light, as if it were the joke she'd waited all these weeks to tell.

"If I said yes," he countered, "what would *you* say?"

"Me," she said, "I can bear it fine."

"Then the answer is no."

"Liar," she said gently, grazing the tip of a finger along the back of his hand.

At that, some random noise—the crack of gunfire, a door slammed shut—drew them back to the road ahead.

It was only Jasper, stopped in a lonely canyon, his hand-drawn map spread out on the steering wheel in front of him. But they watched it for all they were worth, just now, as if to prove they came this far by perfect concentration. In the moonglow pale that bathed their faces, they fixed on the field of vision like a couple of astronomers out to connect the sky. It was queer, how little the moment chose to give them. Just a shot of Jasper, staring out of his Cadillac at the vast surround of the bare rough hills. Yet they watched him— saucer-eyed, finished with grief—as if he would divide among them all the gold he found. As if, almost, he could not go on without them.

Gay & Lesbian Books From Carol Publishing Group

About Face: A Gay Officer's Account of How He Stopped Prosecuting Gays in the Army and Started Fighting For Their Rights By James E. Kennedy $19.95 hardcover (#72281)

Beloved and God: The Story of Hadrian & Antinous By Royston Lambert —Investigates the mysterious death of an ancient Greek boy, Antinous, the lover of the Roman Emporer Hadrian - whose cult-like following threatened the newly emerging Christain religion. $9.95 paperback (#62003)

The Boy Who Picked the Bullets Up; A novel by Charles Nelson—In the insanity of Vietnam, medic Kurt Strom tended to the wounded. In the camaraderie of combat, he seduced them. $12.95 paperback (#62002)

The Gay Book of Days By Martin Greif $14.95 paperback (#40384)

The Gay 100: A Ranking of the Most Influential Gay Men and Lesbians, Past and Present By Paul Russell $24.95 hardcover (#51591)

In Search of a Master; A novel by John Preston—Presents another fascinating investigation of sex and myth, domination and fantasy, and the uniquely human vision that infuses his work. $8.95 paperback (#62005)

The Lavender Screen: The Gay and Lesbian Films - Their Stars, Makers, Characters and Critics By Boze Hadleigh $17.95 paperback (#51341)

A Movie; A novel by Donald S. Olson— Travels a fine line between breathless comedy and bitter tragedy, to a world where movies provide a convenient escape and the ultimate enslavement. $8.95 paperback (#62008)

Panthers in the Skins of Men; A novel Charles Nelson—Continues the amazing adventures and misadventures of Kurt Strom in this 1001 nights' tale designed to fascinate and amuse. $12.95 paperback (#62006)

Pink Highways: Tales of Queer Madness on the Open Road By Michael Lane, co-creator of *Monk* magazine. *"Not only is his account of life on the highways outlandishly funny, it is very well-written. Recommended."* - Library Journal $19.95 hardcover (#72263)

Sappho: Poems and Fragments; Josephine Balmer, ed. $7.95 paperback (#62000)

Some Lovely Image; A novel by Lawrence J. Quirk—Many years after the death of a young 19th century Boston aristocrat, the narrator becomes obsessed with him, soon realizing that he is the lover for whom he had always longed. $9.95 paperback (#62007)

Splendora; A novel Edward Swift—A steamy east Texas town is the setting for this rollicking tale of a man maintaining a relationship with Miss Jessie Gatewood, even while being courted by the town Pastor. $6.95 paperback (#62001)

The Way We Write Now: Short Stories From the AIDS Crisis; Sharon Oard Warner, ed.; Abraham Verghese, fore. $14.95 paperback (#51638)

When the Parrot Boy Sings; A novel by John Champagne—The story of a young New York artist who, through collages, constructs an imaginary world. When it comes to life, he hasn't got a clue where things get pasted up. $8.95 paperback (#62009)

Prices subject to change; books subject to availability

Look for these books at your bookstore. Or to order, call 1-800-447-BOOK (MasterCard or Visa) or send a check or money order for the books purchased, plus $4 shipping and handling for the first book and 75¢ for each additional book, to: Carol Publishing, 120 Enterprise Ave, Dept. 62004, Secaucus, NJ 07094.